PRAISE FOR TH

MW01001718

"Lisa Mannetti's impressive debut novel *THE GENTLING BOX* transp... ...u to another time and place with the same kind of dark magic that pervades the 19th Century world she's recreated, reminding us that it was not so long ago that the terror of sorcery and spectres was very real—very real, and not so far fetched."

–**Hank Schwaeble**, Bram Stoker Award winner and author of *DAMNABLE (Jove 2009)*

"*THE GENTLING BOX* is a brilliantly decadent opium den of mind-bending hallucinations fueled by old-world magic, each page more disturbing and haunting than the previous one. Absolutely stunning! Moving with the frantic speed of a terrified wild horse, this novel will take you on a ride you will not soon forget. If this is Lisa Mannetti's debut, I cannot wait to see what she will produce for us in the future."

–**Gabrielle S. Faust**, *Austin Literary Examiner*

"The dark themes Lisa Mannetti explores come crawling up your throat when you least expect them ... We fall headfirst into a world both abundantly detailed and bleakly hideous for its personal horrors and what man—or woman—may be driven to do for power over others ... it may be a first novel, but it's one powerful and inventive, timeless treatise on darkness of the soul."

–**William D. Gagliani**, *Chizine*

"When was the last time you lost yourself in a book? Lisa Mannetti dares you to enter a realm unlike anything you've dreamed of, a world of gallant gypsies and ancient evil, of passionate obsessions . . . and abject terror. Take that dare. Immerse yourself. The rewards are plentiful. But be warned. Nothing could prepare you for the horror of *THE GENTLING BOX*."

–**Robert Dunbar**, author of *THE PINES and THE SHORE*

"Mannetti's debut *THE GENTLING BOX* is astonishingly well written, richly drawn and simply remarkable. It shares that very rare thing that all the best novels do: the creation of a world, fully formed, familiar and yet magically unique, a world that makes us ache to remain in it for just a few moments longer after the last word is read."

–Stoker Finalist, **Nate Kenyon**, author of *BLOODSTONE* and *THE REACH*

"One of the best books I've read in a long time, *THE GENTLING BOX* is strongly recommended ... The magic in it is as real as horse sweat and ashes, and the reality described as magical as any wild dream ... There is real life in it, and the unblinking way Mannetti portrays it all is greatly to be admired ... this book tells the blunt truth and therein lies its great power."

–**Gene Stewart**, author of *ALAYA'S ASSIGNMENTS* and *ALEXANDRA'S AWAKENING*

"Realistically written, addictive and eerie ... Mannetti had me hooked ... I doubt anyone will be able to put this one down."

–**Nick Cato**, *Horror Fiction Review*

"*THE GENTLING BOX* by Lisa Mannetti—An impressive debut, beautifully written, about old world gypsy curses. There's a pretty intricate structure at work here, and a palpable sense of dread."

–**Greg Lamberson**, *FearZone*

"For the horror enthusiast, *THE GENTLING BOX* can't be beat ... I can't emphasize enough how much I enjoyed this book ... Mannetti's debut novel scores far and above books by many long-standing writers, both within the horror genre and without."

–**Elizabeth Blue**, *Feoamante*

"Mannetti's *THE GENTLING BOX* weaves a magical tapestry that transcends time. This impressive *tour de force* chills the reader and lingers long after the final chapter."

–**Amy Grech**, Author of *APPLE OF MY EYE*

"Brilliantly researched and structured, *THE GENTLING BOX* accurately recreates a world long lost where Gypsies roamed a shadowy landscape filled with superstition and danger. Ms. Mannetti has conjured a heart-stopping tale of magick most black, a terrifying, heartfelt, disarming story that is beautifully wrought and historically correct. I came away from this novel breathless and hungry for more."

–**J.L. Comeau**, *Count Gore's Creature Feature Weekly Web Program*

The Gentling Box

Lisa Mannetti

First Nightscape Press Trade Paperback Edition

ISBN: 1-938644-18-2
ISBN-13: 978-1-938644-18-4

Nightscape Press, LLP
http://www.nightscapepress.com

Introduction by Heather Graham

The Gentling Box is that rare first novel that dares to take many chances, and the result is a Bram Stoker-winning book that combines history, sorcery, compelling characters, and a look deep into the human psyche. It's possibly a horror novel, but it still tells the story of a bygone era, of a time when the true separation of Church and State was not something really conceived, and the very darkness of the world in which people lived allowed the mind to embrace demons and see omens in the phenomena of the earth.

Most importantly, as in all good stories, of course, the tale itself matters only when the characters are so rich and real that they come alive for us. Our empathy for the characters, their honor, their longings, their fears, and the terrors they face take us through this tale without our ever realizing how much we learn along the way, and how our imaginations are piqued. Sights, sounds, and even the breeze become substantial in these pages.

Imre, a half-gypsy horse trader, is a man struggling with torment and torture. While the Age of Enlightenment had come and gone and was replaced by a new Romantic sensibility on the rest of the continent, in Hungary and Romania gypsies were still seen as the despised, as thieves, and, against all reason, as those who are dark, perhaps even evil; liable to consort with ancient demons. In Imre's instance, the extremely malignant forces of culture and ancient times are far too real. As a gypsy, he faces threat from those outside the closed society of his troupe, but he is already well-acquainted with supernatural forces as well: He and his small family have been cursed.

The Gentling Box brings us the chilling atmosphere of misted mountains, fog laden trees, the howling of wolves—all requisite in creating the innate human core of fear reminiscent of the Wolfman and Dracula. It's certainly not to be read while you're on a shrouded hilltop alone in the dark.

While the story is that of demons, living and supernatural, it is also the story of a man. He knows the menace his family faces. He sees his wife overtaken by the curse of a cruel sorceress. He sees those around him afflicted, and he is torn with the same horror that grips any husband, any father, watching a beloved wife or a precious child in danger. His wife suffers the horrors of the damned; he is a man on an urgent mission to save a beautiful daughter from a fate that could prove far worse than death. He is up against the terrible power of a bitter and vengeful witch, but there are even worse fears that will seize hold of him on his journey to save himself, those around him, and their immortal souls.

The Gentling Box is a true page turner, but it is not the literary equivalent of a slasher-flick; its prose is beautifully written and the terrors it conjures are not cheap tricks like those that manipulate us into reflexively shrieking or jumping out of our skins. This is a novel that settles into the bone, and brings forth the kind of ancient fear that still lurks in our souls, no mattered how civilized we might have become. Read carefully—the shadows in your home will have new meaning.

Read, think, and enjoy the chills—*The Gentling Box* will stay with you and haunt you long after you have reached the end.

—Heather Graham
October, 2010

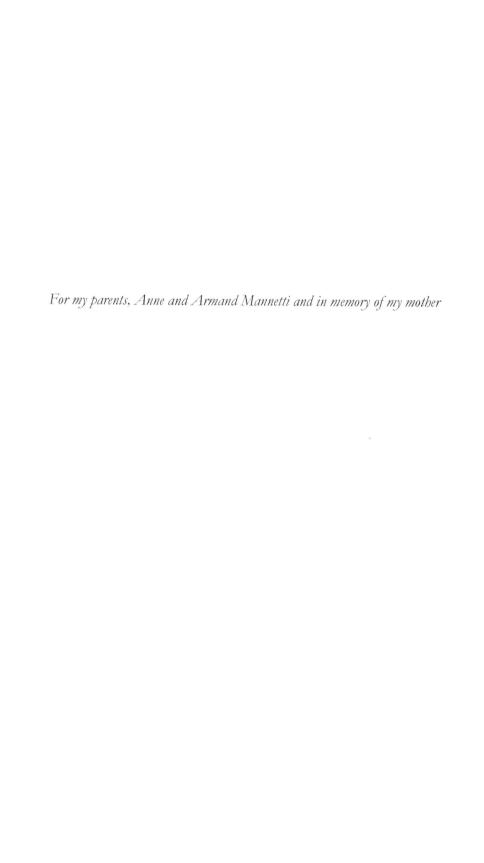

For my parents, Anne and Armand Mannetti and in memory of my mother

Part I

Mimi

All things are taken from us, and become Portions and parcels of the dreadful past.
—Tennyson

1
Nyiregyhaza, Northeastern Hungary: June, 1864

My wife sits mute now in the corner of our caravan, because this morning it is her personality which has come to the fore. Her hands are folded quietly in the lap of her skirt. Just above her left hand is a thick purplish scar that circles her wrist like a hideous bracelet. I don't want to think about the scar, about how it is the source of the evil afflicting our lives.

If I raise my head from the sweat-soaked pillow I can see her bare feet splayed against the worn floorboards, but it is her face I find myself staring at: small, kitten-shaped, dominated by her huge dark eyes. She has gypsy eyes. They were very bright when we were both younger; now they are ringed by deep gray shadows like bruises and filled with pain. Meeting mine, they beg: *Save Lenore.*

My wife is right of course, and she is living evidence of what will happen to Lenore, our daughter, if I don't intervene. But Christ, I think, how can I save her when the foul disease I've taken is ravaging through me like a brushfire? I close my eyes and instantly hear the swish of skirts, so I know she has gotten to her feet, she is moving toward the bed. And now I feel her hand tapping my shoulder urgently.

I open my eyes; her face is full of defiance. Her black brows contract angrily and she points at her wrist. Again.

"Yes," I say, my voice a ragged whisper, "I know." I know we will die shut up in this stinking grave of a caravan and Lenore will be possessed by the same hungry spirit that has taken my wife's life, that killed Joseph and punished me.

No. She shakes her head, and suddenly her thin hands go to her face; her shoulders hitch and great wracking sobs shake her small frame. She is crying, and the wailing voice I hear is the first sound she has made as Mimi, as my wife, in more months than I can count. *She speaks when she is Anyeta,* I think bitterly, *but never as Mimi.* Anyeta has taken that from her, too.

She sinks onto the edge of the bed, her long hair falling forward, and I want to comfort her. I sit up but my chest burns. I cough, my throat a column of fire, but it's so hard to breathe. I make myself cough harder and up comes a wad of greasy yellow phlegm streaked with blood. I manage to hide the clotty mess in a handkerchief before Mimi turns her head and sees it.

I put my arm around her shoulder. Her eyes flick toward my fingers. She whirls around and points at the livid scar on her wrist. I nod. Mimi is reminding me again. She has tried to save Lenore herself, but her powers have fled. I admire her courage. It wasn't failure.

"Not your fault," I rasp before the rumbling cough cleaves me again. We both wait until the fit passes. I let my hand rest on her knee.

All at once, Mimi seizes my wrist hard. Her grip is like iron, like steel pincers, and I'm suddenly terrified the change is on her and in a second her eyes will blink and I'll see Anyeta's demonic eyes, hear her mocking screams and taunts.

But Mimi throws my hand back at me and runs to the oval mirror. She jerks it from the plastered wall so fiercely the nail pops out with a shriek and she nearly loses her balance. The silvery mirror sways between her hands, she holds it to her chest like a shield, she moves toward the bed. She is making a grunting noise, trying to tell me something. I concentrate on her lips. She is moving them carefully, slowly. Then I have it:

"Look, Imre."

In the mirror I see my features are blurred with thick scabs and crusts. My face is overrun with the red weeping sores and I would weep for the sight except I think she has seen it spreading and nursed me and never shown revulsion or fear.

Mimi thrusts the mirror toward me again and makes a furious sound, shapes the word, *"Look!"*

She wants me to know that time is short, that I'm dying, that the pustulent blisters will eat through my lungs, completely consume my flesh—

Mimi hurls the mirror to the floor. The sound is deafening inside the caravan. I see her feet moving among the splinters from the shattered mahogany frame, the chunks of broken glass. She squats. Heedless, she clutches a long sharp shard and I see drops of blood welling from her palm and fingers then running down and staining the white filmy sleeve of her blouse. She points at her wrist with the glass knife, then at mine, and pantomimes sawing.

And then, Christ, *then* I know what she wants. A sick feeling eddies through me, and I feel the vomit rising in my throat. I push it down because Mimi is asking me to be strong, to save Lenore. I look into her dark eyes and I know what she wants. She wants me to claim the hand of the dead.

2

I take a deep breath. We both know that claiming the hand of the dead is no small matter, and I glance up at Mimi, expecting her to be looking back at me with sympathy, with understanding, perhaps a little sadness. But she is already climbing the short flight of wooden steps to the cramped loft space above the bedroom. I hear the creak of her tread on the floorboards over my head. The roof is low, so I know she is bent over rummaging through the boxes and kegs, the rolls of dun-colored canvas we use as tents in summertime, Lenore's outgrown toys. We don't let Lenore go up in the loft. We tell her it's dusty, dangerous. We don't want her to find what my wife has kept hidden up there. Even I don't know where it is, and when I go up to look for a tool or a bit of leather to mend a broken harness, I keep my mind on my business. I don't think about the savage charm.

Mimi is on the third step, standing upright now. And I can see she has the glass-topped box in her hands. My breath catches in my throat.

The box is a rectangle. The bottom is the brilliant orange of hammered copper. It's very old, the finest craftsmanship. I think at one time the top was probably a kind of thin metal tracery or fretwork so the owner could look inside and see the relic. But the soldered hinges show signs of repair, and someone—maybe Anyeta—has had it replaced with glass. It reminds me of a miniature coffin made for a prince or a statesman.

My wife opens the lid, and the caravan is suddenly filled with a sweet fragrance. Briefly, the smell of lilies, tuberoses, gardenia overpowers the sickroom stench—the wet swampy odor of my disintegrating flesh.

She nods at me and sets the box on the low deal table between the bed and the sidewall.

The hand is nestled in a bed of worn velvet the maroon color of drying blood; displayed as if it were a wondrous antique jewel in a shop window, instead of an ugly lump of flesh.

It is black with age and has shrunken in on itself, so that the fingers are curled into a fist. It looks more like the hairless paw of some mummified dog than a human hand. If my wife were to turn it over I would see the fingernails.

They make round, slightly glossy spots like stove windows made of smoked mica. At the wrist two small bits of cracked yellowish bone can be seen.

The thought of claiming it makes my head whirl.

Mimi goes to the wooden door at the rear of the wagon. At the threshold, she turns and looks at me. In the half gloom her face is nearly as pale as her white blouse, and her eyes are the violet brown of pansies. She swallows nervously, then hangs her head a little. She doesn't want this for me, but we are both afraid Anyeta will dupe Lenore as Mimi herself was tricked into claiming it.

There is no air of command in her eyes or her posture, only pleading. She pauses, her hand touching the iron latch, and gives me a small smile. For a second I'm reminded of the young girl I fell in love with.

I don't know if I can summon the strength or courage to claim the hand of the dead. I settle deeper into the feather pillows, my arm resting crosswise over my brow. Mimi seems to know that I want, need, to think about the dark twisted tale of our lives.

I sigh, and suddenly she is at my side, her hand in my graying hair. She leans over the bed and kisses my eyelids one at a time.

"I love you, Imre," she shapes, and then she is hurrying toward the door. It shuts behind her. Neither of us knows whether she'll come back as herself or Anyeta.

Outside I hear Lenore's voice trembling with fear and grief. "Papa," she blurts. "He——?" Her question hangs for several seconds.

"Dying," comes the soft reply. And I know that my child is out there, alone, speaking with a demon that pretends to be her mother.

My eye is drawn to the copper box. The blackened hand seems to vibrate. I feel its power calling me, whispering promises like sighs in the hot wind that blows over the flat Hungarian plain. I grit my teeth. Drops of sweat break out at my hairline. Oh Jesus, no! I don't want this. I shake my head and a sharp steel cough racks my chest.

"Please. I can't."

A constellation of pallid faces—Joseph, Constantin, Mimi, Lenore—crowd the air around my head like cherubs in a religious painting. Their eyes are full of sorrow, begging me to intervene.

"Think of the power." A musical voice hums in my mind—fills it.

"Christ, Christ," I moan. For then I am hearing the haunting sound of gypsy violins. I see the *bosa venos* around the campfire, their faces lit in the ruddy glare. Their heads are canted over the shining instruments. The bows are flying faster, faster. Feet moving over scattered rose petals, the swirl of a gauzy scarf. Mimi dancing. I cover my face with my hands.

"Remember, Imre?"

Yes. After the feast, Mimi danced again—for me alone— in our caravan the night of our wedding. The women had drawn dotted patterns on her hands with red henna for the ceremony; but when I undressed my bride I found she'd privately, daringly rouged her nipples. Her boldness fled, my delight made her suddenly shy. She was afraid the Romany women would show the white nuptial sheets in the morning, and there would be no virgin's blood because we'd been making love, secretly, for months. They didn't. But we stained and reddened the sheets with the henna on her body that transferred to mine. And in the times between our long sweet couplings, I got on my knees and vowed I'd never betray her. I didn't know I was telling a lie. And it *wasn't* a lie until Anyeta came into our lives; I wince hearing a low throaty chuckle bubbling with mockery.

"Look, Imre," the voice croons slyly. I watch transfi xed. The copper box opens, closes, opens, closes. Each time the lid thuds down the caravan walls seem to reverberate. There is another crash, and then I'm lost in the tunnel of memories, hearing the sound of the stranger pounding the door on the night it all began ten months ago.

3
Late August, 1863. Buda-Pest.

I clearly remember the evening Anyeta's messenger arrived. It was toward twilight and I was standing at the long wooden counter in the kitchen, hacking at a fat brown hare and putting the chunks of meat into an enamel stewpot. Mimi and Lenore sat at the table slicing wild mushrooms. Through the window I glanced toward the clearing and saw wisps of drifting smoke from a ring of abandoned campfires mingling with the gathering shadows and the gray mist. The only sound was the wind moving through the trees, or the occasional soft blat of insects drawn to our light and bumping against the glass. Hearing these small noises against the deeper quiet made me feel isolated, a little lonely. There had been a big, noisy wedding feast for Tomas and Helene a few days before, but with the celebrating finished, the rest of our small troupe—some twenty gypsies— had left that afternoon to roam south toward the Lake region with its spas and resorts and tourists. Sometimes I like to think if Mimi and Lenore and I had gone with the troupe, Anyeta's messenger would never have found us, or at least we might have left Lenore in safety with the others, but it isn't true. I'm sure Anyeta's messenger had orders to track us half way across the continent, if it came to that. Anyway, I—we all—wanted to stay in the wooded camp in the hills above the city. There was a rumor circulating that Empress Sisi was coming to the capital. Buda was celebrating the feast of Stephen. Mimi—and especially Lenore—wanted to see her. There were heavy holiday crowds in the marketplace, and I wanted to earn enough money to get us through the coming winter.

"Tourists," I said, thinking of the departed troupe on its way to the resorts, "don't buy horses." I cut an onion into rough quarters and added it to the pot. "It's all right for the others—Rudolph can sell wood carving anywhere, or Kitta can get in a bit of fortune-telling—"

"*Dukkeripen!*" Lenore jumped up from the table, her long braids plaited with brilliant red cotton swinging wildly, her round brown eyes wide. "I'll go right up to Sisi in her glass carriage—"

"They only use that one for weddings, honey," Mimi said, smiling. Lenore had heard that the Habsburgs, Franz Joseph and Elizabeth, had a special glass carriage designed by Rubens and nothing could convince her that the Empress didn't ride in this airy confection all the time. "Why not? If it was mine, I would," Lenore used to say.

Ignoring her mother, Lenore went on. "I'll say, 'Your Ladyship, your Worshipfulness,'"—she mimed bowing her head, dipping her knees in a low curtsy—"'I am but a poor, poor gypsy girl, unskilled in the art of *dukkeripen*, but let me tell your future. You will have many more children and much happiness. You will live to a great age, and when you are finally called, your Highness will make what we gypsies call a good death—peaceful, surrounded by all your beloved children and grandchildren. Amen.'"

At the end of this crazy quilt prayer-speech, Lenore made the sign of the cross, then clamped her hands together at the same time she squeezed her eyes shut as hard as she could. She was so small for her age, and her face was so earnest, Mimi and I were laughing. Curious, Lenore opened one eye to see what we were laughing at, just as I caught the distant sound of hoofbeats ascending the rise toward the campsite.

"One of yours?" Mimi joked.

I'd sold a slicked-up nag the day before to a young farmer whose enthusiasm made him fasten on the gleaming new saddle I'd thrown into the bargain, when he should have been looking at the mare's considerable defects. But dissatisfied or not, my customers didn't seek me out. All bargaining was final I'd tell them before I took the cash or the trade. Now, hearing the horse and rider approach, I wiped my hands on a towel, thinking Mimi had been doing a brisk business with her herbs and tonics; her best seller was a bottled brew she called *Santekash*. It was willow bark and ordinary water, and while it did cure headaches, she stressed its ability to stop a hangover dead in its tracks. Buda on holiday was a big drinking town. Maybe, I thought, it was some drunken Hussar who'd made his way to the gypsy camp looking for a quick cure. Outside our caravan, I heard a man's low voice reining his horse, the creak of leather as he dismounted quickly.

"One of Mother's customers," Lenore said alertly.

But before either of us could make an answer, there was the sharp staccato of bootheels hurrying up the wooden steps, and a fist striking heavily over and over again just below the carvings on the green caravan door.

A Rom I'd never seen before stood shrouded in the gloom of the doorstep. In the dim light I picked out the gleam in his dark eyes, a long sharp nose, a thin sickle of a smile. His face and clothes were streaked with road dirt. A spattered cape swirled lightly around his legs, near the rolled tops of a pair of travel-scarred boots.

"Anyeta sent me," he said, at the same time he thrust one hand against the center of the door, pushing it wide. He stepped high to cross the threshold and brushed past me.

"You've seen her?" Mimi said.

I felt a low dread settling over me like the chill damp in an earth cellar. There'd been no news of Anyeta in Hungary for twenty years—not since before the uprising in '48, when the Emperor brought in Russian troops to squash the revolt. And I realized suddenly that some part of my mind hoped or believed she'd died in the uprising or its aftermath. Shot. . . starved, perhaps.

He came to a stop in the center of the room. There was an eerie stillness in his face and form—all except his ebony eyes, which glittered too brightly. He peered down at Mimi. "The sorceress is camped three, maybe four days east of here, just beyond the Romanian border."

An image of the Carpathian Mountains—dark, steep, wild— that lay between us and the old woman rose in my mind. "And what does she want now?" I asked, but I saw the answer was already glimmering behind the brilliant eyes and sardonic grin.

"What any Romany mother wants." He paused, and his shrewd eye fell first on Mimi and then on Lenore. "A good death," he whispered. I heard Lenore's quick inhale, saw her narrow shoulders stiffen, but before I could intervene, the stranger spoke again.

"Anyeta's dying, she wants her child. She said, 'I want Mimi to have my place in the troupe. Tell her I have secrets.'" His voice went high and reedy. "'Things inside me that belong to her, to her daughter if she has one.'"

There was a sudden silence in the room. Anyeta's voice, I thought, not just her words, but her voice—the quivery way it would sound if she were near death. I thought of Lenore pretending to tell the Empress hers would be a good death, of the stranger's oily insinuating gaze as he'd hissed the same words. I felt my heart speed up. It was as if the old woman had somehow reached across the distance and hidden herself in the room to listen, like a spy skulking in the shadowy corners of things.

"No," I said, "*No.*" I wanted no more talk of the old woman in front of my daughter. I caught Mimi's eye, signaling a reminder that Lenore was in the room.

"Lenore," Mimi said, "go to the bin and get more potatoes for the stew."

"But—" She began to protest, having peeled some half dozen already, but Mimi was firm. I moved to the window and waited until I saw Lenore go on her knees to crawl toward the storage bin under the caravan. Then I spoke up.

"Secrets be damned, Anyeta's a whore," I said, pacing, remembering the night Mimi lost our first child, a stillborn girl. I'd woken alone, to candlelight. Anyeta stood naked at the foot of the bed. "Your wife is *marhime*—unclean. You cannot lie with her all this month," she'd said, grinning. It was not the first time she'd propositioned me and I threw her out. Mimi never knew, but she had no regrets about leaving the old woman or Romania when we decamped a few weeks later.

"Witchcraft." I shook my head. "It's trumpery. She's nothing but a clever whore, and you know it."

"Do I?" His deep-set eyes met mine, and it came to me he'd been cradling one arm beneath the heavy folds of his cape. I heard the faint slurring of the wool as he extended the arm beneath it. The hand he showed was studded with brown bulbous swellings of different sizes. The smaller knobs had the shiny look of tightly stretched skin. The largest—the size of an egg—hung like a soft sac from just above his wrist. He began to roll back his shirt-cuff, and the tumor made a flopping sound against his skin.

"It's pemphigus," Mimi said.

"Is it, *gule romni?*" He'd called my wife a healer, but his voice was thick with sarcasm. "This arm," he said, "only this one, and there is a bloat like the rotting flesh of a fruit in the webbing between my shoulder and chest." He started to undo his shirt.

I felt myself go white. "No, no more." I reached out to stop him. My fingers grazed the brown egg-like sac; it ruptured and began to ooze a thick mucky-looking fluid.

He jerked his arm back, hiding it once more beneath the voluminous cape. He took three long strides to the door, then paused on the threshold. "She's a *choovahanee*, I tell you. Don't do anything foolish; don't keep her waiting. Leave at first light."

"Yes," I said vaguely; I had no intention of trekking across the border. The Romanian gypsies were a superstitious lot, and he'd called Anyeta a sorceress. I didn't know what the course of his disease was, but it was clear he believed Anyeta had afflicted him; he'd brought her message because he was terrified she would do worse.

"But you haven't asked the way," he said, pulling a small paper from his breast pocket. I saw it was a crude map, the route traced in pencil. I put my hand out for it and was suddenly aware of Lenore's light step coming around the side of the caravan. She was singing softly to herself.

"Go on, leave us now," I said, edging him onto the stoop and pulling at the door handle behind me.

Smiling that narrow unctuous grin, he pushed the map at me, then clattered down the stairs. The paper fluttered to the wooden boards. I bent down, scooped it up, found myself at eye level with the Romanian gypsy. Lenore now stood in the thin, trampled grass at the foot of the steps. Her skirt was spread between her hands and sagging a little with the weight of the potatoes.

"*Bahtalo drom*," she said politely, nodding at the stranger. She was wishing him luck on the road ahead.

"Your grandmother's very words," he said, at the same time I saw the phrase scrawled at the top of the map. I frowned at the coincidence. He began to laugh softly, then pulled the heavy wool cape tighter across his chest and moved into the denser shadows. I listened to the muffled sound of his boots in the high summer grass; his footsteps faded, then finally ceased. It was then I realized, with something of a jolt, he had walked off into the night. I had imagined hearing hoofbeats climbing the hill and signaling his approach, but there was no horse in our campsite on the rise.

"She's dying, Imre."

Mimi had spoken first. I knew she would. She doesn't keep things back or brood. None of us had eaten much dinner, Lenore was asleep, and my wife and I sat at the kitchen table, each with a small glass of brandy. The oil lantern overhead made a circle of yellow light against the white cloth, our hands; I looked at Mimi's shadow wavering on the wall behind her.

"You hated her," I countered.

"But she's my mother," she said, getting up and coming round to my side of the table. I watched her shadow flickering on the wall as she paced.

"You couldn't wait to get away from her, from all of them."

"But I was so young. I was nothing in that troupe, I had no status, no place. *Gule romni!*" She spat the words. "Not even that, not even a healer, just a girl puttering and playing with herbs." Mimi lowered her eyes. She looked sad, a little anxious. "Imre, there are things you don't know—"

"What—those secrets? *Dukkeripen*—saying the future? It's ridiculous, too asinine to even consider. You've told me a hundred times it's nothing but keen observation. You watch for the rubbed flesh on the fourth finger where a woman has taken off her wedding ring and thinks she's going to fool you. Or for that slightly anxious look in an old maid's eyes. And then you tell them what they want to hear. Christ, even Lenore knows it—that silly play acting about the Empress—"

"Maybe you don't understand because you're a *diddikai*," she said.

She'd called me a half-breed; well, I was—my mother was English, but my father was a gypsy and I'd lived with one troupe or another all my life. She was a *puro-rati*, a pure-blood, but it was the first time she'd ever made mention of what I thought of as a minor difference between us. I stared at Mimi, but her face was closed.

"My mother—she—" Mimi hesitated, biting her lip. "She helped me get you." If it were true, I thought, recalling Anyeta's naked appearance by my bedside, she would have kept me for herself.

"I had a crush on you," she went on, "but you didn't know I even existed; and then my mother made me a charm to wear on my wrist, to bind you to me. It was a *mulengi dori*, and I tied it into seven knots and—"

As a rule, Mimi was not at all superstitious and I felt my anger rising. I struck the table with the flat of my hand. "Are you going to tell me you believe that a piece of string that someone used to measure a dead man for his coffin brought us together? We've been in love twenty-two years, Mimi! *Twenty-two years!*" I seized her wrist. She tried to jerk it out of my grasp, but I held on. "I'll grant you that it was your mother's influence that forged the bond between us—but it was because you despised her! Have you forgotten?"

I squeezed her wrist harder, and below the fragile bones the flesh of her hand paled, revealing even more clearly than usual a patch of livid wrinkled scar tissue—the faded remains of a hideous burn—in the center of her palm. "Have you forgotten? Have you?"

"No," she whispered. Tears glistened at the rims of her eyelids, and I knew I shouldn't press her, but I did.

"Tell me," I said, "if she was such a great sorceress, if she had so much power, tell me why she had to hold her own child's hand against a cast iron tea kettle while that child screamed and squirmed and begged her to stop?"

"She caught me spying," Mimi breathed, and I thought she looked younger, more vulnerable with the memory. I let go of my wife's wrist and she stepped back, rubbing at the tender flesh.

"And *what* did she say? 'The next time I catch you watching me, Missy, I'll put out your eyes. . . .'"

"Yes," Mimi hissed.

"And is that what you want for our child, for Lenore?"

"No, no!" She shook her head, her dark hair swayed around her shoulders; the shadow behind her rippled in tandem.

"Is this a fantasy then? Grandma Anyeta sitting wrapped in her shawl by the fire telling her beloved granddaughter the old gypsy tales, while you play nursemaid, make honeycake and fluff the pillows?"

"Yes," she said, but too low for me to catch. Her eyes showed it.

"Everything she did healed, forgotten, forgiven? Tell me why you want to go!"

"Guilt," Mimi said. She sat heavily at the table. "If only you know how it makes me feel inside, how the hatred for her is all mixed up with these terrible hating feelings I have for myself." Mimi's voice went high and tight. "You think I don't know what happened the night I lost Elena? She taunted me with it! Told me not to trust you at the same time she was gloating. 'He's delicious, darling, but you'll have to watch him like a hawk—a handsome man like that, and so very good with women. But then, you must know,' and she put her hand low on my belly, like this," Mimi said, touching herself, "and gave it a nasty little squeeze."

"And did you think I betrayed you—with her, with *anyone?*"

"No. But I would find myself flirting, fantasizing about other men, half-wishing something would start up between us, and it made me afraid that deep down I was just like her, a woman who used men, a whore." She shook her head slowly. "And even that isn't the worst. Sometimes," she pressed her hands to her eyes, "Oh Christ, Imre, sometimes Lenore would do some little thing—trying to help, she'd drop a loaf of bread I had ready for the oven, and I'd hear the roaring clatter of the pan against the floor and see the white dough shapeless on the dirty boards, and my mind—I just—" She stopped, grinding her teeth.

"Black anger would spiral, screaming through me, and I'd hear myself screaming, 'I told you to leave it alone, Lenore! And now look at *this*! The bread is ruined, it's been rising all morning, and *now when I'm ready to bake it's ruined!*' And my hand would flash up. Christ, I'd want to hurt her, hurt her bad, and I'd see you." She began to weep quietly. "And at the last second, I'd get hold of myself and stop. I'd take Lenore and hug her and we'd both be crying, Lenore, because I'd frightened her, and me because I knew if I'd hit her, I would lose you forever." She paused, and I sat stunned, silent.

"You were my strength, Imre," she said simply. "Without you I would have been just like Anyeta. But you kept me from it. Because you were loyal to me, because you knew how to love me and Lenore. Because you were kind and good."

Mimi wiped her eyes and I took her moist hands in mine. "These things are more reason yet to stay away from her," I said.

"No, I have to see her. I can't forgive myself until I forgive her—"

I felt another surge of anger. Anyeta deserved not forgiveness but to die, tortured. "Forget this guilt—you did nothing! It was her. Why don't you understand that she did these vicious things, that none of it was your fault—"

"I want peace of mind. I have to go—"

"No, I don't want Lenore anywhere near her—"

"It's twenty years, Imre. People change. Maybe she has no secrets, no place in the *kumpania*." Mimi's dark violet eyes took on a far off look, and I thought about how she'd lapsed into the Romany of her girlhood. "Maybe she just wants my forgiveness before she dies."

"No, I won't have it." But even as I said the words, I knew it was only the last of my anger showing itself against the backdrop of the helplessness I felt, the control I was trying to maintain. I felt my ire draining rapidly. Already I could see myself packing the caravan in the gray gloom before dawn, consulting the stranger's pencilled map.

"My mother needs me. I need to see her." Mimi's voice held a peculiar note and I found myself wondering what really lured her. Did she need to forgive herself for despising Anyeta all these years? To exorcise the specter of those old painful memories? Or was it her mother's dark promise? *Tell Mimi I have secrets.*

"All right," I nodded, giving in. I didn't believe in sorcery. And I expected no deathbed apologies or change of heart from Anyeta, but Mimi was my wife, we were a family, we would go.

4

Romania

"A miserable trip through a miserable country," I said aloud, looking up at the moon casting its harsh light high on the tall alien peaks of the western Carpathians. Mimi had urged me to drive hard, and the days were a kaleidoscope of images: Lenore wailing, "Now I'll never see the Empress!" and taking her last look at the massive stone towers of the Lanchid Bridge when we crossed the Danube from Buda to Pest; the long sweep of the *puszta*, the grassy plains with their herds of wild horses that stretched north to the Nyirseg region, my boyhood home; and then as we crossed the border near Oradea and the land began to rise, the kaleidoscope shifted, revealing bad roads, hurried meals, old, crumbling towns, lumpy women and closed-face men in their crude shapeless shoes bowing at the wooden shrines.

Sorceress or not, with each passing kilometer I dreaded more and more the thought of facing the old woman. Far off a wolf howled and I shivered. Mimi and Lenore were sleeping in the caravan. I had a cold, I was tired. I stopped the wagon, unsure of the way, and leaned out over the edge feeling queasy when I registered the drop.

"Christ." Sheer rock face rose straight up on the left. To my right was a valley, shrouded with mist; here and there trees broke through and glittered darkly. The descent looked menacing. I wanted to stop and sleep a while but there was no place to tether the horses. I curled my toes in my boots trying to warm them a little, sniffled, then gave the reins a flap. The caravan lurched forward. I caught the sound of the wolf's mournful cry; it was still distant, but the lead horse suddenly laid back its ears, snorted in fear and began to bolt.

The rear wheel slewed out until I thought it would buckle under the weight, the wagon tilted and swayed. I saw the sharp outcroppings of the rocks loom up in a second of heart freezing clarity, and then the horses countered the strain, jerking us right, but we were still roaring downhill through the night.

"Whoa!" I stood up, screaming at them to halt, the wind whistling past my ears. My voice echoed and rumbled in the canyons, but in my terror it came back to me as *Run, run, run!*

The team was in a frenzy. I saw their sides heaving, the thick cloud shapes from hard breathing, heard the sound of their hooves and the racketing caravan, and a flash went through me—someone else was controlling the horses, I thought wildly. We were going to be killed. Now moving through dense forest, the road dipped. We rounded a sharp turn and the carriage lanterns bobbed and swayed crazily. Up ahead, lights gleamed dimly through the heavy fog, and for a brief instant I was disoriented. I heard the sound of muffled voices.

"Back, get back," someone warned. A pale hand appeared and faded eerily in the mist.

The road widened through the wall of trees, and in a panic I realized there was another caravan dead ahead of us. I yanked the reins, closed my eyes, threw my arm up and tensed, waiting for the crash. The wagon slewed and jolted against an ancient oak on the right. I felt the blood rushing to my head. Everything came to a sudden and immediate stop at the impact.

In the moments that followed I was groggy and confused. Footsteps and voices seemed to come and go in the cold fog. Through a haze I thought I saw a tall woman in a white gown, laughing with her head thrown back; I thought I heard a man growling at her angrily, "Keep off, you've done enough." But the white figure blurred, then slipped through the trees, and I slipped into a darkness of my own.

"Imre, Imre," a voice called low in my ear. "You passed out."

I opened my eyes, blinking, and an old man's face came into focus. His cheeks were thin, with no pad of flash under the chin; his eyes were hooded, set under heavy white brows. He dragged on a cigarette, and I saw a gold signet ring gleam on his middle finger.

"You remember me?" he asked.

My eyes flicked from the ring to the gaunt face. "Joseph?"

He nodded, absently rubbing one knee. He walked with a limp, I recalled; he was a Lovari gypsy—like my father—one of the skilled horsemen. He was the leader of the troupe Anyeta belonged to. My fingers strayed to the base of my skull where I found an egg-shaped bulge, and his eyes caught the movement.

"Gave your head a hell of a knock." He indicated the rear wall of the caravan. "Lucky you weren't thrown."

"Mimi, Lenore," I began.

"Sleeping—they're all right." He flicked the cigarette over the side of the wagon.

"That's impossible," I started to say, rising from the seat. He laid hold of my coat lapel, his piercing eyes meeting mine.

"They sleep," he said, briefly touching one dry finger to my temple. "And sleeping easily, they dream. Listen."

It seemed to me I heard the sound of breathing inside the wagon—a soft, peaceful riffling. "They're asleep," I whispered. He nodded, and his hand dropped away from my face.

"Your *vurdan's* scraped some, but the wheels are sound." He paused. "I've been waiting here the last two nights for you."

I thought of the flash that went through me when the horses bolted. Had he meant to kill us, stopped in the road like that?

He sat forward, his eyes glittering, and I had the feeling he sensed what was going through my mind. I shivered, dismissing the thought. It was fatigue, the cold, the jarring accident, the damn country—riddled with superstition and dread—all combining to make me confuse fact with fancy.

"Anyeta's dead," Joseph said.

I felt my stomach tighten. We made the trip for nothing, I thought dismally, and slumped against the chill wood.

"It's better this way," he said. "Nobody wanted you to come— nobody wanted Mimi to come. They were beshitting themselves with fright, convinced the old sorceress would give Mimi her powers, and they'd be right where they were before—under some witch's thumb."

"You don't believe that. You're the leader, tell them—"

"My son Vaclav is the *prima*. He leads the gypsies now." He gave a weak smile, and the image of his son—a big, arrogant man—went through my mind. I'd never liked Vaclav. "It doesn't matter what I believe, but you might do well to stay away—'til afterwards. The funeral's the day after tomorrow."

"'Til she's buried, you mean."

"It wouldn't be hard," he said. "You could take the wagon, drive beyond the pass, meet me here two or three nights from now. There's enough forks and turnings that without me guiding, you'd probably miss the camp even in daylight."

"I—" I didn't know what to say. There was something deeply persuasive in his voice, and the idea held a kind of pearly glow, like the deep comfort of a pleasant dream. Yes, I could *pretend* I lost the way, we would see the grave in the woods, Mimi would stand, head bowed, brushing tears from her eyes, and then we would pack our things, take Lenore, and leave the country forever. And then a small nagging voice spiked through me: *She'll know, she'll guess and she'll never forgive you.*

"I can't do it," I said. "Anyeta was her mother. She wanted to come, she deserves to see the old woman one last time before she goes into the ground."

"Suit yourself." He shrugged and began to stiffly climb down from the wagon.

"Look, Mimi's told me the others were terrified of her mother, but you know the Romanians, Joseph—Christ, if you believe them every town has more ghosts than people—and the gypsies are even—" I stopped, ashamed of my slip.

"Worse," he finished. "But seeing more, they have more reason, perhaps." He touched one finger alongside his bony eyesocket. "You're like your mother, Imre. You never believed—not even when your senses might have told you different." He paused, one hand played over the lead horse's nose, the horse nuzzled his palm. "Keep your skepticism, half-gypsy, as long as you can—but don't let Mimi go into the old woman's wagon alone."

"Anyeta's dead—"

"I know," he said, slapping the horse's flank lightly, "but if they catch her alone with the body, there's going to be a lot of ugliness."

Joseph limped toward his barrel-topped caravan. He paused, coughing painfully, then heaved himself up onto the box. *He's grown old*, I thought sadly, clucking to gee up my team, and the old are more liable to superstition. Then his wagon, perpendicular to mine, shot ahead in the early gray light, and for a second I would've sworn the reins were gathered in a knot to one side of the rail, and that he was resting, arms folded, a cigarette idling between his pale thin lips. But that was impossible. No unguided team could navigate the pitted twisting roads in this godforsaken country. I was tired, it was foggy, it was a trick of the light.

5

An hour and half later we drove into the camp. I pulled into the rough semicircle of ten or twelve shabby caravans ringing a communal fire. It was just a little past dawn and I was surprised at the emptiness of the place. A baby wailed from inside one of the wagons, making the tree lined clearing with its dark towering pines seem lonelier still. I was just about to ask Joseph where the other gypsies—what he would call the Vaclav-*eshti*—were, when I turned to see him disappearing through the canvas flaps of a faded blue wagon. Sighing, I unhitched my horses, set them to crop grass, then walked toward the rear of the caravan to go in and wake Mimi, tell her the news.

Behind me I heard a swift rattle of chains. *Someone's monkey*— before I could complete the thought, a short tubby man, dark hair twisted into greasy spikes, leaped out at me, forcing me against the caravan. I heard the slither of the chains at his feet, saw the broken end of one link.

"Wa—re, wa—re," he gibbered in a broken guttural voice. He went on tiptoe, pushed his stubbly face into mine, and I smelled the hot sour odor of decaying teeth. He began to mutter again and I turned my face aside, but not before I'd seen the raw wound where his tongue had been cut away.

I tried to dodge him, moving from one side to the other, but he was quick. His hands shot out, thwarting first one of my shoulders, then the other. I bounced between them like a steel ball rattling back and forth against the pins in a game of bagatelle, while he laughed at me.

"Constantin," Joseph called out sharply. I saw the old man standing at the end of the alley-like passage between the wagons. "Leave Imre alone." The short man backed away at once and stood rubbing his wrists as if he were ashamed. I saw the red marks of handcuffs on his skin.

Joseph grabbed Constantin's arm and attached one end of a pair of old heavy manacles. "Where is it?" Joseph demanded.

The tubby little man made a gurgling sound, shrugging off the question. "None of your nonsense, hand it over," Joseph said. The man hung his head—like a child with a jelly smeared chin caught reaching for a second bun.

"C'mon," Joseph said, putting his hand out. Constantin squirmed his bottom, then reached inside his trousers and withdrew a file. Joseph took it from him and put it in his own breast pocket, saying, "I keep him in my wagon most days—not last night, though. I went in to fetch him from Stephan, who was out cold. Hangover," Joseph grunted. "Constantin saw his chance and cut the chains and cuffs. I knew he'd be here."

"How?" I lit a cigarette to calm my nerves.

"Constantin sniffs out anything out of the ordinary—like the arrival of another caravan." Joseph paused, and he tugged at the gold ring on his middle finger.

Constantin. I knitted my brow. I knew the name. The memory of a plump young man rose in my head. He'd been a great practical joker, a good storyteller. "He went mad?" I breathed.

Old Joseph nodded. "Anyeta did it."

"Say what you want about *her*, but *you* keep him in chains."

"He wouldn't hurt anybody, that's so he doesn't hurt himself— again."

A spurt of revulsion sluiced through me. "He—Constantin cut out his own tongue?" As soon as I said these words, the short man screwed up his eyes and began to weep, his mouth jerked and twitched. The dark stubble on his face shone with a mixture of tears and saliva.

"That'll do," Joseph said, then turned to me. "If he gets to crying hard, he'll start howling. It's hell on the nerves." Joseph laid one hand on Constantin's head, and I had the uneasy feeling I was watching a dog heel to his master. "Buck up, now," Joseph said. Sniffling, Constantin wiped his face with his sleeve and smiled weakly.

I couldn't look at him. The ghostly little grin was more horrible than his tears.

"Two—maybe three months ago," Joseph said, "we heard a big ruckus in his wagon. Shouting. He was screaming, over and over, 'I'll teach that liar's mouth to smart off to me!' and then we heard shrieks, a series of thick babbling grunts, the sound of hammering."

Joseph's lips were tight. "We had to break the door. When we got inside, he was passed out at the table, lying with his face in a pool of blood. He didn't just cut it out—the severed tongue was smashed against the table," he said. "And if you ask me what was worse—the sight of his white face with the blood pouring over his lips, or the sight of the pulverized flesh clinging in flecks and gobbets to the head of the hammer—I'll tell you I don't know." He closed his eyes. "I see them both—his face and the bloody hammer—in my dreams." He paused. "So I keep him with me, keep him clean and comfortable—as much as one man can do for another."

"And you believe Anyeta cursed him?"

"Imre," he said tiredly, "there is much I've seen—more than there's time to tell you. Let your wife do her duty, and take your family away."

He led Constantin off, and I considered what he'd said. The last advice was sound, certainly. I crushed out the cigarette and looked up. In the distance I could see Anyeta's peeling yellow caravan, driven out of the rough circle in the clearing. The whole campsite had a dispirited, depressing air—here and there I saw a rusted chimney flue slanted at a weird angle over roof boards, or a set of stairs made from knocked-together crates—as if times were hard of late, and I thought about how poverty and superstition went hand in hand. Young men dream of the future, of prosperity; it was the poverty that chafed and galled me twenty years ago—and standing there, I suddenly remembered exactly why Mimi and I had left the troupe:

"What's that in the bag?" Mimi had asked. She was too thin in my opinion, recovering much too slowly from Elena's stillbirth. It was dusk and I'd just come into the caravan carrying a large burlap sack, and the smell in the air told me we were about to sit down, for the third night in a row, to another supper of roasted onions.

The troupe was camped in the mountains near Tirgu Mures I recalled, and all that winter there'd been no money in the district, and therefore no horse trading. All of us were pinched and pale— except Anyeta—she looked as rosy as a milkmaid lapping cream night and day. Now it was coming on for spring, but I'd spent another depressing day in town to scare up a few *lei*, and I'd fallen back on what were time-honored occupations among gypsies, but for me strictly marginal work. I'd spent a dull morning shining shoes and grinding knives. In the afternoon I had the choice of two other menial jobs commonly given to gypsies—teeth pulling or rat catching. The idea of chasing around someone's mouth for a rotted tooth seemed even more horrible than grubbing behind dank walls for the rats. And after I consumed a very small loaf of bread and dispensed a very large hunk of palaver, I struck a deal and shook hands over a dirty wooden counter with the fat owner of a cheese shop.

Inside the dank cellar under the shop I found myself wishing I were in a field, listening to the ringing sound of the anvil, the whinnying of horses instead of the squeak and scrabble of rats. With a sigh, I brought out what I privately called the tools of the rat pulverizing trade—a hammer to clobber them and a bag to stuff their bodies inside.

But the rats were cunning at hiding from me, and I'd been so late at it the cheese shop owner finally left, taking his cash box with him and leaving his underling to put up the shutters and lock the door. The shop keeper promised to pay me 50 *lei* per rat when he returned in the morning. I didn't trust the underling—a pimple faced boy of thirteen or fourteen—to keep track of my quarry. In fact, he looked like the kind of boy who could think of several interesting things one could do with dead rats, from scaring small children to seeing how rodent guts splattered when you lay the filthy creatures in the road and watched horse carts run over them. So instead of leaving the dead vermin in the shop cellar, I brought my bounty—four or five large ugly gray brutes—home.

"Is it meat?" Mimi said. I guess my frustration made me decide the countermeasure of a joke was in order.

"Yes," I said, plumping the burlap bag onto the table.

"What kind?" she said, untying the knotted rope that held it closed.

"Mostly dark," I said, at the same time she peered deep into the sack and began to shriek.

"*Rats!*" she shouted. "Oh mother of God, you can't mean you expect us to eat these disgusting rats!"

"I admit they're a little scrawny—but somebody else beat me to the choicer, plumper specimens in the butcher shop—"

She suddenly pressed her hands to her eyes; at first I thought she was laughing; a little hysterically, perhaps, but then her shoulders shook and she began to sob. I took her in my arms. She tried to shrug me off but I held on, saying over and over I was sorry, cursing my stupidity. It had been a mean winter for everyone, and spring had finally come but nothing was better. The thought crossed my mind that she was crying not on account of the rats but because she was secretly afraid she'd lost the baby because of the scant food.

"We have to leave, there's nothing for me here," I said.

"I hate the wandering, the endless roaming," she said, and I nodded, knowing she was feeling edgy and weak and I debated whether or not I should tell her about two incidents.

Yesterday I'd seen a man burning down his own house, the flames roaring against the gray sky when the small bright tiled roof collapsed. It was five years before the revolution of '48, when Transylvania would be ruled by the Habsburgs, but like all uprisings, the seeds were already being sown. He had no money to pay the chimney tax; they would take his land if he didn't pay. "Now I got no chimney, Mister, and I don't owe no tax," he'd said, pointing to the black tumble of stones and spitting on the soft brown mud between his cracked boots. "But where will you go?" I'd asked. His round, chapped face was impassive, his voice dull with resignation. "Up there," he said with a sweep of his arm, toward the towering mountains on the horizon, "to the hills." I wasn't sure what he meant, I guessed he saw the puzzlement on my face, my brows narrowing, and he went on. "To the caves, Mister. I will take my wife and my children to live in a cave." He shivered lightly in the cool spring breeze. "God takes care of the animals, perhaps things will go better next year, or by His grace, the year after that." In my mind's eye I pictured the farmer and his family huddled inside a cold stony tomb like a dark wet mouth and I shuddered. The fact that Mimi and I were living in a caravan was meager comfort. I felt my heart pound lightly with anxiety; I wondered if things would be better next year or the year after that, if telling Mimi about the other incident would frighten her, or maybe make her angry enough to leave—

"We could ask my mother for money," she said, taking my hand lightly; unconsciously she had keyed into my mental debate, and I winced. A month or two before I'd gone to Anyeta to ask for money.

"I don't think so," I said to Mimi, hearing Anyeta's answer, her taunting voice echoing in my head: "Let your wife go whoring," Anyeta had said, her eyes dancing as brightly as the flames behind the isinglass in her stove. She was warming her plump backside by the fire, her hands behind her, fingers stretched toward the glowing flames.

I stood there, feeling her eyes crawl over me and absently turned my black hat in small circles in my hands. I knew she had gold pieces by the dozen sewn inside her mattress.

Filthy bitch, I thought, dropping my eyes, telling myself to try another tack. "Mimi is your daughter."

"Money is money," she shrugged. She didn't add *whoring was good enough for her;* instead, she moved off from the fire, flat hips swaying like a cat's, and let her sensuous walk say it for her.

"She's pregnant," I said, seeing Anyeta turn her back and retreat to the other end of her cozy caravan. "I'm asking for her sake, because there are things she needs." *Ask her for a goddamn loan instead of a gift and get out*, a part of me considered.

Anyeta sat on the edge of her bed and I heard the brief shift and tinkle of coins inside the feather mattress. At the sound, her sharp eyes fastened on mine. "I never loan money," she said. She suddenly lay down on her side, one hand supporting her head with its mass of dark heavy hair, the other lightly sweeping back and forth, tracing a path between the place where her right breast touched the patchwork quilt and one hip rested.

"Loaning money is out of the question," she said again, patting the red and blue quilt, and turning liquid eyes up to mine. "But I might give it—as a favor."

I was a poor excuse for a husband, I told myself, but Mimi deserved better than this degradation—a life of poverty or a life of whoredom.

"And I'm no whore, either," I said, turning to leave. I heard Anyeta's throaty laugh when I shut the door.

Looking at the bag of rats on the table, I decided not to tell her any of it. I would make my appeal based on hope, on the future. I shook my head, "I don't want to ask your mother. I want us to make a life for ourselves." I told her my heart was in Hungary with the wild horses, and in my mind's eye I saw the cowboys we called *csikos* wearing their wide sleeved linen shirts and hairy sheepskin capes, squatting by their campfires, galloping over the prairies.

I don't remember everything I said that night, but Mimi took a chance on me. I never forgot that. She believed in me, agreed to risk the known for the unknown, and less than a week later we left Romania for good.

Now, standing in the tall grass and gazing at Anyeta's broken-down wagon in the distance, I saw her malicious grin, heard her mocking voice in my mind, her contemptuous answer when I spoke of our need: *Let your wife go whoring.* It was twenty years later, the country was still ruined by poverty and superstition.

We would take Old Joseph's advice and leave soon, I thought; Mimi had trusted in me before, she would trust in me again.

I climbed the set of spruce little folding stairs I kept for when we traveled and went inside to tell my wife her mother was dead.

6

Mimi's hand was clenched tightly in mine as we walked through the high grass toward Anyeta's wagon. She'd taken the news better than I thought. She sat with her hands clasped between her knees, nodding vigorously as we all do when we hear something that shocks or stuns us. She didn't say anything. After a few minutes she stood up from the table. Her eyes were misty looking, but she wasn't crying hard.

Now I opened the canary colored door and Mimi followed me into the half gloom. Anyeta lay propped on her bed like a huge wizened doll. Her head lolled against her shoulder. Her dark eyes were open, staring vacantly and I saw that one of them had gone white and droopy looking. It bulged slightly toward her sharp cheekbone. Her scrawny hands were like wax sculptures hooked over the edge of the graying coverlet.

"Christ, they left her in filth," Mimi said. She stepped to the foot of the bed, and nervously fingered one of the tatty muslin drapes that pooled over the warped floorboards.

"She must have been ill a long time," I said, caught on the memory of her plump well-fed face as my eyes ranged over the room that had been once cozy, nearly sumptuous. Now, broken windowpanes were stuffed with balls of fabric. Bedding and ragged clothes were jumbled on the floor, trailing over the edge of the loft. A cupboard door hung crazily, disclosing shelves crammed with a grimy riot of pots and crocks and glassware. On the table I saw a clutch of sticky medicine bottles mingled with dishes of uneaten food, and the dusty remains of blackened herbs.

"The smell," she said, wrinkling her nose.

I nodded. It was something like the gaminess of a wild animal den: a dreadful stench of dirt and feces and flyblown meat.

"It can't be her—her body," Mimi said, "not so soon." Her eyes flicked from the pale wrinkled corpse to the gloomy disheveled room. She moved away and ran one finger over a water stain that swelled and bloated the wood of the right wall. "It makes my heart ache," Mimi said softly.

I agreed. Our childhood landscapes have that power over us, and seeing the place that was home cracked and ruined is like feeling your insides blocked with the weight of hard gray stone. "Let's go," I whispered, thinking this was making Mimi more and more uneasy. "If you stay longer, this will be the memory you take away with you."

She sat heavily on a bench that had been built into the kitchen wall. "They left her to die, the least I can do is straighten the place and sweep it out."

"Mimi," I said gently, sitting down and taking her hand, "after they bury her, they're going to burn the caravan."

"*Yag*," she said, repeating the word for fire in Romany. Her fingers were cold against my palm, she took her hand away and stood up. "You go to Lenore, I'll just carry the mess to the loft, sweep. A few minutes—no more."

I thought I understood. Anyeta had been cruel, but to leave the place in such a shambles would disgrace a beast.

Mimi kissed my cheek, pulled me up. "Go on," she said. "I won't be long."

I was on my feet, nodding agreeably when Joseph's warning flashed through me. *If they catch her alone, there's going to be a lot of ugliness.* Anxiety darted through me. I was her husband, but suppose they thought that was the same or worse than her being alone. I should've brought Joseph along, I railed inwardly; too late now. I sat down, folded my arms. "I'll wait, but be quick about it."

Mimi found a broom, opened the door and began sweeping a great cloud of dust outside. I yawned, leaned my head on my chest. I remembered thinking— only half-humorously—that I hoped no one broke a leg or had a heart attack while we were still inside the old woman's caravan. I peeked at the corpse under my lashes, then drifted toward a light sleep.

"Goddamn them to hell!" Mimi shouted.

I snapped awake. The door was ajar, a great deal of the mess had been tidied.

"Those *bastards!*" Mimi stood holding the bedcovers in one hand, blocking my view of the body.

"What, what is it?" I got to my feet, my spine crickled and snapped, I moved quickly toward the bed at the same time a great racking sob burst from Mimi. She dropped the covers and shrank against the wall, shaking her head in disbelief.

Suddenly she rushed forward again, crying, "Bastards, *bastards.* Christ, oh Christ!" She jerked the covers back and pummeled the bed with her fists, jouncing the body. She slumped to her knees, then sat heavily, clinging to one of the drapes. I saw it strain against the rail at the top of the bed, then plummet in a heap between her hands. "Pull up her nightdress and look," she said in a thick voice.

I tweezed the thin garment between my fingers, and slid it up the old woman's wrinkled flesh. My stomach tightened, I heard the blood singing in my ears.

Above the shrunken cleft of her sex, in the center of her abdomen was a series of long jagged knife marks, as if someone had dragged the knife from her breasts to her belly over and over and over. Dark crusty blood clotted the wounds.

"She was murdered," Mimi whispered from what seemed far away. "They murdered her."

7

"There's no blood on the sheets," I said. Someone had sponged and dressed the body, arranged it under the quilt; I felt my eye twitch, and before I could stop myself, I said, "Now it makes sense, Joseph was afraid you'd find out."

"What?" I heard her scrabbling, getting to her feet. She moved rapidly across the room, shook my shoulder hard. "What did you say?"

"Joseph—he—"

"He *what*? Don't stop, go on—"

"He told me not to let you come in here alone," I said quietly. "He knew, but I don't think he did it." My mind jumped to the image of Constantin, the dangling chains. I told Mimi about him. I sat down on the wooden bench, rubbing my hands over my thighs, trying to think. "Suppose Constantin cut her up, he's crazy, so he's not responsible. Joseph finds out—he's not trying to protect Constantin—only spare you."

Mimi flared. "And they hated her, and she was dying anyway, so if someone killed her, so what?" Her eyes glowed hotly, she paced rapidly, skirts swirling.

"Of course not," I said, wanting to tell her I was sad for her.

"Look at her arms." Mimi seized one limp hand. "No marks," she said, letting it fall. "She never had a chance, she didn't defend herself. They came at her when she was sleeping." Mimi shook her head, then suddenly she was kneeling between my legs, looking up at me.

"Imre, don't you see? It wasn't a madman, it was someone cunning. Someone who knew we were on our way and killed her before she could tell me—"

"Shhh." I grabbed Mimi's arm, heard the sound of someone clumping through the weeds. "Someone's coming." I pushed at her, we scurried up into the rickety loft, lying flat on the floor behind a tower of footlockers and boxes.

"We can't see," Mimi whispered in my ear. But the door was opening, and I didn't think we should risk creeping forward to peer over the edge.

I closed my eyes, listening for sounds—a heavy tread to indicate a man, the sweep of skirts. But whoever entered stood silently in the middle of the room. I could imagine the gypsy looking at the disheveled corpse, at Mimi's work with the broom, wondering if we were still inside, and I expected to hear an earthy chuckle, slow stealthy steps advancing up the stairs.

Instead, the room was plunged in cold darkness—as quick and sudden as nightfall in winter, and I felt Mimi shrink against me.

There was a tinkling of glass—windowpanes being shattered one by one in a dread sequence coursing around the room. The wind gusted up. I heard the cupboard doors flying back, the sound of bottles ringing against each other and falling, of the bed curtains sailing high and brushing the wood ceiling, and I knew something evil had swept in and stood waiting below us.

I heard a low menacing laugh. "Rise," a sexless voice whispered. "Rise," it intoned, and then a kind of brittle excitement infused the voice. "Rise!"

I buried my face against Mimi, trying to shut out sounds: the slow terrible hissing cataract of the falling bedclothes, the double thump of stiff wooden feet striking the floorboards and in my mind I could see the corpse—as pale as the lank white hair that streamed from its head—standing awkwardly in the center of the room and staring blankly with its good eye.

"Who owns the hand of the dead brings healing. Who owns the hand of the dead breeds destruction. Who owns the hand of the dead can take a life or restore it," the voice recited, and the words

sank like acid in my flesh.

I sensed the gypsy was watching, waiting.

Then I heard the creaking sound of Anyeta's jaw dropping: "As you have restored mine," she said, and her voice was utterly empty, desolate. "Ask what you will."

My heart began to beat with a huge hollow resonance.

"*Ask*," she said again, and her breath whistled out of her chest in a high thin screeing—like the eerie moaning of winter wind swirling over rooftops—in the cold, nightfilled room.

8

"*Nooooo!*" Mimi screamed, and I felt her scrambling beside me. The footlocker slid forward, the boxes trembled as she lurched forward and struggled to her feet. I was up in an instant. We heard the boxes teeter and crash below. The caravan was suddenly filled with a thick bone-chilling mist. I peered over the edge and saw a white figure— the same I'd seen at the sight of the crash, I thought—receding through the door. The fog thinned, and now I could see the corpse toppled on the floor, one of the heavy wooden boxes rocking lightly against the body.

Mimi trembled against my chest. "Obscene," she wailed. "Imre, it was so obscene."

I put my hand in her dark hair, soothing her. She pulled away, looked up at me. Her eyes were dull with shock, and it frightened me. I leaned to kiss her or maybe take her face in my hands to let her know I was there, that she mattered. My thumb strayed to the angle of her small jaw, and with the caress I saw something flicker in her eyes. A kind of painful knowledge swept across her face.

She moaned, her hands covered her eyes, and then slowly she lowered the left—the one with the old scar—and stared at it. "I knew," she said in a dusky voice. "I knew. My mother caught me the first time, and she burned my hand against the kettle, but after that I was more careful, and I watched her, and I saw where she hid the glass-topped box." Mimi's gaze went to the ceiling. She nudged a crate into place and climbed up, then leaned out over the loft and tapped at a board in the ceiling. "See the marks."

Under the coating of soot and grime was the outline of a small rectangle cut into the panel over Mimi's head. She was straining to push at it. The sawed rectangle suddenly yielded, disappearing into the dark hole. She gave a little gasp, and I was afraid she'd fall. I darted toward her, clasping her around her thighs, my face buried in her skirts. "For God's sake, be careful," I said.

Above me I heard her saying the same words over and over into the dim recess. "My mother meant me to have it." Her voice had a peculiar lilt—like that of a miser, whispering and sifting through his gold. She went on tiptoe, her hands flailing inside the small space. "The hand of the dead belongs to me."

A shudder racked me, and without thinking I pulled her down from the box. She cried out. I saw she'd skinned one wrist against the sharp edge of the panel. She stumbled against me, stepping on my ankles and feet, throwing us both off balance, but I had her now by one arm and I righted us.

"What are you doing?" she said fiercely, trying to pull her hand out of my grasp. I held on.

"Obscene," I whispered. "You said it yourself." I jerked my chin toward the corpse. "Is that what you want?" She began to struggle toward the crate, crying for me to let her go, and I lifted her up and carried her down the stairs.

I set her on her feet, held on to her arm, made her look at the graceless, crumpled body lying gape-jawed like a mechanical toy that spent its gears and collapsed.

"That's what you want to wind up?" I asked, panting heavily.

"The hand can bring healing," she said calmly, and I felt her muscles slacken under my grip. I let go and she stood quietly.

"Leave it alone." The gypsies would burn the caravan, and with it the savage charm.

"All right, Imre," she sighed, but I saw her eyes lift toward the cutout in the ceiling.

I put my arm around her and led her toward the door. She suddenly stopped near the threshold. "The box isn't there," she whispered. "Someone took it."

"I imagine the woman—whoever she was—thought she'd use it for good, too—" I began.

"I saw a man in here."

"It was a woman with dark hair in a white dress."

Mimi shook her head. "Visions, confusion, it's part of the power—" She stopped. "It was Joseph. He knew we were watching. He wanted me to know he claimed it. Imre, please, just let me look once more—"

"No—"

"Just to see if it's really gone," Mimi pleaded, and all at once I saw a way to end it.

"All right," I nodded. "But you're too short, you'll kill yourself leaning out over the loft." I started for the stairs, moved along the edge. I could see there'd been a railing at one time to prevent falls. The small round dents where the spindles had rested were obvious; some of the boards had a splintered, powdery look and it occurred to me they might be rotted. We'd been lucky—with two of us up there we could've collapsed the whole structure.

I began to move carefully, testing for mushy places. I stepped over the pile of sheets, and now I saw they were stiff, streaked with dried blood. *Hidden by whoever killed Anyeta*, I thought. The boards moaned under my heels.

I realigned the crate Mimi had used, stepped onto it and palmed the ceiling.

Then I leancd over the edge of the loft and felt inside the cutout with my right hand. The first thing I touched was the rectangle Mimi had pushed aside, and I nudged it lightly with my fingertips. I stretched further out, my weight shifting to the arm that was shoved inside the hole, my mind spinning with irritation. I wondered how the hell the old woman had reached it.

"Is it there?" Mimi called from down below, startling me, and I tottered, felt my heart rattle, then caught myself.

"Doesn't seem to be," I said. It came out neutral enough, but a spurt of annoyance rushed through me. I was up here doing what she wanted, couldn't she just let me do it without hocketing at me on top of it all? Buggerandsod, I thought, tell her the thing's gone and get down. I danced my fingers around for effect.

"No." I shook my head and glanced down at her upturned face. "Not here." I prepared to shift my weight back. I leaned, withdrawing my hand carefully, and that was when I felt it.

The copper side was slick, loathsome, but I felt a strange longing to touch it again. I paused, and my fingers crept toward it. It gave off some odd vibration—a low persistent hum I sensed rather than heard—and my fingertips began to tingle.

I brushed the cold greasy surface of the box, and the tender skin of the quicks throbbed the way they do when your fingernail suddenly shears off. I drew my hand back, the pain dulled. My brain pulsed, I felt a power that reviled and drew me, like the sickening sensation of holding ice against the hot battered fingers you've slammed hard in a door. I wanted the copper box with the glass top and yet I wished it were a thousand miles away instead of idling on the edge of my grasp.

"Imre," Mimi began, and I wondered if she'd seen me hesitate, seen the mix of fear and wonder on my face, and guessed. "Imre," she said again, and I heard the hush of caution in her voice at the same time I was aware of the steadily increasing sound of wood and metal giving way.

I turned my head, saw the breach: The floor of the loft dipped alarmingly, exposing a series of bent nails driven into the wall. There was a groan, a ripping sound, the loft swayed.

"It's coming down!" Mimi shrieked.

I swung out over the space, the box skittered deeper into the recess. Behind me I heard the loft splinter and crash. The ceiling was thin, I knew it wouldn't hold me. "Move, move!" I shouted, and let go.

I landed badly, the bottoms of my feet stung like fire. I lost my balance, tumbling backward. A jagged piece of the ceiling plummeted and struck my knee.

Mimi was at my side helping me to my feet, pulling me toward the front of the caravan.

I looked back. The other end of the wagon was a crazy litter of boxes, rubble, sifting dustmotes. The bed was demolished; its dirty drapes lay in a flummox of wood and fabric. One leg of the corpse stuck out from under a broken board. I didn't care if they left the old woman to burn in her caravan or dragged her out of the mess.

My eye went to the crushed stairs, then up to the torn ceiling. *No one can get at the filthy thing now,* I thought. My head throbbed at the memory of how the charm enticed me like a siren song and made me yearn for it. I saw Mimi standing on the crate, whispering *My mother meant me to have it* and realized it had drawn her with deadly fascination when she reached for it. I was sick, thinking I'd touched the slippery box.

I moved toward the threshold gingerly, conscious of the sharp pain in my feet, and I wondered if I'd managed to break one or both arches when I jumped from the loft. My boots seemed tight, the stiff leather pressing on swollen flesh. I limped a little, and it felt good. I eased myself down the first step. "C'mon," I called over my shoulder, and I turned to see her gazing up at the ceiling.

"He tried to kill you," Mimi said.

I shook my head. "The whole place is falling apart."

"It's there," she said, "I sense it." Her eyes were riveted on the ragged hole.

A wave of guilt rushed through me, my throat tightened. "There was no copper box," I said in a thin papery voice.

"How did *you* know it was made of copper?" she asked, staring at me. I looked away.

"Please," I said, "let's go before someone sees us." It was nearly sunset now; the men would be returning to camp, the women bustling around cookfires.

Mimi shut the yellow door, then hooked her arm in mine and let me use her shoulder for support. We ambled down the steps. I was relieved to see the clearing was deserted. A dog barked in the distance. At the entrance to our caravan, Mimi stopped and looked back. Anyeta's wagon was a dark monolith in the dying light.

"It can be used for healing." A little sighing breath heaved out of her. She stuck her hand out briefly—palm up, waist high—and I saw the old scar in the center of her hand, the raw abrasion on her wrist. For the first time I wondered if she'd scraped herself on a sharp corner of the box, not the wooden edge of the cutaway, and whether, like some deadly infection, its power was working inside her.

I wanted to look at her face but I didn't. I knew her violet eyes held an odd capering light, and I knew its source. After all, the lure of the box was strong.

9

"Where's Lenore?" I asked, brushing through the green drapes that separated our daughter's sleeping compartment from the main part of the caravan. I was in the kitchen area, I could see clear to the other end, down the two short steps to our bedchamber.

Mimi's back was to me, and she was rummaging through one of the kitchen cupboards. "There was a gang of kids outside earlier, she's probably with them."

"I didn't see anyone out there," I said.

She shrugged, pulled out a roll of gauze, and patted a wooden chair, motioning for me to sit. Away from the old woman's caravan and the savage charm, she seemed more at ease, more herself, I thought with relief.

I pulled off my boots, a pair of wool socks, and we both looked my feet over. She handed me a jar of salve and wincing, I rubbed it on my feet.

"Hurt much?" Mimi asked, probing lightly with two gentle fingers.

"Call me tenderfoot," I said, and Mimi gave out a small giggle. The Lovari gypsies, the horsemen, used the term to mean a timid man—something like a horse with a stone in its hoof stepping carefully.

I began wrapping my feet with the gauze, and I was luxuriating in the soothing feel of the cloth on my skin.

"Tenderheaded is more like it. You're making a mess of the bandage." She frowned at the trailing white strips and lumpy spots. Mimi took the gauze out of my hands, and I stuck my feet out while she began winding more neatly.

"Some of me's not tender," I said, grinning, and Mimi caught my eye, gave a little smile. I put my hand on her shoulder. "While Lenore is still outside. You know you always relax more," I prompted.

She nodded. We finished the bandaging, and Mimi drew the drapes. She left a plate of supper for Lenore on the stove. We went to bed.

The room was thick with shadows. I was dimly aware of the caravan door opening, and I dismissed it, thinking Lenore had come in for dinner. I heard a series of small movements in the kitchen and kissed Mimi more avidly to distract her from the noises. If she heard Lenore, I thought, she'd get up, and who knew when she'd come back to bed.

I rounded her breasts with both hands, then pressed my mouth to one brown nipple, felt her hands in my hair. She gave a little hum of satisfaction.

"Yes," she murmured, and I felt her hand slide down between us. My heart quickened, it wasn't like her to touch me. I felt myself getting more excited.

Surprised, I drew back. Mimi's fingers slid between her own legs, moving in a slow rhythmic circle. She arched her hips, then suddenly sat up, pulling me with her, rubbing her breasts over my chest. "Umm," she breathed and I felt her slick-damp fingers on my mouth, my chin, poking at my lips, and I sucked at them.

Her legs curved over mine, my hands kneaded her hips, and they seemed softer, more yielding than usual. I pulled her closer, feeling the point of her chin in my shoulder, her hair hanging in a flood over my back.

She was more sensual than she'd ever been and that inflamed me. We slid together smoothly, rocking along on a slow silent tide.

Eyes closed, I rested snugly inside her and savored the last of our lovemaking. Skyrockets and stars, I thought, smiling to myself, and after all these years. I chuckled aloud.

"Share the joke," she said huskily into my ear.

"You were so good in bed I was just wishing your mother would die every day," I said, shifting back, and hearing the soft ripply sound of our sweat damp skins parting.

"Do you?" she asked, and I thought her voice had a throaty sound that was different.

I gazed down. In the twilight gloom, her thighs had an unfamiliar heavy look, her belly was more rounded, topped by large pendulous breasts. "Don't sit like that," I snapped without thinking.

"Wha—?" she sat up quickly, and the moving, blurry face I saw was not my wife's. My pulse throbbed, my head whirled. The woman I saw had dark brows that were more sharply defined. Her full lips were red, pouting. Her hair was longer. I recalled how it hung softly over the skin of my back, and a spurt of panic went through me. I closed my eyes, kneaded my hands into fists.

She got out of bed, reached for a dressing gown, and I heard the whisper of silk. I peeped through my lashes.

Mimi's white dressing gown, which trailed to the floor on her, hung to mid calf on this woman. Tied at the waist, it scarcely covered the bulging breasts, the flaring hips. Not a fat woman, I thought, but lush, overblown like a rose before the faded petals drop. I swallowed anxiously, felt sweat breaking out on my face. You're imagining this, I told myself, you're feverish, fevers can play havoc with your mind.

"Imre, what's wrong?"

I looked up, absurdly relieved to see Mimi's small plaintive face glancing back at me.

"Nothing," I said shivering, hugging her small body. "It's this damn cold." I sniffled, absently rubbing my nose. I caught a vague female scent and I shuddered with dread.

10

That night my half-dreams merged with memory, and I found myself wandering the landscape of older, simpler times, of that sweet green spring when I'd first brought Mimi with me into Hungary. Lying next to my wife, I recalled we'd camped one rainy dusk near the river Tisza, a sort of natural dividing line between the two halves of the prairie:

I was trying to light a fire (it was my youthful brag that I could build one in any weather), and Mimi sat nearby on the steps of our caravan, listening to me tell the last part of an old fairy tale— what we called *paramitsha*. The stories were considered the property of the teller, and I'd inherited it from my Aunt Hannah.

After a while I finished, and we sat quietly; then I said, "I love the rain, love to hear the sound of it. It brings out my gypsy side." I glanced toward her; in the lantern light, I could see some of the color was coming back into her cheeks. The trek was doing her good, I thought. "Back in England, that's just what they call this kind of rainy spring weather—gypsy weather."

I cuddled and babied a small spark of flame deep inside the center of the wood pile. I went on my hands and knees, blew on the coals softly; they began to glow. "And it was my Aunt Hannah, believe it or not, who taught me the right way to light damp wood and make a good hot fire."

"Yes," Mimi said, smiling, "so you've told me. That and how the English Roms are known for storytelling."

"Got it," I said, getting up and going to the windward side to remove the small screen of branches I'd placed there. "I told you, Aunt Hannah's method is foolproof—any night, any weather—"

Mimi was grinning at me now, her eyes sparkling with mirth. Genuinely puzzled, I stopped.

"You got the fire lit," she pointed with one slim arm, then she began to laugh. "And you told me a damn fine story while you did it, but you forgot," she said, actually holding her stomach, "we don't have anything to cook over it."

"Oh, shit," I muttered, running one hand through my hair. I gave her a sheepish grin. She hopped up from the stairs, and put one arm through mine. "Okay, English boy, you showed your stuff, now I'll show you mine."

And that was how my wife taught me the Romanian method of procuring dinner that was quaintly known as *drabbing the baulo*—or poisoning the pig.

"I learned this from my great Aunt Medala," she said, for a tease after she got her "supplies" from inside our caravan. We were on foot, both of us wearing boots and hats to keep the rain off, and we followed the road to a nearby farm.

Mimi set out across a muddy field, telling me to listen for the sound of the pigs in their pen. "Or barring that," she whispered, "the Romanians say you can locate them by smell—in any weather," she giggled, and I pinched her on the can, then waded after her.

Sure enough, after a few minutes of roaming in the dark, she tracked the pigs to their sty. In the distance, I could see yellow light from a window in the small, one story farmhouse spilling out into a swept yard.

"Aunt Medala," she whispered conspiratorially, "says in a pinch you can use ground glass, but personally, she and I prefer the sponge method."

I watched my wife reach under her oilskin cape and extract a flat hard sponge that looked more like a wood chip than anything else. She was careful to keep it out of the wet. Then she brought out a lump of lard she'd wrapped up in cheesecloth. She smeared the dried sponge with the lard, coating it thickly. Then, as quickly as she could, she climbed up and over the rickety side of the pen.

"You want a whole sow, or just a piglet?" she asked me through the boards.

"Just hurry," I said back. You never knew when pigs might turn mean, especially if there was a boar around.

A minute or two later Mimi was clambering back over the boards. On the ground, she put her hand in mine. "I fed it to one that looked just-weaned," she giggled. "No need to get greedy."

"Now what?"

"Now English boy, tonight you have to go hungry, so you might as well make love to me to help you forget your stomach." She began tugging me after her across the field.

"Then what?"

She pulled me close and held on to the lapels of my jacket. "By the time you finish feasting on me, it will be tomorrow, and tomorrow you feast on pork."

"Nice fire, you're a good provider, Imre," Mimi smirked. It was getting on toward noon, the rain had stopped, but the weather was still damp under a heavy cloud cover. The smell of roasting pig drifted on the humid air, set my stomach rumbling, my mouth watering.

"Nice fire, but nicer still to have something cooking on it—plus a wife who's a good provider," I told her.

Mimi nodded, and poked at the slowly blackening carcass with a fork. "Not quite done yet," she said, and then she went on to finish up the story of how she put great Aunt Medala's tried and true method into practice.

"Naturally, when the sponge expands in the intestinal tract, it kills the pig," she said.

"Naturally."

"Luckily, it wasn't a very big pig—sometimes the big ones take longer to die from the blockage. If you have a large group to feed, though . . . ." she sighed.

"Go on."

"Well, I ambled along the road in the wagon early this morning—you know, as if I was just happening by. The piglet was still squealing, and I could hear it even over the noise of the wheels and the harness bells. When I got to the farm, the farmer was standing by the pen. 'Hey, mister,' I yelled, 'you want your future told?'

"He put his hands on his hips, and said in this annoyed voice, 'Lady, it doesn't take a goddamn gypsy to know that pig is going to die.' And he pointed—I swear, right at my pig.

"I said, 'Oh, well, I know a lot about herbs, maybe I have something—some tonic in my caravan—' but he cut me off.

"'I don't have time for tonics—or beggars.' He frowned at me and he turned away.

"This is always the tricky part," Mimi explained, "when you have to be the most cunning—and to do that, like Aunt Medala said, you have to play a little dumb. I got down from the wagon and walked over—but not too near. 'Do you think it's some kind of disease? I hope it's not a disease.' The pig's entire snout was just covered with a scummy white froth," Mimi said, touching the corners of her mouth and chin, "the saliva backs up when it has no place to go.

"The farmer just shrugged," she went on, "but I knew what was coming: The stomach twists up, the pig goes into convulsions, and its heart stops. It was wonderful; about a minute later the piglet started twitching like a possessed puppet. Then it gave one long last hideous squeal and keeled over.

"'Oh fucking Christ,' the farmer muttered, and he was old—but spry, with lots of ropy muscles—and he got right up over the pen, and he hauled my pig out, and then he was standing back on my side of the pen, and the pig was lying on the ground at our feet, and he was staring at it.

"'It's quite a young one,' I said. 'Maybe—'"

"'It was fine, yesterday.' he said.

"'For your sake, I hope it's not some terrible disease that might spread to the others—'

"He grunted at me and said thanks.

"'But you know,' I told him, looking directly into his blue eyes, and reaching in my pocket, 'if you want to sell it, I guess the meat would be good enough for my dogs.' And I showed him a couple of *forints* in my hand.

"I could see he was worried about the rest of his pen, and he flapped one grizzled hand at me. 'Nah, take it,' he said.'"

Mimi began to laugh. "It's always the same—as long as you offer to pay, they give it to you free. Who cares what happens to a bunch of dirty gypsy dogs?" She paused, eyes sparkling, "But would you believe I got him to help me carry the piglet right to our caravan on the road?" Her brown-violet eyes widened. "Aunt Medala would be proud," she snorted. "I got that cart turned around in a jiffy and I got those horses moving." She mimed using the whip. "And the last thing I heard was the farmer suddenly shouting, 'Hey, you said you had dogs! *Hey Lady, where are the dogs?*'

"He probably realized a second too late, there was no barking, no dogs trotting after the caravan, and when I glanced over my shoulder, I saw he'd been running, he was breathing hard and he had one hand pressed to his big chest, but he was stopped in the road, and I knew he wasn't going to keep chasing me."

"I love you," I said.

"Yep. Know what the old Romany gypsies say about 'poisoned pig?'" Her small face was lit with glee. I shook my head. "They say it's the best meat for you in the world."

We both laughed, and in a little while, we stuffed ourselves on the world's best meat.

Lying in bed, smiling to myself, I recalled it was one of Lenore's favorite stories from "before I was born," as she put it, and she always wanted to meet great Aunt Medala. We could never convince her that it was a joke between Mimi and me, that there was no great Aunt Medala, that Mimi made her up because I'd been bragging about my Aunt Hannah.

"Aunt Medala, Lenore," I whispered to myself, sleepily. And I felt Mimi's hand steal out of the dark and lightly touch my shoulder. I turned on my side, then fell into a dreamless sleep.

I woke to the sound of moaning. The caravan was dark. I didn't know how long I'd been sleeping, but for an instant I thought Mimi was crying out in a nightmare; then I heard the rustle of the covers being pushed aside, the squeak of her bare feet scurrying over the waxed boards, and Lenore's voice bleating in the distance. "Mother, Mom—Momma," she groaned. My daughter's voice rose to a drawn out scream. "Mo-o-otherrrr!"

I raced from the bed, tripping over the loosed bandages, cursing under my breath. I caught the wild dance of a swinging lamp, the sound of confusion, a tremendous thump, Mimi's voice shrieking. I tore at the gauze and ran.

At the other end of the caravan, Lenore was sitting up in her bed, bent over, holding her arms at her waist. Mimi was trying to climb into her sleeping berth, a kind of compartment like a ship's bunk with sliding wooden doors. Both of them were weeping. Mimi rocked our daughter. I saw lights flickering outside the windows, gypsies running toward the caravan. An iron that usually rested on the woodstove in the kitchen lay overturned on the floor. Its sole plate was wet.

At the end of the pocketbed lay the foot long carcass of a locust-like insect. Its great head was crushed, exposing a soft yellowish substance the color of rotting honeycomb and dripping thin serous blood. Splats of this sticky-looking fluid covered the blankets, the wall, the ceiling of Lenore's tiny chamber. A dull light shone in its outsize black eyes, and now I saw a fragment of thin, leathery antenna clinging to the heavy iron. The tail—a kind of bifurcated prong—twitched rhythmically, leaking the same pale red fluid in a dribbling spray.

Without thinking I yanked at the covers at the same time I slammed the door all the way open. The body rolled against the moving door, one spindly leg wedged in the narrow gap. The door bounced back, nearly jumping its small track, and sliced the body in two. The head and thorax clumped heavily onto the floor, and I ground it underfoot.

There was a thick crunch, twin sensations: the prickly feel of its shell, the spongy mass beneath it. I drew my foot away and felt something cold and wet adhering to my skin, then saw a viscous string trailing from my heel to the ruined head. My gorge rose, I scraped the mess of yellow slime against the floor.

"The tail, the tail," Lenore moaned.

It was twitching yet. I spread my fingers into a hard claw and raked it from the edge of the bed. It flopped on the floor, and my breath whistled out of my throat. "Christ, Christ." The pain, where the tips of my fingers had grazed the thrashing tail, was enormous. It throbbed in sickening spikes, jolting up my forearm to my shoulder. I seized my elbow, nearly sank to my knees.

Lenore's face was a deadly white, her arms cradled over her abdomen. My stomach rolled with my own pain, the thought the thing had touched her.

I clambered to my feet, threw a great clot of bedding over the blackened body, booted it out of the way. Jostled, Lenore cried out; she stiffened upright, arms jerked high, away.

My gaze fell on the bloody shreds of her nightgown. A great hammering rose in my brain. A round weeping wound—no bigger than an eye—glistened wetly in the downy fuzz between her legs. I swallowed, started to turn away. She was too old for me to see her so frankly. I felt Mimi's hand on my arm pulling me back, forcing me to look, to understand. From the wound, a series of red black streaks ran up Lenore's abdomen, and spidered across the tiny hillocks of her breasts.

Even as I watched, a fine tendril coursed the pale flesh of her throat. Pinpricks of blood hemorrhaged under the skin as it burrowed toward her ear.

I glanced at my hand. The pain was subsiding a little, the flesh unmarked.

"It entered Lenore," Mimi whispered, smoothing our daughter's thick hair back from her forehead.

I nodded, then stopped. "What do you mean, entered?"

Mimi stood up, her breath hot in my ear: "It was on her, its mouth sunk in her belly, the antennae waving greedily over her chest, the tail fastening, grinding into her—her—" She shut her eyes, passed a shaky hand over her brow.

I saw it in my mind's eye: the whip-like feelers, the wicked abdomen arching obscenely, the scorpion tail flicking inside my child.

"We have to save her," she whispered, her cold hand closing over my wrist. My gaze traveled to the humped roll of bedding in the corner.

There was a tap at the window, I turned and saw a crowd of faces, the flare of torchlight.

A hissing noise made me pivot toward the corner again. A narrow thread of smoke wound up from the floor. I took two lurching steps and seized the blankets. Nothing, there was nothing but scorch marks. The squashed jelly of the head smoldered and disappeared. The room smelled of charred wood.

The door swung wide and a crowd of gypsies pushed through, and I stepped back, their voices buzzed around me:

"Is she all right?"

"We heard the screams."

"Joseph saw the flames—"

Behind me, someone gasped. My heart surged in pounding waves, and I turned my head. Lenore's small berth was smoldering, candlewax dotted the doors, dripped down from the bed. The taper itself—separated from its short copper holder—was smashed on the floor. At the lower edge of Lenore's abdomen was a nasty irregular burn with grayish edges. Red marks like scalds covered her chest. The skin on her arms was blistered.

Mimi's dark eyes—helpless, frantic—met mine. I thought, we knew what we'd seen; what had *really* happened. A great leaded weight pressed down on me, another part of my mind took over. My voice when it came had the heavy dull sound of shock.

"She fell asleep with the candle," I lied, gesturing toward the crushed candle on the floor, my mind awash with the memory of the thing's vile head. "We warned her before. She's not to take the candle with her."

Inside her sleeping compartment was a short shelf on the sidewall that held dolls, Lenore's treasures—pretty rocks, a small gilt icon, a fading bouquet of wildflowers. A tawny reddish streak of wax spilled from the shelf onto the wall; I looked again, seeing the congealed smear of blood, entrails, fluids.

"It fell on her while she was sleeping," I whispered. I lowered my eyes, felt the color draining from my face: I was pretending a burning candle tumbled from the shelf at the same time the image of the foul locust falling on Lenore rose up in my head. I felt sick, foolish. I was a terrible liar. The stub of another unlit candle was on a tall stand nearby—clearly outside the berth. They would see through this transparency any second, I thought. I started to shove my hand in my pocket.

Someone breathed in sharply and took hold of it. "But you burned yourself putting out the fire," a voice exclaimed.

I looked down, felt my vision blur, but not on account of my singed fingers. The woman fussing over my smarting hand was the woman with the pouting red lips I'd seen in my bed. The room, the people, the voices receded and droned in my ear like the distant hum of insects.

I felt myself slumping forward, blacking out. Anonymous arms caught me. I fell into them. Someone helped me lay down. Anxious voices, Mimi calling "Cold water, cold water, cold water." Faces above me now, bodies kneeling close to mine. Movement. One face—the one framed with the long dark curling hair that somehow made the pouting red lips seem fuller still—stood out. Her name, her face, an old memory clicked into place in the second before I lost consciousness.

"Zahara," I slurred, "Mimi's cousin." The floor felt hard under my skull.

And then the world was a dark womb I sought for a little while.

11

My unconscious remembered her. Those were the words making the circuit of my brain when I began to swim toward waking. I was confused briefly, then things began to take their rightful focus. I was lying on my back in my own bed. A great weight pressed one end of the mattress, and I wondered if I'd chocked the wheels of the caravan unevenly. The glass window near my head admitted its usual swirling draft, the lantern hanging from the beam was lit.

"He's coming round," a woman said. The weight on the mattress shifted, disappeared. Zahara stood over me, I saw Joseph over her shoulder.

"You've had a shock," she said.

I nodded.

I heard a clinking sound from the kitchen, and made the M shape with my lips. Mimi.

"Shhh," Zahara said and tapped my mouth gently. "Don't try to talk yet."

"It's Constantin," Joseph said, and I saw his eyes turn toward the other room. I heard a kind of burbling noise, the sound of things being hauled from cabinets. "He won't hurt anything." I pictured the tubby little man playing among the pots and pans like a roistering toddler.

My mouth hurt, my jaw ached. "L'ore," I said, surprised I couldn't manage my daughter's full name. Joseph and Zahara exchanged glances.

"You had a kind of convulsion—just one, not long." His ring gleamed, he lit a cigarette. "You strained—maybe dislocated your jaw. Zahara set it right."

"Drink this," Zahara said. I saw she had a plate of soup. She arranged the pillows behind my head, covered my lap with a napkin. The soup—a watery kind of *gulas* with bits of vegetables—was lukewarm, but it seemed to be easing the stiffness in my jaw. I thought she must have laced it with painkiller.

"Mimi is with Lenore," she said. "They're in my caravan, resting. Ithal is with them. He'll come for me or Joseph at once if there's any difficulty. Ithal's quite the young man, now—but then twenty years is a long time."

I found myself looking at her. Zahara was ten years older than Mimi— somewhere around forty-six, I guessed. She was buxom, tall, wide shouldered, and she looked very much the same as the last time we'd seen her. My own brown hair was speckled with a lot of gray, hers was still glossy black. But it was more than that—no roundness had crept into her jawline, there was no hint of wrinkles near her mouth or around her eyes. She saw me looking at her, and she averted her gaze.

"No one would guess you have a grown son, Zahara," I said, sipping soup carefully from the spoon. "How's Frederic?"

"I'm a widow," she said, smoothing her skirts. She was wearing a gypsy bracelet made of small gold coins; they shivered lightly with the motion of her hand. "He's been dead two years."

Joseph looked uncomfortable, I didn't pursue it.

I glanced out the window. I could see gypsies moving about, their caravans were lighted. "We seem to have awakened the whole camp."

"No." Joseph shook his head. "You remember the old saying, 'When the wolf sleeps the flock is safe?'" His hooded eyes looked deeper in the soft shadows in the room. Puzzled, I nodded. He went on. "That is how we lived for many years." He brought his thin arm up, gesturing toward the window. "We moved quietly—at night— when Anyeta was sleeping."

"But—" I started to protest, but his white eyebrows lifted in amusement.

"Old habits die hard." He exhaled a cloud of smoke. I thought of how there was no one around when we arrived, or when we'd sneaked into the old woman's wagon. I started to say Constantin had been lively enough—but Joseph anticipated me again.

"The mad don't live by other men's rules," he said. And I heard the gurgling noise from the kitchen. I looked up, Constantin stood at the edge of the two short steps that separated our sleeping area.

A saucepan dangled from one hand, a white enamel basin was upturned on his head. He'd found a length of some kind of purple material—maybe Mimi had bought it to make curtains—and it was draped Caesar-style over his shoulder. He grinned, slinked toward the bed, and I heard the drag of the metal chain between his ankles. His hands weren't chained, but he wore broad cuffs on his wrists, and they reminded me of old Roman bracelets. He stood blinking under the glare of the light, raised the saucepan suddenly, and pulled a piece of paper from it. He held it out toward me, at the limit of his thick arm.

"Ah, a message," Joseph said, and whispered to me under his breath, "Humor him, will you?"

"What is it, Constantin?" I asked, and he marched to my side, saluted, then held up the dirty paper like an offering. "Good work soldier. Thank you." He handed me the paper. I barely glanced at it, expecting him to retreat, but he leaned over me, pointing excitedly at a series of crude drawings scattered on the page.

"Gee, ghere, and ghere and ghere," he nodded, tapping three of the pictures, and I took it to mean he was saying *See, there.* One was a ball between two peaks. Sunset, maybe. One was a square set on wheels. A caravan? Inside a stick man's head was so close to the ceiling, he appeared to be hanging from the beam.

The rest was a compendium of scratchmarks, badly drawn people, trees. I remembered the days when Lenore drew a big circle with two loops and called it a rabbit; seeing a second piece of paper with the same drawing you'd say brightly "Another rabbit," and she'd tell you gravely, "No, *that's* Mommy."

"Very good, Constantin," I said, handing back the picture. He brushed my arm away.

"Nu—uh." His round face was agitated.

"All right, Constantin, Imre will keep it," Joseph said. Constantin beamed happily, and let the older man take him back to the kitchen. The drawing lay on the bed. Zahara picked it up, and without glancing at it laid it on top of a dresser. She came and sat by my side.

"Poor man," she said, and I agreed, although I got the impression she was saying it for the sake of form and found him repellent. I was a little uncomfortable with her, now that Joseph was out of the room. She wasn't wearing a head covering or an ankle-length, flounced apron, but she was dressed more like the Transylvanian women of the region than the rag-tag gypsies. She had on a long white dress—shirred with bright red, yellow and green embroidery at the bodice and wrists—and it brought to mind the woman I'd seen at the sight of the crash, enshrouded in mist inside the caravan, scantily clad in Mimi's robe. *Your unconscious remembered her,* I told myself, and it was pure coincidence she was here wearing a white gown. She wore white often—always did—and like Joseph said, old habits die hard.

She sat on the edge of the bed, smoothing her fingers; the bracelets chinked softly, and I thought she might be aware of my gaze, but she didn't look up.

I'd had a crush on Zahara when I was a young man and she was engaged to Frederic. Nothing really came of it—except, I remembered, one long kiss under a tree that was definitely more fervid on my part than hers. It was at night, and I recalled I tried to convince her no one could see and to let me feel her up. Her breasts had felt mammoth to my inexperienced fumbling hands. She ran away laughing, her dark hair a shadow against her long wool cape, and that was the end of it. I mooned a lot, fantasized more, eventually forgot her, married Mimi.

I saw a smile tugging the corners of her lips. "Amazing the things your mind can dredge up, isn't it? I was just thinking about the time you kissed me."

"I was too," I admitted, and felt myself blush.

"What were you, fifteen?"

"Seventeen," I corrected, and then got annoyed at myself. What damn difference did it make?

"You were so young," she mused. The mattress creaked when she got up. She moved across the room, leaned one elbow on the dresser.

"We both were," I said.

"I remember thinking you were so—ardent. But I dismissed it. I told myself you were a boy." She turned, rested her head briefly on her arms, crossed her ankles, and I caught myself looking at the pose. Her dark cascading hair hid her profile but her thin waist was sharply defined. Her rump was softly rounded. I could see the shadowy shapes of her long legs through the dress. *Cut it out*, a voice spoke up in my head. *There's no harm in looking*, an equally strong voice countered. Besides—the way she looks—she must have ten overheated swains chasing her. Everybody in lust—from her son's friends to Old Joseph.

"So. You're a widow," I said, wondering if some absurd part of my brain was taking the conversation on a sexual tack. Was I going to ask her what she did for jollies?

"Anyeta killed my husband," she said.

"You sound like Joseph."

"Joseph sees a lot." She returned to the bed.

I thought surely he'd come in at the mention of his name, but he remained in the kitchen. I heard him talking in a low voice to Constantin: "Put the pans away now."

"Did you know Anyeta was a sorceress, that she owned a charm called the *mulengi maulo*, the hand of the dead?" Zahara sat close to me, her voice was low.

"Yes." I heard rattling noises in the cupboards.

"Did *he* tell you?" Her eyes flicked toward the kitchen.

"No—we." I stopped. It might be better to pretend we'd never gone to the caravan. I started to say Mimi told me about it, but she smiled knowingly, her wide red lips parting.

"You went inside the old woman's *vurdan*, didn't you?" she asked. "Something happened?"

I nodded. She leaned over to whisper against my ear, and I was conscious of the warm place where her heavy breast tipped my arm. "You mustn't trust Joseph. He was jealous of the old woman's powers. Constantin knows things, and look what happened," she said. "Old Joseph did it." She made a sawing motion against her mouth, then suddenly grabbed my wrist. "Everyone thinks he claimed the hand of the dead. He—" she stopped.

Joseph stood on the bottom stair. I caught a knowing look in her onyx eyes, and she finished the sentence smoothly, covering the gap. "He's a coppersmith, and everyone says Ithal not only looks like his father, he inherited Frederic's skill." She leaned back, crossed her shapely legs very casually.

"Let the man get his sleep," Joseph said. "He's not used to watching through the night."

Zahara stood up, gathering the empty soup plate. "I'll take good care of Mimi and Lenore. Rest well."

Joseph watched her leave, waited for the outer door of the caravan to shut.

"They'll burn the old woman's *vurdan* at sunset tomorrow. It will make an end of the misery she inflicted." He twisted the bright gold ring on his finger.

"Will it?" I asked, thinking of Zahara's words. Visions, confusion, Mimi had said, seeing a man inside her mother's wagon. I thought of him waiting for us on the road, trying to divert us from coming at all, of Constantin's dog-like obedience.

His gaze sharpened and he stared at me, and again I had the feeling he was probing my mind. "Tell me, Imre, how did Zahara look to you?"

I started to bluster at his insinuation, but he held one bony hand up.

"No," he shook his head. "*I mean, what did you see?*" I gave him a questioning look, and he continued. "She looked the same, didn't she? Even after twenty years?"

"What's that—"

He cut me off again. "Ask your wife what *she* sees."

"Huh?"

"Ask Lenore, ask *anyone.*" He knotted his fingers, toyed with the thick ring. "Don't be a fool, Imre. Don't make yourself a laughingstock. The rest of us see a flabby overblown woman who waddles when she walks. Three of her teeth are missing." He parted his lips, rubbed one finger over his gums. "Her hair is stringy, dull, gray. She looks like any other fat sloppy woman nearing fifty who never took care of herself."

I recalled the sagging mattress, dismissed it. Another trick. They wanted us gone, we would go. They were playing games—for all I knew they were all confederates and wanted only to prevent Mimi from claiming the power. Whatever power lay in that filthy copper box was sick, insidious and they could have it. This was just another ruse. What could I say to my wife, anyway? *Zahara is still beautiful. She looks even better than you.* It had taken me months to convince Mimi the first time I wasn't marrying her to spite Zahara—or so I thought. I shook my head.

"Ask her," Joseph said, and he left, taking Constantin with him.

I got out of bed, moving softly on my bruised feet. Constantin's picture was on the bureau. I brushed it aside, looked at myself in the mirror. My nose was red from the cold, I had hollows under my eyes. I sucked in my gut a little, stood straighter. An old Romany adage whirred through my mind. *Stanki nashti tshi arakenpe manushen shai:* Mountains do not meet, but people do. Zahara. I felt a small thrill vibrating in my belly, but I damped it at once. "You look like hell, chump," I whispered. "Get it through your head. You have Mimi, Zahara wasn't flirting with you."

I looked away, my eye snagged on the scribbles. I reversed the picture, held it upside down. I was looking at a profile drawing of a woman with a heavy double chin, her mouth was open, grinning. Teeth blacked out. Her hair was a pale viper's nest swirling around her head. I squinted. Underneath, stick letters cross-hatched one another. I angled the page, they came clear.

Wit C H

Witch. He'd written witch. I folded the drawing and put it in the top drawer. I lay back down on the bed and stared at the ceiling. I wasn't tired, I wished it was morning.

12

"I have to claim it," Mimi said. Her eyes were hard, the tears glittering at the margins of her lids had an icy look. I put my hands in my pockets, staring around Zahara's small overheated wagon.

It was just after dawn. Lenore was asleep on a narrow cot. Mimi had made a kind of tent of the sheets and blankets to keep them from touching the sensitive skin.

Mimi put her hand on my arm. "She'll die if I don't claim it, Imre."

I felt myself start at the word. Lenore was only twelve, she couldn't be—could *not* be dying. I shook my head. Looking out the window, I saw caravan lights flickering out. I recalled Joseph's words and thought of the strange inversion of day and night the gypsies lived by. I was drowsy myself, Mimi looked haggard. No, Lenore was just sleepy. "No," I said.

"Listen to me!" Mimi jerked my arm hard and pulled me toward the cot. "Look! Look at what's happening to her." She began drawing away the covers.

Lenore's skin was crisscrossed with raised blackish welts. The dark trail covered her face, tracing the network of veins and arteries. The mushy festering wound between her legs—what Mimi called the point of entry—had a wet greenish cast, and below it the evil welts spiraled down over her thighs, her legs. The skin had burst here and there and oozed a pale white pus-like fluid. Nausea rolled through me. I shut my eyes.

"She's dying," Mimi said again. "Joseph did this." From far away I heard myself making moaning noises, heard myself saying over and over, "Not Lenore, oh God, please, not Lenore."

"Stay with her, Imre. Don't leave her."

I nodded dully.

"Talk to her, hold her hand." Mimi put Lenore's limp fingers in mine, and I felt the hot raised flesh beat like a throbbing pulse against my skin.

"Oh, Lenore," I whispered, but there was no answer. She made no movement, no sound, her breathing was too low for me to hear. "Lenore, don't leave us." I squeezed her hand, there was no response. I touched her hair very

53

lightly, and it was then I saw the first thin welt—like the blackened runner of some insidious weed—creeping over her scalp. Realization sliced through me like a knifeblade. The poison was invading her brain, she wasn't sleeping, she was in a stupor.

I was only dimly aware of the sound of Mimi shutting the door and moving down the outer steps.

I sat up and looked through the window alongside my bed. I heard the bare tree limbs click against the pane, the wind rose higher, and I felt cold air swirling over the thin sill. Lenore was crying on the other side of the glass. "Don't leave me," she sobbed. "Please don't leave me."

Her dark hair whipped over her face, merging with the network of black welts. Her nightgown billowed around her legs. Rising from the fanned out hem of the white dress—as if it had a life of its own—was the blurred shape of a second nightgown; then Mimi's small face appeared over Lenore's shoulder. She stepped sideways at the same time Zahara emerged from behind Lenore's opposite shoulder. The three of them stood in a ragged line, wringing their hands and keening. Their eyes were dark with pain, their mouths open as they wailed, the voices lost in the whine of the wind.

I caught a movement: Just above their heads, Anyeta's disembodied face floated like a ball. There was something greedy, watchful in her stare. Her obsidian eyes had a dull, piggy look, her teeth were broken, stained with blood. She's been eating human flesh, I thought wildly. She's grown fat on it. I felt a desperate surge of fear. The old sorceress began to laugh, and the sound was a rough noise like the hideous grut of teeth crunching down on broken glass.

Lenore suddenly shrieked and ran toward me, her left fist shattering the window. I saw the sparkling shards toss and dance over my bed. Lenore's bloody hand fumbled at the latch, her face as sly as Anyeta's. My belly shriveled in a clutch of icy terror, a powerful spasm jolted through me, and I jerked awake all at once.

My forehead was beaded with droplets of sweat, I was sitting in a straight chair next to the cot in Zahara's wagon, but in the eerie way dreams blend with reality, I heard Lenore moaning.

I shot to my feet, leaned across the bed. Her eyes were closed, but now I saw she was grinding her teeth and moving her head from side to side. Hesitating, I stretched my hand out, and I heard her whispering, "Papa."

"She's much better this morning," Zahara said, at the same time her hand fell lightly on my elbow and made me jump.

"How did you get in here?" I said, confused and shaken. I took a step sideways, collected myself. "I mean, when did you come in?"

She shrugged. "A few minutes ago. You were sleeping. I gave Lenore a glass of water, and she went back to sleep—"

"Water—"

Zahara nodded. "She said the pain was subsiding. I don't think she'll have any permanent scars. At her age, burns heal quickly."

"Burns," I repeated, suddenly prodded by the memory of fire the others had seen in our wagon.

"Lots of them are fading, and most of them aren't any worse than sunburn." She took hold of one of Lenore's arms and held it up.

I blinked. The skin was unmarked except for a few dark streaks and reddish patches. I drew the covers back. There were some blistery spots that someone had spread with a greasy ointment, but nothing like the nightmare map of oozing black welts.

Lenore suddenly opened her eyes and sat up. "Can I have more water, Auntie?"

"Of course, darling. Here." Zahara reached for a glass on the nightstand. "This is still good and cold." Zahara sat on the edge of the bed, and held the copper tumbler to Lenore's mouth. "Are you hungry yet?"

Lenore shook her head, wiped the droplets from her lips, and lay back. "No," she yawned, "just tired." She closed her eyes.

I couldn't make sense of it. I paced to the window at the other end of the room, fingered aside a flowered curtain, staring out. The room was hot, stuffy.

"What's wrong, Imre?" Zahara's low voice was close behind me.

I lit a cigarette, but Zahara put her hand out to stop me. "No, don't. The smoke will just irritate her lungs more." I heard Lenore cough weakly as if in confirmation, and I fanned the smoke, pinched out the cigarette end. I found myself staring hard at Zahara, and her eyes met mine.

"Something's wrong, what is it?" she asked.

I wanted a cigarette worse than before but shoved the craving aside. I sat at a small square table and kneaded my forehead. I didn't know how to explain what I'd seen, it sounded stupid, crazy. "There's something so peculiar—so bizarre happening." I paused. "But if I tell you, you'll laugh."

"No, I won't." Her onyx eyes were soft, understanding, and she made it easy for me to talk. "What happened in Anyeta's caravan?"

"That's part of it," I whispered, "but there's more." I told her about the locust-like insect, the hideous welts covering Lenore's flesh.

"Joseph," she nodded.

"Mimi saw him in the old woman's caravan, but I didn't, I—" I stopped, ashamed to say I thought I'd seen her. "We heard him raise the old woman from the dead." I shuddered.

"It's part of the power; they say the animated corpse can prophesy." She leaned across the table, her white hand clutched my arm. "He'll kill you—all of you. Take your caravan and flee, while there's still time." Her eyes flashed. "Where's Mimi?" she asked suddenly.

"She—" I bit my lip.

"She hasn't gone to him? To Joseph?" I felt Zahara's nails digging through the fabric of my jacket. I shook my head. "Tell me!" she whispered fiercely, shaking my arm.

"She's gone to the caravan to claim it herself."

I saw the color drain from Zahara's face. Her skin had an ashy pallor, her mouth was tight. Her voice came out sluggishly. "Claim it?" she breathed. "Oh no, Imre, no." She hugged her arms across her body, and rocked back and forth on the edge of the chair. "Do you know what that means?"

I spluttered helplessly. Images of a rite with burning candles, incantations and mutterings flitted through my head. I

recalled Mimi saying she'd used the dead man's red coffin string to charm me, saw her miming how she sat winding its knotted length round and round her slim wrist—

Zahara stopped moving. "You don't know what she's going to do, do you?"

"She wants to save Lenore," I said, absently tugging at my collar and glancing at the glowing woodstove.

Zahara stood up, pushing her chair away. "Oh Christ, c'mon," she said, and yanked me to my feet.

I looked dumbly toward Lenore, then back at Zahara.

"Your daughter's fine, we have to save your wife," she said.

"Save her?" I muttered. It was so hot, I thought, it was hard to concentrate.

"Yes, save her—" Zahara said, and I saw her mouth moving, but I couldn't seem to hear what she was saying.

My mind went numb, I was rooted to the spot. I felt Zahara's hands shoving the center of my back, urging me toward the door. My legs felt wooden, unconnected to my body as she pushed me along. She was talking, explaining, her voice was like the huge swelling roar of a crowd in my ear. Just outside the caravan she suddenly stopped, faced me and put her hands on her hips.

"Imre, listen to me," she said.

I nodded. It was much cooler outside. The wind ruffled, then lifted a dark sheaf of her hair. Her red lips began to move, and this time I caught her voice over the clamor, but I stood mute, shaking my head because what she was saying couldn't be true. I looked down at the bent, autumn-sere blades of grass, and suddenly she was throttling my shoulders, forcing me to hear, and the panic in her voice rumbled through me:

"Imre," she screamed, "when your wife claims it, she's going to cut her own arm off!"

In my mind I heard the sound of shattering glass, saw the small bloody fingers reaching for me. The dream images of Lenore blurred and became Mimi and roiled in my brain.

When I looked up Zahara was racing through the tall grass toward Anyeta's caravan, and I followed.

13

"She's locked the door!" Zahara shouted. From inside the old woman's caravan came the sound of thick rhythmic pounding thuds. I thought of the copper box lodged in the ceiling: Mimi was shattering the thin roof to get at it. There was the rapid whickering of wood being driven through the air, the huge hollow *crash!*

We screamed her name over and over. I lunged against the door. Mimi must have barricaded it. We pushed and heaved together. It was useless. We could not budge the thick heavy wood.

Zahara ran around one side of the wagon, and I heard her groan with frustration. "She's latched the shutters over the windows," Zahara cried, trying to insert her fingers in a narrow crack, then tugging so hard her face went red with the effort. With the shutters closed, I saw that the surface of the yellow caravan was smooth, solid, impenetrable.

"It's no good, leave off," I shouted to her.

Inside, the battering noise stopped. There was a short sharp gasp. The chilling cadence of a high wild laughter broke over me like a cold wave. The downy hairs rose along the back of my neck, my flesh chilled, broke out in mottled rows of goosebumps.

I felt a sharp pull. Zahara was yanking the hem of my coat, and it seemed to me in a flash we were underneath the wagon, lying on our backs close to an old abandoned hen coop and staring wide-eyed through the cracks in those ancient, warped floorboards.

My eyes adjusted to the deep gloom within the caravan. Mimi had dragged a table into the center of the room, climbed on it maybe to catch the glass-topped box as it dropped into her arms. One of the sheared-off bedposts lay tossed aside, and I thought that was what she'd used to smash the gaping hole in the ceiling.

I could hear her walking back and forth, just out of sight. Her feet were thumping the floor, her skirts trailing. She was whispering. I closed my eyes, listened to Zahara's rapid breathing close by, smelled the dry rot and the sharp tang of guano from the crumbling hen coop just beyond my head.

The footsteps suddenly ceased. I held my breath. I heard the rough grating rasp of something being dragged over the planks, the barely audible creak of an old hinge. Was she looking at the foul charm? Waiting? For whom? Nothing happened for what seemed a long time, and then abruptly the sharp clatter of a belt buckle struck the boards just over my feet. My eyes flew open.

I craned my neck. Mimi dropped her skirt, slowly removed her blouse. She skimmed a chemise over her head; the wispy fabric made a low susurration in the dead silence of that room.

I strained, watching, scarcely aware of the pull of tendons in my neck and shoulders, and then in the most terrible dream-like slowness, she got on her bare knees, and through the dark cracks I saw her lips draw back, saw her grit her teeth. The back of her hand lay still against the floor. She squeezed her eyes shut. A whine came out of her throat.

There was the high silver flash of a glinting blade, a heavy chopping sound: the splintering of bone and muscle and wood. The blood flew up in a bright arcing spray, and I felt it dripping through those old boards, spattering my legs, my chest, and I wanted to scream, I told myself to scream, but my voice was locked inside my throat. I opened my mouth, but there was nothing, Christ there was nothing.

I cringed at the sharp squeal of metal being wrenched from the wooden floor. The blade rose up. And fell. Again.

The blood dripped and ran, dripped and ran, and I was suddenly aware of the thick pit-patter of liquid striking skin. Zahara's cheek was red, drenched. My wife's blood was glistening wetly on Zahara's face, her chin, in her hair. Zahara curled up, turned aside. Her shoulders heaved and I heard the thin sound of violent retching. The smell of vomit mingled with rotting wood, sweet grass, hot blood.

Above me, Mimi's voice was empty—an echo against damp stones in a ruined crypt:

"I claim it, I have given of myself, and I claim the power of the hand of the dead."

In nightmare sequence I saw the ends of ragged flesh, the raw wet knob of bone. The whitened fingers of the severed limb twitched slowly, an idiot crab that would not walk. Mimi's bloody heels skidded over the planks. I glimpsed the backs of her thin white calves.

And, as she quickly passed over my head I saw—in the place where her pretty hand had been—the crude end of the jutting stump.

She hastily tied it up with the chemise. The white cloth bloomed with dark red blots. Shivering, I shut my eyes at last. My mind gibbered, spinning the same words over and over. *I don't think I'll ever get warm again. No, I'll never be warm. Never.*

I heard Zahara turn toward me, sobbing, "No, no, no," and I felt her bury her head against my chest.

14

"Listen," I whispered to Zahara. Overhead I heard the sound of swift footsteps, of liquid being splashed with abandon in the corners of the caravan. The sharp reek of kerosene stung my nostrils. "Christ, she's going to burn it!" I began to push Zahara, urging her to hurry. We squirmed from under the wagon, got to our feet, bolted like fear-maddened jackrabbits, then hunkered down in the tall grass.

I heard the huge *whump!* of air being sucked away in one tremendous gulp. Towering flames shot through the roof at the same time the caravan door— under its massive carved lintel of twisted leaves and vines— crashed open. Mimi began to run, zig-zagging through the clearing.

Zahara cowered more deeply against the ground, holding one arm up to shield her face from the fierce heat. The wagon burned at a furious rate. One end suddenly collapsed, and I saw the brilliant yellow sparks fly up against a column of black smoke.

I stood up, shouting over the roar of the fire. "Mimi," I screamed. A cape fluttered behind her racing form. I could see that her left hand was somehow intact, her arm still wet with sticky runnels of blood. She never looked back, but ran on and on toward our wagon.

"Mimi," I moaned, a lump burned in my throat, and I felt the terrible sadness of despair welling up inside me. "Please," I begged, "please." She didn't hear me. It was too late, she'd found and claimed her mother's power. And there was nothing to be done, no way to turn back. Defeated, I sat suddenly, heavily in the grass and watched my wife's lunatic flight.

Jouncing in her frail arms—sunlight arrowing from the surface in vicious, glaring darts—was the shimmering rectangle of the copper box with the glass top.

Part II

Zahara

For I thought the dead had peace, but it is not so.

—Tennyson

15

It was close to sunset. Zahara and I had gone for a grim silent walk after Mimi left. I sat on the bank of a muddy brook, watching the drifting sticks I'd thrown twist and spin downstream. She seemed to sense my mood—what little she'd said was spoken quietly. After a long while I got up, brushing grass from my trousers, and we slowly walked back toward the clearing.

Now from a distance I saw the gypsies begin to stream from their caravans like bats on the wing in the dying light. One by one they stopped, fastening on the sight of Anyeta's smoldering caravan. A young man ran through the clearing toward Vaclav's oversized wagon and pounded frantically at the leader's door.

The gathering gypsies ringed the blackened corpse of the caravan. I heard them muttering, saw an old woman cross herself then draw a fringed shawl tightly over her frail shoulders. Mimi and Lenore joined the throng. I began to move ahead and felt Zahara's hand blocking me, her palm brushing my stomach lightly.

"Stay back," she whispered. "Mimi's healed herself and the child—there may be those who are suspicious of your wife. Wait."

I saw a hook-nosed man named Old Feri grimace and suddenly spit through his gnarled fingers, and it occurred to me that Zahara might be right—there was an ugly mood in the air. I watched through the thin scrim of trees, keeping one eye on Mimi and Lenore.

Vaclav was suddenly among his people, his big shoulders bulled this way and that through the crowd. His voice boomed, "Christ has sent us a sign!" He pointed at the glowing hulk of the caravan.

"Or the devil," an old woman began to cackle, then fell into silence under the spell of Vaclav's angry look.

"Through the power of the Savior we have been delivered from this evil!" he intoned, and in the wavering torchlight I saw the gypsies bowing their heads, clasping their hands to their breasts. "Is it not written? Thou shalt not suffer a witch to live!" And as if he'd given an order, the men rose up.

Some threw buckets of water over what was left of the wagon. Great clouds of steam roiled upward, fogging the air with the gagging smell of charred wood. Others began to dig a deep pit alongside the caravan, and we saw the gravedirt flying faster and faster.

Full dark fell, and by torchlight we watched the men raising heavy iron hammers. Their faces and chests gleamed with sweat, they battered relentlessly at the metal axles, at the round iron stove—at whatever was left in the rubble.

From inside the soggy pyre a sudden shout went up: "Found it! I found it!" I saw Vaclav turn, and without hesitating he leaped into the midst of the ruin.

He teetered crazily on the back edge of what was left of the caravan—a slanting heap of boards and joists piled atop collapsed wheels and broken furniture. He bent down swiftly, then stood up, holding his thick soot-streaked arms high over his head. "Here!" he screamed. "Here is your witch!"

Like a sacrifice offered to the shrieking crowd, again and again he raised and shook Anyeta's blackened torso between his hands. The head lolled back on the neck, and bits of charred flesh and matted clots of hair clung to the fire-scarred skull. The face was a pitted grayish blur. One leg was gone; the runny meat where it would have joined the hip had fused into a sickening humped shape. The dark stiffened sticks of her arms swung wildly; at the end of each was a small shriveled lump of flesh that had been a hand.

"Here!" Vaclav screamed, and canting his powerful arms back and forth rapidly to give his thrust momentum, he threw the corpse onto the hard packed earth in front of the roaring crowd. It landed and split open with a thick clotty sound like wet cheese spilled on cobblestones. There was a momentary hush, and then the mob began to caper and shout triumphantly, shaking their fists at the sky. An old woman delivered a sound kick to the rib section. A youth with flashing white teeth ground his heel into what had been the shoulder. I saw Old Joseph leap up from his campstool and, linking arms with one of his cronies, he danced a whirling jig.

She's gone, it's over, I thought, and a wild glee raced through me as I stared at the wavering flames of the torches, the dark shifting shapes of the crowd.

"Maniacs, maniacs," I heard Zahara whimpering, at the same time I found myself mesmerized and drawn by the sight of two smoke-stained faces: Vaclav's lit with a kind of unholy joy, and Mimi's glazed with horror—as the gypsies pulled the corpse to pieces.

I saw Lenore shrink against Mimi, saw my wife's protective arm around my daughter, screening off the sight of the frenzied gypsies destroying the carcass. *Mimi needs me* I thought, taking two quick steps toward the clearing. My jacket snagged and I stopped. Zahara tugged me back, and I turned to see her reeling, on the verge of passing out. I caught her, she sagged heavily against me.

"Christ, Christ, I can't stand it," she breathed. "Imre, take me out of here, please." Her knees buckled again and I steadied her.

We walked a looping path away from the madness and toward her red caravan. Inside, I helped her ease onto the bed, and lit a lamp. Zahara's eyes were closed, her lids fluttered lightly; her skin was very pale, and I wondered if she'd fainted.

Outside the screams and cheers rose louder. I glanced out the window, seeing the gypsies heave the rubble into the pit of the grave. More water was poured over the remains to hasten rusting; they dumped in barrel after barrel of quicklime—it rose up from the hole as white as smoke—to destroy what was left of her body. They would destroy it all, because they believed anything left— any possession— might allow the old woman to find her way back into the land of the living.

I remembered Old Joseph's words: They'll burn the caravan at sunset, and it will make an end to the misery she made. In the end, I thought, it wasn't a funeral—only a mock ceremony made by apes. Zahara groaned and I turned back to her. She opened her eyes.

"All right?" I asked.

"Yes," she nodded. "Just. Queasy. A moment there." She drew deep breaths between the words.

"That's right," I said. "Take nice slow breaths." I sat down, lightly took her hand, and patted the knuckles.

"They're burying it, aren't they?" She began to sit up.

"Shhh, lie back, rest yourself," I said, touching her shoulder gently. Her eyes flashed on my hand, then looked into mine. I saw that she wanted me, but she was waiting for me to begin whatever might be between us. Her lips looked very full, very soft. I swallowed nervously, closed my eyes.

Outside, there was a great hollow booming—the sound of someone beating a drum. Wild violin music joined the rhythm. I opened my eyes. The gypsies were tamping the grave with the flat backs of the shovels, then stamping the ground more firmly with their bootheels. A moment passed, I focused on the scene beyond the window, while a sharp voice inside me shouted *Mimi, Mimi* over and over. My hand fell away from the round softness of Zahara's shoulder, and I leaned back. A curious mixture of relief and disappointment flooded over me.

"Stay with me awhile," Zahara begged. I nodded, unable to meet her eye, then waited what seemed a long time before she dropped asleep.

I was just shutting the door to Zahara's caravan when I saw Mimi. She was crying. One hand held a white cloud of handkerchief pressed to her lips, the other firmly clasped Lenore's arm. I was certain she'd seen me on the steps. I called out to her, but she wouldn't look at me. She was hurrying toward our green wagon, her small face dark with fear and pain. And thinking of the terrible moments both inside the caravan and afterwards, I wondered which of us was the source of her evident grief—Anyeta or myself.

16

"You have blood on your shirt," Mimi snapped. I walked into the kitchen, glanced down seeing the smudgy blots where Zahara had rested her head against my chest while we lay under the old woman's caravan.

"It's your blood," I said, beginning to unbutton my white shirt and to remove my grue streaked pants and spattered jacket. The blood had dried—especially on my trousers—leaving stiff patches that lay unpleasantly against my skin.

"Is that what you did—take off your clothes to fuck that bitch?" She hurled at me, banging a fry-pan heavily on to the cookstove, jarring me into silence. "I saw you coming out of her caravan! I thought I could trust you—"

"Lower your voice," I said, nodding toward Lenore's end of the wagon. I moved toward our bedchamber, opened dresser drawers rummaging for clothes. Behind me, I heard Mimi picking up the cast-offs.

She ran toward me carrying the blood smeared white shirt. "These are smudges, not drops. You were holding that slut in your arms!" Mimi shook it between her fists.

I shook my head back and forth, not in denial, but in trying to shut out the memory of staring up through the cracks in the floor, of seeing her maddened, naked, kneeling—and of witnessing the hideous amputation. "A moment of comfort," I started to say.

Mimi's arm whipped out. The bleached muslin shirt caught me across the face. I felt the bone buttons flay my cheeks. The fabric stung my eyes. I made a fumbling grab, missed. The shirt dropped to the floor with a small clicking sound. I stared at her; her chest was heaving, her color high.

"That's enough," I said. "Nothing happened." She glared at me while I pulled on a pair of dark gray flannel trousers. "It's all over now. In the morning we'll pack the caravan and go back to Hungary."

"No." She shook her head. "No." She folded her arms across her chest.

My hand shot out, seizing Mimi's arm, my face pushing close to hers. "What more do you want?" I shouted, squeezing the thick purplish scar that braceleted her wrist. I felt my face turn violent red. "She's dead, Mimi, for the love of Christ your mother's dead!" Flecks of spittle flew, landed on her shoulders, her dark hair. My chest hitched, I began to pant. I suddenly pushed her away, and my voice cracked. ". . . Burnt up, gone," I said, my anger draining.

Mimi brought her arm up, slowly wiping the dots and flecks of saliva. I felt the tension mounting in the room.

"She's no-o-o-o-t-t-t-t!" Mimi shrilled at the top of her voice. The sound of her scream rang in my ears. "She's *not* dead!" Veins throbbed in her temples, she clenched her fists, her face was a leering mask. "It's her, it's her, it's her!" she howled, leaning back and tilting her head toward the high ceiling. Her mouth was open in a grimace, her eyes closed.

Her head suddenly snapped forward and she turned on me. "Don't you understand—it's been her all along!"

I felt a part of my mind withdrawing, I narrowed my eyes. "What are you talking about?" I asked in a low voice.

"There is no Zahara!" she said. Mimi's mouth opened, a deep choking sob came out. She suddenly rocked forward, covering her face with her hands, and I heard her weeping as if her pain was so great, so unspeakable, it was beyond any sorrow she'd ever known.

Pity surged up inside me, and I gathered her small form in the circle of my arms. "Shhh, shhh, now," I soothed. I held her while she cried, put my fingers in her hair. She looked up; her face red, her lips trembling.

"Imre," she began, then hesitated. Her huge violet brown eyes met mine, I saw frozen glassy tears, heard the arctic sound of winter wind in her voice. "Zahara was the one," Mimi whispered, and I felt brittle frost closing round my heart at the dread words.

"Zahara claimed the hand of the dead, herself—and then she killed my mother."

17

She's gone mad, I thought, raking my hand through my hair, and if I keep listening, she's going to make me crazy. Unless it's too late already. I sighed, only half listening to the hum of her voice.

"I sent for Joseph's son—for Vaclav," Mimi was saying. "If you won't believe me, at least listen to him!"

I was distantly aware of knocking, footsteps. She stopped talking, and it was the silence that made me look up.

It was Lenore and Vaclav. Dwarfed by the leader's towering bulk, she looked even tinier as she stood on the edge of the steps leading to our bedroom. She cleared her throat as a kind of signal to us announcing his arrival, and retreated. He nodded his big shaggy head in a curt greeting and Mimi pulled me toward the kitchen.

"Zahara's been trouble for years," Vaclav said, covering his glass with his hand when Mimi lifted the decanter to pour another round of brandy. "She's always been a restless, fretting woman. She made her husband's life a misery, I can tell you that."

"Let's talk about Frederic for a minute," I said. "She told me Anyeta killed him."

Vaclav stretched his long legs, then tugged the tight roll of a Romany *diklo*—a blue silk scarf—at his throat. "Well," he drawled, "that depends on your perception."

"Like everything in this damn country," I said sarcastically, reaching for the brandy. I'd never liked Vaclav—now, having witnessed his barbaric antics, I despised him even more. I poured myself a drink.

"Anyeta whored around a lot, it was how she got her way, got certain things from men—"

"Men like you?" I asked. "Or your father?"

"Imre—" Mimi interjected, but Vaclav put his big hand up.

"Yes," he said, "me included; not that it matters anymore." He stared at me. His eyes, a rust-rimmed brown, protruded slightly, moving restlessly in their sockets. "From where Zahara sat, Anyeta looked like she was having a grand old time. Plenty of money, plenty of lovers. And Zahara was bored with her own marriage. So she made a pact of some kind with Anyeta, and in exchange Anyeta killed Frederic." Vaclav grunted. "Make up your own mind who murdered the man."

"And what did Anyeta get?"

He shrugged. "Who knows? But the more Zahara got involved in sorcery, the more she liked it. She knew Mimi was coming and she wanted to grab the old woman's power herself. My father says she did."

"There's no scar on Zahara's wrist," I said evenly. I felt Mimi's eyes searching me for clues of infidelity.

"Oh, it's there, Imre. You just haven't seen it yet." He grinned, making his huge brushy mustache twitch. I felt loathing well up at the thought of this arrogant oaf sitting at my table, spewing his nonsense.

"She won't stop," Vaclav said, "until she has all of you under her thumb."

I began to see the game they were playing. Joseph wanted power— for himself, for his son. I looked at Vaclav, trying to gauge the depth of the man. Was he afraid to claim the hand of the dead? Was that it? I was suddenly certain Joseph had done it, that he wanted to get rid of Zahara. She knows too much, I thought wearily. I was tired. I downed my glass, excused myself and went to bed.

"Don't go," I heard Mimi say, "Vaclav has more to tell you. Anyeta—"

I flapped my arm to still her. It was on the tip of my tongue to shout, "And I guess you have a thing or two to tell *him*—" but I didn't. I was sick of accusations and intrigue, and that was part of it; but I was also worried about what they might do to Mimi if they knew. I shuddered; in my head I heard Vaclav screaming: *Is it not written? Thou shalt not suffer a witch to live.*

I lay tossing on the bed, unable to sleep despite the soothing cadence of their low whispering. Toward dawn, I heard Vaclav yawn, the sound of his chair grating on the wood floor as he stood up to leave.

Sleep began to descend on me, my eyelids grew heavy, the feather pillow seemed softly cool, inviting. I heard Mimi escorting Vaclav to the door, fatigue evident in her voice, her tread. Pale light filtered over the threshold through the parted drapes, I could make out Vaclav's bulking form, he was poised to leave when the quiet in the camp was ripped apart by the sound of screaming.

I struggled to get out of the bed, but an invisible weight pinned me down. "Christ, it's some kind of spell," Vaclav said. I saw him moving slowly like a man wading through chest-high murky water. Mimi looked up vaguely, her reaction out of synch with the piercing cries.

I saw the glowing ball of the sun suddenly loom above the twisted alpine peaks. At the same instant, Vaclav sank stone-like onto the steps, his head nodding heavily against the door jamb. Mimi gave a little cry and staggered back. Her face went dreamy, she sat down, then quickly stretched full length, her hands cradling her face.

The screams rose to a hideous strangling cry, then abruptly ceased. I blinked at the blaze of daylight, my arms flailed at the weighty counterpane, and then, powerless to resist I dropped heavily asleep.

Sunset. My eyes opened wide. I was lying on my back, my arms crossed on my chest. My joints seemed stiff and cold. I sat straight up, rising from the waist like a coffined vampire in the old tales. I began to rub my hands and wrists, and as twilight dimmed into darkness I felt a tingling sensation that turned to heat suffusing my limbs. Outside, I could hear movement in the camp and I recalled the screams. Lenore was just waking, throwing off the heavy sleep. Mimi and Vaclav were already gone. I dressed quickly and left the caravan.

There was a great knot of muttering gypsies outside Zahara's small wagon, and I edged toward the group, then elbowed my way inside.

An overturned chair with one cracked spindle lay against the boards. I had a glimpse of dangling feet, blood. Two men supported the long torso and the limp, brown booted legs while a third was in the act of cutting a makeshift noose. The body suddenly slumped, and over the men's high shoulders I saw a ruined face. Two dark gaping sockets. Furrowed cheeks sheeted with blood. The tongue was a bloated sausage protruding from flabby lips. The eyeless head was cocked at a sickly angle. Ithal. It was Zahara's son Ithal.

As the men turned him completely around to lay him on the bed, I heard a high excited chattering. Constantin leapfrogged from a bench to the center of the kitchen area. His stubbly face was flushed with excitement, his mouth working. Still asquat, he bounded around the room, squealing and clapping his hands. "Wi—" he trilled, "wi—rgh."

"She's a witch, all right, she killed 'im," one of the men said in a sullen voice, and Constantin gurgled the word over and over until I broke in.

"What are you saying? Where's Zahara?" I asked, leveling my gaze at the gypsies, at the same time I wondered where Joseph and his son were.

"Taken. We've had enough of her dirtywork. No one's safe around the likes of her," Feri said, wiping his blood-caked hands on his pants.

"How could she kill him? How could she lift him?" I paced toward him, grabbed one of the old man's ragged sleeves, and pointed at the frayed twist of rope hanging from a nail in the ceiling joist. "It would take someone strong and tall to hang a struggling man—someone as big as you—or Vaclav—" I began, then stopped, remembering that Vaclav had dropped asleep on my doorstep when the screams began at dawn. I heard their deep rumbling laughter.

"Cunning, she is," Feri said, and I saw the others nodding. "Spells us into sleep at dawn, sends him a vision perhaps. *Armaya*, a curse; because with a curse it's not what you say, it's what you think, eh? But something malignant, something black enough to make the lad tear the eyes from his own head. And then," he patted Constantin's greasy hair as if the ape-like little man had a lucky life, "climb on a chair, kick it away and take the swing." Feri nodded solemnly, and Constantin began to chirp.

They can't be right. She wouldn't kill her own son. This was more of Joseph's work. "Where is she?"

"Tonight, the old man's caravan. Tomorrow, with God and St. Mary's help, in hell," Feri said, and I saw him raise one dirty hand and fork the evil eye.

Hurrying, I turned, shoved my way through the roiling crowd of gypsies. They bumped and nudged at me and I stumbled down the stairs. The moon was a narrow white sickle floating in the starless sky. I sprinted toward the sagging barrel-topped caravan with the broken ribs that belonged to Joseph. I heard taunts and catcalls from the ragged band of gypsies huddled around Zahara's caravan. I felt their savage eyes watching me.

An old woman shouted my name in a cracked voice, "Hey, *Lovari*—horse dealer!" she shrieked at me. I kept up my pace, ignoring her. A thin sharp stitch pierced my side.

"*Yekka buliasa nashti beshes pe done grastende*," she squealed. I didn't look back, I knew she was raising her skinny brown arms, hoisting her skirts and bending over, making an obscene gesture. "You understand? With one asshole, you can't sit on two ponies!" she trilled. "Hey! Hey turn around!"

I had a fleeting glance of her bony arms angled out like the handles on a jug, she shook her thin backside. Her gaudy dress swished back into place. "Both of them, pony boy!" the old woman yelled; the rest of what she said was indistinguishable, lost against the clot of dark pine-infested hills that surrounded the clearing. I frowned, then began walking faster. Behind me I heard the distant echoes of their low laughter.

Twenty yards away, angry male voices rose inside Old Joseph's wagon. Zahara shrieked. Holding the cramping muscle in my side, I broke into a painful run. I heard the sounds of struggling, her white face appeared between the tattered canvas flaps. "Stay back, stay back, it's a trap!"

I stopped, my heart racing madly. She cried out in pain, her head snapped. She was jerked backward out of sight. I heard the garbled sound of Mimi's voice cut off, and then, before I thought to spring forward, I heard the crack of a whip and the caravan lurched beyond my reach.

From the other side of the clearing I heard Lenore scream, saw the long rectangle of yellow light from the flung open door to our caravan. She spilled down the steps, arms outstretched, calling my name, sobbing. "They took Mommy," she wept in my arms.

I held her, saw the satisfied Roms come untethered from Zahara's abandoned wagon—like horses set free to crop they roamed away, nodding smugly. I held my daughter in my arms, fingers moving over the crown of her head, I touched her scalp. The skin felt hot and damp with crying.

Looking out over the tumble of her dark hair, I pressed my daughter more tightly to me—as if I could somehow shield her from the flickering shadow of the barrel-topped wagon racing through the night. Lenore trembled against my chest. "They took my Mommy," she said.

And I wanted so much to take away her pain.

18

"Both of them!" Lenore said, pounding her small fist against her knee. I nodded, thinking of the old woman's screeching words, but not really listening. We'd been following the trail of Old Joseph's caravan all night. At daylight we found the small signs of encampment: the remains of a cookfire, the scattered bones of a roasted hare, a forgotten mug that once held coffee or tea. But mostly Lenore and I watched for the light scarring of wheel ruts or looked at overhanging branches for clues to their passage: bent leaves, snapped twigs.

"The gypsies went the other way," Lenore said, pointing at their *patrins*—heaps of twigs and stones the troupe had left as trail markers along the way. I caught a hint of anxiety in her voice.

"Probably meeting Vaclav and his father at a pre-arranged place. I want to get your mother away before they meet up, and then all of us—Auntie Zahara, too—will go back to Hungary." It would be so much easier to take on the old man and his son alone, without the rest of the troupe. In my mind's eye I saw Vaclav and Joseph sleeping in bedrolls close to the caravan; I would creep up on them. My hand went to the pistol I'd shoved in the waistband of my trousers. Guns were quick; the hulking Vaclav and the old man were slow.

"I didn't know he meant both of them," Lenore said miserably, and this time I left off planning my ambush, and looked at her. Her mouth was set in a small tight line, her eyes dark with worry.

I halted the rumbling wagon and turned to her. Under my gaze a cringe swept up her shoulders, over her face. Fear touched her eyes.

"Lenore," I prompted, and her voice spilled out in a rush.

"I couldn't sleep," she began. "I heard Mother and Vaclav talking. mommy didn't seem to like Auntie Zahara," and I nodded, aware that Lenore had heard our violent argument. "Vaclav said Auntie Zahara was a witch, that a witch made up her spells and curses with the plots she hatched in her head. 'When it's over, we'll be free,' they said. 'We'll be free of the demon inside her brain!'"

Lenore's hands twisted helplessly in the lap of her ruffled skirt. "It didn't seem so bad, I didn't think it was a bad thing if Auntie turned into a quiet woman." She paused. Her eyes flitted anxiously, her gaze fell on the stilled horses. "I swear it. I didn't know that Vaclav was lying, that he was a traitor, and he meant taking mommy and—"

Panic spiraled through me. "Lenore, Lenore," I said, grabbing her narrow shoulders. "What are you saying?"

She collapsed against me, her voice was thick with crying. "Gentling," she sobbed, "they said gentling was the only—"

"*Gentling!*" I shrieked. "Oh, Christ!" A shudder wracked me. I was suddenly cold, shaking.

"I didn't tell you I overheard them, because I kept telling myself Auntie Zahara will be all right—only a little different—like the horses. You told me once that lots of horses live through it."

Remembering a day when Lenore was helping with the horses, I felt the sting of my own tears. "What's that, Papa?" she'd asked, pointing one chubby finger. It was for my work, a gentling box, I told her, glossing a truth I thought was too painful for a five year-old child to hear. It was for my work—but I never used it, never gentled a horse, never told her how it was done. For some horsemen, the gentling box was a tool of trade—no different from the grinding stone used by a knife sharpener; but for me it was so much more sinister—a hangman's noose, an executioner's axe.

"Lenore, Lenore," I said, mourning inwardly, not wanting to punish her for what was partly my fault. Out of kindness we lie to our children, and those lies come back to hurt us most.

"And then I didn't tell, because I was afraid you'd be mad at me for not telling sooner." I understood she'd been suffering more than me during our long campaign through the night. Wanting to do the right thing and fear of my anger had made Lenore feel she was in a steel-jawed trap.

I soothed her while Vaclav's words rose and fell like hammer-strokes in my brain. Thou shalt not suffer a witch to live. Old Joseph and his son knew Mimi had claimed the hand of the dead, I thought, as an icicle of fear plunged through my belly; and they'd used Mimi's anger at Zahara to trick her.

"I didn't know he meant Mommy, too," Lenore wailed again. I put my arms around my daughter to keep from seeing the haunting, broken look on her face that said she was sorry now and knew— because she learned the hard way—that too late was always too late.

I felt her move from my embrace. I clucked to the team and the wagon began to move slowly over the road. Lenore found a handkerchief, blew her nose.

"Are these horses gentled?" Lenore asked. I caught the note of hopefulness in her voice, and without wanting it to be so, my mind and heart were dragged back in time:

There's hardly any light. It's very early in the morning, and while there's a part of me that is still a sleepy boy of eight who would rather be sitting with his mother eating porridge by the fire, listening to her soothing voice, waiting with her while she waits, baking bread, then filling the caravan with the smells of a good supper, I'm proud to be walking alongside my tall father. Mother is at home, waiting for both of us: My father has told me I'm old enough now to be learning there's more to the business than camouflaging a mare's gray muzzle. We're going to gentle some horses.

There's a mat of frost on the ground, and the soles of our boots make a muted crumping sound as we cross the fields. My father's big hand suddenly snakes out, halting my forward progress. I look up at him, seeing the dazzle of gold hoop in his right ear, the small cloud of breath forming around his black brush of a mustache. "See there," he sighs softly, and my gaze follows his pointing finger.

On a distant slope is a small herd of wild horses, grazing, nickering lightly, tossing their heads. Watching the moving pattern of the grass, I know we're downwind; and although we see the shapes of the horses, they're not aware of us.

"Move softly, Imre," my father says, and I watch him hoist the leather strap that holds the big rectangle of the wooden gentling box a little higher on his shoulder. We skirt the edge of the field to advance on the wild horses at an angle. I'm trundling a small wheeled wagon heaped with hobbles. Some are made of iron—sets of rings joined by links; some are made of leather—thongs attached to wooden posts you hammer into the ground. My father, who is an expert, will do the roping. I will set the hobbles. "Keep out of kicking range, son," he reminds me in a whisper, as we hunker on the edge of the field, the gentling box set on the ground between us.

The sun comes up and I watch my father swing the rope time and again, and each time the rope spirals through the air like a slow glittering snake and he snares a horse, I bolt up out of the grass and fasten the heavy rings or the leather thongs to those angry, spirited forelegs. I'm happy with the joy of running, with the feel of the wind stinging my cheeks, with watching my father's graceful work, with his praise at my deft movements as I tether the herd.

I count fifteen. There are no more hobbles left on the small red wagon, I call to my father, and he moves toward me.

"We'll let those go," he says, sounding a little winded after his labor, and jerking his head toward some half dozen or so horses circling in a mad dash across the field.

Grunting, my father hefts the box onto his shoulder and approaches the first horse. I walk at his side. "Steady now," he says softly, and the horse gives out a huge chuffling snort at the same time it dances sideways; but its legs are caught in the iron ring. Its eyes are rolling in fear.

My father opens the wooden box. "Get a browband on him," my father says, sifting through the gear, "and keep away from his mouth." My father means I should take care I'm not bitten, and I'm cautious, on the alert for a show of those long teeth.

I'm told I'm a tall boy, but it's a stretch for me to reach up and attach the harness works—the browband, the strip of leather we call a crown piece—and twice before I can slip the iron bit in place, the horse nearly knocks me aside with its great head.

"Ready," my father calls. Moving forward swiftly, he attaches a round wooden ring to the browband. He cinches the worn crisscrossed leather straps that fasten it to the crown piece behind the horse's ears. "Here, stand on this," he says, pushing the gentling box toward me with one nudge of his foot. "Hold the cap steady." I climb on to the box, find myself level with the top of the horse's ears. My hand moves along the thick jaw, over the horse's smooth brown hide. I make soft noises with my tongue and teeth to soothe him.

"Hold the cap," my father says again, and my eye is drawn to the circle of the wooden band. Now I see there are really two bands— like circles nesting within one another—separated by a small metal flange.

"The outer band keeps the pressure steady," my father explains. "See those holes?" I stand on tiptoe, crane my head and nod. There are two holes drilled in each of the bands.

"Line them up," my father says while he is twirling the wing nuts on a pair of big greasy screws sticking out from either side of the wooden bands like gray moths. It's simple, the bands slide clockwise, they rotate easily, but I concentrate on getting them right.

"Right," my father says inserting the two thin needle-nosed spikes he has hammered on his anvil into the holes on the outer band. I watch not really comprehending, but before I can ask my question, the needles pass through the inner circlet, rest against the broad bony expanse of the horse's brow.

"Hold the cap steady as you can," he says, and his big hands come up, quick as a heartbeat. His broad thumbs twist the screws, and suddenly, all too suddenly, I understand the mechanics of this contraption.

I hear myself screaming, "No, don't!" and my hand jerks wildly, knocking one of his off balance, and he is screaming at me, "There's no pain if it's done right, they're animals, they don't feel a thing!" But the horse is screaming, screaming in terror and pain, nearly going down on one knee, his great head rolling, his eyes glazed, his lips drawn back, his body flecked with sweat. And my father is screaming at me, that if I'd held the cap steady this wouldn't have happened, it's nothing, it's like going to sleep. His voice is rough, his movements swift and hard; he brushes me aside, I lie stricken on the ground watching his hand reach sideways and his fingers turn the other screw. I hold my breath.

The second needle penetrates the hide, the skull.

The horse staggers, the sound of its scream is cut off. I see the light in its eyes die out—as quick and sudden as snuffing a lamp. I hear my father saying, "The horse is going to be as gentle as a lamb and on its feet before we finish the next."

The light in its eyes is dead, and something in me dies. Two thick runnels of blood drip down the length of its dazed face. The horse stands dully, blinking back the bloody streams.

My father picks up the box, I watch his retreating back as he moves on to the next, already wall-eyed from the smell of blood and men and terror. I see my father's head turning toward me, and I know he's going to tell me to be a man, to be a *Lovari*, a horse trader, but before he says those words I'm on my feet running.

A small boy with a gold hoop in his ear, white sleeves billowing, I'm waving my arms and running; running toward the horses, wanting them to run. The wind is a sob in my ear, my eyes are blurry with tears. "I didn't know, I didn't know what it was!" I cry, and the herd goes skittish, the horses take short awkward hobbled steps.

"I didn't know what it was," I shout, lifting my own small eyes to their huge glossy ones. They look back at me with something like sorrow, like understanding.

My father is cursing under his breath, calling me a worthless boy. There is a high whinnying shriek, then the sound of one of the horses I helped hobble falling to its knees. The smell of blood and horse foam drifts across the tips of the waving grass.

"I'm sorry," I whisper to a pale long-maned mare, her head dips twice, daintily, like a woman's when she nods. Soon her creamy face will be red, slick with the trails of blood, and it will be too late. My hand reaches out to slip the peg, release the tether.

I hear my father's heavy tread, his hands and clothes are dotted with horsehair and blood. I hear the wooden bands, the metal spikes rolling inside the box.

Hurrying, I tug at the hammered peg. He sees what I'm doing, shouts, "Stop it!" The peg comes out of the ground bringing up a huge clot of earth. I slap her flanks hard to make her flee.

The horse runs in one direction, I race off in another. Out of breath, I stop, cup my hand over my brow: I see the top of her pale head rocking over the field, and it makes me think of the rush of the white-capped sea. She made it, I think, when she's no more than a flying speck in the distance. Around me I see the work done by the gentling box. They were wild horses, now their eyes are dead, dumb. They nose each other, sniffing clotted blood, placid as milk cows. They plod along, as lead-footed as the sullen, foolish farmers my father will sell them to.

I run toward the woods. Behind me I hear my father shouting, "What's the matter with you? Come back here! After it's done they don't remember." And I keep running. Because somehow, that seems most terrible of all.

"Are they, Papa? Are they gentled?"

Lenore's voice broke through and pulled me back from the hellish vision of the worst memory of my life. "No," I said, praying with all my heart that it wasn't so; because, she, of course, meant the horses, but I was thinking of Mimi, of Zahara. I clucked to the team, flapped the reins, got them running. Visions of my small wife and her pretty cousin flitted in my brain: I saw them sitting under a tree shoulder to shoulder, their long hair mingling across their breasts. Their eyes were closed like those of sleeping saints. Round their heads, malignant haloes kept watch while the blood dripped down their faces.

A groan escaped me. In my mind's eye, I was seeing them in death: the long needles meant for the thick skulls of horses impaled their waxy brows, penetrated too deeply. But if they lived—my thoughts broke off, and I saw Mimi's glittering violet eyes dulled to idiot vacancy, her mouth turned up in a fool's perpetual grin. I saw Zahara dragging her feet, shuffling like an old bewildered woman who suddenly finds herself in her kitchen and begins to weep because she has forgotten how she got there, or why she came. Dear Christ, if they lived! I screamed inwardly, a lump burned in my throat.

Afterwards they don't remember, my father's voice echoed in my head. And if they were gentled, if we were too late, I thought, driving the team in a fury, that would be most terrible of all.

19

It was Lenore who first saw the smoky skybound trail of their campfire above the trees. I pulled the caravan to a halt. The old man and his son were less than a quarter of a mile away. The brush and trees along the road formed a dense, impenetrable thicket. I could see a bridge in the distance. It seemed likely Joseph stashed his rickety caravan by the water, while he and Vaclav went into the woods on foot. Were my wife and her cousin penned in the wagon? I was fairly certain Mimi and Zahara had been force-marched through the woods, but a mistake on my part might cost their lives. I would check the old man's caravan first, and if they were inside I would get them out and disable the wheels.

I handed Lenore the reins, slipped down from the box, formulated my plan. "Do you see that bridge?" I asked.

"Yes," she said, holding the worn leather reins tightly between her small fingers.

"There's a chance Vaclav left the caravan there and followed the stream into the woods."

"To be near water."

"Yes. If it's there and if your mother is inside that wagon, I'm going to fire three shots in the air. Then—and only then, Lenore, I want you to drive toward the bridge. Otherwise stay here."

"If she's not—" Lenore whispered, biting her lip.

"Then I'll take her and your aunt out of the woods and bring them right here." If only, I thought, Joseph didn't use the power of the hand to sniff me out and stop me.

Her eyes drifted over the lonely road, the darkening sky, the thick brush, then rested on the carriage lanterns. "Will you light the lamps before you go?"

"Yes," I said, thinking the light would be a comfort to her, and there was little chance Vaclav or Joseph would see the glow. If he knew I was coming, it wouldn't matter anyway. "Are you afraid, Lenore?" I asked, lighting the roadside lamp.

"No," she said trying to sound brave at the same time she nodded and her eyes showed yes. I looked at her, and she ducked her head. "A little," she said. She leaned across the box and I kissed the top of her head. She put her small hand on my shoulder. "Don't be gone long, Papa," she said softly.

"I won't be," I said, adjusting my pistol, and checking my pocket for ammunition.

"I'm afraid of wolves," she said and I saw her round eyes lift to the dark blue horizon where the moon was a dull lamp barely visible in the sky. "All day I've been worried about wolves."

I couldn't tell her not to be, but I said, "I didn't hear any."

"I did," she breathed. "Sometimes I thought it was the wind, but it wasn't." She shuddered, closed her eyes, as if she heard their mournful cries rippling in the steeps. Then a small tired smile touched her lips. "You'll be quick," she said. "I'll wait. Unless I hear the shots."

I nodded, marveling that my daughter could tell herself the parting words, the reassuring things I'd been about to say. I kissed her again. "Very quick," I said, then started down the road. I turned once, gave her a final wave.

"Wolves," she said, her voice barely audible. "Be *careful* of the wolves, Papa."

Months later, her words came back to haunt me. But that night I was thinking about the old man's power, about his clairvoyance, forgetting we all have a little, overlooking my daughter's share.

Near the bridge was an old cart path used by drovers to take their teams down to the water. Vaclav had followed the track and left the wagon near the bank. Mimi and Zahara weren't inside the caravan, but I felt better for having checked it to be certain. I began walking downstream, looking for a place to enter the woods different from the one they'd used. I didn't want to run right into them, I wanted to scout the edges of their camp. I used the moon as a guide, and quietly threading my way through the heavy brush I began moving up on them. A half hour later I was in earshot of their lair. A careful parting of the greenery showed me the two men sitting by a fire just outside the entrance of a small cave. The old man's attention was focused on some kind of handwork in his lap. Vaclav was angry.

"What's taking so long?" Vaclav said, then got up and paced rapidly before the cave.

"Precision is important," the old man said, holding up one partly constructed gentling device. My heart lifted with the gesture.

"I don't care if she dies." Vaclav spat. "I don't care if the goddamn spike gets driven out the other side of her fucking head!"

"I cannot take a life—not even hers," the old man replied evenly, then turned his slow hand to drilling the holes.

"I could've made a dozen of the damn things by now!" Vaclav said in a lower voice. I saw his eyes flick toward the black mouth of the cave and reasoned the women were inside.

"Yes, if you knew how, but you are not a *Lovari.*" Joseph blew on the shavings and began drilling again.

"If you don't hurry," Vaclav said with a glance at the moon, "he's going to find us before we can do it." His mouth turned down in a furious mask of frustration.

"There's time yet," Joseph replied. He stared toward the trees, nearly making me start. I was glad for the darkness and the heavy brush. I wondered if he sensed how close I was. I saw his gaunt face break out in a grin, then I watched him insert a spike into the hole he drilled. Testing carefully, he turned and locked the device. I saw the thin needle click home.

"I'm through waiting," Vaclav shouted. He stooped suddenly and retrieved something I couldn't make out. Was it a spike, a second device? I didn't know. He shoved his father backwards with the heel of his hand. Joseph wailed in protest and tried to heave himself onto his feet. In the firelight I saw his face go violent red, a coughing fit took him, and he fell heavily onto his hands and knees. Vaclav took two long-legged strides into the cave.

I heard the sound of female voices shrieking in alarm, and my heart jolted in my chest. Seconds later, Vaclav had Zahara by the hair, and he was dragging her trussed body back out of the cave. The gentling cap circled her brow. She tried to twist out of his grasp. Her head jerked free of his bunched fingers, and I saw her swivel her jaw, bare her teeth, trying to bite. He clamped down on her shoulder, then drew back his other arm and pummeled the side of her head. He flipped her on her stomach, seized the ropes that held her hands behind her back, and pulled her through the dirt. I saw the dark gleam of blood covering her face.

Mimi suddenly cried out. "Hurry, *hurry!*" she screamed from inside the cave. I flashed on the thought she'd used the power of the hand and sensed I was there. Relief washed over me, she was unharmed, she was begging me to save them both. I didn't dare wait, didn't dare stop, think. Instead, I broke my cover and leapt into the fray.

20

Mimi ran from the cave. She shrieked Vaclav's name. I felt a trembling vibration that seemed to be gathering force and bearing down on all of us. Her voice rose into a hectoring scream, her small hands flew to her head, and I saw something pass with the speed of wings between her and Zahara. Zahara's face screwed up into a mask of terror and agony.

I saw the old man rising to his feet, saw Vaclav raising his arm to twist the screws, when the camp was suddenly rent by the sound of crackling thunder and a huge blue flash that sent Mimi and the old man sprawling backwards and knocked Vaclav across Zahara's body. At the same time I heard a high pitched snapping yowl, the sound of heavy pads racing over the ground. I turned to see the feral gleaming haunches of a wolf pack break out of the tree line. Their eyes were lit with a deadly blue-green luminescence. I caught a glimpse of bared fangs, wet lolling tongues. Three of them sprang on the instant. The leader clamped his long jaws onto Vaclav's body. The others tore into his thrashing legs.

"Do it," Mimi shrieked. "For the love of Christ, do it!"

My first bullet shattered the leader's snout in a mass of splintered teeth and bone. Vaclav screamed. I saw clots of hair and blood rain over the screaming struggling humans. I aimed, cocked the gun, fired twice more, blasting the heads of the others into a bloody mash of brains and fluid. The air was suddenly filled with thick black smoke.

Nerves jangling, I pivoted, facing emptiness. The smoke grew heavier, spinning here and there in swirls and thready patches. I heard the sound of shrill laughter and turned to see Zahara yanking the device from her head.

Beside her Vaclav lay unmoving, streaked in a glistening slime of blood. The lower half of his jaw hung by one drippy sinew. Broken teeth poked up from the shredded gums. His left eye socket was a fist sized bloody hole. At the side of his head, a long ragged flap of scalp flesh was flung backwards showing pulverized bone and leaking brains.

"You killed him!" Mimi screamed at me. "He was going to do it—"

"Wolves," I babbled, at the same time I heard a low hissing. I saw the three crumpled bodies—the great furred paws splayed out, their bloody heads slack jawed in death—waver for an instant, then disappear. My eyes bulged. No wolves, there were no wolves, only a vision, I gibbered inwardly, and I shot him . . . one eye stared blankly at the moon, the top of his head was torn away, his jaw ruined like the blasted snout of the wolf . . .*Do it, do it*, Mimi's voice clanged in my head, and I realized with a sickly kind of dread she had not been exhorting me to use my gun, she'd been urging Vaclav to hurry. I saw there had been one device—meant for Zahara alone.

The air seemed to ripple. Through a shifting haze I saw the dead wolves lying on the ground again. I saw Vaclav's big hands still clutching dense fur, his head thrown back in agony, his long body crushed under the dead weight of the beast. My mind suddenly reeled, I felt the gun slipping from my hand, my knees went weak and watery.

"Fight it, fight it!" someone screamed.

But the smoke-filled air went hot, hotter, seeming to suck every sound, every sight around us, until there was nothing left. I felt my chest being squeezed, then slowly crushed with a weight like a stone slab. I gasped, barely able to breathe in that dead air. I sank to my knees, and I thought, this is what the silence of death sounds like, and then I heard a voice whispering low in my ear, breaking through the poisonous fog.

Arms pulled me up, pulled me along, set me running pell-mell through the woods. I never felt my feet moving over the ground. "This way, this way," the voice called out to me. Behind me I heard the sounds of pursuit. Confusion wracked me, I couldn't shake the terrifying image of slavering hungry wolves running us down. All around me, the night was alive with the deadly sound of throaty growling, moans, flesh being torn and snapped from bones. The stink of their pelts, of hot breath rolled over me. Something snagged at my leg, my heart vaulted in one long, looping, erratic lurch, and I staggered and fell full length. I felt the shock of icy water, heard my pulse drumming in my ears.

My collar was jerked back and up, my shoulders lifted out of the stream, and I realized I was with Zahara. "We have to run!" she panted. "Get up, Christ, Imre, please get up! Don't you hear how close they are?" I got to my feet, she pulled me after her. We ran the length of the stream, splashing clumsily through the shallow water. I remembered thinking the water would stop the keen-nosed wolves from tracking our scents; I remembered being shoved onto the box of my caravan, then hearing the crack of the whip as we sprang forward. But beyond that—until I woke to a life that was forever changed—I remembered nothing at all.

21

woke to the thickest darkness I'd ever known. Lying on my back, I held up one hand in front of my face and gasped, genuinely astonished at the sensation: I knew it was there, I felt the pull of tendons in my forearm when I turned my palm to and fro, but I couldn't see it. The velvety blackness was like a cloak thrown over my head, dampening my emotions, muddling my thoughts. I felt numb; as if something that was an integral part of me was suddenly missing. I took a deep breath.

I was alone in my bed. The caravan was still, silent. Slowly, wisps and tatters of memories floated in my head: sprawling in the stream, feeling the flood of icy water drench my skin and clothes. The madcap flight through the dark woods. The sound of feet moving through the underbrush. Wolves. In my mind I suddenly heard Mimi screaming *Do it!* and the sense of shock fell away as easily as you might pull down a sheer, sun-rotted curtain.

Mimi was in league with Joseph, I thought, feeling anger rise in my throat like a bitter juice. Together with Vaclav they plotted gentling Zahara. How could Mimi consider it? She knew what it was. I shook my head. Mimi believed Zahara had killed her mother, but Christ! Christ, there was nothing on the face of the earth that could bring me to gentle a human.

For the first time in all the years I'd known her, I felt a terrible sense of disappointment in my wife. Her wanting Zahara gentled was like a dagger to my heart. How could you, Mimi? I mourned, at the same time an answer was bubbling to my lips. Joseph. Joseph had bewitched my wife all along.

For some reason I couldn't begin to fathom, Joseph wanted all the power in the troupe. He was hideous. Evil. This was my father's friend, this bastard, this *Lovari*. "He sent the vision," I whispered, feeling the truth of it welling up inside me. Joseph sent the vision of the wolves and he wanted me to kill his son. Wanted to reclaim his place as the *prima*.

Where was Mimi now? I wondered. My anger gave way to a depression as black as the night around me. Where was she? I felt my heart speed up, and suddenly, a new fear, another anxiety caught me, made me cry out in my agony, bellow like a wounded animal: "Lenore," I screamed, "Lenore, Lenore, where are you?"

A lighted candle moving through the darkness. The sight of fire-pinked fingers shielding the flame, the ghostly outlines of a shadowy face, the sound of bare feet whickering over the floor. I threw the covers aside and sat up on the edge of the bed. My pulse raced and fluttered.

Zahara stood over me. I took one look at her dark brimming eyes and I knew.

"Gone," Zahara said, shrugging her shoulders helplessly. Her voice was tentative, pain-flecked. "Lenore—she's not—she wasn't here." Zahara reached out with one shaky hand and touched my arm lightly, and a knife-edged sorrow sliced through me.

"Gone, both of them gone," I cried, covering my face with my hands.

It poured out of me: all my suspicions, my hatred of Joseph, how he'd used my wife as a pawn. Zahara sank on the bed, her hair hung down over her shoulders, the tears rushed down her cheeks and dark-spotted the fabric of her blouse. She wouldn't meet my eyes. She begged me to stop. "No more, please," she whispered, "I can't bear it."

But it was inside me: festering, ugly, raw. "My fault," I said, plucking uselessly at the bedcover. "I told Lenore, 'Drive on if you hear three shots.' And then, and then—" I wept harder. "The wolves, Christ, the goddamn wolves; he knew and he sent them. I saw three attack Vaclav. Three of them," I repeated. My chest heaved, I bent over and clutched my belly. A sickly nausea spiraled through me, my brain was giddy, whirling. Oh, mother of Christ, the depths of the man's cunning.

"Lenore, she—oh God, she heard the shots and she drove, because I told her—she thought it meant Mimi was inside his wagon." In my mind's eye I saw Lenore running up the rickety steps to the old man's door, saw her small hands turning the knob, trembling with anticipation, calling to her mother, and then—then what? Did she see an illusion? I didn't know. I closed my eyes, gritted my teeth.

"Oh God forgive me, she was so worried, so frightened, she must have gone right inside his caravan to see her mother, to make sure Mimi was all right. She wanted her mother! and I did it, I sent my daughter to this—to him—"

"No, no," Zahara clutched my wrist. "No, he did it, he did it! Don't you see."

I shook my head. "Mimi," I said, sniffling back my tears. "She was good, a good woman. The things she did for me . . . and for Lenore." I paused. "Once we were in Old Buda, in the city. Lenore saw a porcelain doll in one of the shop windows. It had blonde hair, a tiny string of pearls around its neck, white gloves. We couldn't pull her away from the shop. Then Lenore was seeing dolls everywhere. Every time she saw some well-dressed little *gajo* girl carrying one of those fancy dolls around, she cried that she wanted a real doll, too—not another shabby homemade rag baby like the gypsy girls had—but one with yellow curls, a picture hat, pantalets. I don't know where Mimi found the money, or what she sold to buy it, but on her feast day, Lenore found that satin-dressed doll sitting on her chair when she came in for breakfast."

I sighed, once again hearing Lenore's whoop of excitement when she saw the beautiful doll. Talking in a high, eager voice, Lenore sat at the table, held the doll on her lap like a baby and fed it spoonfuls of the porridge she was too excited to eat. I remembered the joyous, satisfied look in Mimi's violet eyes, and how she took my hand in hers while we stood watching our daughter's delight.

"I loved her," I said. "Mimi filled the house with love, she—" I stopped. "Oh goddamn that bastard! He's destroyed everything, taken everything I love—"

"I loved her, too!" Zahara cried out. "Mimi was my cousin. She loved me, and Joseph poisoned her against me." Zahara shook her head back and forth. "I can shut my eyes and see her, dancing the night of your wedding, her saucy mouth smiling, laughing behind the silky veils. She was so in love, so happy."

"The wedding feast," I said. But no one had seen her dance for me in the caravan. The hot light in her violet eyes.

"And do you remember your betrothal? The *pliashka?*"

I nodded, seeing the bottle of brandy covered with the red silk scarf and festooned with a necklace of gold coins. We drank from it to seal our engagement. I saw Mimi's face, her eyes locked on mine.

"And she told me," Zahara said, "she told me about Sighisoara—"

I closed my eyes, lost in the old memory. Sighisoara was a medieval fairy-tale town set high on a hilltop and less than a day's drive from Tirgu Mures. Not long after we became engaged, I took Mimi there. I recalled that summer afternoon spent climbing up the narrow winding streets; Mimi's delight in the ancient clock tower; the turreted houses—like minarets—with their mosaic tiled roofs; the crumbling citadel perched above the town like a brooding cormorant. I remembered holding Mimi's hand while we stood in a jewelry shop, her fingers squeezing mine (for yes, that one!) when the girl who ran it showed us a necklace that was a small crescent moon hung on a silver chain. I bought it, then fastened the links about her slim throat. Mimi smiled, preening. The shop girl nodded, saying it looked lovely on her, so becoming! I recalled wanting to lift the heavy mass of Mimi's dark hair to kiss the place on her nape where the small white clasp rested; regretting I couldn't because we were in a public place. Later we paid a penny for a tour of a huge old ochre-colored house that a withered man with a squeaky voice told us was the birthplace of Romania's bloodthirsty hero, Vlad Dracul.

At dusk, it was cool in the mountains. I took her to a *levnerker*, a public house, for supper. I smiled, now, recalling how I'd set out to get her drunk on *tuica*—brandy made from plums. She knew I was trying and she let me; she giggled, only half-pretending to snatch away the glasses I filled for her as we sat by the fire.

"Get us a room, Imre," she crooned. She was at that stage of tipsiness where a whisper has the force of a shout. I was tiddly myself, and her voice was loud enough so that by the time I turned my head to look for the bald-headed innkeeper, he was already popping the hinge to raise a section of the mahogany bar, then striding toward me and rubbing his hands.

"A room, yes, for the night? My wife serves a very fine breakfast—" He was holding two long-knuckled fingers up.

We glanced at one another; we were only engaged, we could not stay out all night. I put up my index finger, "A room for one—for a few hours, so my wife can rest before we journey home." He didn't look happy but he agreed, and I counted the money into his hand.

I let the bald-headed proprietor show Mimi up to the room, and as soon as he was out of the way I went bounding up the wooden stairs, scratched at the faded blue door marked 3 in rusty brass. The room was paneled from floor to ceiling with narrow wainscoting painted a cloudy white. The windows were pushed outward, open. Pots of brilliant red geraniums filled the sill. I stood just beyond the threshold, waiting, scarcely breathing. Mimi opened her slim arms, welcoming me onto the narrow iron bed. She was a virgin when we'd set out that morning. I made love to her twice.

It was one of those rare days we are sometimes given, when each moment, every impression stands out—perfect, discrete: the leisurely drive along the peaceful, country roads, the sight of the oxen plodding in the sunshine; the old glass lanterns fastened to graceful iron arches and set directly into the buildings; the way the lamps glimmered at twilight in the steep streets; the sound of the bells ringing out the hours; the rhythm of young bodies that seek pleasure and find delight.

We both loved—and neither of us ever forgot—Sighisoara; and on our way home, we stopped the caravan on the side of the tree-lined road and made love in the moonlight. Mimi, my bride-to-be held me against her small chest, met my ardor with an urgency of her own.

I remembered fondly looking down at her body under mine, seeing her pale hand—silver in the moonlight—dart up to smooth my cheek. I saw her quick smile, heard her tease: "My own, my Vlad Tepes."

It was Vlad Dracul's other name; she'd called me Vlad the Impaler. Then she raised her head swiftly, her wet lips touched mine for the space of a heartbeat, and we both laughed.

"Yes, she told me about the first day, the first time—the private joke about Vlad the Impaler," Zahara said, and I was too surprised to blush. I turned it over in my mind, thinking her cousin must have meant more to Mimi than I ever knew, if Mimi had confided this . . . .

"She came to me, right before the wedding," Zahara went on, "she held my hands in both of hers. 'I want you to know,' Mimi told me, 'of all the troupe I love you best, and I have something for you.' It was her wedding, and she had a gift for me. It was a pendant."

I closed my eyes, seeing that dusty shop in Sighisoara, the gleam of Mimi's smile, the charm winking against the darker skin below her throat—

"Silver, the shape of the crescent moon," Zahara said. Her hand crept toward her collar, and she loosened two tiny shell buttons. "You never knew she gave it to me," Zahara said in a voice that was husky with emotion, "but I have it still." She fingered the fine linked chain at her throat, tugged slowly. And I saw the silver moon

I'd given my beloved rise up from between her breasts.

Sighisoara, I mourned inwardly. A fairy tale.

It came into Zahara's hand, we both stared at her palm, at the fragile ornament lying against her skin, and I heard her voice hitch. "It was Mimi's and because she loved me, she gave it to me."

I bent to touch my lips to the silver shape in her hand, and as I inclined toward her, I had a sudden glimpse of the flesh below the frilled cuff of her blouse. I felt the ache of despair, and a moan escaped me. Zahara's wrist was white and smooth—as white and unmarked as Mimi's had been before this terrible evil assaulted us.

I stopped, gazing up at her. Her onyx eyes met mine, and I saw a questioning light there. "Oh, Zahara," I whispered, "Mimi said you claimed the hand of the dead."

"Joseph—" she began.

"Joseph made her think so," I finished sadly. I closed my eyes, my head fell forward, and her arms were around me, comforting me. Her voice was soothing, a murmur. She was saying Mimi's name over and over. The sound of my wife's name was like the distant roll of waves breaking on the shore; I felt as lonely as a man who is cast adrift to drown in the night sea and who yearns for light, wants to touch land, hears the haunting peal of the ship bells fade, then finally cease.

"Mimi," she breathed again.

We held each other. My hands found her hair, turned her face up to mine, and weeping for Mimi, I kissed the salt from her skin.

22

We made love. And, that grief-filled first time, it was for Mimi—as if we both made love to my wife. But the second time at dawn was ours, for the years of buried passion that had risen again between us.

I woke gradually. The room seemed to hang suspended in the time between night and day; lurid streaks of light vied with deep pockets of shadow. The sun picked out scatterings of clothes—trousers, a filmy chemise, a white, work-worn shirt, cotton stockings. Zahara leaned over me, and I felt her lips nuzzling the tender flesh just under my ear.

Her hand played over my chest, fingers idling in the graying twists of short wiry hair, and I closed my hand over hers. I turned to meet her gaze and felt her full lips press to mine. She smiled behind the kiss as if she had some sweet secret, and the gesture was so girlish, innocent and womanly all at once that it inflamed me. Slow, I reminded myself, and let my eyes fall shut.

I caressed the nape of her neck, let my hands sift through her thick shining hair. It was cool, gossamer soft against my fingers.

"Imre, my love," she sighed into my mouth, and her breath was warm and comforting, her tongue luscious against mine. I felt her shift, straddling me lightly, and I opened my eyes to look up at her. Zahara's head was canted back, her face serene with a half smile. Her skin was a dusky olive. I brought my hands to her breasts, rounding them slowly, gently scissoring the dark brown nipples between my first and second fingers. Far away, I could hear her uttering a kind of deep, sweet humming.

She leaned forward. I tasted her breasts, felt their round weight against my lips, my chin. I slipped one hand between her legs, the flesh of her thighs gave off a warm soothing radiant heat. She was slick. Wet.

I felt her turn, take me in her mouth, her hands moved over me slowly, at the same time I slipped my fingers inside her, skirled them around and around the small hot button of flesh. I heard her breath coming harder, the sound of her light sighing moans, and I felt myself shudder, nearly come to climax. I was aware of the wetness her mouth left on me when she pulled away to straddle my loins.

I felt her fingers guiding me, and then I was inside her, helping her lift her hips that we might lift and fall more delightfully. She shifted her weight, we clung to one another, took a slow spin, and I was on top, feeling the whole wondrous depth of her. I looked down. Her eyes were closed, her lips redder with our kisses, her dark hair was a rippling fan against the sheets. I felt her teeth, the slight pull as she nipped, drank up the skin of my throat. Her legs opened and closed around my back, I bent my lips to one nipple, and the image of myself at seventeen kissing her breasts beside the nightskin of a gnarled tree rose unbidden in my mind, and I felt the beginning of that letting go that brings you to the end.

Afterwards I lay on her chest a long while. Her hands moved slowly through my hair, across my shoulders, up and down the tender skin of my back.

"I'm in love with you," Zahara whispered, tugging lightly on a small tuft of my hair, and making me look into her dark obsidian eyes.

I stared into them a long time. I smiled, but I made no answer.

She was lying on her back sleeping when I woke some hours later. I never eat breakfast, my stomach is a much later riser than the rest of me, and the very idea of food in the morning registers as a faint queasiness inside me. But I was hungry that day, and the flashing image of scrambled eggs, fried potatoes, sizzling chunks of meat, brown coffee set my stomach growling and brought a grin out on my face. She was sleeping heavily. I would fix the food, I thought, popping out from under the covers and hustling into my clothes.

I was bent over and had one leg stuffed into my pants when I heard a thick gobbling sound, followed by the riffling of a protracted snore. It startled me briefly, and I chalked it mentally to save as a tease. Just about everybody snores sometimes, but we keep it private, a secret—along with the rest of our noisy body signals. Smiling, I pulled my trousers up and glanced across the room.

The window by the side of my bed admitted light, but the sun had gone round to the other side of the caravan, making the room duller than it might have been. Zahara's skin had an unfamiliar pasty look, thicker somehow than I remembered it, with a greasy whitish cast like lard. The sheet made a rumpled dividing line over her belly. One arm was thrown back over her head.

I moved closer and the room was suddenly much darker, dim with shadows as if the unseen sun had gone behind a patch of heavy clouds. Under the sheet, her legs and hips appeared to have taken on a bloated swell. Her belly and midriff were wide, round, pocked with dimpled flesh, marbled with tiny capillaries that gave it the faintly pink look of butcher's pork. Her breasts hung slablike, pulled out of shape by their ponderous weight. I saw a deep fold of slack skin at the point of her shoulder where her arm was raised over her head. The elbow was pudgy, wrinkled. I sucked in my breath. But that only happens when a person is enormous—Christ, you can waddle around for years before the fat begins to deposit at your shoulders, your elbows—

—*The rest of us see an overblown, sloppy woman who waddles when she walks*—

Joseph's words jumped in my head. I felt a slow churning in my belly. No, he planted the idea in your brain, and it slowly ripened with time into black fruit—

I stepped nearer the bed. Her mouth was open, her chest rose and fell sluggishly, her breath came out in short heavy puffs. In the gloomy light, her hair was mousy, shot with gray, her teeth took on a sickly brownish tinge—

—*Three of her teeth are missing*—

For a second I saw the dark gap, the shrunken stunted pink of her gums where the teeth had fallen away, her tongue turned and clicked in her mouth, her lips came together with a tiny flapping sound. I leaned closer, breathing in a foul cloud. Gagged on a stench that rose from *sordes*, the crusts that jacketed her rotting teeth and gums, from the accumulated gases deep within her.

I drew back, turned away and clapped my hand over my nose and mouth. Impossible, I told myself. It was guilt making a slow subterranean course through my brain, finding its way to the surface in the memory of the old man's hideous words.

—*What do you see, Imre? The rest of us see*—

The right side of the mattress sagged beneath her humped body, listing under a vast weight. I moaned inwardly. A man would roll to the center of that, fetch up against the meat of her. I felt my mouth twitch. A mental image of my hand playing between great jiggling thighs, of kissing a broken sour mouth creased with wrinkles rose up. In my mind's eye I saw Constantin's picture of the fat, chinless woman, her splintered grin in profile. The snaky writing spun up at me. *Witch.* I shuddered, telling myself Constantin's a madman, and closed my lids.

I rubbed my hand against my brow, forced myself to look again, then breathed a sigh of relief. I saw her full reddish lips turn up, Zahara smiled in her sleep and settled on her side—her slim body undulated in a long slow curve—like any love-sated young woman.

I shoved my disquiet aside and left the room, walked up the short flight of stairs to the kitchen. Moving softly I took out the tin pot, then set coffee on to boil. I stood by the window, absently looking out while I waited for the coffee. In the glass I caught sight of a tattoo of bluish-purple marks—love-bites—dotting my throat. I lowered my eyes from the reflection, began buttoning up the collar of my shirt, and as I brought my hand up I smelled the dank odor of her sex on my fingers. I felt a spurt of fear rising up inside me; I went to the basin and began to wash, an old Kalderash gypsy saying swirled inside my head. *Kon khal but, kal peski bakht.* He who eats much, eats away his luck.

I was only dimly aware that my appetite had left me.

23
Late Autumn, 1863

Day after day I drove the caravan through country lanes and mountain passes, always searching for some sign of Mimi, of Lenore. We asked in towns; spoke to grim-faced farmers nodding tersely as they leaned over broken fences, shook my hand, wished me well. We stopped at the fairs and marketplaces. Always the same result. No one had seen her, seen a young girl, seen an old gypsy man pass through driving a beaten wagon.

Zahara never said a word to me about this long fruitless search; I never mentioned that I had the feeling Mimi was trying to find her way to me.

It was getting close to November. We'd camped near Deva. In the distance, the mossy ruins of the old Citadel loomed above the hills. Zahara was in the caravan; toward sunset I unhitched the team and led the horses to a meadow to let them graze. I watched them crop a while, their mouths working at nibbling the hay stubble; then I saw that a chestnut mare was favoring her right foreleg.

"Stone, for sure," I said, advancing, and taking a pick out of my pocket. As I stooped to examine the hoof, I heard my name drifting over the silent yellow fields.

Imre, Imre.

I looked up, oddly certain it was her, that Mimi called to me. But there was only a covey of quail taking sudden flight. As if they'd been routed, they rose in a flapping cloud, vented their shrill cries, and I felt a mad skittering in my heart. I looked out over the meadow.

There was an ancient stunted tree in the center that made a rude shelter for cattle during summers. The wind blew up, and I heard the bare limbs rattle against each other with a skeletal sound like the bones of dead men. The top of the oak blazed with fierce red light, the bottom lay in thick twilight mist. The sun dipped over the horizon all at once, and I felt a keen excitement all along my spine, as if some moment that was out of time was bearing down on me.

And then I saw it. The old man's barrel-topped caravan was there; a wavering image rising out of the gray mist beneath the tree. I held my breath.

The skin of the canvas seemed to disappear, and then I was seeing inside. Pale ochre light from a rusted lantern spilled in a circle over the table. Mimi got up, filled a white soup plate with stew from an iron pot on the small black stove. She carried it back, set it in front of the old man. Lenore smiled, held up her dish for a second helping.

I took one long step nearer, the caravan seemed to fade into the swirling fog, and a groan was wrenched out of me. I stepped back, the vision returned and I was suddenly aware that I was hearing them—

"He will come to it in time, my dear," Joseph said, patting Mimi's wrist, and I saw the gleam of his gold ring on his thin finger, the sly look in his hooded eyes. Did the old man think I would claim the hideous power, too?

"It's so long, so wearying," Mimi sighed. "This endless waiting," and I saw her glance at Lenore, as if there was something my wife was torn between telling our daughter and keeping from her, too. Mimi's face was too thin, she looked weary, pain burdened. She told Lenore to finish her supper and get ready for bed. My daughter— her hair hanging in thick brown braids—stood before Joseph. I saw the old man kiss her brow, and I felt a sickly dread in my heart. He's bewitched them, set his mark on their minds, gives them kisses worthy of Judas.

Mimi moved toward the doorway, crossed her arms at her waist, and I saw her gaze out over the darkening field and I wondered if her eyes found mine, if she saw me. A moan came out of my throat and I began running toward her. With each step the caravan dimmed, until at last there was only the single silhouette of Mimi's form— the froth of dark curls around her head, the bell shape of her long skirt—the fading sound of her voice, a sigh, and then a whisper—

Imre, Imre

—that became silence.

There was nothing under the oak. I searched the ground, tramped in circles around and around the trunk. My eyes bulged, my head ached with the strain of trying to see in deepening shadows, of looking for trampled grass, a forgotten handkerchief, a scrap of food— for a sign, for just one more glimmer, the merest touch.

Were they here now? I wondered, striking the tree with my fist. Had they been here before, or were they coming some night in the future? I didn't know, I was reluctant to leave. For me that autumn-clad field was a romantic, haunted place; the nearest I'd come to finding Mimi and Lenore. And I think I might've spent all the sunsets of my life in the meadow waiting for them; but in some deep part of me I knew no vision would come there again. There was no denying the sudden emptiness of the place, the sense that its magic was fled, and after three more lonely evenings, I gave it up, feeling sad and heartsore.

If my days belonged to Mimi, I will tell you frankly that I was a divided man—and that division was just as sharp as the line between light and shadow in the tropics—so with the growing darkness of the season, my nights belonged more and more to Zahara.

We made love with an abandon I had never known, but out of that wildness a sickly thing grew between us. Like a fat leech, it fastened and fed on our sweat and groans and cries.

It began innocently enough, like the larking adventures two daredevil children might share. We'd been teasing each other—and getting steamed up—all through a long supper that we had sitting side by side on a bench. Zahara was wearing a white linen shirt of mine; and if the sight of her bare legs wasn't enough, the thought that she was naked under the shirt was. Every time she leaned or shifted the shirt collar flapped wide and gave me a tantalizing peek at her breasts, at the smooth expanse of skin just below them.

"Oh, here I went to all this trouble and you're not eating," she said, giggling, shaking her head at my food laden plate, a *sarmale* of cabbage leaves stuffed with rice and meat.

"Cooking is not the trouble you went to," I replied, pointing at her. "Dressing—or undressing, I should say, is what you concentrated on." I leaned back against the wall of the caravan and nudged my dish toward the center of the table.

"Did it work?" Her eyes were bright with mischief. She suddenly faced me, her chest held high. "Did it?" she whispered, lightly nuzzling me with her breasts.

"Yes, I wonder if my plan—" I felt her hands scrabbling in my lap, and I gave a small groan.

"Yes, you little witch, your scheme worked," I said, at the same time I tore the buttons of the shirt away and bent my mouth to her breasts.

She snaked away from me. "Catch me," she cried, and ran naked toward the bedroom, the torn shirt flapping like a sail in one hand.

I stumbled after her. She was lying on the bed, knees drawn up, her hands behind her head. "How's the view," she said, rapidly opening and closing her legs a few times.

"Divine."

"Want to see it better?" she teased, patting the sheet to invite me. Her face sparkled with naughty intent while I began to undress and I saw she was going to spring out of the bed.

My pants were half down, my shirt hung open, I flopped on top of her. She squirmed and churned underneath me, then managed to wriggle away. "Got you," I triumphed, diving and grabbing one ankle as she tried to vault out of bed.

"So you think," she laughed while I wrestled her back down and sat astride. Her feet flailed and thumped behind me. I pulled her arms high over her head, my hands held her wrists wide, I shifted my weight so that she was pinned beneath me, our eyes met.

"Tie me down," she said.

"What?" I heard a croak in my voice.

"Do it," she nodded toward the tattered shirt, and God help me, my hands shook, my heart pounded, but I tore the cloth into ragged white strips and wound them over her wrists and around her ankles and strung her in an X across the bed like a man crucified in ancient Rome.

And then I had her, and Christ save me, even then I knew it was wrong, that it was the beginning of something sour and black and deadly, of dark fantasies we spun together that made me wince and heave by morning when my hands shook and my conscience twitched, but I couldn't help myself, and that was the beginning.

24

Zahara drew me in deeper and deeper because some of what she did wore the face of innocence. She took to wearing costumes, and once, I recall, she was decked out in a yellow gown like an English woman from the 18th century. Her waist was cinched, her bosom drawn high. She wore white stockings, simpered behind a black lace fan, powdered her face and neck and pasted a tiny patch—like a beauty spot—near the corner of her mouth; another sparkled just below her right eye. She rented a tall white wig and served me tea.

Suddenly in the midst of the play-acting and coquetry, a strange, wondering expression came over her face. She stopped, scratched her head briefly, seemed to dismiss whatever she'd been thinking about. She poured tea in a thin blue cup. "Aren't you curious about all this lacy underwear?" she asked; and the same puzzled look came into her eye, and then, instant, dawning awareness:

"Shit!" Zahara screamed, yanking the wig off, and flinging it halfway across the room. She bent all the way over and shook her head back and forth rapidly, plunged her hands over and over in her black hair. "*Oh, shit, the damn thing's full of bugs!*" she shrieked.

Deposed vermin crept willy-nilly across the pale yellow satin skirt of her dress. She stood up and began wildly brushing at her lap, her eye fell on the infested wig and she began screaming again. "When I get hold of the bitch who rented me this . . . . " she raved, and then, since I'd already given into loud hysterical laughter, she began to laugh, too. She pulled off all her clothes, threw them in a heap out the window, and tugged me onto the kitchen table with her. "No sense," she said, "in spreading them to our bed." After we made love we scrubbed the caravan down with a solution of hot water and lye soap and took baths before we slept on our sheets.

But there was a darker side to the play-acting, the costumes. I came in one night and found her dressed in a tightly laced whalebone corset that pushed her breasts high up on her chest and exposed them completely. "Ever had a whore?" she breathed, tweaking the ball of her right nipple.

"No," I said.

"Want to pretend?"

"All right." I swallowed; with her looking like that, there was no will in me to refuse. The ivory corset ended at the hip line, and a pair of frilly garters stretched downward accenting the dark curling tendrils between.

"How much would you pay?" Zahara asked, sitting propped against the pillows while she toyed with the smooth flesh that showed over a pair of black stockings. My eyes were riveted to her fingers sweeping lightly over her skin.

"Anything."

She laughed at the rasp in my voice. "How much?"

"A lot," I whispered.

She stood up and preened, balanced on one high heel, lifted one long stockinged leg up onto the bed. She looked at me over her shoulder, wiggled her fingers. "C'mon then, pay." Her voice was liquid, sweet with teasing.

I chuckled and stepped toward her, put my hands around her waist, then pulled her against me to feel the tautness of her buttocks, to caress her. My fingers slid between her legs.

She turned and hissed. "What do you take me for, huh? Pay or get out."

"Pay?" It was a game, I thought. I wasn't sure what she wanted of me.

"Are you daft? It's pay as you go. Empty your pockets."

I put my hands in my trouser pockets, accidentally turning them inside out so that the coins spilled from my clumsy hands and rattled in a hail on the floor.

She glared at me. "Pick it up."

I got on my knees and began gathering up the money. A coin cartwheeled out of my grasp. "All of it," she sneered, and I snagged the rolling gold piece.

I held it up to her, and for a second I thought she'd slap it out of my hand, dash it on the floor, laugh, clasp me to her. Instead, she reached between her breasts and pulled out a small pink striped cotton sack with a ribbon drawstring. She put the money inside the bag, and stuffed it down into the corset.

"All right." A hard smile came into her dark eyes. "You bought the whore, you get the whore. But this," she patted the waist of the heavy girdle, "stays on."

"It's foolish, that's why!" I shouted. It was two weeks later. She had not relented one inch from what I called the whore game. "The money is yours—take it from me—everything I have is yours! But don't make me do this."

"I already told you," she said, sitting, legs wide apart on a chair. "Straight lay is what you get." She was wrapped in a tattered red negligee, staring into a small mirror while she rouged her lips, her nipples, with the abandon of a practiced courtesan. "You want a blow job, you pay for it in advance. You want to eat my pussy," she grinned, knowing her crudeness both shocked and thrilled me, "then pay." Peering into the glass, she stuck the tip of her finger in the rouge pot, then dabbed the corner of her rosy mouth.

"But why do you make me stop? Why can't I—why can't I pay for—all of it at once?"

"That's the way I do business," she said, not looking away from the mirror and hitching the robe back onto her shoulders.

"It's cheap," I began helplessly, sick at the thought that I'd already done it again and again. Paid her. Then gotten out of bed, gone to my wallet, and paid her a second or third time to feel her mouth on me, to put my mouth on her.

"You're tired of this, aren't you?"

I nodded wearily.

"Maybe if we rented a room it would seem more real to you."

I looked at her, not comprehending.

"Yes," she said, "that's what we'll do." She saw me shaking my head. "Are you saying no, you don't want to rent a room?"

When I nodded she gave me a sly, knowing look and said, "Well, then, we'll just pretend."

Two nights later, she had her way and it was real.

I blew on my hands, paced in a drafty hall stamping and stirring my feet to keep warm. Then I knocked on the door, waiting patiently until I heard her voice telling me to come in.

The whitewashed room was lit with a single candle. The ceiling was low, streaked with soot from the brick fireplace. Wooden shutters lined the windows, here and there slats were missing. There was a rude, stinking chamber pot in the corner partly covered with a graying towel. There was a chipped pitcher and a mismatched green basin on a small rickety stand. The bed was small, the covers pulled up sloppily. She was lying on the bed, barefoot, naked from the waist down. The rounded tops of her breasts showed over the neckline of a snowy chemise. Her dark hair curled softly over her shoulders.

"Oh, Zahara," I said, wanting to tell her none of this was necessary, asking her to end it.

"Shut up," she said. "Put the money on the dresser." She pointed with a metal nail file she held in her hands. I walked across the room slowly, sighing, my feet creaking over the wavy boards, and put three gold pieces in a porcelain tray painted with red flowers.

"Come here," she said, and I approached the bed, dreading what I knew came next. I stood before her.

"Take it out of your pants," she said.

I unbuttoned my trousers, held myself aloft while she held the light close, seeming to inspect the flesh for signs of disease.

"All right."

I squeezed my eyes shut, hearing her fumble among the vials and bottles that cluttered the top of the nightstand. I heard the sound of a cork being drawn. I felt the wet sensation of being doused with something that smelled like alcohol and stung like fire. I don't know what it was, she said all the whores used it to prevent disease. It dripped and splashed over me, leaving a huge splotchy stain. I felt it trickle through the cloth of my trousers onto my thighs.

"You can undress," she said primly, and I heard her lay back.

Twenty minutes later I was in the hallway, nearly tripping over a bald-headed farmer who was leaning against the wall. I stumbled down the passage toward the stairs, too dazed and humiliated to think about my addiction to her, about the way she thrilled and repulsed me, until behind me I suddenly heard Zahara calling, "Come in."

I turned in disbelief to see the broad retreating back of the farmer crossing the threshold. It's a joke, it can't be, I told myself, pattering back down toward her door. I caught a sudden surreal whiff of bad cooking from the kitchen in the tavern below, heard the clatter of pots, the sound of tinny music.

"Open up," I shouted, rattling the knob, startled to find it locked. "Stop it!" I screamed.

From inside came the sound of her low voice: "Put the money on the dresser."

The farmer's voice was the heavily accented twang of the country. "They said you was big," he yawped approvingly, "I like a big woman."

Sick, I ran from the tavern.

25

I sat on the bench, one eye vacuously scanning the small black book in my lap, the other sharply alert for Zahara. I had begun following her out of a jealousy so keen it made me queasy. My thoughts ran in a compulsive circle, like gnawing rats they rounded the wheel of my head, my belly. *Who was she with? What was she doing?*

She was haunting the graveyards, I discovered over the month we journeyed eastward toward Sibiu, an old Gothic town just above the Carpathians. And just before noon, I'd seen Zahara pass through the high stone towers flanking the entrance gates to the cemetery, and this time I'd followed her inside, settling on a fancy wrought iron bench to watch from a safe distance.

Now I had a fleeting glimpse of Zahara's head, dark curls flying up in the wind. I craned my neck. The cemetery, like the town, was built on several connecting levels amid sprawling hills. She disappeared behind the high rectangle of a white mausoleum, then I saw her ambling slowly, her black cloak fluttering at her heels, moving down a steep gravel path.

Nearby an old woman laid a small bouquet of blood-colored mums beside a narrow, sunken plot. A pair of smudgy gravediggers walked past me, lugging their tools. Far off, I watched them discreetly skirt the edges of a ceremony that was presided over by a tall priest, and I smiled at that: I was dressed as one myself. I'd hit on the idea that I could track her wanderings through the cemeteries more easily if I wore a habit, and I'd broken into a secluded country rectory one night and stolen the local monsignor's black cassock, his cape and the book of daily prayers—the breviary.

Occasionally, Zahara wandered out of my sightline, but I sat in the anemic winter sun, feeling the unaccustomed sensation of the dark cassock skirt billowing around my legs waiting, watching. She was winding through the tree-lined walks, searching for recent graves, the telltale signs of newly laid stones, mounds of earth that had a naked look. I saw her linger near several of these. I had heard of graveyard prostitutes, and I fumed angrily at the thought she was like a streetwalker working the byways and lanes in the cities of the dead.

I knew the whores pretended to be stunned by grief. They waited for a likely mark, then acted out a quiet charade: they sobbed over the new tombstones, sometimes lost control and pretended to faint. The man, like as not, would come to their assistance. A clever woman could tell him anything: my mother died of a wasting disease, three days ago my fiancé killed himself, my husband, a promising young musician, was run over by a speeding carriage.

From feeling sorry for the distraught woman, it was only a short step to buying her a hot drink, a late supper. In places like Paris, London, the whores pretended the gentlemen aroused their passions: *"Oh, God forgive me, it's wrong with Allan barely cold in the grave, but I cannot help myself."* Soon the men were bringing presents, paying for clothing, furniture, apartments. On the road, I guessed, Zahara might turn the trick by pleading sudden poverty and getting their money, or stealing it. I felt my mouth turn down in a tight line. Either way, the man would be too embarrassed to go to the constables, and she would be gone—if not that day, then the next.

My stomach contracted in a tight knot. Zahara's movements gave the impression of purpose, and I wondered if she knew the place by sight or reputation. Had she done this before? Been here before? Only yesterday I'd seen strings of gaudy gypsy caravans on the old city road, heard the jingling bells of their horses.

She was kneeling by a tall ornate marker, dark dress and cape pooled around her knees, and she lifted her eyes each time she heard footsteps sliding on the path. Once, a young woman approached, and for one numbing second I thought it was Mimi, but Zahara's face was calm, serene; and I dismissed it, telling myself I'd only imagined the likeness because I'd seen the caravans.

A few minutes later, an old man tipped a crippled-looking hat in her direction. Zahara smiled weakly at him, then lowered her gaze.

Not that one, not him, no, she wants somebody *rich*. I felt a hot anxious sweat break out along my spine and under my arms. In my mind's eye, she snagged one of the local aristocrats, a courtly man with white hair, a narrow silver mustache. He carried a rolled umbrella and wore gray gloves. At his midriff, the gold chain of a watch gleamed. He took Zahara's arm in his, helped the grief-struck widow to her feet. Her face was pale behind the black veil, her lip trembling. I could see myself leaping up from the bench and chasing them down for the confrontation: *"Whore! Whore!"* I screamed, and conjured up a tortuous fantasy of shouting, scuffling, punches, torn clothes, bloody cheeks. My head spun giddily, and then my thoughts turned to the loathsome possibility I would only slink away—a beaten man that learns the difference between suspicion and discovery. I was suddenly afraid I would see her with a man and say nothing, do nothing. My breathing went shallow, my heart began to race when I thought of accusing her, confronting her.

What if she denied *me* her favors? Worse, I thought, and the force of the idea struck me like a blow, what if she left me? I saw her white and naked and rolling under me, making me groan with passion and I felt my stomach cramping in hot waves, heard a wailing voice inside. No, no, Christ, I can't risk it, can't risk losing her. I gritted my teeth, a wave of longing went through me.

The wind gusted sharply, riffling the pages of the breviary, casting a chill on my sweaty skin. I shivered, told myself I only had to wait and then I would know for certain—who she was with, what she was doing—and if confronting her meant I lost her, well then, so be it. There would be no love lost between us, she wasn't my wife. My hand tightened on the book, my nails leaving scars on the worn leather spine. She wasn't Mimi. She was only a whore with a soul as black and false as the bogus veil on her head.

It was twilight. As the afternoon grew darker I'd told myself I was glad of the cassock, the heavy cape—I would be still less conspicuous in the lengthening shadows. But gradually the cemetery began to empty, and I was aware of the wind moving through the trees, scattering fallen leaves so they skirled and clicked dryly against the gravel paths.

I was on the verge of giving over my watch and going home for the night, when I saw her creep toward a small gray ruin of a chapel, her face anxiously turning to and fro. She was moving stealthily, with the consciousness that comes from knowing you mustn't be seen, mustn't get caught. I saw her try the door, then step back and tilt her head up. What did she want there? The tiles were gone from the roof, and the dark upthrust joists gave off the bare skeletal look of a rib cage. She dropped her gaze, then gathered her skirts and began to run quickly, flitting between the trees, the monuments, always stopping to glance about before moving on again.

And suddenly I was aware there was danger for both of us. Even playing a priest, what reason could I give for being in a graveyard after dark in a country where it was believed no sane man would come there—unless he had traffic with the devil.

The church bell tolled the hour—a hollow clanging that echoed over the square. I heard the squeal of iron, and in the thickening shadows, I could see the sexton swinging the heavy gates closed, hear the rasp of metal on metal when he lowered the bar and fastened the lock. Then his bootheels tapped over the stones as he hurried away toward the dim glow of lamplight, toward the safety that lay in the heart of the living city.

I turned my head, hearing the creak of tendons in my neck, saw Zahara moving, a black wraith among the trees. I suddenly recalled the night we crashed, the night we'd seen Joseph on the road, the sight of the white-gowned woman fleeing through the woods. I felt fear ticking in my chest. She hesitated, and I picked out the shadow of her dark cape against the white marble of a tall mausoleum. I heard her rattling the lattice-work of the bars. And then there was a tiny flash of yellowish light—like the first flare of a match in complete darkness it was quick, startling, nearly blinding in brilliance—and I found myself straining to see more clearly, but the black shape of her cloak, her veil was only a moving blur.

Low and distant, I heard the soft screak of metal being gently, carefully drawn over stone. And I knew she'd gone into the tomb.

26

I took two long running steps, then stopped, puzzled. From inside the mausoleum I could hear voices. My heart thudded in my chest. What was this? Some tryst with a rich toff, a pervert with a taste for necrophilia? Had she suggested the tomb to make the pretend seem more real? In my mind's eye, I saw Zahara lying atop a blanketed slab of marble. She was very still, scarcely breathing. Her eyes were closed. A young man with wavy brown hair leaned over her, eyes riveted on the sleeping figure clothed in the dark dress. One of his hands crept from his side toward her. His ringed fingers began undoing the buttons. He held his breath, stroked the winter chilled flesh of her breasts, traced the curve of her belly. A fevered thought jumped into his brain. You can do anything you want to a corpse, yes, anything at all.

I clenched my fists, paced closer. A dim yellowish light gleamed inside the crypt, I saw the checkered shadows of the bars faintly etched against the ground. The archway over the door had been draped with a swag of black crepe, and I watched it stir, billowing lightly in and out against the marble facade. On the entry step were two bronze urns, and now in the dull light I saw they were banked with great masses of drooping flowers—frost stung roses, spotted lilies, the faded tumbling stalks of tall gladiolus. Someone was buried here recently—my thoughts broke off.

From within came a low shuffling sound that drew me closer. Passion rising, would he tell her not to move? I wondered. And then I heard a man's thick guttural voice, the words clotted in his throat. "Ask," he wheezed heavily, *"Ask of me what you will."*

And I ran forward.

In lightning sequence, I saw her standing before an open stone sarcophagus. A man sat on the marble edge, feet dangling to the floor. Behind him I saw the upraised wooden lid of an ebony coffin. Zahara's hands were clutched deep inside the lapels of his black suit, her face hidden against the gleaming silk of a cravat. Over her shoulder the man's head lolled downward, pale frizzy locks banding his shrunken scalp.

My fingers were hooked through the bars, and as I stood there I was nearly overcome with the smell of rotting flowers, the ripe sweet odor of decay—

"*Ask,*" he moaned, and the sound was no more than a piteous wail. At the same time his face came up, lids fluttering—

One blue eye had gone filmy white and lay sunken deep inside the dead socket. His mouth hung agape, the blackish tongue unraveling from the dark shriveled lips. His face was the dark gray of tainted flesh that has begun to rot, his limp hands were livid, purpling. My eyes widened, bulged. I saw a maggot worming at the root of his nose. My jaw dropped with a painful snap and I screamed.

Zahara turned, hissing, her face contorted with anger so black I felt it like a blow caving in my temples. The corpse toppled sideways all at once, thudding heavily into the padded coffin with a sound like a felled tree striking soft earth.

She began advancing slowly. I was frozen to the spot, my hands locked onto the icy steel of the bars. Her heels clicked against the stone, her dark dress seemed to swell large and larger, her mouth turned up in a grin, and then a terror so great it crashed the walls of my mind took me.

She was all things at once. Like the subtle images of a nightmare kaleidoscope, I saw her sweet, supple—the dreamy girl of my youth. The body and face shifted, bloated to monstrous proportions. Her gray hair lay dank against a thick scalp, her smirking mouth became a crumbling hole. Her hair went white. I saw the gleam of her scalp through the thinning strands. Her body shrank, narrowed, her skin lay pinched and wrinkled over the time eroded bones like glowing parchment. She walked stiffly with the measured stoop of age. Mimi's words spiraled up inside me with sickening speed: She's not dead! And at last I saw, I knew. She was the old sorceress-whore. She was Anyeta.

"Visions," Anyeta crooned, one hand floated up dreamily. I felt her dry fingertip brush mine. My head whirled, an inarticulate cry rose up in my throat. Zahara stood before me, tall, broad shouldered, the thick curling mass of her hair making the full red lips look fuller still.

I leaned heavily against the bars, ached for her, and of its own accord my head turned and yawed, tilting to take a lover's kiss. My eyes closed. I felt a delicious warmth coming off her skin as she drew closer, closer.

From far away I heard myself moan, a deep yearning welled inside me. The soft skin of her lips nearly brushing mine, tingling, the bars between us somehow arousing something dark and hot and passionate inside me. I saw myself wanting her, straining to clutch her breasts, her body, my desire growing, until it was like an agony and I could bear it no longer, and I had to pull the door aside and take her.

Her lips trembled on the verge of touching mine.

She laughed lightly.

And on the cold air came a smell that was the stinking miasma of charnel houses, of decaying teeth and foully crusted gums.

My eyes flew open.

An aged Zahara looked at me with greedy piggish eyes, dark slits nearly hidden in the chunky flesh of her face.

And I fled.

27

Afterwards I never remembered the details of my flight. I could call up vague notions of trying to scale the rusted fence, taking off my boots, tossing them over and pushing myself higher and higher with my bare feet, my frozen fingers. Landing with a rocking thump on the cobbled street and running for what seemed like half a mile, my boots clutched in my hands, until I stopped in a doorway, my breath heaving, a stitch in my side. I sat on a stone threshold and my naked feet burned with the cold and the pounding frenzied run, and I put my boots on and I walked the streets for hours, too stunned and dazed to think, until one idea took hold of my brain. Drink. I wanted to get stumbling, falling down sodden drunk to blot out the hideous memory of the tomb.

I found myself in the steamy lobby of a tavern. It wasn't until I went into the bar room, my mind on fire with the idea of blessed, numbing brandy that I realized I'd half registered the sight of a red and black gypsy caravan hitched to the curb.

Constantin was there, his back to me, his small round face barely cresting the top of the tall bar. Laid out between his hands were what looked like several flat wooden tokens, painted and cut in the shapes of an ale stein, a wine glass, a tumbler. He gave a small grunt and pushed the likeness of the tumbler toward the innkeeper. A brandy bottle appeared, the bar-keep filled his glass with *rachia*, the really strong stuff. Constantin raised his arm in a little toast of thanks, took a swig and grinned.

He tapped the tumbler again. The barkeep motioned for the glass to refill it, but Constantin pulled it away, covered it with his hands and shook his head no. "N-n-nuh," he muttered. He pointed ahead at a rank of clean glassware ranged along the shelves.

"N-no-t muh-e," he tapped his chest, shook his head again. "Fre-ehn." I saw the puzzled look on the barkeep's face. Constantin's voice was low and muffled, thick in his throat because of the missing tongue. But I knew what he was saying.

He turned around suddenly and pointed at me, his face beaming with delight. I began to walk across the room. The barman's face cleared with sudden understanding.

"Want to buy a drink for your friend, do you?" he said, and Constantin nodded cheerfully. "All right."

I moved alongside, Constantin clasped my arm, said hello with his eyes. The barkeeper set a cork coaster out, filled the glass he laid on it with rachia brandy.

I raised the heavy tumbler to my lips, watching the barkeep suddenly duck his head, nervously swab the wood counter with a polishing rag. His eyes floated up to mine, and I nodded a greeting.

"Friend, right," he muttered, and his gaze dropped to the swishing cloth. "But there's twenty people in here," he said, lifting frightened eyes, looking over the tables, toward the roaring hearth. "The door's been swinging open half the night. He never turned around— not once. So how did he know you was in the room?"

Constantin smiled at me, then his eyes tipped closed like those of a small wise buddha.

"He was waiting for me," I told the barkeep, and in the act of saying it, I felt the truth of it shine, like a small brilliant gem. I recalled the brightly painted wagons I'd seen the day before; the rest of the troupe was close by, but Constantin had sought me out.

"Oh," the bartender said. His face showed his mind was still working how that could be. Then he let it go and moved down the bar toward another customer.

I thought of the pictures Constantin had drawn, the old woman, the hanged man, the stick writing: Witch. He wasn't mad, merely different. Mad—that was my word, not the truth.

I turned to Constantin and we clinked glasses. The tinkling sound rang in my ears, kept time with the simple thought humming through my mind:

Constantin knew things, had a kind of clairvoyance, I guessed.

28

"Anyeta," I said, pointing to the drawing of snaky-haired woman kneeling in front of another figure.

Constantin nodded.

We were sitting at a table near the fire. I'd asked the bartender for pencil and paper and Constantin was trying to answer my questions with sketches.

I looked at the picture, feeling something like a missionary trying to read a sand map drawn by a savage. Anyeta was staring up at a body that floated over a rectangle. "Coffin?" I said.

"Y-uh," he nodded, and sipped from his glass.

"What's this?" I pointed to a bubble enclosing a scattering of hatchmarks that streamed from the body's mouth.

He mimed talking with his hands, pointed to his mouth.

Like a newspaper cartoon, I thought, and nodded. "She makes it speak?"

He shook his head. He touched his lips again, furtively, and now added a sawing motion. I swallowed, yes she'd taken his tongue, I thought queasily, and tapped his arm to show I understood.

"N-nn-o," his head turned back and forth in a sharp negative.

He pointed to the rendering of the words, tapped his chest. "J-uh," he muttered, then laid one finger along his nose.

"Joseph?" I asked. I couldn't read his face. Constantin suddenly smiled, his round face looking ruddier in the fireglow. There was a rush of cold air as the heavy door wheezed open. I followed Constantin's gaze.

I felt the hairs rising along the back of my neck and shivered. The old man himself came into the tavern, his great cape swirling around his thin body. Without meeting our eyes once, he walked directly to our table.

"Where's Mimi?" I said. I wasn't sure how much I liked this intrusion. Constantin had laid his hands on my arm several times, blinking to signify Joseph could be trusted, called him friend, and bought the old horse dealer a drink. But as I watched his gaunt impassive face, I wondered if Joseph had managed to fool the younger man. Constantin had a child's trust. "Where is she?"

"Not far." He tapped a cigarette against the tabletop, lit it.

"I want to see her."

"She's very angry, jealous; sick with jealousy, if you want to know the truth," Old Joseph said, and a wave of guilt swept over me.

"In her mind Mimi understands," he touched his brow, "that you were tricked into sleeping with an illusion, but emotionally," his long bony index moved to the center of his chest, "it cuts her."

"How does she know?" I glared at him.

"She knows because over time the power of the hand grows. She knows because she's seen it." I started to say it was more goddamn likely that he'd told her, planting evil seeds of doubt between us for his own purpose, but he held up his hand to stay my interruption.

"This is what Anyeta wants—to divide us." The old man's dark eyes pierced mine.

My hand tightened on the glass, I gave a small grunt.

"Whatever you feel about me—now is the time to cast those feelings aside." He paused. "If you have the desire to put your life— your family's life—together again."

"Lenore—" I began, and felt his thin hand and Constantin's small warm fingers touch my wrist at the same time.

Joseph spoke gently. "It will be better for you to fight armed with knowledge than to blunder in ignorance," he said. "Will you listen?"

I nodded. I would.

"Anyeta owned the hand of the dead for years," Old Joseph said, leaning over the table. The bar was emptying, the fire burning low and hot. "But there is something in the charm that works in the mind, fastening, feeding on it. Like a worm in the belly, eh?"

"Yes."

"At first Anyeta was like a woman given a treasure—happy to look at it before she sleeps or when she wakes. Then she needed to see it. She went to it more often, touching the copper box, stroking it, singing to it."

In my mind's eye, I saw the old woman compelled to run her hands over the shiny metal, the brilliant glass, groaning with a mixture of delight and fear; I realized I was seeing it through Joseph's eye as he—and Constantin—had seen it.

"As power grows, so does knowing, and Anyeta was dying when she learned the secret of the hand."

I saw a muscle working in the old man's narrow jaw, felt my pulse quicken. I recalled the day in the old woman's caravan when I'd seen the corpse raised. The words bubbled to my lips. *Who owns the hand of the dead brings healing.*

Who owns the hand of the dead breeds destruction. Who owns the hand of the dead can take a life or restore it."

Joseph nodded, and I felt a tiny click in my head—his mind locking into mine. He went on. "Yes, the dead can be raised to life. And the purpose is prophecy."

I saw now what Constantin had been trying to tell me with his drawing—the body floating, words streaming from its mouth.

Recent graves, I chuckled bitterly; if the body was too far gone, it was useless, and—

I suddenly stared hard at Constantin, remembered the old man's words. He cut out his own tongue.

Joseph's dark eyes glittered. "How much more powerful to raise the corpse of a clairvoyant, eh?" He touched Constantin's hand. "She was trying to kill him."

My stomach turned over, he'd pretended to be mad, mutilated himself to save his life. Zahara's son, weaker perhaps, had been driven to suicide and hanged himself. "Prophecy." I shook my head. "All to see what lies in the future."

"You're forgetting, part of the power lies in taking a life."

"Killing—"

"No *taking* it. As Zahara was taken." Joseph twisted the gold ring on his middle finger, took a deep breath. "Anyeta was afraid Mimi wouldn't come to her in time. She needed a victim. So she tricked Zahara into claiming it."

"If the old woman wanted the power for herself, why would she—"

"Because to die owning the hand of the dead is to suffer eternal torment, unless another life can be found. Zahara realized the old woman duped her. She went into the caravan . . . ."

As the old man talked, I saw it. Zahara claimed the hand of the dead and was suddenly overwhelmed by the knowledge of a terrible secret. I sensed Zahara's frenzied panic: she'd cut her own hand off, healed herself, then had a terrifying vision of what her own death would be like. She felt her coffin swaying as the gypsies carried it to her grave and lowered her down inside, heard the thick clots of earth covering the casket, heard the muffled sound of their footsteps moving away in the sunlight while she lay buried in the cold earth, the flesh falling from her hands, her mouth locked in a silent scream, while her mind churned endlessly in the cramped space where she lay paralyzed, trapped.

Through Joseph, I saw her creeping into Anyeta's wagon, jerking the covers back from the sleeping figure. Zahara raised the knife-blade. "You lied to me," she screamed at Anyeta, "I didn't know what it was!" She plunged the knife into the dying woman's breast and belly, dragging it through the puffy flesh. Anyeta's black eyes jerked open, her hands fluttered around the haft of the twisting bloody blade. The glittering knife rose and fell over and over.

"Die, I want you to *die*, you goddamn bitch! Betrayer! You'll go into the ground a stinking, rotting corpse. Suffer throughout eternity, awake, aware in torment," Zahara shrieked.

I saw blood fly up, spatter her clothes, her face. Zahara's breath came heavily. She threw the dripping knife aside, it clattered on the floor. She stood panting, staring at the ruined corpse. One arm came up, she wiped her mouth, smudging the blood across her lips. Reflex, impulse, habit. Her tongue swiped at her moist salty lips, and in the instant, she staggered back, stunned, felt the change, heard Anyeta's mocking voice inside her head, the shrill trumpeting laugh of triumph.

I can make you do what I want, whenever I want. I own you, girl.

Zahara screamed, her hands flew up to her ears, trying to shut out the voice. She clamped her eyes shut but she couldn't shut out the picture. She could see Anyeta capering, gloating, see the old sorceress as if the two of them stood side by side before a mirror in an empty room.

Who owns the hand of the dead can take a life; I sighed. Zahara had killed the old woman in a fit of vengeance, hadn't known it was the most dangerous thing she could do, and Anyeta's spirit had found its way inside her.

"There was no scar on Zahara's wrist," I pondered aloud. I felt Constantin's hand clamp my arm.

Joseph said, "There was no Zahara, not really. She was weak-willed from the beginning. Anyeta just sucked her up over time, drained her dry, and made herself stronger in the process. My boy, you were sleeping with the old sorceress whore herself."

We'd ordered another round of drinks but they sat untouched before us. I pulled my dark gray coat tighter around me, not knowing if the cold I felt was from the lateness of the hour or the hideous tale.

"She's haunting the cemeteries because she's trying to find out if there's a way to take the life of one who never claimed it," Joseph said in a low voice.

"Can she?" I asked, my mind suddenly seized by the sound of that thick inhuman growl, *Ask of me what you will.*

Joseph shook his head. "No, but her powers are great and she'll try to convince someone to claim it. Someone young, beautiful."

I nodded, realizing it was something of a strain for Anyeta to maintain an illusion constantly. In her sleep, I'd seen the real shape of the body she'd taken— gross, obese. Zahara was nearly an old woman herself.

"I think she's also trying to find out if she can take a life without dying herself," Joseph said. "She had enough of a taste of that torment when Zahara stabbed her."

"Is that possible?" I tried to work it out. How could she escape? I thought of those poor wretches who spoke to themselves on the streets, seemed to change personalities. Some called them mad, others said they were possessed—an icy chill suddenly gripped me, and I shuddered.

"That I do not know," Joseph shrugged. "We can hope." I saw he was thinking now of Mimi. She would face that endless torment unless she found her way into someone else. An air of gloom seemed to descend all at once on the three of us. "I only know that you must go back to Anyeta—"

"She saw me in the tomb—"

He waved away my protest. "And yet, she has a hold on you; Anyeta knows that you can be turned to her own purpose. She will use you to lure another."

"Another woman?"

"Or your wife."

"I don't think I can do it," I whispered, remembering the way she made me want her in the tomb. "She—she preys on my fantasies, she—" I swallowed, seeing the Zahara of my youthful passion undulating beneath me.

Joseph gripped my shoulder. "It's much worse than you imagine," he said. "Anyeta has set the wheels in motion, and Mimi has already claimed it."

In my mind's eye I saw Mimi enraged with jealousy, stabbing Anyeta, the blood flying in a spray over our naked writhing bodies, sheeting Mimi's face in a viscous red mask. I saw her tongue creep between her lips and I screamed—screamed at her to stop . . . too late. I grieved inwardly, made myself push the image aside.

"You have to kill her," Joseph said.

Constantin made a grunting noise, twirled one finger in a wide circle around the top of his head.

"No," I said, suddenly aware, sick at the thought.

"It's the only way. She cannot take another's life if there's nothing—"

"Oh, Christ, don't make me do this!" I thrust my head into the cradle of my arms. "I can't," I whispered. My blood went cold, my mind suddenly numbed to the point of blankness. I felt Joseph's hand at my shoulder, and I sat up. "Oh, Jesus," I cried out, afraid to meet his eye.

They wanted me to gentle her.

29

I was walking through the dark streets, the gentling device Joseph had given me cradled uncomfortably under my coat. My anxiety was growing, my thoughts centered on where I could hide it if she was already inside my caravan, if I saw the lamps lit. In one of the bins lashed underneath the wagon? Somewhere in the tangle of laprobes and leather harness jumbled in the lidded bench on the driver's box? I shook my head. I was really trying not to think of all the things Joseph had told me.

"Her ego is vast," he said when I protested that she'd take one look at my face and read my thoughts as easily as a child scanning a first year primer.

"She has power over you—she showed you the wolves, the attack on Lenore—even at the tomb, you saw her as the Zahara of your youth."

I threw up my hands in exasperation. "I don't want to go back! I don't want to be a slave to her passions!" I felt disgust roil inside me like a nauseating stew. "Why don't *you* do it," I sneered. "You *and* Constantin, read her mind, come at her when she's sleeping or knife her when she's in the bath, the way Charlotte Corday assassinated Marat."

"I cannot." The old man shook his head back and forth, his eyes were dark and brooding.

"I saw you making the device! Vaclav was on the verge of gentling her when I—" I raked my hands through my hair. "When the wolves came," I finished feebly.

Joseph nodded, sympathetically I thought, as if somehow he not only understood but forgave me.

"Vaclav slept with her," he said simply. "I did not."

"Slept with her! What's that to do with it?"

"Every sexual relationship has elements of the struggle for power. My son slept with her under a thousand different guises—like an Arab lord choosing among the women in his harem. Yet there is choice, free will. In the end, he chose to see her as she was."

"What are you saying?" My mind conjured images of Vaclav laying his long youthful body over that old one, kissing the withered breasts, burying himself in the flesh of age. She would smell old, a dry unpleasant scent like yellowed newsprint.

"To see her as she is—that is to break to the spell, the power she wields over you. Perhaps you will come to it yourself, Imre." He toyed with the bright ring on his finger.

"And how do I do that?" I said angrily. "How do I screw that old whore—without her knowing I'm not under her spell? Huh? The first time my hand twitches with revulsion when I put it in her, you better believe she's going to know I'm not dazzled."

Joseph only raised his white eyebrows, gave a weak smile.

In a fury, I shoved back from the table, paced toward the hearth. "Choice! You dare tell me I have a choice!" I advanced on him, my face close to his. "We both know you never chose." I drew back and watched his face darken at the thought of the old memory.

When I was a boy, Joseph was accused of adultery. His wife, a huge terrifying woman, caught him on the edge of a pasture grinding away over one of the troupe's raven-haired beauties. In those days, an adulteress was sometimes beaten and dragged behind a caravan. In Romania I'd seen women whose eyes were a constant well of misery, their faces forever marked, their ears cut off, their nostrils slit. The *kumpania* shaved the head of the young woman who tempted Joseph; still, his wife and her cronies weren't satisfied, and she was further punished by having her teeth smashed and broken. I remember seeing them pry open her mouth with a stick and battering her jaws with an enormous stone. But life isn't fair; in most countries the wayward man wasn't punished at all—except in Hungary, where the Roms were given the choice of being shot in the arm or leg. When the morning of his punishment came, Joseph was standing tall against a spring green hillside, looking brave, while the leader of the troupe stood ten paces away and leveled the gun.

"Arm or leg?" the *prima* said, cocking the trigger.

My eyes started. In the space of a heartbeat, I felt a flickering: Joseph had taught me a lot about horses; I recalled what he'd said over and over: *When you ride, you must be one with the horse.* He would need his legs to guide and work the horses, and he could wind up a cripple, but the arms and hands were important too, for the work with the reins. I held my breath.

"Which?" the leader asked, and then I saw something I never forgot. Before he answered, Joseph's eyes flicked toward his wife's, her eyes narrowed, and very casually she lowered one hand slowly to her thigh. I saw the daunted look in his eye, knew what he'd say before the word came to his mouth.

"The leg," he whispered, lowering his head. The shot rang out, and he fell backwards, blood flowing from the wound to his knee.

In the tavern, his eyes met mine and held me. "We both know why you limp, old man, and who chose that day," I said.

"Yes," he said, "I let my wife choose, and she did it cruelly, waiting until the very last second before she named my punishment. It was a mistake I regretted all my life; and yet, that moment changed me. Since that day I have let no other person choose my destiny." He paused. "My own son Vaclav fell under Anyeta's spell. I did not. My powers are not great, but sometimes it's given to me to see things, know things. Ask yourself this—even if the gain of my power would be a small one, do you think during all those years Anyeta never tried to lure me?"

I saw her gliding through his dreams, arms undulating, hips aswirl, heard the demonic sound of wild violins while she danced the old gypsy rhythms that made men grind their teeth and sweat.

I slumped back in my chair. I knew she had tried to entice Joseph, and that he had resisted.

He'd given me the hideous device and I'd left shortly after that, feeling as low as I ever had. Now, walking along the damp streets, his words echoed in my head. *You can choose, Imre.*

The gentling cap felt harder, more unyielding under my arm and against my chest than it should have, I thought. I stopped and took it out to look at it, my breath whistling harshly out of my throat. Benign, I told myself, like all mechanical contraptions. Nothing but wood and leather and steel. It was nothing—no different from a cider press or a spinning wheel—until the deadly needles were triggered.

And then it came to me, there was a way to catch the old woman off guard. Think of her as Zahara I told myself, and keep the knowledge she's the sorceress whore like a small steel hidden deep inside you. I stashed the ugly cap under my coat and headed for my caravan.

"Zahara, Zahara," I whispered in time to my pounding feet. I crested a short rising hill, and in the distance I saw the shining shape of the caravan gleaming in the moonlight.

Si khohaimo may patshivalo sar o tshatshimo. There are lies more believable than truth. I took a deep breath. She's Zahara until the moment is ripe, I told myself. And then, I would let that hard steel inside me spring up and out as swiftly as a switch knife, and I would make an end of Anyeta.

30

Zahara opened the door, and as I stood on the threshold I was aware of the warmed air from inside the caravan mingling with the frosty chill outside. Behind her one lamp glowed softly near the bedside. She smiled at me and held her hand out. The movement was slow, graceless. The hand I saw was spotted, studded with thick blue veins. I swallowed, briefly narrowing my eyes, looked again and felt relieved. It was all right; the image wavered, and she was young. Just like the trick of seeing patterns in wallpaper; a flower shifts to an open-mouthed face, a leaf on a stem turns into a man leaning on his walking stick, and once seen, you can hold those new images forever.

I followed her inside.

The gentling device was wrapped and hidden in the folds of my greatcoat which I was carrying rolled up under my arm. She paid no attention to it, never even glanced at it and I decided to leave it on a chair, hide it under the mattress later.

She stopped inside the darkened kitchen and turned to face me, put her arms about my neck. I felt the tips of her breasts tingling against my chest. Zahara, Zahara, I breathed inwardly; lies more believable than truth.

"Ever think about having two women?" she whispered, then stepped back and held up her fingers in a vee, turning them back and forth. "What do you think would happen?" she asked, and my mind gave a lurch. Vague fantasies filled my head.

My mouth went dry. Her voice whirred and hummed, "What do you think would happen? Would she kiss my breasts . . . lick me? Would you be jealous like you were of the farmer at the inn? Or would it be like paying me back? Getting even?"

I felt my pulse racing, I licked my lips, then felt her wet mouth on mine. Her hands slid over me, one led mine under the crossed facings of the red robe she wore, guided me between her legs where my fingers touched warmth, wetness, and I felt myself go hard at once. She pulled me toward the bedchamber, a mother leading a child sleepwalking. She's Zahara—

Zahara—her name filled my half-dreaming mind.

"Zahara."

I opened my eyes at the same instant the young woman on the bed called to her again. Her brows were plucked, her mouth and cheeks made up with a startling red, but she was dressed in the quaint peasant clothes of the region. A pale embroidered blouse contrasted with a dark apron. She raised her arms casually and removed a headdress like a long white veil banded with a blue ruffle. She set it on the bed, the train cascaded to the floor. Her waist was narrow enough to emphasize the curves and swells above, below. The girl stared at me with large liquid eyes.

"I found her for you, what do you think?" Zahara said. She licked my ear, whispered, "She's not more than seventeen, eighteen at most."

She was so young she wrung my heart. But it wasn't her youth, not really. Her hair was dark, glossy, her face a tiny oval, dominated by the startling violet-brown eyes. She could have passed for Mimi at the same age.

"Do whatever he wants," Zahara said sternly, and I heard her step out of the room.

I drew her up from the bed, put my hands into her hair, kissed her face, her mouth, the tender skin of her throat. Far off, I heard myself give a small groan: her hair, her flesh, that indefinable scent: she even smelled like Mimi, I thought, not caring if it was one of Zahara's illusions or real. Bewitchment. Mimi, I breathed inwardly, eagerly. If I closed my eyes, it was like holding her again, hearing her again:

Swear to leave when we no longer love, swear to love as long as we live.

My heart's own.

Swear it . . .

I heard the pleading note in her voice and then, as the rest of that old memory rose up in my mind's eye, I saw myself transported back in time, standing on the summer prairie, watching a small herd of half-wild horses cropping lazily in the distance. The sun was glaring, the hot wind carried the dust, and I felt the small granules peppering my sunburned cheeks, filming my dry lips.

It was the 13th of July, the feast of Saint Paul, and I had promised Mimi I would be home in time for the celebration.

Was I going on the cattle drive? she'd asked, when I left the small town near Debrecen the week before. There was a twitch of nervousness in her voice, and my heart gave a start at the question.

No, I told her. I'd always wanted to—some of the drives went all the way to the markets in Hamburg and Paris. And because the *csikos*—the cowboys—were loners themselves, they were more tolerant of itinerant gypsies than most *gaje*. But no, I wasn't planning to spend weeks and weeks in a saddle, living rough among horses, cows, dogs, cattlemen. My intent was to get hold of a few horses to sell to the men who needed mounts for the drive.

And just downwind, I thought, staring into the distance through a pair of binoculars, were three or four likely beasts. They had the look of horses that had perhaps broken through fences, and then wandered, seeking pasturage. Here and there under their dusty hides I saw dark patches that looked like healed over scars from brambles or wire; two roans had marks that appeared to be old brands. I wouldn't sell those two, but the brands told me the herd was probably at least partly domesticated. It wasn't exactly thievery, I told myself; more like selling a gift—everything you made was clear profit.

Mimi had another baby started and we could use the cash. I hunkered down to camouflage the movement, wiped liberally at the sweat stinging the back of my neck. I barely glanced at the filthy handkerchief, just balled it up and shoved it in my pocket. I'd been out in the grassland for a week and this was the first prospect I'd run on—surely she would understand if I missed St. Paul's day. I hoped she would; it was also a big day for the Roms who took up the Christian custom of feasting and celebrated the cult of *Bibi*, an old fierce woman whose name meant Aunt in Romany. She was said to drive men and women to insanity, to cause illness and all kinds of bodily evil. Some of the Bulgarians made ritual sacrifices of sheep and hens to appease her; but for most gypsies it was just a kind of excuse to make a feast of cakes and food—maybe put a gilt icon with a favorite Saint or the Virgin on display. *It was one day, one party*; Mimi would get over it, I told myself.

I began planning how I'd go about roping my quarry. Still squatting, I planted my elbows against my knees and raised up the shabby, leather-clad binoculars: experience had taught me it was best to decide ahead of time which three or four horses I wanted most, which would be easiest to separate from the herd of a dozen or so.

Through the glasses I saw the gray brown dust rising in small puffs around the herd. The ground was uncomfortably hot and dry under my feet, but that was typical of the prairie—centuries ago the Turks had burned what had been forest, and all that was left was the patchy, grassy scrub that would grow out of scorched earth.

The dust hung, tawny as a lion's back, seeming to slant on a broad plane in the vicious light. I felt a hot blast of wind rising sharp and sudden; it coated the glass with grit so fine I couldn't see. I lowered the binoculars, rubbed them with my shirtcuff, glanced down. Alongside my right instep I saw a small pile—like an anthill— of gray brown silt. There was another banked against the sole of my left boot. The wind picked up and I saw the dust slowly swirling, accumulating fraction by fraction. I watched, fascinated; it was an optical illusion so quick it was impossible to tell if my foot was sinking into soft earth or if the dust was rising, creeping higher, burying the black toe of my boot. I began to raise the binoculars, saw my hands and wrists slicked with brownish grit like a fine wash of sepia; saw it clinging to the hairs on my skin, to the skin itself.

Then I heard a low sound—the sound of deep pitched humming mingled with a barely audible hiss, and I thought of the singing sands in the deserts, the sound of the wind moving over the sand, the endless drone that was also a whisper. I looked up to see the sky gone dark.

In the distance, a horse let out a nickering cry, broke into a lope, shaking its thick neck and head. I saw the dust rising from its mane. It began to run. The sky went darker; the swirling winds carrying tons of that alkaline soil becoming a roar. The air was filled with sand, a hot stinging fog. I was gravel-blind. I pulled my jacket over my head, tried to make myself as small as possible. The dust, the wind swept against me, a steady drag that pushed the grit right through my clothes where it stuck against my damp skin like a membrane of ash. I heard the engine-like sound of hooves pounding the earth, the brassy neighing of fear. I knew the horses had fled, trying to outrun the storm.

Mimi was standing on the wooden stoop outside the caravan when I returned on foot the next morning. I was perhaps a quarter of a mile away, standing on a hillock looking down toward the slight hollow. She was stock still, her arms folded at her waist, her head lowered, eyes downcast. I could see the dark green enameled door behind her, the thick carved fruits and leaves mounted like a swag above the entry.

For the space of a minute, it seemed to me I heard the last desultory gasp of the wind, the sound of a storm on the ebb. I saw drifts of sand like dunes half-burying the yellow wheels of the caravan, the door was dull, grimed, the carvings obscured by wind and dust. And when I looked at her it seemed to me she was like some half-eroded statue perched on the flat edge of the desert, her features blurred. The sandy bones of her arms melting against the pitted slab of her brown figure. And everywhere lay the dust. Everything had turned to dust.

Her head came up. She cried out, I saw her arms lift. The hideous image died away, replaced by the sparkling greens of caravan and grass. Mimi ran toward me and then her face was burrowing against my chest, she was crying in my arms.

"When you didn't come back, when you weren't here for the feast I thought—I thought you'd gone. Because here, in Hungary . . ." She wept, unable to finish, but I knew.

In Hungary, there was no ritual, no custom for a final leave-taking. A man who wanted a divorce packed his things—or not— and left. Years later a woman might appeal, and in most cases the marriage was considered legally dissolved by the *kris*, the law court of the Roms. But there would be that endless waiting, the mixture of futility and hope. Was he lost? Gone?

"No," I whispered, "Never." She pressed against me. I kissed the crown of her head. My arm around her waist, I walked her toward the steps and we sat.

"I was caught in a dust storm, lost the horses I was trailing, lost mine. I walked the whole twenty miles—all night."

"Last night? But Wednesday the 13th was three days ago."

"That can't be right," I said at the same time wondering if I'd lost track of time; certainly I hadn't been confused, wandering through the dusty circuit of the plains . . . *Bibi*. Her name jumped in my head. A she-demon who drove men—women—mad. Her feast, held to celebrate—to appease—I thought, and felt my stomach tighten.

"I was sure you weren't coming back." Mimi stood up, hugged her arms against her waist. "Oh Imre." Her brown violet eyes dimmed again with tears.

"The storm—" I began.

"There wasn't any storm," she said. "Every day I went to the village; I even rode to Debrecen. I spoke to the smiths, to the breeders, to the cattlemen riding in off the plains. The drive left yesterday—no one, not one *csiko* spoke of a storm—"

"Dust—"

"Look at your clothes! Did you wash them, wash your leather pack?" She pointed at the kit I'd laid on the stoop alongside us. I glanced down expecting to see that poisonous rime of gray brown adhering to my pack, my coat, my skin. There was grime, I saw my hands were streaky, my gear dirty with a week in the rough, but there was nothing like that cakey powder of clinging dust.

"*Detlene*," she whispered. "The storm you saw was the *detlene*, the dark wind that is the souls of the still born, the aborted, searching for an entry into the world, crying for mother love—"

She's pregnant, I thought, and my eyes widened with alarm. I took hold of her narrow shoulders, felt my fingers squeezing her flesh. "What are you saying? Mimi, what are you saying?"

"I'm trying to tell you," she said. "When you didn't come back, I thought." She stopped. "I didn't want to be a woman on my own with a baby—"

"You didn't." No, I told myself, she wouldn't, couldn't. "You didn't take anything? Do anything?" Maddening images of poisonous tonics, long sharp blades revolved in my brain.

She shook her head. "I prayed to *Bibi*, 'Send him back to me, let him return—'"

"But a prayer, a wish," I began.

"In my country," Mimi said, "we believe She gives—but only with the left hand . . . *Bibi* demands sacrifice—"

"The smaller animals. Hens, dogs, lambs . . . and sometimes—"

"The child," Mimi said, pressing her hand lightly to her flat belly. "The pains started, the blood came. Wednesday, while you were out in the storm."

"A coincidence," I said.

"Was it? A storm that no one else saw?"

"It was coincidence and nothing more." I shook my head at the same time I heard that sound, the sighing moan that was a whisper.

The dark wind. I saw the sun blotted out, felt the brown dust blowing around, through me; covering me like a soft shroud. Mournful, lonely. *Detlene*—the souls of the stillborn. Again I saw the frightening dusty vision; Mimi immobilized, the fused shapes of her face and body half buried by sand and time. We shared a child, had we shared a mystery?

"I thought you left me," she said again. "In my country a man who wants to divorce tells his wife. There are customs, ceremonies. There is a witnessing of their end—no shame comes to either. But here . . ." She swallowed uneasily, shook her head.

"Mimi. I love you—"

She turned her dark eyes up to mine, took my face between her small hands. "*Swear to leave when we no longer love, swear to love as long as we live.*" I felt her lips touch mine. "Swear it," she breathed.

Yes. I held her close, clutching her small frame to my chest. Then I lifted her up and carried her to our bed inside the caravan. She was my wife, I felt her pain, her fear, her sorrowing loss for the child that would never be. I loved her, and I would own that love, that oath in the ritual of our bodies. Gently I lay my wife inside the downy swells of the white coverlet.

"Mimi," I whispered, seeing her, my daughter's mother, whole and perfect. I didn't care if I was playing out the unraveling of one of Zahara's plots, her schemes. I kissed her deeply, lifted her light body onto the bed. And then I was no longer aware that the youthful dark haired woman that Zahara had found, that I held in my arms was not my wife. "My heart's own."

Swear to love as long as we live, she'd murmured.

And I felt my passion rising like the dark wind to overtake me.

31

When I woke I was lying on my side, naked under the heavy quilts. The caravan was dark. The room was cool, but I was aware of a delicious warmth barely a hand's breadth away. I opened my eyes, smiled, was about to reach toward Mimi. I stopped before I made any movement, heard soft whispering. Not Mimi, some young woman. A whore. Then I was aware of the more maddening whisper of a hand slowly moving over skin and lightly brushing the covers. Giggling.

Zahara was in bed, the young woman was between us, facing her. Quiet—except for the sound of hands moving, the young woman's breathing, a light kiss. Still, I sensed whatever was between them was over, had happened while I slept.

Then Zahara's voice, low and soft, broke in. "If you did claim that relic I was telling you about, you could live forever."

"Emm, that's nice," the woman replied absently. "Feels nice." She shifted slightly. "Do the other," she whispered, and I heard Zahara's hand stroking gently, the knuckles grazing the sheet.

"There's such power in it . . . ."

"Power?" Her voice was weak.

"Powers yes, to do anything, be anything, have anything . . . ."

"Rich?"

"Certainly."

"Lovers?" The voice was a sigh. "I'd like to have lots of lovers. Real ones, not the kind who pay. I want a man to love me."

"And you shall."

The young woman sat up suddenly, put her arms around Zahara's shoulders and hugged her. "You're the only person I know who's ever been nice to me."

"Would you like to see it?" Zahara asked, smoothing the girl's brow, then letting one hand linger in the soft tangle of dark curls. "Hmm?"

I guessed she was nodding, Zahara's voice overlapped the motion. "All right, then. Come with me."

Hand in hand they moved softly across the room, then began mounting the stairs to the loft. There was the sound of a match being struck and I knew Zahara was lighting an old horn lantern that hung on a nail. She briefly rummaged among the boxes and barrels. I heard the sound of a lid opening, the copper box being withdrawn, lightly scraping the inside of a wooden barrel. My head began to pound.

I heard the woman gasp. She was running her hands over the glass lid. Zahara showed her how to spring the catch. I suddenly smelled that sweet fragrance—lilies, gardenia, tuberoses, jasmine—

"Beautiful, isn't it?" Zahara asked.

"Yes."

"Yours if you want it. A cut that's nothing, you can heal yourself in the blink of an eye, and then . . . ."

"Riches. Lovers," the girl whispered, her voice taking on a lilt, and I imagined her eyes looking far off, shining with the light of a hundred shimmering visions. "And I'll live forever."

"Yes," Zahara said. "Oh yes, indeed."

"Give me the knife then."

"No." I heard Zahara taking the box, and the girl gave off a faint mewling cry. "He's down there," Zahara said. "He mustn't see."

I knew she meant me and felt my heart speed up.

"Tomorrow," Zahara said, and I heard her replacing the copper box that held the hand in its hiding place. Joseph's words rushed pounding through me. She'll try to lure someone young, beautiful. She found a girl who's vulnerable, who looks like Mimi, and has a body Anyeta could be comfortable with for years. From Anyeta's point of view the girl was better than Mimi—she was only seventeen and was already a whore.

I heard them on the stairs, closed my eyes, breathed deep to mimic the slow paced rhythms of sleep.

"Tomorrow we'll get rid of him. Leave it to me."

The covers slid back, the mattress creaked, they settled in each other's arms.

"Then we'll share our secret."

"Tomorrow," the girl whispered.

And I echoed the thought; tomorrow I would send the girl away on some pretext—say anything, do anything, give her money if I had to—and kill the old woman.

I lay awake in the dark a long time, until I was certain they'd fallen asleep. Then, moving as quietly as I could, I made my way into the kitchen. I unraveled the wad of my cape, took out the gentling cap, and left the cape in a crumpled heap on the chair. I held the device loosely in one hand, felt my way back to the sleeping area.

The blankets trailed over the side of the bed like a skirt, and I got on my knees and stashed the gentling device just under the place my head rested on the pillow. Easy to grab, I thought.

I was getting to my feet, knees creaking and popping when the girl gave a shudder in her sleep and muttered something. I half jumped, ran a shaky hand through my hair. She sat up all at once. Her eyes were wide, staring, the whites of her eyes faintly luminous in the pre-dawn light.

"What. What are you doing?" she slurred dreamily.

"Using the chamberpot," I said, quickly dragging the china basin from under the bed.

She nodded and lay back down.

On the off chance that Zahara heard us, I forced a few drops of warm urine into the pail, replaced it under the bed as far from the gentling cap as I could, then slid under the covers and lay on my back.

"Is it tomorrow?" she whispered sleepily, and I heard her yawn.

"Not yet," I said, thinking it soon would be, while my pulse set up a steady restless thrum, and the image of the wooden bands, the sharpened spikes, circled and knifed through me.

32

"Going into town to work a trade this morning?" Zahara asked.

It was already full daylight. I'd overslept and now her question put me on the alert. Nervously, I climbed the steps into the kitchen area and sat at the table. The young woman was still sleeping soundly, but their conversation roiled in my head: *Leave it to me. I'll get rid of him.* Zahara knew my habits—she was simply taking the most direct line to assure herself I'd be gone most of the day dealing horses while she worked her mischief. Now she acted very casual, poured coffee into a tin mug, set it down in front of me and turned back toward the stove.

"No, it's not a market day, there's no fairs about," I said, trying to sound equally natural, and grinned at her. "I'd rather stay here and toy with you." I reached playfully for her hips, then stood up and caressed her waist from behind. If Zahara fell into a deep post-coital sleep, I thought, gibbering to myself, I could get the girl alone, send her away.

I nuzzled her neck. Her hair felt brittle, and I caught the faint sour smell of old dirt rising from her scalp. My stomach tightened, and as I drew back I saw the line of her shoulders suddenly droop into a thick dowager's hump. My fingers twitched deep inside a fleshy roll of her midriff. I was afraid of retching. Oh Jesus, don't let me see this, I gabbled inwardly, and squinted. Her image quivered, settled into the familiar shape of my fantasy.

She leaned back against me, raised her hand to touch my cheek. "If you stay home, where will you get the money to pay for me?"

"I've paid you plenty," I said, sliding my hands over her belly. "C'mon," I urged with a little squeeze, "give me a toss on credit—"

"No." Zahara shook her head.

She'd said it lightly enough because she was really only trying to get me to leave, but a kind of low grade panic began swelling inside me. I needed to talk to the girl alone, and what the hell was I going to do?

Zahara turned, sucked in her cheeks and gave a little pout. "Mamma says no," she said again, simpering. She pinched my cheek, and all at once I felt frustration roaming through me like a restless tiger. "Business——" she began to say—and I cut her off.

"Fuck *business!*" I gripped her elbows hard, squeezing, then suddenly pushed her aside roughly. She tottered toward the steps, put one scrabbling hand out against the wall to catch herself from falling. Her head swiveled up. She looked at me furiously and her eyes flashed hard and bright.

"I don't need you! I'll fuck the girl," I shouted and felt my own anger rising still higher with my voice. "It's all the same to me.

She's younger anyway," I sneered. I gave her my back and stamped toward the bedroom.

Zahara grunted heavily, and then she was on me in a flash. She jerked my shirt backward. I felt her nails clawing at my skin through the cloth.

I spun around and seized her flailing arms. I used my height and weight to force her backward and half-dragged her toward the door.

"You son of a bitch, let go of me!" She screamed at the same time I hooked one leg around her ankle and pushed. She tripped forward, thumping knees and hands, then striking her chin against the floorboards and crying out.

A line of blood flowed hot and glistening from the corner of her mouth, her eyes had a dazed look. I didn't wait. I got my hands under her shoulders and hips, scooped her up, kicked the door open and didn't put her down until we were on the steps outside.

I raced back up the stairs, saw her struggling to her feet and slammed the door, sliding the bolt home at the same instant she hurled herself against the stout wood and began pounding.

"Open this door," she screamed.

"See how you like it!" I shouted, knowing she would think it was my way of paying her back for what she'd done that night with the farmer. "I'm going to savor every single second with that girl! I'm going to lap her up like cream from a saucer."

I heard her moving off the steps, trampling through the tall dry grass. I stood stock still, listening. She was walking to the right, I thought, heading off, no, she was turning—going to the window! Oh Christ, she was trying to get in through the kitchen window I realized with a sudden bolt of awareness that electrified me. My heart hammered madly in my chest. I galloped into the other room.

Her face floated, round and moonlike up at me. Her bleeding tongue crept between her lips. She was grunting with effort. Her thick arms were high over her head, hands grappling to raise the heavy wooden shutter. I threw the casement upward, the glass rattled and shook in the frame. I leaned out, wrenched and twisted the shutter from her grasp, ripping two of her nails and bruising her fingers. She yelped with the pain and skittered backwards.

"Choke on it, Zahara," I screamed, banging down the shutter, then threading the metal hook and eye and locking it from inside. I ranged through the caravan to fasten the rest.

"You bastard! You're a bastard!"

Her voice sounded farther away. Cautiously, I unlatched one shutter—half afraid her hand would come clawing through the opening—and saw her walking in the direction of a small spring we'd camped near. She was going to wash the blood off her face, I guessed. I would have to be quick, the spring wasn't far at all.

The girl was sitting up in bed, the covers drawn to her shoulders. She was wide eyed with terror.

Christ, I thought, I forgot the window by the bed. All Zahara had to do was knock on the glass and tell the girl to let her in.

"I'm not going to hurt you," I said, advancing across the room and breathing a long whistling sigh of relief—the shutter was closed, locked after all.

"Here, get your clothes on," I said. "You have to get away from here."

"But—"

"Look, there isn't time!" I closed my eyes, drew a deep breath, decided to plunge ahead. "I know what she told you about the hand of the dead." I stared hard at her. "It's all lies."

The girl nodded. "She said you'd say that." Her slim fingers moved sluggishly over a row of tiny buttons at her neck.

"Have it your way. But if Zahara was telling the truth, don't you think I would've claimed it to take all that power?"

"You're afraid. Like the others."

"It doesn't matter if you believe me, will you just go? I'll pay you whatever you want."

She sat on the edge of the bed, in the act of lacing her shoes, hesitated. Then she said, "There was power in that box. I felt it. Zahara, she's very pretty she is. She's the only person who's ever been nice to me."

"Well then use your head, and ask yourself why—"

"I'm like a daughter to her—"

Anyeta. Wanting my wife, settling for a naive substitute. I suddenly groaned. "That," I said, feeling a dark sorrow inside me, "is the only true thing she told you."

The girl turned those huge, liquid eyes on me, scanning my face. "Why are you being nice, then?" Her voice softened.

"Because you remind me of someone I loved."

"Loved?"

"Do love. But I let her down—badly." I paused, thinking, *Christ, just say it you coward.* "I betrayed her."

"With Zahara?"

"Yes. I don't know if I can ever set it right again, but—sending you away, is the beginning of trying to find my way to her." In Hungary, a man who wanted a divorce packed his things—or not— and left. *Swear to love . . . .*

She cocked her head, the great mass of curls tumbled to one side, and again I had the feeling she was trying to size me up. "Loyalty's a good thing," she said, standing up.

"You believe me then?" I put one hand on her arm, lightly.

"I believe you love this woman. What's her name?"

"Mimi." I looked away briefly. "What's yours?"

"Catherine." She drew on a shabby faded shawl, and I saw she was giving in, going. She followed me up the stairs through the kitchen, through the curtained alcove to the front of the caravan.

I opened the door a crack. Zahara was nowhere in sight. "Catherine," I said. "I won't forget you."

"Not me, it's her you've got to keep in mind." She shrugged. "I've knocked around. I've seen a lot of men fall from grace. But a good man—his woman will nearly always take him back."

I took her hand, pressed her small fingers. I tried to shove a stack of gold coins in her palm, but she wouldn't take it from me, waved me off. "Your fortune's free today, gypsy," she said, and her small mouth curved up in a bright smile.

I leaned over and kissed her forehead. "Bless you, then."

She nodded, suddenly looking more mature and worldly than her years. "Remember her."

"Mimi," I said.

"Mimi."

Then she was gone, moving lightly down the stairs. I watched 'til she was out of sight, then sat down to wait for Zahara.

I heard the knob rattle, and it jolted me out of the visionary plans I'd been hatching. I made myself be calm, lit a cigarette, crossed one leg over the other. I'd left the door unlocked and now Zahara opened it.

"Where is she?" Her voice had an edge to it.

"Up in the loft," I replied evenly, and watched Zahara's jaw muscles tighten in reflex. Her eyes scanned the length of the caravan, traveled upwards. "A little fantasy of mine," I said, stubbing out the cigarette and getting up. "A game."

Her lids drooped a little, she stared at me, let me go on.

"You and I are making love," I whispered, and reached one finger up to stroke the curve of her breast. "We're very intent, so intent we don't hear her creeping into the room," I said against her ear, while I rounded her belly with my hands. "You're my whore, my dirty girl." I began drawing her toward the bedroom.

"What's the game?" she whispered.

I chuckled lightly. "She's my wife, and she catches us. After all . . . she looks a *little* like Mimi . . . ."

I felt her start, told myself to keep going, keep her off balance. I kissed her lips.

"And she's very angry," Zahara said.

"No," I chortled, thinking ohchristforgiveme, shoving my repulsion aside and pressing on, "No, in my fantasy, it's a little game I've worked out with Mimi, and you pretend to be frightened at being caught, but she wants you, too." I saw the wheels in her mind turning, told myself to reel the whorebitch in. "The girl says she'll do it."

"Do what?" she purred.

"Whatever you want," I said, easing her so she sat down on the bed. I knelt between her legs, rounded one breast, then pushed her skirt up and buried my face in her thighs. I felt her hands in my hair, my mind began to jitter and skid. How slow should I go? How long could I keep her distracted before she called for Catherine? I had no illusions about forcing the gentling cap onto her head; I'd hidden a long knife alongside the device. It was on the floor just under the dragging blanket. I could feel the rounded tip of the bone handle grazing my knee. Immobilize her, I told myself, one slash across the eyes or throat, anywhere, wherever my hand found flesh, and then while she was down, the cap. But it had to be quick—

"Quick," she murmured and I felt my heart skitter madly in my chest. Dear mother of Christ, she'd picked the thought randomly from my brain as easy as you'd pluck a bad grape from the cluster.

"Want it quick, do you?" I asked, running my tongue over her thigh, trying to divert her, to stop the swift tide of fear that was rising in me. The deep pores of her skin swam into focus. I saw the dry, sagging flesh whitened with countless lines and wrinkles, forced myself to shut my eyes. I nipped and sucked, her skin rolled inside my mouth like a loose wad of sacking, and I felt myself gag. Zahara. Lies more believable than truth. "Suppose it was slow, lingering?" I breathed. "Nearly endless . . ."

"Endless," she said, and I heard a catch in her voice.

Her hands suddenly clenched in my hair, and then before I could stop myself my eyes lifted and met hers.

Panic rushed through me. I saw the hard light of awareness begin to glimmer in those dark ancient eyes. There was a pause that was both infinitesimal and eternal, and I screamed inwardly *Now, now's the time to do it, Christ, do it!* so that at the same time my hand seized the knife under the bed, her eyes flamed with full understanding. "No!" she gasped, flinging one arm high and shuddering backwards trying to heave herself out of the way

but the knife was already a glittering arc risen high and

and Anyeta screamed as I screamed

and drove it with all my might into the center of her chest.

Blood geysered from the wound. Her jaw spasmed and dropped, her eyes went glassy. Her fingers fluttered weakly, opening and closing around the protruding handle, then she collapsed back against the bed, arms and legs splayed, knees bent over the edge.

I stood up, panting, breathing in that sharp coppery scent and watched the blood running in a thick ropy stream from her breasts to her belly. It seemed endless, that red pulsating wet flow.

There was a gurgling sound in her throat. Her eyes bulged wide in their sockets. She strained, trying to lift her head, and I saw the cords standing out on her throat. Her head dropped back heavily against the bed. The blood coming out of her chest bubbled, then slowed to a trickle.

She was dead, I thought, but I knew better than to put my ear close to listen for any faint stirrings inside her. Joseph had said he doubted the old sorceress could possess anyone who hadn't claimed the hand of the dead, and her attempt to trick the young whore made me think that was the case, but I told myself not to take chances.

My hands were slimed with blood and I wiped them carefully against my trousers. I went to the mirror and peered at myself, using my shirtcuff to dab at the red flecks and smudges. Afterwards I'd burn my clothes, the bedsheets—anything that showed a single drop of her blood.

I took a deep breath and told myself the worst was really over. The old bitch was dead, all that remained of the job was to send her to the hell she deserved. And all I had to do was take the cap from under the bed.

33

Don't think about the gentling, just do it I told myself as I peered down at her body sprawled across the blood-spattered bed. She was the Zahara Joseph described to me that long ago day. Her hair was filmed with gray—even her brows and lashes were dull with aging.

Her mouth, hanging open, revealed the dark gaps in her teeth. Her thick body slumped awkwardly in death. Yet I felt no repulsion now, only sadness that her dreams had grown as grotesque as her body and betrayed her into death.

My eye fell on the bloody knife sticking up from between her heavy breasts, and my hand came up to pull it out—then I thought it was better to leave it. I hunkered down and took out the gentling cap, placing it on the edge of the bed.

I knelt over her, smoothing the wiry hair away from her brow with my fingers. Then I picked up the hideous cap. My stomach did a slow roll, my mouth went dry.

Joseph had sewn two wide leather strips at right angles, making I supposed alterations to fit a human head. There was something very ugly about that raw-looking thick brown leather. From far away I heard myself grunt. I saw he'd used a dark heavy wood to shape the bands—walnut or beech perhaps, and smoothed it a little, but it still felt rough and grainy when I ran the pad of one finger along the outer curve. Hideous thing, really—I shoved aside the image of Zahara screaming in terror that night in front of the cave while Vaclav tried to force the cap on her head.

It's the only way.

I held the crude device between my hands and lifted my arms to place it on her head, but I was practically straddling her and the position was very awkward. Her head was nearly in the center of the wide bed.

I paused. It would be better if I turned the body around. I slid backward off the mattress, then bent to shift her, swinging her legs around. I put the pillow under her head and now, lying lengthwise, she looked more natural, like a woman who'd fallen asleep. Much better, I decided. I watched her a while, then told myself to get on with what had to be done.

My breathing went shallow, my hands felt thick, awkward. I tugged the cap into place. The wood bands arched across her forehead. The criss-crossed leather pressed so tight it seemed to change the shape of her skull into something sickly and inhuman. An evil contraption, a filthy thing. Leather, wood, steel. Like a torture device dreamed up during the middle ages. I looked at her, lying so still, eyes wide, and swallowed uneasily.

"Give her some dignity," I muttered out loud, and the sound of my voice startled me. I crossed her legs demurely at the ankles, arranged her hands so one clasped the other at her waist, pushed her mouth up and into place. Her skin was very pale, a grayish blue, but at least when I posed her she had the look of someone who'd been cared for, attended to. I stood back, hugging my elbows, watching a while, thinking of myself as the sole mourner at a funeral. Then I was suddenly conscious that the floor felt cold and hard under my feet. I shook my head, told myself leave off daydreaming. It was best to get on with it.

I'd taken the long metal spikes out of the bands earlier, now they needed to be refitted. I tweezed them from the mattress, one at a time, rolling them lightly in one moist palm. They had a weighty feel, the slightly greasy touch that steel has at times.

My pulse throbbed at my temples, I lined up the holes on the bands, slipped the thin needles into place. Riding lightly, without breaking the skin, they still dented the flesh of her brow. And when they went in—I closed my eyes, gulped, shook the thought off. Christ it was hideous, though.

My hands came up to turn the screws, my fingers trembled, my palms were sweaty. I lowered them, wiping them against my trousers, lifted them again, then leaned over her.

My face was so close to hers, my own breath came back at me, warm and light, and for a second I stopped and jerked away thinking, she's alive, good Christ, she's alive.

I took a long step back, stared at her. You could almost make yourself believe her chest was rising and falling, however slowly. It was barely detectable but I watched the tip of the bone white handle slide up and down by fractions. My eyes went blurry. I blinked, cleared my vision. Anything, I told myself will seem to move if you stare hard and long enough, because your own eyes—

Her eyes. The thought clamored in my head. Her eyes were open. It was making the job harder to do. It's as if she's glaring at you, reproaching you. It would only be the work of a second to close them and then I could do what needed to be done, stop this crazy fooling around.

My knuckles grazed the ashy cheeks, I brought my thumbs up to push the lids down and found myself gazing into the black irises.

There was mystery in the those dark, subterranean depths—a moonlit lake that descended forever.

All at once my breath came hard, I was suddenly crushed by the memory of kissing her wide red lips in springtime. I smelled the warm living flesh of her breasts, musk mingling with the scent of newly washed clothes and perfumed hair. She was twenty-one, an older woman to a callow youth of seventeen; she had plaited a scattering of tiny golden coins the size of teardrops here and there in her hair. I heard the gold pieces chiming softly when she shook her head, heard the high sweet chirping of nightbirds, saw the moon—white and round and full—over her shoulder where she leaned against the rough black bark of an old knotty elm. I felt her tongue meeting mine, her hands were warm and soft on my back.

"*Tikno*," she whispered against my mouth. "Little boy." She touched my face; I wanted to tell her I was no boy, that I loved her. The words stayed locked in my throat, burned inside my head. I reached one hand up; I thought I would stroke her hair, touch one shimmering coin. Instead my hand fell clumsily on her breast, and from far off I heard a groan issue from deep inside me.

"*Te na khutshos perdal tscho ushalin*," she teased. "Don't try to jump your own shadow. It's not love, little boy; it's only lust."

Then she was running, laughing lightly, the gold in her hair ringing sweetly, the hair itself a glossy tangle against the moving blur of her cape, and my heart was beating hard and fast and I knew that for me, she would be that Zahara forever.

One kiss, I thought, just one before I—I—to say goodbye. Here and there her pale face was flecked with blood, but her lips were tinged with it, making them redder still. Surely even Joseph wouldn't begrudge a kiss given to an old love. I peered into her eyes, the light seemed to flicker and dance there briefly, as if she were waiting for my kiss. I closed my lids, leaned toward her. Delicately, I put my hand behind the nape of her neck, inclining her face up to mine, thinking, just one, quick and light, one single kiss. My lips lightly poised to touch hers, I drew her closer. Something like a sigh wheezed out of her throat; air passing from the lungs through the vocal chords, I told myself, at the same time it seemed to me the sound of the voice was the low and distant song of ship bells on the sea. Haunting. Romantic.

"Ah," I breathed, verging on the kiss, my warm hands pressing her head forward to make her mouth meet mine, then suddenly and completely registering the feel of that chill flesh—

I was consumed, shuddering with horror: The muscles of her neck were beginning to stiffen. Under my fingers, her jaw was rigid, stony. I winced away, shaking. Her head fell woodenly against the pillow, a long moan escaped the mottled lips, the voice an anguished whine, but Christ, how long had I been just standing there in the shuttered gloom of the caravan, staring?

Hours and hours. I raked my hand through my hair, thinking it couldn't be. But it was. I popped a shutter; the winter sun was low in the sky, the light illuminating the bed, feeble.

Gentling. It's the only way. Joseph's brooding face wavered before me.

I shoved my hands into my pockets, seeing the corpse of a blowsy, overweight woman, and exhaled sharply. I understood that behind the obsidian eyes Anyeta seethed, churning with impatience to be released, that she was playing with me, tormenting me. That even now she might be capering with greedy delight: But I couldn't do it. It didn't matter if she—if both of them—had bewitched me all these months. I couldn't do it to Zahara. I couldn't savage the memory of the shining girl that danced in my heart. No. I could not bring myself to gentle any living thing, any human.

I shook my head, took two long steps, wrenched the hideous cap from her head and flung it away. It tapped and clattered maddeningly against the floor, came to a stop, and the atmosphere in the room was suddenly filled with a silence that seemed blessed.

After a long time, my hand went up and out, smoothing Zahara's hair gently. "Poor thing," I whispered, stroking, and then her head suddenly turned under my fingers. Her cheek buried itself against the pillow, I heard the feeble creaking sound of her jaw dropping wide, and I hissed, jumping back. One eye glared up at me, the light giving it a wicked glint that matched the smirking grin—

Anyeta.

"Leave me alone!" I shouted, my voice echoing harshly in the stillness of the room.

I shivered, began to pace, jabbering to myself. "No. She didn't move, no, you were patting her head, you did it yourself!" My eye snagged on her leering face, a mocking death's-head. Anyeta.

I turned away, sinking heavily to the floor, then I lowered my head and wept.

34

I pounded my clenched my fist hard against my knee. There had to be another way, I told myself. And there was still a job to be done, even if I couldn't— couldn't dishonor Zahara. I grimaced, catching sight of the vile cap. Joseph didn't know everything. I just had to think of some other way. Something cataclysmic. Final. My brain teemed. My teeth were chattering, I felt feverish— my thoughts broke off, I felt myself break out in a wide grin—the idea took hold and bloomed in my head: Fire. Yes, fire would consume her so there was nothing left. All right then, I nodded, I'd wait till full dark and then take her body from the caravan. Burn it. Just as I'd planned: Blood splotched sheets, bedding and all, I'd *yag* it, and that would make an end of Anyeta.

I hoisted myself onto my feet, began to make my way up the ladder of stairs to the loft. The rags, the kerosene, scrap wood— everything I needed would be there.

I tossed the shovel aside with a heavy grunt, looking down at the shallow oval pit I'd dug twenty yards from the caravan. My eye measured the corpse shrouded in the blood soaked bedding. The grave was five or six feet long, it sloped unevenly down four, maybe five feet deep at the bottom; big enough.

I began tossing scraps of lumber, and they landed with the sharp clattering sounds of wood striking wood. I arranged the boards in the rough shape of a pyre. Still stooping, I paused, smudged the back of my hand against my forehead, then I reached behind and grabbed the round red can that held kerosene. There was a rag stuffed in the spout, and the instant I pulled it out my eyes began to water from the acrid fumes, and I coughed. Breathing through my mouth, I began dousing the wooden boards, watching them darken where the liquid soaked in.

I got to my feet, turned toward the body, considering. It had been something of a struggle to maneuver her dead weight, and I'd gotten her to the edge of the grave by shifting her into a small wheeled cart that Lenore sometimes called her pony trap. Now that the spurt of emotion that carried me through the job was gone, I thought it would be harder to lift her out of the boxy cart to place her inside the grave. Easier to burn her, cart and all, I decided, looking briefly up at the dark sky, hearing the wind rustling the leaves of the trees.

I bent over, locking my knees, grunting and lifting the handles of the wagon. Her head and neck were jammed against the backboard, her knees and feet flopped over the low edge on either side of the handles. I could feel the cold flesh of her calves bumping against the backs of my hands and it made me uneasy. I swallowed, and began pushing. The cart swayed under her weight, and I steered it toward the pit. It stuck in the soft dirt on the lip. I strained, getting my legs and back into it, heaved it up and over the edge. It jolted down the slight incline. The wheels struck one of the boards, and under the heavy awkward weight, the cart tipped on its side, spilling Zahara's body out of the loose shroud and across one edge of the pit.

In the moonlight, I saw her face resting against the naked boards. Her body was jack-knifed under one edge of the cart. Don't look at her, I told myself. I hunkered down and began wadding the rest of the bedding and the clothes I'd worn in and around the wooden boards. I splashed more kerosene, feeling slightly queasy when it spattered her arms, legs, her face. I could imagine the flames, the roaring sound they would make consuming her. There would be the smell of roasting flesh. If I stayed to watch, I knew my gaze would be drawn helplessly to the sight of her blackened flesh shriveling back to show the teeth, the grizzled scalp and filmed-over eyes. I shook my head, knowing deep inside myself I'd never strike the match while I could still see her face.

I sighed. There was nothing to do but to crawl down inside the grave and cover her. First the shroud, then pile more wood and don't think about the red-hot center, about her body feeding the lunatic flames.

At the bottom was the cold dank smell of earth, the sharp reek of kerosene. I told myself to step slowly, carefully among the boards as I moved toward her.

I jerked one corner of the spread, wincing at the stiff feel of the cloth where the pooled blood had dried. Her body shifted and there was a tinkling sound— the soft ping of metal on wood, and I stopped, puzzled. Then it came to me: it was the silver pendant around her neck, the one I'd bought my wife that long ago day in Sighisoara, that she told me Mimi had given her on our wedding day, and I suddenly wanted it. Take it, a voice inside me urged, and grimacing, I felt among her clothes until my fingers closed on it. I jerked the chain, snapping it, and shoved it deep in my pocket.

I looked down; she was lying on her side. The moon picked out the gleaming edge of the knife handle, her arms and hands flung in a grotesque sprawl. For the last time I saw her face, one eye gazing darkly, her mouth open, the jaw slightly askew. I covered her with the sheet, yanked the boards over her corpse and scrambled out of the grave.

I stood on the edge, felt the wind lifting my hair. I lit a cigarette, took a long drag, savoring the harsh smoke and peered down. Nothing of her to be seen, and nothing would be left.

"Goodbye," I said. *"Akana mukav tut le Devlesa o Beng*—I leave you to God—or the devil." I tossed the flaming match into the pit.

There was a pale blue light, very nearly like a droplet of oil striking water, a sudden brief yellowish flare that expanded then seemed to contract just before it exploded into rushing lines of fire that raced along the boards.

I sat on the ground twenty feet away, feeling the warm draft, watching the lurid flames flicker and spurt against the sky. It would take a long time—maybe the rest of the night—for the body to burn completely, and I'd stacked wood and brush nearby to feed the fire at the first sign it was dimming. I would wait, there was no hurry now. I wrapped a blanket shawl-fashion over my shoulders, snugged the end underneath my hips and legs.

Then I took Mimi's pendant out and looked at it, a silver moon gone red in the firelight.

I dreamed of myself as a boy in England where my parents traveled one summer in our yellow caravan. It was England where they'd met years before I was born. My mother came from a district in the north, near York I think it was. She was a cottage girl—all I really knew of her youth was that she'd slipped from that life into my father's. The intrigue and mystique of gypsy ways held her in its thrall, I suppose, but that summer she showed me England, and one of my most vivid memories was of a field glowing at sunset while hundreds of brown rabbits hopped madly around us, scampering into the hedgerows, and it was this old dear memory that found its way into my dream, then shifted.

Time collapsed on itself, so that I was suddenly aware I was no longer a boy but a young man, standing amid the summer washed green clover and sweet grass. I watched the gamboling rabbits in sheer delight, saw the buttery flash of paler fur from underbellies and tails, a wide smile on my face, my hands held high and wide as I pirouetted with joy.

In the way of dreams I heard the low slinking jingle of a tambourine, and then, far off at the edge of the red horizon I saw Mimi. Arms outstretched she ran toward me. I saw the long colored ribbons streaming like banners, trailing from the tambourine she carried. Her face was lit with a wide smile, she'd threaded wild flowers in her dark braided hair, and I saw the gleam of lavender, blues, whites, pinks, sometimes falling away, as she raced toward me, barefoot, laughing.

I ran too, and we met in the center of the field and rocked into one another's arms.

"Dance with me, Imre. Dance with me," she said, laughing up at me, and I felt her hands on my hips, while she stepped sideways, twirled, her long full skirt floating gauzily, a summer kaleidoscope of pale rose, yellow, cool green. A thin gold bracelet shimmered at one slim ankle.

And then my arms were around her, tighter than before, she was so warm against me, flushed with running and joy, and she pressed her lips to mine, and I heard her moan, softly, and the red sky was alive around us and then there was the light sweet tinkle of the tambourine slipping from her hands, like the chime of bells on a gentle breeze—

—and I felt sad and cheated when I saw the gentle English meadow change for the barren Romanian steeps, the brilliant sky was only the glow of the old sorceress' funeral pyre; but I was surprised that my dreaming mind still held on stubbornly to the jingling sound of bells. Now I heard the soft scattering of hooves, of wooden wheels moving over hard ground and seconds later a dark caravan came into view, stopped in the shadows.

A figure jumped down lightly, skirts swirling around slim booted legs and turned toward me. Her eyes were shining. I held my breath and yet the name came to my lips, "Catherine," I began to say, hearing a kind of hushed wonder in my voice and feeling my eyes widening, my pulse begin to hum at the same time I got to my feet and began running, because I suddenly realized in the very depths of my heart what I'd known all along: It was Mimi, standing there, in the full flood of her youthful beauty—arms outstretched to catch me—

—Mimi lowered her arms slowly to her sides and I felt a pang of disappointment, then slipped out of that half-dreaming state, found myself still sitting on the ground, now fully awake. I looked up. The night sky had gone cloudy, the moon was no more than a misty light. In the ruddy glare of the fire I saw Mimi's face was grim, her lips pressed in a tight line, her shoulders drooped with weariness.

I moved toward her, aware that the smile on my face felt unreal, the way it always does when you grin from nervousness. I never glanced back at the fire, told myself what she doesn't know can't hurt her. I nodded hello, and the sad dark eyes that looked into mine were tentative, but I took my wife in my arms.

"The place stinks of her," Mimi said when I opened the door to our caravan, and I felt a wave of guilt and sorrow contracting my stomach. "Christ," she brought her hands over her nose and mouth, "it smells like home—not our home—but the hellhole I lived in with her when I was a child."

She sat heavily at the table, and I watched her draw a finger through the dusty surface, gaze blankly around the disheveled room. For the first time in all these months I was aware how unkempt, how dirty it was. Cast off clothes and graying smeared towels were bundled here and there—even in the kitchen. Pots and pans and greasy dishes lay in crooked slanting stacks on the counter, caked silverware poking out between the rims. The stove was splattered with bits of dried food. There was a long ragged tear in the green curtain that separated Lenore's sleeping compartment—I winced thinking of how it had gotten torn when I pawed one night at Zahara.

"Funny, isn't it? She brought her smell with her and it stayed," Mimi said, lowering her eyes. "I didn't notice it when I was here before. Or maybe I made myself not notice it."

She'd already told me what part of me had known all along; Joseph had sent her as Catherine, not so much to lure Anyeta— although the old woman's greedy desperation led her to believe she'd found a willing victim—as to use her own power to help me. I hadn't thought about it, but now I realized she'd kept Anyeta from blasting me to shreds, using a sort of steady but inexorable counterforce, and keeping the old sorceress off balance so there was no time for her to think, react.

"You can train yourself not to see certain things, I guess," she said a little sadly, and I saw her glancing at me. "Oh well, might as well get to it." I knew she meant to clean and scrub before she would let Lenore back in, before she thought of it as our home again. She took off her gloves, then pushed back from the table and started to get up, and I put my hand out, inadvertently catching hold of her scarred wrist. We both stared at it briefly, and our eyes met.

"Mimi," I said, letting go of her hand. "I—"

"What's done is done, Imre." Her voice had a wooden, hollow sound that frightened me.

"Mimi," I stood up, then buried my face against her, "Oh Christ, oh Christ, can you ever forgive me?" I cried, felt tears that wanted to come burning hot and hard in my eyes and throat. "Maybe not yet, but someday? Just tell me if it's in you to forgive me someday?" I hung my head, afraid to meet her eye.

"Imre, look at me."

I lifted my head, her hands hung limply at her side. "Do you see this?" She suddenly pushed her sleeve back and gripped her forearm tightly with her fingers. The thick ugly scar circling her wrist went a deeper purplish red. "This is your answer."

"What do you mean?"

"My death will be one endless torment, an eternity of suffering, trapped inside a rotting body, a dark, stinking grave. That is my future—the only future I have. Do you think I'd let the days of my life—what days I have—be a second river of agony?"

I shook my head.

"Then you know you're forgiven," she said, moving away, and tying the strings of a dirty white apron over her dress.

"But your voice . . . it's so hard—"

"I have said I forgive you, and I will clean up this mess and pick up what I can of the life we had—"

"She bewitched me, it was an illusion," I said. "Mimi please, it wasn't real—"

"And I will go on—mostly for Lenore's sake, and—"

"The first time—even the first time—I pretended it was you, please oh Christ, I'm sorry, so sorry, she tricked me; and even with you—when I thought you were Catherine, oh dear God it all came back to me and it was you I wanted, you I was making love to, even the scent. I saw it in your eyes; you know I was reliving that first summer we went to Hungary! We're sworn to love as long as we live—you know that part of me sensed it was you, please—"

"And what about the part that shook with heat and writhed in passion and dabbled inside that cunt of a whore that was my mother?" Her breath came out hard, her eyes glinted with pain.

"You wanted her!" she screamed, suddenly weeping into her hands, and I tried to take her in my arms, but she shook me off and sobbed. "Dear Jesus, you wanted her more than you wanted any woman your whole life."

"No, Mimi, it wasn't real, not even the desire was real. It was—" I spread my hands in a helpless gesture, "it was only an old memory she twisted and brought to life inside me." I put my hand on hers. "I thought you loved her. Zahara told me she loved you—"

"Loved me? *Loved me!*"

"She showed me the silver pendant, said you gave it to her the day of our wedding—" My hand burrowed deep inside my pocket.

"She stole it from me! The way she took you . . . . It was *armaya*, a curse, don't you understand? 'Love what you hate, love she who makes you angry, she who makes you cry.'" Mimi shook her head. "But it isn't love, it's the power to deceive; she pretended to care to trick me, to trap you—"

"I have the necklace," I said, pulling the moonshape from my pocket. "I have you, we're together now—"

She struck it from my hand. It clattered noisily onto the floor, the glittering silver rattling and tapping; emphasizing the silence, the space between us.

Mimi stepped back. "I keep seeing you with her." She closed her eyes, brought her hands shakily up to her brow. "Seeing you like some half-crazed creature slavering over that grotesque flesh—her mouth—yours, I—keep seeing it, remembering it."

I pulled her hands from her face, held them tightly between both of mine. "Don't! Mimi don't—we both have to learn to forget—" I stopped, shivered, suddenly aware of the oppressive atmosphere, of the smell in the caravan, a miasma of rank sex, grime, spilled blood, thinking for her it must be a thousand times worse.

"It's like she's still here, and I'll never be rid of her, never." Mimi groaned, swayed a little, sagged weakly against me, and I caught her in my arms, and then I lifted her and carried her to the one clean place in the caravan, the one place I never sullied with Zahara—the small ship's berth of a bed that was Lenore's.

I laid her down gently and we cried in each other's arms, and then, oh thank God, and then, the healing began between us.

35

I couldn't undo or change what had happened between Zahara and me, but I could make Mimi know that she mattered, that I loved her. Regrets and apologies can only carry a man so far, after that it's the loving that lets his wife know what he feels. And so, we began to make love tenderly, sweetly—like the very first time—although our bodies had known one another long and well.

Mimi leaned against my shoulder. I stroked her hair for a long time, until gradually I felt she was freeing herself from the spell of tension, and we kissed, gingerly at first. My hand moved over the soft skin of her cheek, her throat, then slid to the row of buttons. I began undoing them slowly, wondering when the last time was that I undressed her, that she might savor that small but electric thrill.

She sat facing me, her blouse unbuttoned to her waist, and I let my hands linger at her breasts while we kissed, until I heard her breathing begin to quicken. I opened my shirt, felt her hands moving softly beneath the mat of hair.

I caressed her thighs, her small buttocks, felt her skin growing warmer through the rustling fabric of her skirt.

"You're taking such a time," she whispered.

"Impatient?"

She shook her head. "No. It makes me feel more desirable—as if I were a *tschai*, a girl, and you wanted me to be ready but weren't sure how far I would go." She laughed lightly.

"We have all night," I said, and then I moved my hand slowly and deliberately between her legs, listening to the silky whisper of the fabric under my fingers, savoring each separate and discrete sensation.

"I love you, Mimi."

I knew it would be a long time before I allowed myself the pleasure of touching the moist flesh there, longer still before I tasted it with my tongue. I closed my eyes, kissed her, thinking toward dawn we would both be naked. I would feel all of her against me, smooth and warm and deliciously damp. Our bodies would meet, drift on that delightful tide before they finally parted.

I don't think either of us was aware of the sound of sleet gently pattering off the roof. It was harmony for our unhurried romance, the anticipation we savored; we were both looking ahead to dawn.

My hands found the bow shape of the ribbon drawstring and delicately plucked it, then drew her underpants down to her knees, but not off, not yet. Under the skirt, I caressed the skin of her belly, felt the small bones of her hips. I rounded the tender flesh of her inner thighs, let one finger move leisurely against the slick center. Inserted the tip.

"Rockets and stars," she murmured. "And after all these years."

It was our best time, but I, we, didn't know it was nearly the last time we'd ever make love. Perhaps that was just as well.

I came awake smiling, my hands instinctively seeking Mimi. I wanted to kiss the sleep from her eyes, feel her touch, her warmth. I rolled toward her but there was only the shape of her body imprinting the feather mattress, the sensation of fading heat. I heard her stirring somewhere in the caravan, the sound of a few notes hummed softly. I grinned. Mimi was a light sleeper, I would have bet my hat on the fact that she'd gotten up and decided to quietly begin straightening up the wreck inside the kitchen. But that wasn't fair, not a bit, I thought, swinging my legs over the edge of Lenore's pocket-bed. We'd begun healing what was between us, I didn't want her wounded again by what she'd find, what she'd see. They're your dirty sheets, you clean 'em, I told myself. I raked my hand through my hair, yawned, pulled on a pair of trousers, brushed the torn curtain aside, pattered out.

She was in the bedroom. I felt a ripple of guilt, began moving toward her. Her dressing gown was tied at her waist, she was bent over, back to me, probably picking up one of Zahara's tattered

corsets, I grieved inwardly.

"Hey let me do that," I said, pausing on the top of the stairs.

She straightened up, turned, and now I saw what she held in her hands. The gentling cap.

"You didn't do it," she said softly.

My eye was drawn to the circle of wood, the dangling leather straps. I swallowed uneasily. "I couldn't." I looked away, saw the light glinting off the metal spikes that still lay on the wooden floor.

"When I saw the fire I thought you burned her afterwards, after you gentled her—"

I felt my jaw tighten, didn't answer.

Mimi's gaze was drawn to the window, to the smoky glow of the burning grave beyond it. She took a step nearer, and I looked through the glass too. I could make out the black triangle shape of the smoldering pile of boards; they were thinner, whittled down by the flames.

I took hold of her arm and gave her a small shake. "What are you thinking? There's nothing there, now—"

"You should have done it—the sleet," she began. "The fire's nearly out."

"She's gone! The flames were twenty feet high—"

Mimi shook her head, looked down at the cap.

I grabbed it from her, flung it aside. "It's useless, I tell you there's nothing there—"

"I have to be sure," she whispered, and then before I could stop her, she turned and ran from the caravan, slippers clacking over the boards.

I grabbed a shirt, yanked on a pair of boots and raced after her. She was already at the grave when I reached her. The smell, even in the frosty morning air was sickening, and I fumbled in my pocket, found a handkerchief and held it to my mouth and nose. The center gave off a reddish glare, there were small crackling sounds, once a large pop! as a knothole exploded. The sleet had stopped but the pyre was a half-burned soggy ruin. I saw the wet brush and wood I'd heaped alongside to keep the blaze going, felt a wave of guilt.

"She's there; can't you feel it?" Mimi said, squatting at the edge, one hand bracing herself to keep from tumbling in, the other wielding a long stick. She poked it through the rubble. Mist and smoke mingled, rising in a noxious cloud. Several of the charred boards gave way. I heard her gasp, looked in, felt my gorge rising up my throat.

The fire-scarred body, on its side, was still intact. The clothes had mostly burned away, but here and there dark shreds and tatters clung to the black flesh, making the whole sight worse and reminding me that I'd set fire to a human being. I saw the skin was gone from her feet and hands; the thin black bones curled in on themselves, like the claws of a hideous bird. One skeletal foot had separated and lay at a small distance, I guessed it had fallen away when Mimi stirred the debris.

The head was nothing more than the bloated shape of the skull; one ear was gone, the other a vague lumpish nub of seared flesh. It was like unearthing some ancient petrified mummy. The dark withered skin rippled unevenly over the bones, the face seemed more prominent under the denuded scalp. And it was her face that held me. The eyelids had been burnt away, exposing two viscous looking sockets, a runny smear on one cheek that might have been an eye. The nose was only a thin pinched-looking rill above an open mouth drawn back in the agony of a silent scream.

I staggered backward, my stomach contracted in one long painful spasm. I bent over, clutched my belly and vomited. The smell rising on the steamy air made me sicker, helpless. I fell on my hands and knees, weakly; my jaw convulsed, I opened my lips in a wide rictus—like her, I thought, seeing the image of the burned gaping mouth—and then wave after nauseating wave rushed through me.

After a while I was conscious of a series of movements; out of the corner of my eye I saw Mimi lift the can of kerosene, heard the liquid sloshing inside. She was going to finish the job for me, I thought, feeling bad about it, simultaneously trying to wipe my mouth and get up on my feet.

Mimi stood on the edge of the pit holding the red can; one hand firmly clasped the handle, the other clutched the bottom. I saw her arms go back, then plunge forward in a swinging gesture. I started to call to her that it was dangerous, at the same instant a long thin stream of liquid snaked out of the spout, hung briefly in the air, splashed downward into the pit—

There was a flash, the air went thick.

"No!" I shouted, trying to throw my arm over my face. I saw the kerosene can leaving her hands, but slowly, too slowly. It spun a hand's breadth away from her, she was trying to back up—

Fire arced back along the trail. The can exploded with a huge noise. The air was heavy, hot, filled with roiling black smoke, and her clothes were suddenly alight with the fury of a torch. She was lifted screaming into the air and then thrown backward onto the ground.

I ran toward her, shouting her name at the same instant the smoke seemed to rise above the pyre in a bubbling mass shaped like a ball. It hovered for the space of a heartbeat, then burst into a scattering of shiny black droplets. I saw what looked like the tattooed outline of a woman's form against the gray sky. Then it darted and raced along the line of the firetrail, consuming it, homing in on my wife's flailing arms and legs, her panicked shrieks, and arrowed straight down her throat.

A tower of flames suddenly shot up from the center of the pit in a terrifying blast of heat, a wild concussion. I fell to the ground, deafened by the roar. A hot wind buffeted me and flame-studded debris rained down, sizzling against the wet turf.

Through the smoke and a glaze of heat-blurred air, I saw Mimi running away in a crazy looping flight, trailing fire, her face a mask of terror. I raced after her, screaming her name over and over. The cords on my neck strained with the effort of shouting, I felt a hot stinging sensation at the back of my throat. I knew my mouth was open, and my tongue moved, yet I was aware I couldn't hear the sound my own voice.

I closed in on her, dived headlong to wrestle her to the ground. She collapsed under me, writhing. My heart drummed with panic. I rolled her back and forth, back and forth trying to smother the flames. Her mouth was open, she was screaming, moaning, weeping all at once. Under the layer of soot her face was red, blistered with whitish patches, her hair was a clotty, frizzled mop, half of it gone. Her legs were badly burned from the tattered robe, now smeared with damp earth. But I saw that her hands and arms had taken the worst of it and I felt something turn over inside me. One was a wet-looking runny mass, and oh sweet Christ, I wept—her nails were no more than brown crusted patches, her fingers fused into a molten clump.

She was still thrashing, her feet tapping and bouncing against the icy turf. "Still," I whispered, wanting to touch her, to soothe her, and not knowing if somehow I'd hurt her more. "Shhh, try and lie still." I gripped one shoulder lightly, trying to blink away my tears. There had been no time in my life I'd felt so utterly helpless. I didn't know what to do. I was afraid to move her, afraid the motion would kill her. I was afraid she was dying and if I didn't do something quickly I'd lose her.

"Mimi, Mimi," I said, my voice a shadowy rasp I could hardly make out amid the ringing clamor in my ears. "Please help me. Tell me what to do."

She wasn't responding. I anguished inwardly, saw the hellish flames still raging in the grave, and cursed myself. My failure brought this to her, I thought. Oh Christ, dear Christ, you can't punish her, not for my weakness. "Please," I said again.

I heard the sound of air being drawn in a tortuous wheeze through her chest. I knew what that meant and I closed my eyes, felt a hot pain daggering my heart: Her lungs were burned. Oh Christ, she's not going to make it, she's dying.

"I love you," I said, my voice cracking. "Don't leave me." I carefully squeezed her shoulder and I felt her stir; then her dark, pain-wracked eyes lifted slowly to meet mine.

Her chest heaved, again I heard the low sound of that gritty sigh, and it filled me with such hideous sorrow, so much aching, I wished my throbbing eardrums had shattered, that I might not hear what she was suffering.

Her eyes stayed on mine, she was trying to speak. Her jaw was clenched, her teeth tightly pressed together. Her mouth moved stiffly, opened a fraction. "In . . . ne," she breathed.

I looked at her, thinking she was trying to say my name, but no, that wasn't it. Her eyes flashed at me as if she was confirming my thought.

"In ne," she repeated, at the same time she made a feeble motion, a slight downward tilt of her head toward her chest. She tried to lift one arm, couldn't manage it.

I tapped my own chest. "You, yourself." She closed her eyes, gave a barely discernible nod. She was trying, I hoped, to tell me what could be done, what I might do to save her. "Yes, yes," I said, putting my ear close to her lips. A hot pulsating glow radiated from her, and it made me dizzy: No one could be burned this badly and live. I shoved the thought aside. "Tell me."

I closed my eyes, concentrated, and this time I caught the words in the clogged rale that was more growl than voice: "In me."

I sat back, puzzled. There was something that told me she wasn't talking about the fire that seared her inwardly. I felt my eyelid twitch. "In you," I repeated, and again she gave me a faint nod.

"What are you saying?" I felt low hysteria spiraling through me, growing. "Mimi, what are you saying?"

"An-*yeta*," she whined, her eyes moved sluggishly to indicate her chest.

Panic seized me. "No, NO! It's impossible!" I shot to my feet, saw the smoke fragmenting into those glassy black dots—hard and shining like thousands of tiny obsidian eyes. They spun and whirled, coalesced into the shape of a woman. I shuddered, remembering: They'd swarmed over Mimi's face like a cloud of angry bees, then rushed down her throat.

"It can't be," I said, but the words sounded like a lie falling from my lips, and I felt the truth, like a nasty snickering inside me. Joseph had been right all along: *Gentling was the only way.* I saw Zahara licking blood from her lips. My mind reeled. The old woman had done it a second time; her spirit found its way inside my wife.

I looked at her lying on the ground and a mix of anger and grief trembled inside me. I clenched my fists, felt myself losing control. It flashed through me to lash out, pound her, as if somehow I could shake her loose, pry her out of my wife's ravaged body. "Anyeta." I spat the name.

Mimi suddenly exhaled and went limp, her head settling toward the cradle of her shoulders. Her eyes fluttered closed with the swiftness of a shade being drawn down.

A tremor coursed along the length of her body.

The eyes flew open, and I saw a malicious glint sparkling in the dark irises. "NO!"

I saw her lips begin to move, muttering the words of the spell. I stood mesmerized at the transformation. Like a snake rising from the fakir's basket, it began at the feet; the burned flesh fell away, disappeared with a quick sibilant sound and was instantly replaced by skin that was whole and healed.

Lying on her back, she wriggled and twisted against the ground, and at each undulation another part of her emerged unscathed, until at last the words poured from between the delicate lips, and the voice I heard was strong, powerful.

"Who owns the hand of the dead can bring healing."

I watched, stunned, my eyes bulging. Anyeta got to her feet. The blasted robe clung to Mimi's figure, revealing glimpses of smooth flesh. Her small hands danced up and down her body—not to cover her nakedness but to glory in it.

Anyeta looked at me, and without thinking I stepped toward her, holding my hands out to touch her. She chortled, and I recoiled as if I were stung, thrust my hands behind me in confusion.

"Mimi," I said.

"She's here inside me." Anyeta grinned, tapping her chest. "What do you want, her body or her soul?" She clutched her breasts, squeezing them together. "Don't you want them anymore?"

I looked away, sickened.

She put her hands on her hips and faced me. Then she threw her head back, the long thick hair rippling down over her shoulders. Peal after riotous peal came out of her mouth. She was laughing at me, at my plight; cackling in shear deviltry because she was free.

"You're pathetic," she said, and began striding across the field. I stood there, dazed, hearing her cruel laughter float back at me.

And the sound was like the sharp jangle of glass in a windowpane that shattered and fell crashing over and over, again and again.

I knew I would hear it always, the rest of my days.

Part III

Joseph and Constantin

Depart not—lest the grave should be, Like life and fear, a dark reality.

—Shelley

36

I watched Anyeta crossing the field, my heart racing. She reached the steps of our caravan, and suddenly from a distance I saw her hands going to her head at the same time her feet slid out from under her. She crumpled to the ground, and I heard her screaming.

"Shut up, shut up!"

"Make me! I know what you are, I know what you did to her." The voice, higher, went on shouting.

I stood puzzled, watching. There was something different, I thought, and then realization welled up in me all at once. I saw Mimi struggle to her feet, then collapse onto the stairs and I began running toward her. Her face was contorted with pain.

She was gasping for breath, small hands clutching at her chest. She shook her head, waved me off. "Run," she panted, as a second spasm flitted over her features. "Bring Joseph."

She plunged her hands deep inside the thick black hair at her temples and screamed. "I can't hold her! Oh, I can't." Mimi rocked back and forth. "Hurry! Get him."

And then before I could say a word she was flying up the steps into the caravan. The door slammed behind her, jarring the wooden frame, sending a shuddering vibration down the length of the caravan.

Anyeta's voice rose to a shriek. "Let me out!"

I heard the sound of fists pounding against the door, the heavy grunts of labored breathing. And then the iron bolt clanged down, and I knew Mimi was buying herself the precious seconds she would need when Anyeta was loosed like a raging demon within her. And I ran.

Joseph's caravan was on the edge of a high field on the outskirts of the town. Christ, let him be there, I thought. My lungs were raw with running five kilometers, a stitch burned in my side. I raced toward it, my mind awhirl, and pounded frantically at the sidewall, shouting his name, then lurching up the rickety stairs toward the canvas flaps.

He was standing by the table, in the act of drawing on a gray cloak. I took one look at his face and saw that he knew I hadn't used the cap. Suddenly I was overcome with anxiety. Lenore. She'd hear me, know something terrible happened. My God, was I crazy shouting that way?

My eyes flitted over the room to look for her, at the same time I felt that subtle mesh of his thoughts with mine and he said, "Constantin has taken Lenore to the village. A street fair with mimes and jugglers." He looked deeply into my eyes. They had known I was coming, spared my daughter the scene.

I felt the full weight of my failure to gentle Zahara all at once. "I couldn't do it," I said, lowering my gaze, afraid to see the sad reproach in his.

But he never said a word against me, only put his hand lightly on my arm. "Your daughter is safe here with us, until you can bring her home."

"Mimi," I began, stealing a swift upward glance, and I broke off. I saw that his eyes were filled with anguish.

"The sorceress has taken her," Joseph said. "I know." He finished fastening the cloak and began moving toward the doorway.

It was the cloak—so much like the one I'd carried the gentling cap under— that triggered a surge of fear in me, and my hand lashed out, grabbed at the thick woolen folds. "You can't! You're not going to gentle her," I screamed, strangling on the half-question.

"No," he said softly, shaking his head. "Come, we will see what can be done."

I hesitated. "Mimi's stronger than Zahara was. The old woman— she wasn't there—it was Mimi when I left."

"That strength will be her blessing and her downfall, I fear." He passed through the worn canvas flaps, held one high for me, but I stopped.

"What do you mean?"

"The time has come for you to put all your trust in me, Imre," he said.

For a brief instant I felt my old suspicions flaring up. What was in this for the old man? Then I remembered it was Mimi herself who asked for him, and she was suffering. "All right," I said following him down the stairs. We began walking over the wet field, the wind gusting and crying around us, and I thought of tortured souls lost, wailing.

"Do you know the work of the disciples of a German physician named Franz Mesmer? No? Then let me explain."

I hung on every word.

It was Mimi—hollow-eyed and weary—but it was clearly Mimi who unbarred the carved door and let us in.

I saw the old man's dark brilliant gaze scrutinizing her, then he nodded. "It's her," he said, raising one thin hand to touch her cheek lightly. He swung the cape from his shoulders and said, "You understand I couldn't be sure until I saw her for myself."

Mimi blushed.

"I know my own wife—" I began to say, but he cut me off.

"Perhaps. But another mind—a very cunning one—has access to hers now."

"Are you saying Anyeta could imitate her to fool me?"

He nodded, and turned his attention to Mimi. "Tell me what you can. She has been out since Imre left?"

Mimi nodded slowly. "I feel a pressure, here" she said, bringing one hand to her head. "A kind of storm—like snow swirling and rushing faster and faster, and a cold, burning pain; then everything gets blotted out in all that white."

"Can you see her—see what she does?"

"Yes."

"Hear her?"

I saw her slim throat tighten, and she swallowed. "In my head, she says things, taunts me—like the voice in a nightmare that never stops."

"Can she hear you, see you?"

"I don't know."

"Can you feel her now, or see her?"

Mimi's eyes took on a faraway misty look. She lifted her head, whispering, "She's veiled, hidden."

Joseph sat back, considering. "Anyeta will use the secret byways of the mind to push you aside. Think of Zahara, how she used the woman's old longing for Imre against her. There may be things inside you that you don't know about yourself—and yet, she will do the work silently, burrowing deeper to get at dreams, fears, desires. Forewarned is forearmed, we must find out all we can."

"Yes." Mimi placed one small hand across her chest. "I feel her chipping at me. Do you know that old tale about eternity? That it's like a great silver ball, as large as the earth, and a single bird circles it, tipping it with one wing; and that as long as it would take the bird to wear out that monstrous orb—that is the beginning of eternity." Mimi's face went fierce. "I feel her will inside me—iron hard, determined, saying, 'And if it takes that eternity, so be it. In the end I will break you and laugh when I crush your bones in my fist.'"

"There will be things Anyeta fears," Joseph said. "And those fears can be used against her."

"Mesmerism," she said, and her eyes flashed onto his. She took his gnarled hand in her small one, and I saw their minds were meeting in a place I could not go. "Put me in a trance, then."

Joseph looked grave. "You may not remember what happens when you wake—"

She nodded. "But you'll tell me."

"If she comes out, we could lose you." He paused. "You know that?"

Her eyes fluttered closed, and I saw the line of her dark lashes against her pale cheek. "Say my name. If I can hear it, I'll come back."

37

I didn't like what they were up to. It seemed too dangerous, too risky. I paced back and forth in the caravan.

"You never told me she might be called forth!" I shouted at the old man, but he only shook his head. I rounded on Mimi. "If all it takes is saying your name, why did she laugh at me? Don't let him do this," I said, pleading, grabbing her hand. "Why are you doing this?"

"She'll get out, Imre," Mimi said. "And I have to find a way to keep her back."

"How do you know she will?" I folded my arms.

"Because I know what she did to Zahara."

"And what was that?"

"Terrified her until Zahara retreated so far, she was a speck; Anyeta took the last of her powers, and then for Zahara there was nothing."

"Nothing?" I kept after them, but they ignored my objections and went about setting up the caravan, drawing the shutters closed, lighting one short candle.

Joseph had made an easy chair out of the wooden bench by stuffing it with pillows and blankets for her to sink into, and now he answered me. "Nothing but the dark place that was the sum of her fears."

I shivered, feeling gooseflesh breaking in cold waves over my skin. But there was no time to protest further, they were ready to begin. Mimi settled in the chair, facing Joseph, and I watched anxiously. He counted backwards from ten, led her gradually and slowly to a place deep inside herself, while I sat peering at her still face in the gloom of the caravan. I chewed at my fingers, wishing I'd kissed her smooth brow while I'd had the chance.

Her head lolled toward the cradle of her shoulder. Her closed eyelids fluttered lightly, then stopped. The small hand resting in the lap of her skirt was as motionless as a statue's.

"Mimi," Joseph said. "You can open your eyes, talk, move about the room. Yet you will remain within that safe, silent place inside you, until I call you to waking." He paused, and she nodded slowly.

Her eyes opened with the sludgy mechanical lifting of a doll's. She was waiting for him to guide her; her face was as blank and vacuous as her eyes.

"All right," Joseph said. "Can you tell me exactly what she used against Zahara?"

"Dark, cold." Mimi whispered, her head tilted backward suddenly, her pale mouth gaped in a silent scream.

"Where are you?"

She cringed, huddling deep against the bench. "Don't leave me," she whimpered.

I stared, feeling half-enthralled myself. It was like looking at the image of Zahara. The face seemingly filled out, Mimi's sharp cheekbones diminished under heavy pads of flesh. The eyes were smaller, darker, filled with the helpless terror of a trapped animal. The shoulders had a rounded, drooping cast to them.

"Hear them?" she asked, and now I heard a huskiness in the voice, watched her shiver. "They scratch at the wood," she lifted one hand, miming a claw. "They'll get in soon."

"Earth," she said, and there was something so desolate in her voice I felt myself go cold. Oh Christ, I thought, she was seeing, feeling that eternal unrest that was the curse of claiming the hand.

"It's so hard to breathe, the air is heavy. Rings," she said, clasping her fingers. "Feel like bands of frozen steel. They hurt. They hurt. It's always night. Always. And I hear the sound of rain—far off, high up." She trembled. "The scratchings and the tunnelings of the worms. I hear the first one bore through the wet rotting wood, and the rest pour in like a flood. Swarming. My flesh," she wept, her body going as rigid as a stone effigy. "They eat my flesh. And I cannot move."

Joseph turned to me. "This is the vision the old woman used to terrify Zahara, to shove her aside and weaken her. She will find a more powerful way to get at your wife."

"Is that—was it Zahara?"

"No," Mimi said. "Only the reflection of a memory behind the sorceress. An illusion." The voice was toneless, empty, dead—there was nothing human left in it.

"Where is Zahara?" I cried.

"Waiting. In the earth. Always," Mimi said, and I felt Joseph's hooded eyes piercing me, saw the panged look that said if I'd gentled her, she would have found peace. *Afterwards they don't remember!* My father's voice rattled in my head, and I saw the metal spikes protruding from a horse's skull and a woman's brow; saw the punctured flesh, the bright runnels of blood dripping down dazed, confused faces, and I shook my head. Old Joseph was wrong. My father was wrong, I told myself: peace and that the hideous state of un-being were not the same, must never be confused. I was sorry for Zahara but I had no regrets about the gentling cap. I heard Joseph sigh, and I looked up.

"Now I want to ask you, Mimi, can you see Anyeta?"

"Yes. She's sitting in a bare room, just beyond the gauze of the veil."

"Can you hear her, hear what she's thinking?"

"Yes. Run with the wolves when the moon is high. Lope over the fields and run. Into the town to take—take whichever one I want, and I will run."

Joseph's eyes went wide, and I saw his bewilderment. "Take, run," he repeated slowly. "What does that mean?"

Mimi got up, and now her face had a sinister look. The dark brows narrowed to a slash, the lips drawn into a cruel half-smile. She began to snicker. "First the animals. Bite deep. The blood fills your mouth. First animals." Her voice was a growl, thick with saliva as if she was excited at the thought. She made a sucking sound. Her eyes gleamed with a vicious light, and she gave a sudden snort.

"Animals," Joseph said. "And then?"

But the face went sly. "And then we will see, we will see what the other one changes into."

"Who are you?" Joseph demanded at the same instant he grabbed my arm, warning me, holding me back just as I was on the verge of saying her name. "Don't even think it," he snapped at me. "Who are you?"

"Heh-heh-heh."

The voice was an evil chortling sound, so eerie I felt the hairs on the back of my neck stand out. I held my breath. The face took on a weathered look, and now I saw the hair was paler than Mimi's. Lank greasy strings lay damply over her shoulders. Her white face shone with droplets of sweat, the eyes were glowing pinpricks in the shadows. "You know," she crooned. "Say it," she shouted.

Joseph shook his head, no, my pulse was racing. I saw her eyes flick toward me.

"Say my name and I'll tell you." She came and sat on my lap, her body like a small hot furnace. She leaned her mouth against my ear, whispering. "Lost. Lenore will be lost." Hectic fingers stroked the curling hairs at the base of my throat. "Like her beloved Empress. Sisi," she chuckled. Her son, a murderer and a suicide. Her sister trapped in a theater, killed when a gas lantern explodes. Her life a broken one; a sham marriage and a life of endless wandering.

"There will be no good death." She peered into my eyes. "Not for Elizabeth. No. Only an assassin's knife." She snickered, tapping her finger against the center of my chest. "Say my name, save your daughter if you can."

I closed my eyes, afraid to move, wondering if it could be true; no, the Empress' son, I thought, was scarcely more than a toddler . . .

"Mimi wails inside me, waiting in a place more silent than the grave she yearns for. Say my name . . . I have secrets. They can be yours, only say my name—"

. . . and I felt that hot dry breath, and I thought, Oh Christ is this what Mimi's hears, the subtle voice of the desert wind, swirling, inexorable, grinding her to dust, to the sand that is the wind itself. *Detlene*, the dark wind. I thought of the vision I'd had that day, seeing Mimi immobilized like Lot's wife on the stoop of the caravan; waiting for me. Lonely, frightened, begging me to swear—

"Say my name," she breathed, and at that instant I felt my jaw drop, the name rising, coming to my lips and tongue, and I saw something greedy in those obsidian eyes, felt her thin burning body writhing against mine eagerly.

"Yesss—say it." She opened her mouth for a kiss. My hand lighted on the back of her head, but the image that rose to my mind was a hard sun-whitened skull filled with sharp teeth. I gasped, flailed my hands and pushed her away.

She stood up and laughed, seemingly undaunted. "Not now." She waggled her sharp finger at me. "But I will make you say it." Her eyes blazed. "And I will make you regret not saying it now." She turned hissing, seeming to dissolve into Mimi. "Remember, you might have known . . . ." And then she was gone, and Mimi blinked her eyes, twice, and shook her head. Her face was blank, as if she were still looking inward at something.

"She's waking," I started to say, but Joseph cut me off.

"Quiet," he commanded. "We must be quick, before she comes out of the trance. What is she afraid of, Mimi?" He pressed, "What does she want?"

"Sharp," she muttered. Her shoulders twitched, fingers clenching tight enough to break the skin. "Hand," she said, gazing down dreamily at the bloody indentations in her palm; and then the blank look was gone and she was staring hard at both of us.

38

"She wasn't out all the way," Joseph said, pacing, hands knotted behind his back.

I wasn't so sure. "Christ, she felt like a bag of bones sitting on my lap, even the smell—" I stopped, catching sight of my wife's face.

Mimi's violet brown eyes had a sad, haunted look. "It's me," she said, slowly. "My body. And yet you feel revulsion."

"It's you—I know—but it doesn't seem like you," I said helplessly. "You look different."

She uttered a little "oh," and I saw I was upsetting her more, making her feel more cut off, adrift. Was there any way to explain the terror Anyeta invoked in me?

Joseph held his hand up. "I know this is hard. But we have to face it, you especially, Mimi. If she can find a way through your defenses, she won't rest until she wears you down."

He turned to me. "And she will use you, Imre. Any ploy she can think of— if she emerges even part way, you must never say or think her name."

"Did she speak the truth—will the Empress—" I swallowed. My God, the sheer power of the thing. I thought of Anyeta raising corpses in the cemeteries, heard their howling voices. *Ask. Ask of me what you will.*

Joseph would not answer, he only gave me a hard stare, and I thought I saw his jaw tighten, as if he knew, saw. Then he turned to Mimi, hunkered down. He took her hands lightly in his, mindful of the gauze bound over her palms. "You did well, my brave one." He leaned over kissed the knuckles, in turn. "Can you do a little better, do you think?" His eyes twinkled.

"This is the worst flattery," she giggled, and I saw she was feeling better, more at ease. "But, yes, I'll try."

"Good! Don't listen to him, the sorceress was only out part way. What I want to know is this—were you still linked to her, and if so, can you tell me what she was thinking?"

Her hands still rode lightly in his, she closed her eyes, concentrating, then exhaled and shook her head. "No," she said.

"Patience," he said under his breath. "Don't pull back, this time let yourself flow into her thoughts."

She moaned softly. "No, I don't know."

I saw tears well up in her eyes. Joseph brought one hand up, brushing at them as delicately as any mother. He smoothed the sweat-damp hair, slowly, rhythmically. I wondered if it was to comfort her or to guide her back toward the relaxed state she felt in the trance.

"Shhh, all right. Easy, now," he said, and Mimi closed her eyes. "What does it mean, run with the wolves, to bite animals first?"

She shook her head.

"Tell me what comes after animals."

"Children." Her eyes flew open in alarm. "What does that mean?"

He shrugged it off, then softly moved his big hands round and round her temples. "What about sharp or hand, the words you said when you were coming out of it?"

"Nothing. Can't tell," she said, and I thought that was the end of it, but something struck the old man.

He stood up, twisting the gold ring on his middle finger. "Can't tell," he repeated. "Mimi," he said, his eyes flashing sparks, "will you let me put you under once more, briefly?"

"Now?"

"Please." He nodded and she agreed. He began to count, before he reached five, she was breathing deeply.

"What does Anyeta fear? What does sharp mean?"

"Can't tell," she murmured in a high tight voice. "No, mustn't tell." She shook her head back and forth, reminding me of a worried child who wants to confess but feels afraid. Was some part of Anyeta holding her back?

"Then show us," Joseph said.

She began to mime seizing a knife and stabbing at her own chest. A low moan came out of the old man's throat, and he nodded, slowly, painfully. I looked at him but he wouldn't meet my eye. "And what does she want, what of the hand?"

I watched in amazement as she raced lightly up the stairs to the loft, rummaged among the barrels, then returned with the copper box. She opened the glass lid and the room was filled with that inexplicable sweet fragrance— lily of the valley, roses, gardenia. She leaned over, and I saw her fumbling in the inner corner of the box at what appeared to be a small brass button. She depressed it with the tips of her fingers, slid it out of sight. It was a crude release mechanism, I realized, watching her lift away a shallow wooden tray; it was covered with the maroon velvet that outlined the hand of the dead.

Beneath it was another compartment. But there was nothing in it but a brownish, dry looking substance—like the bark of a tree but twisted into a fantastic shape.

"Is it a truffle, some kind of mushroom?" I asked, poking one finger out.

"Don't touch it," Joseph said, but the tip of my nail had grazed the surface.

A drop of blood suddenly welled up, then ran quick and bright over the humped shape, pooling against the copper bottom of the box. Under the rill of fresh blood, the thing took on a pinkish hue.

"It's flesh," he said.

"What kind of flesh?"

"What did she say?" Joseph raised his eyes toward the ceiling. "First animals, and we will see what the other one turns into. First animals, then children."

Deep in the trance, Mimi moaned, swayed on her feet.

"Wake her up," I said, feeling anger roiling inside me.

"No, let her dream a while. I'm afraid it's all the comfort she'll have for a long time."

"What does this mean, all this wild talk of knives and wolves and flesh?"

For the first time in my life I saw him angry. "It means, you stupid man, when the body is controlled by Anyeta she will run gibbering and kill—animals, babies, eat their flesh." He glared at me a long time, then the hot light in his eyes began to dim. The expression on his gaunt face softened. "Do you remember when I told you Anyeta was looking for a way to take someone who claimed the hand without dying?"

I felt my mind spinning. "But how?"

"When you go to mass and take the host, are you not one with the Christ? Has no priest told you of that miracle?"

"Of course, but—"

"And do you believe you are one with Him?" He didn't wait, but went on in the same crushed voice. "Then there is your answer. If she eats the flesh and blood of one who has claimed the hand, they are hers."

"She's already in Mimi," I said, thinking aloud.

"Mimi is strong, Anyeta wants someone weak she can overpower, obliterate. A child." He paused. "Lenore is a child," he said dismally.

My eyes locked onto his and in a mindless fury I bolted from the chair, grabbing his frail shoulders. "You said it yourself, old man," I shouted, shaking him. "Mimi is strong, Mimi can hold her back! Not Lenore, not Lenore!"

He began to laugh, a long bubbling sound rising higher and higher, startling me, so that my hands fell weakly to my sides and I realized the laugh had become a throaty bray of hysteria.

"Yes," he said, "your wife can keep her at bay by using the old woman's fears against her. And what is Anyeta afraid of? Pain, stabbing," he spat each word, and his dark eyes glittered with fear. "So tell me what you'll do the first time you see Mimi, with the *tshuri* clutched in her hands, cutting herself and grimacing with the pain to keep that she-demon inside?"

I had no answer, there was no answer. Only the sinking feeling that between us, we'd opened some hideous door that yawned wide and would never close.

39
Winter, 1864

"Sisi has one like this," Lenore said, fingering a long strand of garnet beads the shopkeeper held up for our inspection. It was getting on toward little Christmas, the feast of the Epiphany, and just lately Mimi had seemed more like herself, less prone to the wild outbursts and violent mood swings that signified Anyeta was on the rampage. "But Sisi's has gold spacers and those," Lenore made a squiggly line in the air with her index finger, "filigree caps—like little hats around the beads. Mother would like this one, though . . . ."

But no, not another necklace, I thought. Anyway, the price on the discrete cardboard tag was out of my reach. I shook my head to signify no, wondering if we should try one of the other shops in the cobbled square.

"The young lady and her Madame Mere admire the Empress?" the proprietor asked. He was as long legged as a stork, and he took a sideways step at the same time he spread his narrow hands with a flourish to point out another case—but Lenore had already lighted on the target and was dancing on her toes in excitement.

"Oh," she cried out, "it's the most cunning, the darlingest . . . ."

While Lenore crooned, the man's eyes rolled up to mine. I was his real customer, the one with the folding green; I was sure he wasn't about to hand over the diamond brooch in the shape of a bouquet of miniature roses for her to look at, but he slid open the wooden door behind the case and brought it out, laid it in her hand. "It's not real, of course," he said, and I nodded, both of us pretending I'd known it was sham. "Austrian crystals, but of a nice quality—and set in silver—not platinum. But it is an exact copy of the one the Emperor gave his bride."

"It's very brilliant, and just like diamonds," Lenore prompted. "Is it terribly terribly expensive?" she asked.

I'd already seen it wasn't, guessed if I bought the brooch for Lenore plus another item I had in mind there was room for some bargaining to be done.

"Please?"

"Well," I hesitated, knowing it wouldn't do for Mimi; she disliked gaudy jewelry, and the pin was as ugly as it was garish. On the other hand, I knew that Lenore's heart's desire was to have a mauve colored velvet dress (like Elizabeth's, only not so grand, she begged showing us a copy of a lithograph torn from a newspaper) like the one the slim-waisted twenty-six-year-old Empress had worn to an Autumn cotillion. But there was no velvet in the local shops, and Mimi had even written to a seamstress in Buda. The letter had come back three days ago marked "unknown," and we'd both felt bad about it. Then I'd found my wife standing in the middle of our caravan. The room was an explosion of shawls, blouses, dresses, petticoats yanked from a trunk and strewn helter-skelter like a display of second hand clothes in a Turkish bazaar, saying, "Where is it, where is it?" At first I thought Anyeta had come to the fore, but no, it was Mimi and she'd hit on the idea of cutting down and remaking one of her old dresses for Lenore. It wasn't velvet, it was a sort of shiny cotton, but it was lavender. It would do. And the fancy pin in the shape of a bouquet and made from crystals would be just the thing for a certain young lady to pin on the bodice of her new dress. I had to get her out of the shop, though.

"Have you bought anything for your uncles?" I asked, my hand going to my pocket for coins.

Lenore began ticking her fingers. "I made each of them a clay dish and painted it. Uncle Joseph can use it as an ashtray, and I suppose Uncle Constantin can put gold pieces in it. Also, I drew some pictures—"

"Go on now," I said, handing her the money. "Go get a little something for each of them. I'll meet you in the square in a few minutes."

"Are you trying to get rid of me?" Her small face was wreathed in a huge grin.

"Nope."

"I like jewelry, too, you know, Papa," Lenore said, moving toward the belled entry of the shop.

"I know you do," I said, laughing. "Now, scoot." There was no fooling Lenore: As she passed the store window I saw the lilt in her walk, her broad smile, her upturned eyes and knew she was lost in a happy vision of possessing the facsimile of the Empress' brooch.

Twenty minutes later I was out in the square, leaning against the base of a bronzed statue of a rider on horseback, waiting for Lenore. In my coat pocket were two drawstring pouches; one held Lenore's brooch, the other, a pair of small amethyst earrings I thought would accent the violet light in Mimi's eyes.

I saw Lenore crossing the square, went to join her; we turned down a narrow alley, the tiled roofs of the crowded shops hanging low over our heads, the tiny slitted windows like eyes peering down on us.

"I bought Uncle Joseph a pipe," Lenore said, walking along and unwrapping a straight stemmed pipe, its bowl rough-hewn of some dark burly wood. "Don't you think he'd look nicer with a pipe, instead of those nasty brown cigarettes?"

I nodded, and she put it back into her cloth purse. "And a game for Uncle Constantin. It's called *opre t'a tele*—ups and downs; it has little wooden cubes and it's just like snakes and ladders and he can play it with me."

I saw she was serious, hid the bark of a laugh that was threatening under a cough, and said, "Those are good choices."

Lenore suddenly stopped, murmuring, "Oh no."

"What's wrong?" I said. I saw the hurt expression on her face, the color draining from her skin. I followed the line of her vision. Across the pavement was a butcher shop, I saw the carcasses hanging in the window; plump, skinned holiday fare. Lambs and goats and chickens . . . .

"Mooshie," she whispered, pointing, at the same time my eye picked out a long string of ducks tied by their feet, their dark bills draggling downward.

"Lenore," I sighed. We all knew, thanks to Lenore's chatter about the Empress, that Elizabeth was wild about all kinds of animals, and 'Mooshie' was a pet Constantin had given her. The week before, Lenore had carried the big white duck outside for a breath of fresh air, and it had squirmed out of her arms and gotten away. She tried chasing it down, but in the end she went to bed crying— Mooshie was gone. All of us—Joseph and Constantin and myself—felt bad about it, and we thought that was pretty much the end of the duck, but there was worse in store. A day later, they told me they heard Lenore screaming. Constantin rushed out of the caravan. Something—a fox perhaps—had attacked the duck, then dragged him into the weeds nearby, and Lenore had found him. He was still alive. There were deep bites in the soft flesh of the abdomen, and one wing was crushed and broken. They came for me. Except Lenore, we all knew the duck was dying. I made a sort of splint for the wing, tried to bandage the wounds. It was a bad, clumsy job at best, with the duck feebly trying to get away from me, Lenore weeping.

"Mother would make a poultice," she said. "Sowthistle and agrimony is for internal complaints, and the other one, I forget," she cried, gently stroking Mooshie's head. "But it's for blood poisoning."

Yes, she'd make a poultice, I thought, or if Anyeta let her she could just heal the damn thing. But there wasn't anything I could do except let Lenore grieve, cradle her stricken pet on her lap, stroke its ruffled feathers.

When it was over, Constantin and Joseph buried him for her. She had seemed all right since then, but now the row of ducks in the butcher shop was bringing it all back, and I saw tears glittering in the dark fringes of her lashes. She brushed at them, and then to my surprise, I felt her small hand stealing into my coat pocket.

She plucked out the red leather pouch that held her Christmas gift. I knew what she was going to do, but before I could stop her she was opening the pouch and shaking the crystal pin into her hand. "Uncle Joseph told me about it," she said, as if she were answering an unspoken question. "He said it's the Romany custom when you're reminded of someone you loved, you give something away to the first stranger you meet. The Lovari, the horsemen, buy a harness or a saddle; sometimes the women make a meal, or give away a blouse or shoes. . . ." Her voice was low, sad.

It was the custom: to show that you loved someone who'd died you gave something away in their memory—and the more precious the gift, the more you relived that love.

"But, Lenore," I began, nearly blurting *Not the brooch! Not for a damn duck*; the words died on my lips. I was suddenly caught on the memory of Mimi, scarcely past her girlhood, giving away the anklet of gold coins that was her wedding gift after she lost Elena.

It was in a village in the Tirgu Mures district, shortly before we left for Hungary. I recalled feeling her hand tighten in mine as we walked along the high street: two silent mourners made a poor man's procession following a coffin drawn by a single horse. The black casket was no bigger than a bassinet. "Elena," Mimi whispered; then she turned, gazing through a window, cringing when she saw two children—a brother and a sister—begging at a restaurant table for the scraps some fancy dressed ladies left on their plates.

A thin sour-faced matron in a black dress suddenly shouted and went after the children with a broom, literally sweeping them away from the white-clothed table and out the doorway. "Get out of here! Go eat garbage, but leave my customers alone!" She shook the broom at the children, I saw a lock of her gray hair tumbling messily from one of its pins.

Then I watched as my wife unclasped the narrow bracelet and held the string of coins in her palm. She went over to the ragged children, who had moved a few yards down the street and were loitering in front of a glove shop.

"Don't be afraid," Mimi said, stooping down so that her long skirts brushed the curb. "What's your name?" she asked the girl, a gamin with dirty blond hair and mahogany colored eyes. The girl sniffled, brought a grubby finger up to her nose, wiped, and sniffled again. "She don't talk," the boy said. "She's seven, I'm eight."

"What do they call you?" Mimi asked the boy.

"Ion. She's Eva." He jerked his thumb at his sister.

Mimi put her hand gently on the girl's head. At the same instant I saw the boy's hand fly up. He snatched at the length of bright yellow coins Mimi held in her other hand and began to run toward the church. His sister seemed stunned for a second, her jaw dropped into an O, and then she streaked away after him. They turned a corner, disappearing from our sight.

"It doesn't matter," she said, coming up to me, when I commented that the Romanian people always blamed this kind of thing on gypsies; any beggar, any thief was a gypsy. "It doesn't matter, Imre," she said, "because the money was in memory of Elena, it was for them, anyway."

In the narrow street of Sibiu, I looked up, saw Lenore handing her brooch to an old beggar woman sitting in a doorway, knees sprawled under a ragged gray dress, while she rattled her cup. In a low voice I heard my daughter say the Romany words her mother had whispered twenty-odd years before: *Te avel angla tut . . .* she began reciting. *May this brooch be before you and in your memory.* I knew she was thinking of what she'd loved, of what she'd lost.

It had snowed the day before little Christmas, just enough to make a stingy layer like a gray-white net over the frozen grass that poked through the crust. But the temperature had dropped, and on my way to Joseph's caravan I saw sheets of ice in the gutter, the water barely flowing beneath the surface. A fountain I passed had the look of an arctic field, greenish chunks bobbed and collided like miniature floes; the spray had dwindled to a soft bubbling, bright and glassy in the sunlight.

I climbed up to the field where Joseph's caravan was parked. Below me, the bells from the tower were ringing out the Epiphany, and from a distance I saw villagers moving leisurely over cobbled streets. Faces lit with broad holiday smiles, babies lifted from their prams for inspections and kisses, old women with fat arms carrying packages, white pastry boxes carefully tied with string. My boots made a crunching noise as I hurried toward the wagon. Then I saw a flurry of canvas flaps—Lenore sticking her nose out. She disappeared and I heard her voice drifting on the cold air. "He's here, it's Papa."

"'Outside Hungary there is no life; if there is any, it is not the same,'" I quoted. It was late afternoon, I sat leaning—sprawling nearly, at the table, fingers loosely curled around the stem of an oversized goblet filled with brandy. "Even the Romans knew it," I said. "'*Extra Hungarium non est vita—*'"

"Shhh." Joseph held one finger against his thin lips. I nodded drunkenly, mumbling sorry. He grinned at me, rolling his eyes toward the other end of the shabby wagon where Constantin and Lenore— her "Empress" dress spread round her legs like a pale lagoon—sat playing the game she'd bought. I heard the wooden cubes rattle and bounce, Lenore cackling with glee when the score rose in her favor.

I refilled my glass from the bottle on the table. "I still say this is a miserable damn country." I'd awakened that morning expecting Mimi to come here with me; instead I found the caravan cheerless and cold. The fire in the stove had guttered out, Mimi was gone and I was alone. She had seemed nearly well these past few days, I had been harboring the secret hope we could have Lenore home again soon. And now it was Christmas, I mourned, and no sign of my wife. I dressed sluggishly in the dismal gloom of the caravan, thinking I'd tell Lenore her mother had relapsed, was ill with another bout of fever.

On the kitchen table I'd found the large pasteboard box that held Lenore's dress tied with a dark green ribbon. Visions of Anyeta raging and cursing flickered in my mind. *I don't have to stay here another minute! I don't have to live with some fool of a jackass!* she'd scream while bundling herself into one of Mimi's shawls, lacing up thin leather boots. Sometimes in the middle of the commotion Mimi would emerge, looking slightly puzzled. Why am I wearing my shawl? Where are we going? The words would no sooner be out of her mouth when she'd realize. "Oh," she'd say in a small, resigned voice, one hand rubbing her temple, *"Anyeta."*

I hesitated, my hands around the box. It would be like Anyeta to do something vindictive, I thought. I imagined Lenore excitedly untying the green ribbon and hearing her voice break when she found the lavender dress shredded into pieces with scissors. I felt my pulse throbbing in my temple, untied the ribbon, pushed aside layers of tissue. The bodice of the dress, neatly stuffed with more white tissue lay on top, the long wide skirt folded beneath. I rewrapped it, told myself over and over: Here was proof of Mimi's love, she had kept Anyeta in check and she would find her way to us.

Now in Joseph's caravan, I felt my disappointment turning to anger. Part of me had waited, trembling with hope during all the day: watching Lenore open her gifts; showing me the decorations she and Constantin had hung; hearing her high sweet voice singing an old carol while Constantin played his violin; both of them excitedly turning over their dinner plates to find the coins Joseph had placed there. The afternoon wore on, the light fading early from the sky. Then Christmas was nearly over, and Mimi hadn't come.

"I'm grateful for all you've done," I said to the old man, "but more and more I think I ought to pack it in and go back to Hungary."

"With Lenore?"

"Certainly," I said.

"And with Mimi?"

I shrugged one shoulder. *Swear to leave when we no longer love, swear to love as long as we both shall live.* Well, I did love her. I didn't want to leave her. It was Anyeta I wanted shut off, the miserable country I wanted to flee. I felt Joseph's gnarled hand touch my wrist lightly. His eyes were soft with understanding.

"Hungary," he said, plying a match to the pipe bowl and sucking smoke, "has a special fascination for you. I see it differently. 1848—the year Franz Joseph ascended the throne—the same year as the revolution and its aftermath is very clear in my mind—"

"But Kossuth, the leader, was right—"

Joseph hushed me with a sideways wave of his hand; I sensed he was trying to tell me something, but I wasn't sure what it might be. "Yes, calling for the end of aristocratic privileges, of censorship, and demanding a constitution—all of it was morally right; but the world is not made up from morals, it is steeped in politics. I was in Buda then, and what did I see? Imperial soldiers entering homes, bayoneting old women; spies pretending to be partisans in order to arrest those who supported the revolt; a reign of terror; prison and death sentences. La Tour—the Minister of War—was dragged from his house and hung on a streetlamp; the people tore his corpse to pieces with their hands."

I had a mental vision of the gypsies ringing Anyeta's fire-scarred body, ripping it apart . . . were the Hungarians so very different from the Roms after all? A feeling of unease swept over me; Old Joseph seemed to key into my thoughts.

"People said when the Russian Czar sent his soldiers to help the Emperor, he saved Hungary for Franz Joseph—but he turned it into Siberia. It didn't feel like home to me anymore. It was hateful . . . dreary. That was why I left."

I nodded.

"I know that the Emperor—now that he's over his worst fears— has become a sort of kindly ruler; that the Empress is beloved. I know that living in the North, in the Nyirseg, you were largely untouched by those things." From across the table, he paused, looking at me carefully, and I felt the penetration of his brilliant gaze. "That even if you had experienced the fear and privations I faced, you would go there—because despite its problems, Hungary is a place that you love."

"Yes." I closed my eyes, briefly seeing the sun dappled plains, the grazing herds.

"Tell, me then," Joseph said, "do you think when Anyeta is out, Mimi also goes to a place she loves?"

I shook my head. Joseph puffed quietly on the pipe.

"Well, where does she go?" he asked, and I found myself imagining some dismal Siberia of the soul, thinking a man doesn't leave a place he loves—much less a person—

"What kind of vigil does she keep? Does she sleep? Watch? Wait?"

"Oh, Christ," I murmured, knowing he was right, and I felt the wellspring of my anger ebb.

At nightfall, I sat soberly at the table in my caravan holding the small glittering gems before me, slowly turning the deep purple amethyst earrings to and fro, watching the facets refract the candlelight. Thinking of the violet hues, the light in her eyes. Remembering other holidays, other years:

Mimi, making an enormous batch of poppy seed tarts filled with honey. Lenore (aged four) and I crowded round her, pretending to help, both of us egging the other on as we stole fingerfuls of raw dough from Mimi's big blue mixing bowl. Mimi laughing at the same time she swatted my hand lightly with the back of the sticky wooden spoon.

"Go on, get away, the two of you," she giggled. "There won't be enough for a single tart."

"Do we care, Lenore? I mean does it matter if it's raw or baked as long as we enjoy it?"

"Nope," she shook her head, grinned. "Look Mama, there's a bat at the window." Mimi falling for the ruse—or pretending to—while I made a squeaking noise to simulate the bat. Lenore whooped, then plunged her whole chubby hand deep inside the dough and clapped it to her mouth, chewing fast.

Mimi laughing, the words "Lenore, you're going to make yourself sick," coming from her lips at the very instant Lenore's face went nausea green and she clutched her tummy and bolted for the washstand. She was so tiny, she had to stand on tip toe to aim at the basin.

She coughed, spit out what was left of the huge wad of dough, then let out the most un-girlish belch I'd ever heard, a deep baying that sounded like a bullfrog suddenly released from the depths of a swamp.

"Ahhhhhhhhhh," she made a carking sound, burped again, patting her round belly. "*Tshailo sim*—I am replete."

It was what the old Roms said, their stomachs bulging like water barrels, having gorged for hours nearly to bursting.

The spoon fell from Mimi's hand, both of us bayed laughter and hung on each other's shoulders. Lenore stooped down in a child's careful way, slowly picked up the fallen spoon, then wedged herself between us in the middle of our hug.

"What's so funny," she asked, tugging Mimi's skirts. "What's so funny, Mama?" In her other fist, she clutched the sweet dough smeared spoon, waving it around baton-style as we stepped apart. It appeared to catch her attention. She paused, staring at the spoon, and then we saw her wee pink tongue come out for a final lick. Mimi and I laughed until we cried.

That memory faded, but my mind played over a whole series of images. The sight of Mimi, her narrow waist looking smaller still, as she reached high to place a bright red vase filled with holly on a shelf. Candles, flames glowing yellow soft, their copper bases rising out of pungent evergreen boughs. The white and gold clothed table filled with food; Hungarian delicacies like *toltott paprika*, meat stuffed peppers served in tomato sauce; or *racponty*, a devilled carp with vegetables and topped with sour cream. Mimi, smiling, heaping our plates.

I recalled Mimi and three-year-old Lenore setting up a small paper crèche in the middle of the wooden kitchen table. But Lenore did not want a "centapiece," she told us. Because she was not allowed to play at the table, and she wanted to play with the "mange," and therefore, didn't we think it would look much better on the floor under the tree? But no, Mimi told her, that wouldn't be nice. Good children did not play with Mary and Joseph and the baby Jesus, and sent her off to bed. Later that night Mimi and I followed our own custom and sat under the lantern at the table drinking sweet wine. Mimi kept fiddling with the star on the roof of the stable and rearranging the tiny painted figures and saying, "Something looks wrong," while I told her she was too much the perfectionist. And both of us giggled the next morning when we found Lenore asleep in her berth—with most of the cows, the Three Wise Men, and all of the camels spread around her, a white sheep scrumpled in one fat hand.

All those years of comfort, of companionship, of merriment. And alone now, I sat at the same table, keeping a custom. A bottle and two unfilled glasses rested on the bare boards. I twirled the tiny gold posts of the earrings, watching them reflect the lantern light. Where was she? Surely if she kept a vigil this cold, forlorn Christmas, it was in no place she loved. Joseph's voice echoed in my head. *Does she sleep? Watch? Wait?* Thinking of her pain, her sorrow, I held my wife's gift in my hand. It was so little measured against all she'd given Lenore, all she'd given me.

I would not sleep, I told myself; but I would watch, and I would wait. For her.

40

"Must you?" Mimi asked, biting her lip.

I nodded sadly, began unwinding the long smooth strips of sheeting, not wanting to look at her frail body strung out over the bed. She knew what happened with Zahara, and that made it worse for both of us.

"Even when you know it's me? You do know it's me?" Her arms were already fastened, she raised her head awkwardly, straining and twisting her shoulders to look at me.

"Yes . . . " I began, but my voice trailed off. I did know it was my wife whose mind had control of the body. But there was no help for tying her down. I puffed air between my lips, thinking of that feral, growling voice. *Run with the wolves. Bite deep.* Anyeta, we now knew was more likely to emerge when Mimi slept; there was no way to guard her all night, every night. "We agreed," I said, "it's the only way."

"It's been two days this time," Mimi said.

I wrapped the strip of cloth over her small ankle, making a series of tight knots, looped it to the bedpost, tying it firmly. Mimi was wearing a pair of red woolen socks; she said her feet got cold and cramped when she slept because of the unnatural position. I lashed her other leg, then began walking around the bed, jerking on each of the four strips with a hard yank to make certain they were secure.

"I can tell when she's coming," she said sullenly.

I said nothing. In my mind I heard last night's conversation: Mimi begging, *Don't, don't tie me down, she won't come tonight, please.* Both of us crying as I fastened her. I lay down on the white featherbed in the corner of the darkened bedroom, listening to the sound of her sobs—harrowing, desperate. She cried a long time, while I tossed uneasily on the makeshift bed. The last thing she said was, *When she's coming out, I feel giddy for hours before, a kind of dizziness—the feeling of being unwell before you get the flu—then headaches. I know when she's coming out,* she finished, and when I didn't answer, she said, *Imre, please, sleep with me, untie me and sleep on the bed with me, I'm afraid to sleep alone.* I didn't do it, though; she was not alone, I knew—not really. Still, I thought, Anyeta had not come.

"Please," Mimi said again, when I arranged the pillow under her head, and tucked the quilts around her. I leaned over the bed, kissed her goodnight. "I love you," I said, stroking her cheek softly with the backs of my fingers.

She turned her face away. "We can't live like this forever," she said, gritting her teeth.

I blew out the candle. Mimi lay quietly. I began undressing in the dark, hurrying a little because of the chilly air, the wintry drafts that swept over the windowsill, eddied up through the floorboards. Sighing a little at the thought of another bad sleep on the lumpy pallet, I turned toward it and heard my own sharp intake of breath: the featherbed lay in a spill of brilliant moonlight, looked whiter still in contrast to the deep black shadows. *When the moon is high. Lope over the fields and run.* I felt my eyelid twitch. From the bed came the sound of rhythmic breathing. She's asleep, I told myself, then moved stealthily toward the window and peered up into the slate-colored night sky. The moon was out last night, I reminded myself, and nothing happened.

It was just a little past the full, one thin slice edging it toward the ragged gibbous phase. Now the light was white, hard, shiny; toward dawn it would soften to yellow, drifting down through the veils of mist.

I got into bed and turned the hem of the sheet over the stiff, heavy covers—then stopped abruptly: From across the room came the sound of a low snicker. I listened carefully, but there was only the drumming beat of my pulse. I lay back, the cotton a rustling noise against my ear, but under it, low and ominous, I perceived the distinct sound of chuckling.

Eyes wide open now, I lay rigid in the dark straining to hear, concentrating. The wind rushed past, rocking us lightly; from under the eaves came the thin screak of wooden joists; a mouse scurried through the loft, tiny nails clicking fast against the boards.

There was nothing else, not a sound from the bed where Mimi lay. I stayed awake all night, would take an oath I never moved, never slept.

At dawn I went to unloose her; Mimi always wanted the chamberpot right away, even before I finished untying her— but she was still sleeping. I yawned, my eyes stung, I had that faraway clotty feeling that comes from lack of sleep. I stooped down to reach beneath the bed for the flowered china pot and came awake all at once with eye-popping speed.

On the floorboard was the bloody imprint of a human foot. Someone had stood there, first flexing, then springing onto the bed: The round red circles from the toes were more sharply outlined than the heel.

Red wool socks, I thought, and I knew I would have to keep my hands from trembling when I untied her, look without her knowing I was looking for tell-tale signs. I felt my mind tilt. It couldn't be, I told myself, tugging at the handle of the pot with a shaking hand, it was impossible. Over my head came the sound of Mimi's voice wishing me good morning.

"Does she know you saw?" Joseph asked me later that morning. We walked through the woods near my caravan. The old man had been stopping by every few days, sometimes bringing Lenore for a visit.

I couldn't see the green caravan but found my gaze drifting uneasily in that direction. "I just made small talk; I hardly glanced at her feet."

I'd already told him the dried blood on the socks was easily overlooked against the vivid red wool, the dark flecks and slubs in the lumpy knitting. I tried not to imagine what they would have looked like if they'd been white—but it was too easy to see the pale stocking shapes clotted with streaks of gore. Her skin under the wool must have been drenched with it. I felt a queasy roll in my guts, then spat to clear my mouth.

The blood was caked on the soles of her feet—like she'd been standing in a puddle of it. The thick wool was matted down, and I'd pretended not to notice the stockings were hard—stiff with crusting blood—when my hands brushed them.

I recoiled now, thinking of the blood, of the sharp coppery smell that assailed my nostrils when I bent low to pick at the knots, and frowned with disgust. "How the hell is she getting out?" I said, at the same time I wondered uneasily if she'd done it before, whether it was the first time I'd noticed.

"Tonight I'll stay with her," Joseph said, sitting down on the edge of a rocky outcropping, and leaning heavily on a black walking stick. He rubbed one hand over the other briefly, and I saw he wasn't wearing the heavy gold signet ring. His finger was slightly narrowed, the skin faintly shining where it rubbed under the ring all those years. I was about to comment, ask him if he'd lost it, but he broke in on my thoughts. "Tell her you're going back to town, to be with Lenore. Then, if Anyeta spells me into sleep, it won't matter."

"Yes," I said, catching his drift at once. I would lie in wait, watching the caravan.

I looked up at the blazing ball of the sun, and for a brief instant the sky went black; I saw the duller light of the moon. I squeezed my hand in a tight fist. If Anyeta left to run with the wolves, I'd know about it. And I would follow.

I stood at the window of the caravan, just beyond the line of the shutter, peering through the glass. Beyond the bedchamber, I could see the dull red glow of the fire in the stove. The old man had tied Mimi to the bed, then warmed himself with a glass of brandy. He blew out the candle and sat fully dressed, cross-legged on the feather bed in the corner.

Mimi was asleep. Joseph was silent, watching. Twice I saw his head drift toward his chest, then snap forward with a jerk. There was a stillness, a cold heaviness to the air, and I felt myself getting drowsy. I blew on my hands to warm them, and with a glance toward the sky thought of moving off toward the woods to watch from a distance with the spyglass Joseph had given me. I was about to tap lightly on the glass to signal the old man when I saw him go suddenly rigid.

His arms and legs slowly stiffened straight out, his shoulders canted backwards. His breathing went shallow. His eyes were wide, staring. I leaned closer, watching, and at the same time I realized he was sound asleep I saw his frail body rising from the floor.

It was slow. He was lifted like a wooden puppet controlled by a child's hand; his legs draggled against the floor, the bootheels knocking on the wood, his head hanging forward over his chest.

On the dresser a candle flame sprang to life, and I saw Anyeta sneering through Mimi's features. "Want to play, old man?" she whispered.

A shiver coursed along his body, but there was nothing else—not even a flicker in his unmoving eyes.

The bonds that held her began unwinding themselves with slow sinuous movements. Like four small white columns they turned and fluttered rising straight into the air.

Anyeta sat up, rubbing her wrists absently. I saw her grin. She gave a sharp nod and Joseph's body floated backward until it touched the wall. His arms were high over his head, his legs wide apart. His eyes were fixed, unblinking; a small runner of tears dribbled down one thin cheek. Like a specimen pinned to a dissecting board, he was sprawled against the wall.

Anyeta began to laugh as if she'd thought of a capital joke, then she turned, narrowing her eyes, concentrating: The white strips of sheeting slithered through the air with a quick hiss. They began wrapping themselves around the old man's cruciform wrists and ankles and throat. I suppose it was a mockery—the bonds were as much a useless decoration as her own. He was nothing more than a broken doll, a toy for her, and I closed my eyes, sick at the thought.

"Are you watching, old man?" she said, "Dreaming you're wide awake and alert? And what do you hear? The beating of your own heart? The wind in the trees? Nothing else?"

The front of the bed jerked high and fell crashing back against the floor. Instantly it rose again and smashed downward, over and over, until the noise and vibration was like echoing thunder in the room.

"Did you hear *that?*" she asked, and began to snicker. Joseph's face was blank, the eyes hollow, dulling with the glaze of unblinked tears.

"You watched all night and you saw *nothing!*" Her jaw gaped in mock surprise, her voice was filled with disbelief, shock.

"You have to watch more closely," Anyeta said, snapping her fingers and his dark eyes began dragging back and forth in the sockets, moving to and fro like the ticking of a pendulum.

She got up from the bed, yawned behind her hand, then crooked one finger idly. A hairbrush danced off the dresser and flew to her waiting hand.

The old man's round black irises shifted right and left and right and left, the endless circuit of animated clockwork.

Outside the window, my heart picked up the rhythm and I clenched my fist in a hard knot and told myself to wait. The moon was on the rise. And when she finished amusing herself, she would run.

41

The door to the caravan swung open. I froze, pressing myself against the side wall, heard her clattering down the short flight of steps.

From the crest of a low ridge came the sound of howling. I turned to look, with the odd sinking feeling she was doing the same. The moon had climbed a little ways above the horizon, it was low and brilliant, canceling the stars in the east.

On the ridge I saw their shadowy forms. The light glinted off the silver streaked fur when the wolves paced, snuffling over the ground, or sat on their haunches and tilted their sleek heads against the sky. Here and there I picked out a pair of glowing luminous eyes, the white of saliva-slicked teeth.

The pack howled and she answered. Then she began to move with preternatural speed. I heard the sound of brush snapping under her tread, of her feet striking the ground, of air rushing past her racing form. And then she stood on the ridge, upright, among the cringing wolves. They crowded close to her, oiling softly, like dark water breaking against rocks that rise out of the sea.

She flung her arms back, lifted her head and bayed. Hers was the only voice lifted in the silence of the night; it rose high and piercing, echoing in the cold air. Less than a second later, she sprang forward with a great leap, her long hair drifted out like a dark cloud, and all of them—Anyeta, and the wolves—began to run.

There was no keeping up with them, but twice during the night, before I confronted her, I found their handiwork.

The first kill was a small flock of sheep huddled on the lowest plateau of a hillside. Before I saw the slaughter, I heard their terrified bleats, the swift jingling of the bells as they broke into a run and scattered; the sound of the rams and ewes trying to climb to safety, their hooves making frenzied clicks against the rocks, a rain of pebbly shale sliding down.

I stood briefly, looking at the carnage. A dozen or more were dead. They lay on their sides, fat tongues lolling from their narrow mouths. The wool streaked and clotted with shiny black blood where throats had been ripped or guts torn from soft underbellies.

Below me, from a strip of forest closer to the town, I heard the sound of snarling and fierce barks, and I started down the mountain toward it.

I picked my way stealthily through the woods, moving through the trees, alert for sounds. The first carcass I came to was one of the wolves, its body savaged, one haunch nearly torn away. In the distance I heard a sharp yelp—suddenly cut off, and guessed this time they'd set on a pack of wild dogs. Edging closer slowly, I stayed downwind, and now I hunkered down in a small pocket of land. Around me the night was alive with the sound of the wolves' feast. The crunching snap of jaws against bones, the soft wet ripping of flesh, the menacing gnarr and aggressive barking when one protected its kill from the rest.

I clutched myself, huddling with terror, afraid of the pictures in my own mind. The blood-soaked stockings, the sound of the greedy voice. *Bite deep. The blood fills your mouth.* I moaned softly. Overhead the moon was splotchy with the black shapes of its mountains. Like an enormous tooth, it gleamed: white, hard, spotted with a darker gore.

Anyeta suddenly barked the signal, and I heard the pack breaking into a swift purposeful run, their feet moving over the forest floor toward the hard-packed winding road that led to the town. A bolt of fear shot through me, I saw her teeth bared in that wide grin. *And I will take—take whichever one I want.* My chest heaved, my breath hissed between my lips, and I let out a long curse. Shit, shit, I wanted to heave myself up and race after them. But I took a deep breath, swore again and made myself wait. I knew if they saw me on their trail, they would turn—with the smooth efficiency of a driven wheel—and tear me to pieces.

Ahead of me, I saw the soft glow of streetlamps. The road abruptly changed from dirt to paving. But I'd known for the last half-mile the wolves had departed; the spoor was gone. Prints vanished, there were no more droppings or gobbets of flesh. High up, far off, I heard their cries tune up, then trail off. But something—some feeling impelled me to walk through the town.

I passed a tavern. Inside, a short rotund man wearing a towel across his hips apron-style turned off his ale taps and mopped the bar. One old man sat in the dull glow of the banked fire, the inn keeper urged him to finish his drink, and the old man frowned behind his tumbler, sipping slowly.

A shout came from the second floor. "Gregor! Come to bed," a woman's deep voice bellowed. The owner rolled his eyes toward the ceiling, the old man held up his glass with a shaky hand.

"To your wife," he said, throwing down the drink and smacking his lips with a chuckle.

"Come to bed!" she called again, and next door, from a lighted room I heard the sound of a window being raised. A woman leaned out between the second-story shutters, laughed down at me.

"How about you? You want to come to bed?" she said.

I shook my head, kept walking. Rounding through the steep, curved streets; watching lights blink on, off. Listening to the sound of my footsteps echoing off the buildings; hearing now and then a signboard creaking on its chains, a man's shout, a cat mewling, asking myself if I was patrolling like some lunatic night watchman, or if I thought she was here. I stopped, realizing I *did* feel her presence—like the steady throb of a pulse.

My pace quickened, I turned down a narrow alley; a clump of ragged weeds sprouted from one corner of a building. I picked my way through broken glass. A dog nosed through a heap of refuse— he lifted his head, flattening his ears and growling at me when I passed. On the right was a low house giving off a dirty light. I peered through a small mullioned window. In the middle of the bare floor I saw a rag burning dimly in a saucer of grease.

There was a sagging bed in the corner of the room; on it a half-naked woman lay in a stupor, one hand dangling over the edge like a signpost for the empty brandy bottle that had slipped from her fingers.

A sudden scraping noise made me pivot. And then I saw her.

She was standing before a boarded over fireplace. Her head was down, and she was clutching what looked like a small bundle of rags close to her chest.

The whole lower half of her face was red with smeared blood—as if she'd dunked it, and I felt my gorge rise, thinking of the gutted animals, of the champing jaws, her mouth gnawing flesh, fur, bone. Her teeth were whiter against all that the darkness. The ends of her hair were clotted with drying blood, had traced idiot patterns across her shoulders and chest. The skirt of her dress was grimed with long smears.

Small gory hands twiddling, she drew back, grinning. Her mouth parted, and now I saw the blood lining the cracks of her teeth. Head lunging forward, she burrowed through the rags to expose a thin white chest. I heard a faint cry. Oh Christ, it was a child. I saw the cap of baby fine curls, the round blue eyes and I screamed, punching my fist through a small pane.

"Stop! For Christ's sake, stop! Don't, Mimi! *Don't!*"

Her head came up, the eyes glinting briefly in the bluish light. She blinked rapidly, and then she had the look of someone waking from a deep dream. Her glance fell on the toddler and she suddenly shrieked.

She flung the child down, its small hand struck the bedpost. I heard the thin snap of a bone and let out an anguished cry. The child wailed for its mama, breaking into hoarse hysterical sobs. The figure on the bed began to stir.

Mimi shook her head back and forth, her hands thrust behind her back. "No, no, no! I didn't!"

She leaped forward, pulling the blood slimed clothes aside. The baby cried louder, now sitting up, leaning against the bed, his legs spread wide. The boy's dirty face was streaked with tears. The tiny chest was unmarked.

Mimi's bloody hands flew to her face, she stood in the center of the reeking hovel and screamed over and over.

Lights flickered in nearby houses. I raised my leg high, kicked hard to shatter through the rotting window frame. Glass and splintered wood sprayed over the room. I pulled myself over the ledge, jumped inside, grabbed hold of Mimi and dragged her back out with me.

I heard the sound of voices, someone pounding on a door on the other side of the wrecked room, rattling the metal knob, calling on the missus to let them in.

I jerked her arm to make her run, propelled her ahead of me down the alley. Steered her through the cobbled passages, taking her on a spiral farther and farther from the center of the town. Her low voice as we ran was a broken sob in my ear. "Oh, God, I hurt that *chavo*, oh God forgive me, forgive me, I might have killed him. Oh God."

42

"Do you see what she has done?" I held my hand out toward Joseph. The gray pre-dawn light filtered in the caravan windows, revealing his thin body immobilized against the wall.

Mimi closed her eyes, let out a sharp exhale.

The strips of white cloth fluttered when we neared. I craned my neck to look up at the old man. His gaunt face showed signs of exhaustion. His skin had a sickly greenish cast. There were great hollows under his eyes, throwing his sharp cheekbones into even greater relief. His mouth drooped slightly, the corners slick with saliva. His chest scarcely moved; I wondered what it cost him to take a breath, to fight the pain, the drag of gravity. Only his deep brown eyes showed any life, drifting endlessly back and forth.

"He's dying," Mimi whispered. Her head sank forward and her brow touched the damp wall. She reached high with one arm, her fingers rested briefly on one of his bony ankles, and I thought of the old women with their beads in church who prayed to the saints, touched the cold marble statues when they left. Mimi turned around,

then leaned her head against the wall again.

"Do something," I said. "Use the power of the hand."

"Don't you think I tried," she snapped. "Do you think I stood by last night, watching her do this and didn't try to stop it?"

"What are you saying?" I felt the first tendrils of panic like a black growth in my brain.

"She's eating at me, Imre. Whittling my power, adding it to hers." Mimi sat on the edge of the bed; her small hands writhed and twisted against each other in her lap. Her eyes, huge with fear, met mine. "Do you know how many times she came out since you pulled me from that room?"

I shook my head slowly.

"Who suggested I stop and wash the blood at the stream? Was it me?"

I groaned softly.

"Anyeta," she said. "She came out twice more. Once when I saw a smear of blood on a leaf, the second time when we passed the crest of a low ridge."

I took her hands in both of mine. "Do you know why?"

She nodded savagely, breaking into harsh sobs all at once. "The kill," she wept, "and the place where she meets with the wolves." Her eyes took on a glassy look. "I see it over and over in my dreams, knowing the worst—that it's not a dream, that it's real." She looked sadly at her hands, as if they were still stained with blood; she gave a small desperate cry, and then she rubbed viciously at the corners of her mouth. Her voice, when it came, was low and mournful, I had to strain to hear it. "The guilt," she said. "This guilt will be with me always, and there is nothing that can take it away."

I sat beside her, looked deeply into her eyes, felt her pain. What was there to say? That she hadn't butchered the child was no comfort.

"She gets out," Mimi said, "and I hear myself telling you lies: saying it was me—and even as I say it, I wish my tongue would dry up in my mouth, but I cannot help it. She has a hold on me; loosening my tongue when she wills it, or binding it, if that's her pleasure." Mimi sucked in her breath. "Last night was not the first time she killed, not even the second or the third." Her hand clutched at my wrist. "I don't know how many times it's been. I only know that it was the first time she dared to try a human—if you hadn't come—"

"But I did." I squeezed her hand.

"Yes," she gave a bitter laugh. "Last night, yes. What about tonight, tomorrow and all the nights that remain? Can you chase me down a thousand times? Ten thousand? How many, Imre?"

"I don't know."

"How many nights will there be before she tires of the game— for her it *is* a game, you know. She will delight a long time in eluding you and making you suffer. But when she gets angry or bored—and turns on you, what then?" Her gaze drifted to Joseph's spent body. "This—or worse?"

"Where is she now?"

"Sleeping," Mimi said. "Like a drunken man stuporous with wild revels." She gave a weak smile. "That's why I'm telling you this—while I can."

"Take her power then," I said. "Use it. Let the guilt be washed away in salvation, save him." I saw a flicker in her eyes. "You told me yourself, the first day in the old woman's caravan. It can be used for good, it can be used for healing." She stood up and slowly walked toward the dying man. She stopped in the center of the room.

Her body was ramrod straight, I saw her chin lift, her violet eyes narrow, and the atmosphere in the room was suddenly charged, electric. I felt the air grow warmer. There was an unpleasant tingling sensation in my veins, I heard the sound of humming in my ears, louder and louder until it rose to an unbearable shrill whine, and my head roared with sharp pain.

I saw the body shudder, the eyes suddenly cease their restless tracking. Joseph blinked, and a low moan came out of his throat. He blinked again. "The pain," he cried, and I thought of all those long hours he hung crucified, his eyelids forced wide. "The light, the light." His head rolled tipsily toward one shoulder; one brown eye drifted slowly down, like a dull marble sinking in a water-filled tank.

"Blind," he rasped. "I'm blind!" His black pupils dilated wide until they nearly filled the muddy circle of the iris. At the outermost margin, a streak appeared, like a jagged rip in a dark curtain. And then the irises themselves began to bleed.

The room took on the glowing heat of an inferno, the noise jumped in intensity—shrieking, drilling in my ears.

Joseph's body trembled, his breath rattled in his lungs, his bony chest heaved up and outward. There was a convulsive spasm, his arms and legs jerked.

"No!" A ragged cry was torn from Mimi's lips. Her eyes clamped shut, she staggered back.

His body crumpled all at once, plummeting gracelessly to the floor like a wounded bird suddenly felled by a rifleshot. It was that quick. Legs bent, he lay completely still, one arm caught under his back, his gaunt face turned up to the ceiling. Two slender filaments of blood trickled from the wide, unseeing eyes.

The room lapsed into eerie silence, there was only a dull buzzing in my ears.

Anyeta's sly features rippled over Mimi's and broke through. Her eyes snapped, the narrow chin took on a vulpine look, the lips were thinner over the white teeth. She saw me staring and she laughed at me.

"Gone," she said, and I knew she meant Mimi. "Hugging herself and helplessly crying like a senile fool—"

—and for a second, I saw Mimi's shattered face, weeping in shock and confusion; she looked old, worn out—

Anyeta tapped her chest. "No one usurps me, *no one*, do you hear? Tell that stupid bitch if she tries it again, I'll kill her."

She pointed to Joseph's twisted body lying on the floor. "And I'll make her suffer twice what he did before I let her die."

She stalked to the other end of the caravan, I heard the door slam.

I sat on the floor, and it seemed good to know there were wooden boards, solid and slightly cool under my fingers. I found my mind drifting out toward the truth, and then it would pull back. I sat staring a long time; I knew it was useless, but I couldn't help it.

My wife was gone, my friend was dead.

43

I lifted Joseph up. It seemed to me his body in my arms weighed no more than a large bundle of sticks—as if he'd been ill a long time. I lay him on the bed and gazed down at him; he looked frail, vulnerable. I felt the rough sting of my tears, but they were nothing to what he'd suffered. His blank eyes were bloody pools. The red streaks had dried to a dark maroon crust on his cheeks.

"Ah, Christ," I whispered. The rubbery lips were pulled back to show the teeth. His mouth, I thought sadly, was like a scream. I cupped my hand under his chin, slowly eased his jaw up, feeling it click against my fingers.

And then I began to prepare his body for the grave, the last kindness any of us ever know.

Two cotton pads covered his eyes. I'd sponged the blood from the angular cheeks, shaved the flesh carefully, set a gold hoop in his fleshy ear. I went to my clothes press and removed my only other suit; I sniffed camphor in the dark gray wool, but there was a sprinkling of moth holes. Still, it would have to do I thought, picking at a loose thread in the lapel. I laid the suit at the foot of the bed alongside a clean shirt.

There were Roms that were afraid of handling or in any way touching the bodies of the dead, and some of the old-timers—at great pains—knowing that none would come near them, actually heaved themselves off their death beds, washed, dressed themselves in their best. On account of my English mother I had not been raised to that kind of superstition, and of course I'd known Joseph, my father's friend, from childhood.

Glancing at his rigid body, I recalled suddenly that one autumn, he and my father had been worried about having enough money to manage over the coming winter. It was back in Hungary, the troupe was camped close to Eger, a district known for its wines and fine country inns. The local aristocrats patronized these *csardas* heavily— often as trysting places to meet with their mistresses. It was fairly typical of the time and place that after dinner, gypsy bands were brought in to entertain. My father and Joseph had heard that given sufficient enthusiasm and plied with the local red wine, the gentry rewarded the performers by throwing gold coins at them.

Both were only so-so fiddlers, but they were *excellent* organizers—and they assembled the finest *bosa venos* in the region, promising each man a share in 75 percent of the take, with the two of them dividing equally the remaining 25 percent.

"You should have seen us," Joseph said, telling me the story while we sat by a campfire one starless night when I was a boy. "Your father thought we'd earn even more if we brought along some of the dancers, and in the end there were twenty or thirty of us. The women wore gold embroidered shawls on one shoulder, left the other arm and shoulder utterly bare. We men had on purple and red and yellow silk shirts, and all of us had on our finest jewelry. We had pride and we wanted to look our best, *be* our best in front the nobility.

"Well, after the gents and their ladies had eaten, the innkeeper pushed the tables back into a wide ring, leaving a huge space in the center of the room. We were all a little nervous entering, I suppose; I was used to the confines of a *vurdan*, and I remember feeling awed by the size of the place, the expensive furnishings, the smell of the perfumes and flowers; then we started to play.

"We played one song, then switched to another gypsy tune. The women shimmied and swayed, the music got wilder and wilder. The room was baking hot—there was an enormous stone fireplace dominating one whole wall—and you could see the sweat shining on the dancer's bodies, on the *bosa veno's* faces. And the men in the audience were stomping and shouting. I remember, Imre, suddenly realizing, *knowing*—aristocrats or not—we *had* that audience in the palms of our hands.

"You know what the Romanians say when the *bosa venos* play, don't you?"

I nodded, he gave out a small grunt.

"Right. *Beng* the devil comes and makes a link that tight," he said, pasting the heels of his hands together and squeezing his fingers, "between the audience and the players. When the devil descends into that room, the *bosa venos* begin to play better, and the audience gets more and more frenzied. I tell you, boy, whether you believe that or not: never underestimate the power of the gypsy rhythms. I saw it that night.

"The place was on fire. People shouting, clapping, cheering. The Romany women shaking their dusky flesh. The *gaje* men rose up and we saw the coins streaking through the air like gold hail. Your father caught my eye, gave me a look that said it was just what we'd expected, just what we'd heard the Hungarian aristocrats did, and we'd get more money when we played the soul rousing finale. I gave the signal to the band and we launched into one of the most famous gypsy melodies of all time.

"We had them screaming. One old man in a white uniform got so excited he leaped to his feet, waving and brandishing his sword, the gold decorations and medals on his chest jumping and bouncing. 'My God,' he shouted. 'My God, these men are playing nearly flawless Liszt!'

"I'd heard that was what the *gaje* thought—that it was simply amazing that a bunch of untrained, uneducated gypsies could learn to play the masterworks. The Romany opinion was *not* that we played 'nearly flawless Liszt,' but that old Franz—shrewd as he was—copied our classics and here and there accidentally put down a few *wrong* notes.

"Anyway—it didn't matter, because the old man was in ecstasy and whipping up the audience for us, and that meant the layer of coins piling up could only get bigger, brighter, deeper. We played as if our shoes were smoking.

"But what we didn't know, what we'd never heard was that past a certain point the nobles stopped throwing money. Money was for a *pleasing* performance. But when the *gaje* were ecstatic, they smashed mirrors and threw dishes.

"And sure enough, seconds later, the audience was pulling the mirrors off the walls, snatching plates from the massive hutch in the corner. Dishes and crockery sailed and crashed around the room as if a hurricane had hit.

"We stopped playing. They stopped the breakage. There was a dead silence in that room.

"'Well, why don't you go on playing?' a young blonde haired man asked.

"None of us knew what to do. We were so uncertain, so embarrassed. Perhaps that's when the devil fled—or arrived—depending on your interpretation of what happened. Anyway, finally we started playing again, but it wasn't the same, and eventually most of the *gaje* left, taking their women to the rooms upstairs.

"It was only later on that we found out these country inns actually kept an extra supply of mirrors and dishes on hand for the aristocrats to break.

"Your father and I were such fools," Joseph said, shaking his head. "We thought it was our fault the *gaje* had been driven to a frenzy, and the only honorable thing to do was to let the innkeeper take back the cost of the damage from the coins the men had thrown for us. By the time he made up his accounts, there was almost nothing left."

"Was the devil there?" I asked him, hugging my small knees closer to my chest.

"Maybe," Joseph said thoughtfully. "His mark was certainly on that innkeeper's black heart; a man low enough to take advantage of our ignorance and pride, our meager hope of earning a little money. You see, the innkeeper got the price of the broken dinnerware and gilt mirrors twice. Your father and I, we didn't know it was all *standard*—right there on every bill—the cost of the plates and the glasses was added to the price of the food." He shook his head.

Years later, some of the bitterness at being cheated gone, he was able to see the humorous side and laugh about it. But I remembered it was one of the reasons he'd left Hungary. He was, he said, tired of wandering, of living in a country where gypsies—constantly accused of stealing—were themselves the victims of hold-ups. No, it wasn't safe for the likes of a lowly horse trader; not when you considered that even a man as important as Bismarck needed an imperial escort to protect him from the bandits and thieves.

Looking at his still face, I thought about the depths, the great sensitivities inside him, about how in one form or another he'd been badgered, hounded, bedevilled his whole long lifetime. And saddest of all, I grieved inwardly, that had also been his end.

I turned back to my work, sighing a little, stripping his shirt from his narrow old man's chest, then beginning to struggle with his trousers. I crumpled and slid them down to his ankles. Holding the cuffs in my hands, I jerked hard. From the corner of my eye I saw something fly out of the pants pocket, soar across the room. I heard the sharp tink of metal striking a wall first, then bouncing off the wood of the floor. There was a rolling clatter.

My eye fell on Joseph's flung out hand, on his denuded middle finger and I turned. On the floor his ring was chittering in smaller and smaller circles, the gold flashing with every spin. It wobbled briefly, then came to a stop.

I let the pants fall and stood looking down at the ring. He hadn't been wearing it yesterday, I recalled, and for some reason he'd put in his pocket. The seal on top of the ring was his own initial, a heavy Germanic J. I remembered he'd shown me once what was written inside: *Deus Vult*. God wills it.

Constantin should have this, I thought, stooping down. My fingers closed on the cool metal. There was a small blue flash; I registered a shock and drew my hand away. Friction, I chided inwardly, rub your feet on a carpet, touch something metal, and—

But not gold and not bare boards, another part of me spoke up, there's no rug.

I seized the ring, closed it inside my palm. It was warm against my skin.

There was a kind of vibration—something like the resonance of a tuning fork—but felt in the flesh, rather than heard. I gave a weak smile, thinking it was the drum of my own pulse.

God wills it…

I held the ring up, peering through the circle at the faint inscription. His fingers were thinner than mine. I slipped it over my littlest finger. It was a tight fit.

I was aware of a rushing sound; louder then fainter.

"It's like the whisper of the sea," I said aloud, and suddenly I realized I was hearing the whisper of a human voice. It repeated the same low desperate cry, over and over. *Help me. Please. Help me.*

"It's not possible," I said, staring down at the ring, then gazing at the old man's blank, patched eyes looming over the ashen cheeks. I was tired,

overwrought—

"Please," the voice begged. *"Help me."* I closed my eyes feeling lightheaded, a faint nausea churned my belly. I swallowed uneasily.

Constantin should be here, he loved the old man like a father. He should have the ring, I thought, pulling it off, shoving it deep inside my pocket.

I finished dressing Joseph quickly, then I left to seek out Constantin. I walked along the road, aware of the ring's weight like a lead drag in my pocket. It lay beating faintly like a small hot heart against my thigh.

I scratched on the worn canvas and Constantin lifted the flap to let me in; I had the sense he was waiting for me, and in the dim lamplight I saw at once he already knew. He was crying, his eyes were red-rimmed, his round face puffy.

I started to speak, but he put his finger to his lips, signaling me to be quiet. The caravan was smaller than mine; there was only a strip of fabric to separate the sleeping areas, and Lenore's bed was just on the other side of the curtain.

We slipped outside and drove off. The horses jogged over the fields and the harness bells seemed like a slow mournful music to my ears. Constantin sat quietly next to me on the driver's box, his hands on his thighs, his short legs dangling several inches above the floor. He lifted his round chest and heaved a long sigh. I reached over to pat his arm, and suddenly I felt the weight of all of it—Mimi, the filthy sorceress, the old man's death—bearing down on me.

"Shit," I said. "Mimi tried. She tried to save him, Constantin."

"Y-uh," he said, nodding fiercely.

"Then that bitch came to the fore and killed him!" I flailed one hand helplessly, I was making him cry harder. "He was a joke for her. Maybe he was already dead when Mimi tried—I don't know."

Constantin pricked up, "N-uh." He brought both his stubby index fingers to his eyes, then drew two lines down his cheeks.

The blood, I thought, realizing he was right. Anyeta wanted Joseph to suffer, to take that final agony to his death. His eyes burning like the desert, bleeding from wounds that felt like glass knives. My pulse began to throb and I suddenly thought about the ring in my pocket; how the old man had taken it off before he came to my caravan. "Constantin, did he know? Did Joseph know—before?" I breathed.

He nodded, and I thought, Oh Christ, this man knew and he'd come anyway, sacrificed himself on the altar of my life. I looked up. Constantin's round face settled into a frown, he was tapping his chest, telling me he had known.

"You knew?" I repeated.

"Yu-uh," he said sadly. He mimed touching his mouth, made the talking fingers flap like a bird flying off. Then he tapped my temple.

"Your thoughts," I said slowly. "Like talking inside Joseph's mind?"

"Y-uh," he said, making the gesture of striking the hand, the *coor dur duk*—a Romany oath broken only at death. They were brothers . . . more than brothers, he was saying. They were one. He suddenly stared hard at me, as if he had something he wanted me to know. He pointed to me, to my ear, mimed talking. "J-uh—Juh-sef?" he said.

"Can I hear Joseph?" I said to Constantin, thinking it didn't make sense, couldn't be right.

He tapped his middle finger, mimed twisting a ring, and I felt sweat breaking out under my arms, trickling down my spine.

I reached into my pocket; my fingers, touching the ring, were moist. I drew it out shakily, turning it between my hands. *Help me. Please. Don't let—*

"I guess he meant you to have it," I said dropping it neatly into Constantin's waiting palm.

"J-uh—Juh-sef," he said. His eyes were very wide, he squeezed it tight in his small fist and held it against his chest. Then he cocked his head.

"You hear him?" I whispered, telling myself it couldn't be. His eyes searched mine as if he were surprised that I didn't hear the old man. But before I could say anything he suddenly groaned, clutching my arm.

"Witch," he mumbled, jerking his chin forward, across the field toward my caravan.

"She's there," I breathed. "The sorceress."

"Y-uh." He mimed lashing at the horses, speaking in his halting stifled voice. "You drive fast, now." I thought of the ring, the thrumming vibration, the words echoed in my brain. *Help me. Please.*

I saw the caravan in the distance, the windows lit by a ruddy glare, and my heart lurched with the sway of the wagon, kept time with the horses' pounding hooves.

Constantin's eyes were locked on the caravan ahead. He kissed the ring, then grimly shoved it deep inside his pocket. "I keep him," he said.

44

We crept toward the caravan on foot. It was preternaturally quiet and as we crossed the field I could hear the horses stamping lightly in their traces. The low sound of their riffled snorting carried on the chill air. I wondered if Anyeta heard it too, was conscious of our sliding steps, our labored breathing as I followed the dark outline of Constantin's broad back.

He paused alongside the bedroom window, his arm came up to hold me back briefly, and we looked in. The room was lurid with red fireglow. There was a dance of huge black shadows that flickered and played against the white plaster of the wall.

The image of thin arms rose and wavered in silhouette. A woman's head in profile tilted backwards—as if she were uttering a silent laugh—I saw the black shapes of her teeth larger than life. There was a low snicker, and then the sound of her voice.

"Rise," she whispered, and on the wall Joseph's elongated shadow lurched and sat up in the bed. One of the cotton pads I'd used to staunch the blood arced through the air and landed on the floor with a wet sounding plop.

I strained at the glass and now I saw Joseph, his head slowly turning on his thin neck, his pallid face a mask of pain, his eyes raw gashes over the trembling mouth.

"Ask of me what you will." His voice was a rattling sigh, mournful as the winter wind.

"Where's the ring, old man?" Anyeta demanded, stepping into view.

Constantin screamed. "Mimi!" he shouted, wrenching the window out with a jerk. Anyeta turned, her eyes blazing with anger. I didn't wait. I bounded away, racing toward the front door, praying it wasn't locked.

I rattled the knob, felt it suddenly yanked hard from the other side, and I spilled into the room. The door swayed under my shoulder. I tried to catch myself and went down, one knee striking the floor hard enough to make me wince. I crawled forward, swiping at her ankles. Laughing at me, she skipped away from my swinging arms and retreated toward the kitchen. Anyeta capered out of reach and backed up against the table.

I glanced up and my eye fell on the row of long handled knives in their wooden rack suspended just over the counter. Just let me get a little closer, I prayed.

I started to get to my feet; Constantin was climbing in the window. She saw me avert my gaze, heard his movements and turned her head. It was time enough. I leaped up, plunging desperately toward the knife rack.

She was so quick our flailing hands knocked it aside at the same instant. It fell onto the counter with a crash. Three of the blades dumped out, jittering from the narrow slots.

She was bent under me, her long hair trailing over the edge of the counter. I felt her breasts against my ribs. Out of the corner of my eye I saw her knuckles clamp down, clutching around the black handle of a knife.

I stood up, seizing her wrist and jerking it straight up over her head. She cried out.

At the level of my ear, the knife blade glittered dangerously in the red light. I bore down on her thin white wrist. Her breath was coming hard. I edged a knee between her thighs, used my height and weight to force her backward away from the counter.

"Drop it," I warned.

"No!" she gasped, and in the instant she said it I pushed hard against her midriff, knocking the wind out of her, upsetting her balance. She fell back, I grabbed her wrist with both hands and wrenched the knife away.

We stared at each other across the small space, lightly swaying on our feet. I kept her at bay with the knife, her eyes followed the shifting blade.

Anyeta made a sudden dart toward the bedroom. I made a grab and my fingers tangled in her hair. I dragged her back, snaked my arm through both of hers. I held the tip of the knife against her throat.

"Go ahead," she said. "Kill your wife."

There was a kind of wavering in the figure's face. Mimi looked up at me, her eyes rolling with fright.

"Imre," she wailed. "Don't!" Her mouth dragged open. Then she suddenly disappeared as if she'd been sucked back inside the gaping maw of Anyeta's lips.

I stepped back, groaning.

"Go ahead," the sorceress taunted, holding her hands up submissively. "Don't you want to, half-gypsy?" She began edging toward the door.

I shook my head, the hand clutching the knife fell weakly to my side.

She began to chortle. "I think that's wise," she said, "and wiser still to remember this night in the future." I looked up at her. "Even if she dies, I live." Anyeta grinned, tapping her chest. "And when Lenore bends near to kiss a dead mother's lips, it is *me* she will taste and I will take her."

She fled through the open doorway and I hurled the knife across the room. It glanced off the wall, then fell clacking and rattling onto the floor. At the same instant Constantin cried out and I heard the sound of Joseph's body dropping back heavily against the bed.

From outside, Anyeta's eerie laughter floated back over the night-clad field.

I'd driven the wagon Lenore slept in closer to ours, then lit a fire on the grass between them. We'd kept a watch for Anyeta, but now Constantin and I were lying on makeshift beds we fashioned out of the benches and chairs in the kitchen. We'd gathered up all the spare pillows we could find, stretched the blankets over our toes. Neither of us was comfortable. Constantin played with the ring, idly staring a long time at the embers in the stove.

Near dawn he called my name softly, and I saw his hand reach toward me in the half gloom. I stuck mine out, thinking it was his way of saying goodnight, suddenly surprised to feel the weight of the ring in my palm. He smiled at me, then settled down to sleep.

Absolutely nothing happened when you touched Joseph's body, I thought. My hands had ranged up and down his narrow chest, the age-dried skin of his wrists, his throat. I'd been trying to duplicate the thrumming vibration I'd felt, then heard. I'd laid my ear over his heart but there was only hollow silence.

I sat up, looking at my palm. In the dim light the gold winked like a small bright flame. "Is it the ring?" I asked, closing my eyes, slipping the band over my knuckle. "Does it have power?" There was a hush, a very small sound like the ratcheting of a miniature gear, then softly his voice filled my mind.

"Anything worn a long time becomes something like the person himself, absorbing thoughts, feelings, dreams."

I nodded.

"Constantin gave it to you because he thought it would bring you comfort, Imre—the same way it does for him." Joseph sighed. *"I talk to him about our memories, things we shared in the past—a hunting trip, a bottle of brandy, firelight, the old tales and songs. That's what he thought he was giving you."*

I felt a dart of anxiety. *What, then?* I asked inwardly.

"I do not want the sorceress to profane my body again." He paused, and I shivered, remembered the thrill in her voice commanding him to rise, saw his ash-gray corpse rigid against the bed, suddenly jerked upright. "Ask of me what you will," he'd whined, and I saw the nodding white head of a puppet.

"To be raised up is more terrible than you know. All the desolation in the world sweeps like a night wind howling through the vast emptiness that is your being. And there is only the will of the one who commands."

There was a quick rush of air down the chimney, the flames made a hissing sound and rose higher. I stared at the shifting fire-shapes and for a second, I thought I heard a wailing like the distant cries of lost souls. *What do you want, Joseph?*

"*I'm going to ask you once again to put all your faith in me; to believe that what I ask is for my sake. The power of the hand is great, but where there is no mind, no soul—there is nothing for the sorceress to glean. In destroying me, you put me beyond her reach. And I want you to do it, knowing that you give me peace, that you have done the last thing I shall ever ask anyone on earth to do. Be my son—*"

"Don't ask it! I cannot gentle you—" The words slipped out, and I heard Constantin toss and fidget in his sleep.

"*Don't let her profane me. Please. I stayed that night in the caravan because I knew Anyeta was restless, glutted with animal flesh. She wanted more. And I knew that Mimi loved you, that if you followed her there was the chance you might call her back and save her from that hideous sin. Mimi couldn't have lived with that guilt, Imre.*"

In my mind, I saw my wife broken, weeping; her voice a well of sorrow: "I see what Anyeta does in my dreams, knowing the worst, that it's not a dream—"

"*The battle lines are being drawn, and I do not say that in the end Anyeta will be defeated, but we cannot let her take us—one by one— like so many cards drawn from the deck and thrown away—*"

One by one—the phrase was like the dead march of wooden feet. Mimi was a shell—easily crushed. Joseph was gone. She was going to kill us all. The room went hazy, my mind was spinning.

"*The sorceress wants Lenore, and you are the only one standing in her way now, Imre*"

I was numb with dread. "You can't! You can't abandon us. Please." My voice broke. "For Lenore—"

"*I tell you,*" Joseph shouted, "*she will raise me up and have it all from me— every last thing. If you cannot destroy the body for my sake— then do it for your own. The more she learns of what lies in the future, the harder your task will be.*"

"What task?"

I thought he smiled—a little sadly—and I flushed guiltily. Christ, this is what Anyeta plots and fumes over.

"*The dead have secrets, Imre. They see into the minds and hearts of humans. They see what has been and what will be—*"

I felt a wavering, a rippling sensation that coursed through both my body and my mind, and I saw the Empress Elizabeth, years from now it seemed to me. She was still thin, but the light in her blue eyes was mostly gone. She was dressed in mourning, wearing no ornament but a heavy necklace of black wooden beads; a small medallion held a rosette that had been woven from pale human hair. *My boy. Rudolph.* Her fingers stroked the silken hair, the touch brought her the bitter mix of comfort and grief. As suddenly as it came, the odd vision left, seeming nearly to fade from my memory—

"*But let the future be a dark veil for you. Some things are better not known. And that is as God wills it.*"

Against my skin the ring seemed to burn like thin fire.

"*Mimi needed help. I gave it. Now I'm asking you to be strong, to give me the peace I seek.*"

I closed my eyes. *Please*, I begged inwardly, bearing down hard on the flat gold seal, *Not gentling.* I slid my jaw forward, grinding my teeth.

"*There are other ways,*" Joseph said evenly. "*Tomorrow, Constantine will make the casket. You will go to the town to make arrangements with a priest. And you must be quick. Before he reads the service there are certain things I want you to do . . . .*"

And then he went on to describe a destruction so horrible, for the first time I wondered if gentling might not be easier.

45

I was on my way into town to see a blonde-haired middle aged priest Joseph had described to me. I knew he was going to refuse Joseph burial in the churchyard, but I went to ask him anyway. I glanced down at the old man's ring, his voice whirred impatiently inside me.

"This priest is very devout—he'd say no, even if you offered him enough gold to bury twenty men, and tell you if the bishop got wind of it, they'd only have to dig the body up again, but go ahead and ask him. There are eavesdroppers in his rectory—"

I walked along in the pale sunlight and sharp wind, pulling my coat tighter against my chest. "What difference does it make then?" I whispered.

"The priest will confirm we're Catholic, that I wanted to be buried in consecrated ground. That even if we are gypsies, the townspeople have nothing to fear."

There's been no trouble, why should they suddenly be afraid?

"There's talk in the town—in the bars, the taverns, the shops—that the wolves are running. Farmers speak of finding gutted sheep, maimed cattle. Winter is hard upon the land, and when their prey grows scarce, the wolves seek weakness among men. Already there are rumors that the child attacked in the alleyway that night was set on by a wolf that the neighbors frightened away."

"But it was us—we ran, Mimi and I—" He cut me off.

"So much the worse. Watch their faces, Imre, they believe a gypsy can turn himself at will into a wolf or a fox. There is danger here—not just from the old sorceress, but in the very heart of this country itself."

The road turned to cobbles under my feet, I moved through the narrow lanes, heading toward the church. For the first time, I felt the eyes of the townspeople looking through me, and I wondered if Joseph was right, if they were afraid. I tried to seem casual, but I watched closely to see if they forked the evil eye or blessed themselves quickly when I passed. If they were calling on those old superstitions, I didn't see it—but their faces were edgy, lined with a tension I hadn't noticed before.

I saw the steeple of the stone church looming ahead and I passed under an old archway into the cobbled square.

"*The priest is inside hearing confessions,*" Joseph whispered. "*Look sad, light a candle, the old women who pray there notice everything.*"

I hesitated briefly, then climbed a set of bulky stone stairs and opened the heavy iron-shod church door, reminding myself this was the easy part. I laid aside the fear of what was yet to come.

There was a small glass votive lamp flickering on a stand mounted outside the confessional box. It burned with an eerie blue light. Joseph was right, the priest was still inside, and now and then I caught the sound of muted voices begging forgiveness.

Keeping one eye out for the priest, I knelt at the nearest side altar, my mind spinning on what the old man wanted me to do, his words racketing through my head.

"*Oil of vitriol,*" Joseph had said. "*But they won't sell it to you. You'll have to break in to steal it—*"

"Why?" I'd asked, a low dread winding through me.

"*Because . . .*"

Now trying to stop the flow of memory, I glanced up at the altar. There was a painted statue of Christ, his sensitive fingers cupped to show the Sacred Heart—a brilliant red the color of fresh blood, the gilded rays around the heart like daggers. I was suddenly overcome by the heat, the thick smell of melting wax from the ranks and ranks of burning candles. My head tipped forward giddily, and I let it rest on the edge of the cool marble rail. It's not the heavy suffocating air making you queasy, I told myself, or a gruesome statue. It was hearing his voice in my head—

"*They won't sell it to you because oil of vitriol is concentrated sulfuric acid.*"

It was knowing what Joseph wanted me to do—

My fingers were clasped, but now they jerked and twisted together in a painful spasm. The exposed heart in the statue seemed like a live thing, beating and pulsating. And for a brief instant I had a hideous vision of molten flesh, of a ruined body that was a shifting tide of bubbling blood and white bone and rippling skin. Oh Christ, I thought, Joseph was right, the acid would destroy him.

I heard the soft swish of velvet and I turned to see the priest brushing the purple drape of the confessional box aside. He blew out the candle, and I moved toward him.

We sat in the priest's tiny overheated office in the rectory. "You understand," he said. "The church forbids it. And if my bishop were to somehow hear of it . . . ."

I nodded absently, brushing at a tear and thinking Joseph knew, he knew what the priest would say. *The dead have secrets.*

"And the villagers," he sighed. "You know Romanians, they're so superstitious." The priest spread a pair of hairy, freckled hands, gave me a look that said we know better, you and I, but what can I do—

I'd tuned him out then, my mind repeating the word acid, acid— like a dirty refrain, my mouth dry with terror.

I glanced up and saw his blond head bobbing. "Yes, I'll be there the day after tomorrow," he was saying. "I don't imagine there'll be many mourners, but can you arrange to have the casket brought to the potter's field?"

"A potter's field," I repeated. I looked down at the gold ring, and twisted it as I'd seen Joseph do a thousand times. My hands were moist with an oily sweat and it turned easily. *Are you sure you want him?* I asked inwardly.

"He's the pastor. His word will carry weight."

I saw the priest's mouth moving, my own face felt tight and stretched and I guessed I was giving him a fool's grin.

Let the future be a dark veil.

We moved across the room. Like a sleepwalker I put a numb hand out to say goodbye. But his blue eyes suddenly darted toward the doorway. Something creaked in the hall.

The priest put his finger to his lips, motioning me to be silent, and cat-quick he yanked the door wide. A fat housekeeper with bulging eyes was in the act of straightening up. Her ear had been laid against the keyhole I guessed, and she'd mistimed the end of our conversation.

"Well?" the priest said, glaring at her. "Haven't I told you if I caught you spying out here again you were out of a job?"

She stared back, and her hands, holding a feather duster went to her wide hips. "You ain't going to read service over one of tem," she challenged, pointing to me.

"They're God's children too," the priest said evenly.

"Eh. More like devil's spawn. Didn't my own Lidia say to me dere wass a gyp woman peering down at her son when she walked the child in hiss carriage? Wheedling around, the gyp was. Marking de boy. Lidia said if she turn her back one instant de *untdelmn* gyp would snatch the baby!"

"Don't be ridiculous—" the priest began.

The housekeeper ignored him. "Look to your missus, gypsy! If even one small thing happens to my grandboy you will answer to my man! And we will have your head on a plate same as John the Baptist." Her face, under its crown of pale carroty braids, went a dark dangerous red.

The priest hustled me out the door past the raving housekeeper. I heard a hawking sound from deep in the well of her throat, felt a thin splattering on my coatsleeve.

Joseph was right I thought, the townspeople were afraid. I couldn't ever remember being spit on. I glanced down and saw the sticky globule, feeling a low disgust.

"Forget it, get out, get the acid," Joseph urged, and I left the rectory.

The church bell tolled eight, and from the sheltering recess of a store front, I watched the apothecary across the way locking his shop. He pocketed the key, hefted a lumpy sack higher in his arms, and moved off down the street. He stopped, briefly, speaking with a tall-hatted watchman. Their voices in the dark seemed loud and grating.

I had a quick mental flash of the acid hissing and smoking, and I shoved my fear—of handling the dense clear liquid, of getting caught—aside. I clenched my fist, leaned against the door, deeper in the shadows, waiting for them to pass so I could get on with what Joseph wanted me to do.

I heard the watchman tap his stick and bid the apothecary a good night. He walked past me, whistling softly.

I moved out from the shadows, crossing the narrow wet street, and my anxiety rose with each quickening step.

The apothecary hadn't left any lights burning in his small shop. I took a deep breath, then leaned my forehead against the cool glass. "Don't make me do this," I whispered, but there was no answer from Joseph now, only silence that seemed as sharp as an admonition.

The front window was a tall three-sided bay lined with shelves. I could dimly make out the shapes of glass jars and canisters filled with murky liquids that would show green or red or blue by daylight. None of it was acid, I was sure— that would be kept in the back. Still, it was going to make a hell of a noise and a huge mess when I broke in.

I had a vision of slipping on the floor and getting badly cut, or worse, hurrying on the way out and falling on and shattering the bottle of acid. People died from acid burns. I felt the muscles tic in my jaw. I remembered hearing about a man who was hanged for murder; the vitriol thrower, they called him—

"Break the glass," Joseph said, cutting in on my thoughts.

I stood sideways to the narrow panel nearest the door and wadded my coat protectively around my right elbow. I got my shoulder into the swing, bunching the muscles of my forearm, and battered my elbow against the glass, shattering the window, sending apothecary jars to the floor with a wet crash.

In the deserted street the sound was very loud. I hesitated, waiting for lights or the watchman's shout, but there was nothing.

Broken glass crunched under my feet. I reached through the window, toppling another shelf lined with heavy bottles.

"*Be quick,*" Joseph urged; I ducked through the window and entered the shop.

There was a door behind the long wooden counter; I opened it, feeling carefully along the jamb on the right. Most people are right handed, if they hang a lantern or tinderbox inside a doorway, it's almost always on that side. My fingers brushed a round bulbous shape that was glass, I heard the soft screak of a metal handle. The apothecary used a lantern. I shut the door and lit a match, then took the lamp from the hook.

I was in a kind of windowless closet with yellow plaster walls. The air was heavy with the fumes of drugs and chemicals. There was a workbench littered with small vials, stacks of paper labels, instruments for rolling and cutting pills. Next to it sat a deep gray stone sink under a set of crude shelves crammed with hundreds of pottery crocks, sacks filled with herbs, jars and bottles. Nothing labeled, everything helter-skelter, it would take me a day to paw through the apothecary's stock.

Where is it?

There was a pause, as if the old man were scanning the shelves with a wary eye.

"*Top right, the brown glass bottle.*"

I reached up, took it down. The dark bottle had a long thin neck and wire clamps over the stopper to prevent accidental spills, I guessed. When it was topped up it might have held a liter, but it was only about a quarter full. I held it up to look more closely, tipping the bottle gently, then bringing it upright. The liquid sloshed softly against the side, then shifted back and forth like the motion of a small evil tide. My stomach suddenly rolled, and I felt drops of sweat breaking out under my arms.

"There isn't much—" I started to say.

"*—Enough . . .*"

"It wouldn't take long. I could look around, he might have quicklime—"

"*There's enough—for the purpose.*"

I grasped his meaning at once, and closed my eyes, feeling sicker at the thought, at the same time I chided myself inwardly. Christ, what did you imagine it would be like, did you think you could just toss him in a vat of the stuff? Would that be easier? I groaned. It was ridiculous, but it was true. The mind is such an endless rationalizer, capable of absurd distinctions: It would be a lot less horrible to drop him into a barrel—as if the liquid were nothing more malignant than water; a lot *less* terrible to stand by the pit of his grave shoveling quicklime that you could pretend to yourself wasn't all that different from earth. But in this one slim bottle, there was—

Enough

—Just enough to gelatinize the tissue of his face, to eat through the muscle, the bone, sink hissing, deep into the brain.

"Oh dear God," I whispered, my fingers trembling around the neck of the bottle. I can't do this. I wanted to hurl it into the stone sink and rush from the place. I clutched the bottle, raised my arm . . . but his voice rooted me to the spot.

"*This is my wish. And you have to be strong for Constantin's sake, Imre.*"

A sound that was part laugh, part sob caught in my throat. "Constantin. He'll fight me to the death before he'll let me do this, old man."

"*He will understand if it comes from me. You know the old Romany saying, half gypsy: The soul remains with the body?*"

"Yes," I said, feeling as though he'd wrung the word from me. I lowered the bottle calmly, as if in a dream, blew out the lantern, found myself ambling like a sleepwalker slowly through the door.

"*When I'm truly gone, I want you to give the ring to Constantin. It will bring him comfort—for a while.*"

But when you're gone, when we—I do this, I grimaced, *he won't hear anything, will he?* I asked, barely aware of the sound of my heels tapping over the shop floor, crunching shards of glass underfoot.

"*Do you tell the child that the friend he imagines he can hear, see, talk to isn't there? Constantin is like a child, and he will think of me and speak to me, and—*"

What's that old gypsy saying? When the last person who remembers you dies, you die again, I said, fingering the gold ring, feeling my irritation rise. *Tell the truth!* I demanded. *You want me to give him the ring because you're afraid, because that old saying comforts you!* A gust of cold air peppered my cheeks.

"Yes," he breathed.

And for a second, I felt a kind of triumph. And then I realized he'd made me angry intentionally to mask my fear. His will was stronger than mine. I'd wanted to smash the glass, hurl the vile stuff into the chemist's sink, but I was already on the deserted sidewalk, hurrying along, the brown bottle of sulfuric acid cradled safely in my arms.

46

I saw the glow of torchlight first, then as I neared the caravan I heard the zith of a planing tool, the sound of hammering. Constantin was fitting the last few boards for Joseph's coffin. I saw him bent at the work, his face red with cold, his nose streaming. He set the hammer down and pulled a handkerchief from under the end of his sleeve, ruffled it under his nostrils, then shoved it into his pocket. I stood in the shadows, watching awhile. He worked with the plane, a spray of shavings followed the sweep of his hands, and I realized there was a kind of tenderness in his gestures. Performing a final service, he wanted to honor his friend, and he had: Joseph's casket wasn't a crude knocked-up thing. The joints were beautifully dovetailed, the surface, even without finishing touches, was smooth, the wood grain gleamed.

I rubbed my fingers over the gold ring. I knew it was the last time, the last night he might ever have with Joseph. I wanted that for Constantin. I slipped the ring off.

He turned when I called to him, resting his broad hands on the planked lid, then he pointed at me, mimed a quick genuflection, crossing himself. "You see—?"

"The priest?" I asked, and he nodded. "Yes. The funeral's in two days. In a potter's field."

"Fu-fiel?"

"A place for outcasts, paupers, nameless nobodies. It's going to be bleak," I said, trying not to think of what I knew would be harder still. "It's cold tonight. You want me to finish this?" I tapped my fingers against the open edge.

"I—I finish—" He tapped his rounded chest, then rolled his wide eyes toward the caravan. "For him."

I took his hand, turned it over, then laid Joseph's ring in the center of his palm. "You keep him tonight."

"Nu-uh," he shook his head back and forth.

"Yes," I said, closing his fingers around the ring, and insisting. "Yes."

He cocked his head, gave me a questioning look.

"Talk to him," I said. "Go on."

Constantin closed his fingers around the ring and shut his eyes. A soft hum welled up in his throat, passed his lips—the sound of a man suddenly in possession of the thing he wants most in the world. The corners of his mouth came up in a wide grin. Then he nodded, jauntily shaking the gold ring closed in his hand like a pair of dice. He opened his eyes and smiled at me. "O-kay. I keep."

When I went toward the caravan, he was leaning against the edge of the casket, listening eagerly. I heard him laugh, looked over my shoulder to see him wipe tears of mirth from his eyes. He chuckled again, picked up the plane, and nodding cheerfully as he listened to the last echoes of Old Joseph's voice, plied it with long careful strokes.

Constantin had left a lamp burning in the old man's caravan, and I guessed Lenore was there when I saw her berth was empty. I made my way down the steps to stand awhile by Joseph's body. He was lying on the bed dressed in the black jacket and trousers that were too big for his gaunt frame. I saw Constantin had knotted a brilliant red silk *diklo* around his throat, neatly tucking the ends of the scarf.

It was only his body and nothing more, I told myself, there was nothing for me to hear; after tomorrow there would be nothing for Constantin, either. Guiltily, I removed the bottle of acid I'd hidden in the folds of my coat. The liquid had an oily, viscous look. Sinister. I swallowed uneasily, and now I was suddenly afraid to look at Joseph's ashen face, to think about what he wanted of me, but my mind seized on small details—unearthing the casket, opening the wooden lid, standing over the night-darkened skin, removing the glass stopper, seeing the vitriol ooze up along the sides—

"Don't do it, Imre."

Mimi's voice startled me. I gave a shudder, my hand shook, and I felt the glass skitter between my sweat damp fingers. My heart lurched, I flailed with the other hand, catching it. The glass pinged lightly into my palm, my clutching fingers. I let out a long exhale, swore under my breath.

She was standing in the shadows at the top of the stairs looking in. Her clothes hung flapping as if she were made of sticks instead of flesh and blood. Her black hair was a mare's nest of whorls and spikes. Her eyes were glazed, great hollows like bruises shone out against the pale skin.

"Don't do it," she said again. Her gaze drifted toward Joseph, then swung back to me, and I understood at once she meant the destruction of the body. I felt my face go white. Christ, I thought, it's Anyeta.

She gave me a sickly grin. "It's me, Mimi," she whispered, moving toward me into the pool of lamplight. She put one hand out, and it was then I saw both her arms were bound with strips of ragged bloody gauze.

"No," I said, taking a step backwards; in my mind's eye I saw her in the trance stabbing herself. Joseph's words rose up in my head. *Anyeta is afraid of pain, but what will you do the first time you find your wife, knife in hand, to keep the sorceress at bay?* "Oh God," I murmured, wincing. Beneath one of the unraveling strips I saw the edge of a crusted wound oozing a mix of blood and wet yellowish pus.

"You know it's me," she said, holding her hands out like a woman submitting meekly to being bound. "Here is my proof." Her face was weary, her shoulders bent. "That I'm here now, speaking with you, standing by his bed has cost me more suffering than I hope you'll ever know."

"Why, Mimi?" A soft moan rolled between my lips, I let one finger lightly trace the gauze, and she flinched.

"Anyeta's getting stronger," Mimi said. "That's part of it. But I wanted to be here—for Joseph, for what happened to him and my part in it. But also for Lenore." She gave a little smile seeing the stunned expression on my face. "Lenore loved Joseph, Imre."

Christ, I'd run out of the caravan this morning and hadn't even thought of Lenore's reaction. She must've seen Constantin making the casket, I thought. "How did she take it?"

"I found her in here this morning, barefoot and in her nightgown. She came running in when she saw the caravan parked here— she thought it was a surprise—that we were both here, that I was well."

I flushed guiltily.

"Apparently she screamed when she saw the body. But by the time I came in, she'd calmed down. She was holding Constantin's hand. They were like two children helping one another be brave, and he was telling her not to be afraid. Lenore tied the red scarf around his neck and placed the pipe in his hand." She paused.

"I didn't want to upset her. I told her Joseph had a stroke and she accepted that."

"What about these," I said, nodding toward the white bandages.

"She doesn't see them, Imre," Mimi said. "I don't let her."

"You—"

She cut me off, bristling. "I have some power, yet." Her eyes met mine darkly. "Did you see through Zahara?"

"No," I said huskily.

She nodded. "All right then. Weak and damaged as you see me—as I am— today at least, my daughter had the mother she needed. At the funeral we'll mourn his end together—"

His end. Not the sane ritual of a funeral I thought; no, funerals are pretty. His end would be the wild work he demanded from me. "Why did you say I shouldn't—destroy him?" I said, my voice sinking to a whisper..

She shook her head back and forth. "I don't know." She squeezed her eyes shut, her mouth was drawn tight. "Something with Anyeta—but I don't know what. The idea makes her . . . restless, angry."

I felt myself go cold, thinking if she says anything more I'll never do it. "Please. Don't make this worse for me."

"All right," she said quietly. "I'll keep Anyeta out of the way." She laid her small hand against my cheek sweetly, briefly. I kissed the palm, knowing what she meant to do. I saw her straighten her shoulders—bravely, I thought; and then she turned and left the room.

A little while later I heard the sound of her breath coming in short hard gasps. There was the sharp high whisk of a knife being drawn rapidly against flesh. She gave a grunt, and I cringed, thinking of her pain.

I hung my head, laced my fingers in my lap. Then I heard the slash again and closed my eyes, knocking my palms one against the other in frustration.

God wills it.

I glanced at the old man's corpse; his gaunt features looked softer in the dim light, as if he were at peace.

Some things in the future are better not known, not seen.

I didn't have to see into the other room—see my wife— to know that from her gashed wrists the blood spattered, and made a pattern of round spots and thick drops that were shining darkly on the floor.

47

When it came to a funeral, the Roms spared no expense; and Constantin had fitted out four of the horses with waving black plumes and brand new leather traces studded with round brass medallions. We put the open casket on a sledge and the team dragged it into the woods. Now in the gathering twilight, we'd come to say goodbye— Mimi, Constantin and I. Mimi brushed Joseph's pale cheek with the tips of her fingers. She leaned over and kissed his bluish lips.

This was the funeral (wild work!) before the funeral, I thought, looking at the old man lying in the coffin; but Constantin didn't know it yet.

I'd taken Joseph's signet ring from Constantin earlier. Now I pressed the gold, felt the metal cutting deep in my flesh. *Help me.*

Please, I whispered inwardly. *Give me strength, because this is going to break his heart.*

Mimi stepped back slowly, and I felt the weight of a terrible sorrow, knowing it was time.

"*Tasaulor,*" I began, putting my hand on Constantin's shoulder, "tomorrow, after the funeral we're going to leave. I'll hitch the wagons in tandem, then all of us will go back to Hungary. So this is a kind of good bye—a private ceremony, just for us—not like tomorrow in the field—"

His round jaw dropped, his mouth gaped in growing panic. "Leave?" he shouted. "No! No fiel! No f—ff-un-ral! No 'lone!" His hand fell heavily on the coffin edge. "No 'lone! No leave! You take heem!" He pounded the wood with the flat of his palm.

I thought of the acid wrapped in my cape, lying nearby on the grass and for a fleeting instant I considered it. We could go now, take Joseph with us, I thought excitedly—

(Let the future be a dark veil.)

—But the priest was expecting us, fleeing would arouse suspicion and they'd be on our trail like a pack of bloodhounds. "No," I shook my head.

"No 'lone," he sobbed.

Alone. I thought of the old man in the potter's field with its patches of bare, humped earth. The rows of rotting wooden crosses. His body would lie in an unmarked grave, far from all of us. He would be unknown, nameless. Year after year, the seasons would do their slow silent work.

Constantin was right. There's no sadder feeling than the thought of someone you love buried away in the earth, away from sunlight. Alone—

"No 'lone for Joseph," Constantin moaned.

"Talk to him," I said slowly, holding the glittering ring out toward Constantin. *When the last person who remembers you dies*, I thought, *you die again*. I cleared my throat. "Tell Joseph we love him. Tell him we will remember. He lives in our memories. And we carry him with us—always—in our hearts." I felt a spurt of painful grief—for the old man, for Constantin—rise bitterly on my tongue.

The wind gusted up, blowing the old man's hair in a random silver spray, fluting the dark clothes of his suit. They lifted lightly flapping in the breeze, and it was a terrible sound, the sound of loneliness. *Joseph*, I begged, *you promised. You've got to tell him. Please*, I said, and inwardly I felt him nod.

The ring left my fingers, and Constantin clutched it to his chest.

He stood by the coffin, murmuring, one hand nervously stroking the old man's white hair. His eyes were wet with crying, the lashes matted.

I felt Mimi's fingers twine in mine, squeezing.

"*Nuh*," Constantin said suddenly, in his broken guttural voice. His head tipped backward and he bayed. "No! Joseph! No! D-on't make me!"

The image of the brown bottle and hissing acid rose before me. I felt a thick lump in my throat. Oh God help me, I thought. I knew what Constantin was hearing.

"Take him away," I whispered hoarsely. "I'll do it."

Mimi moved toward him, her face grim. She spoke low in his ear. "NO!" he screamed sinking to his knees. He threw his arms out and clung to the side of the coffin. After a long time, she helped him up. His face was ghostly, his eyes blind with helpless terror, his fingers clutching her arm hard enough to turn his knuckles white.

They moved past me, deeper into the shadows. I stooped down and slowly began unwrapping the brown bottle. The glass was a dark gleam, the wire clamps shone dull silver. I stood up, holding the bottle by its neck, my fingers trembling against that cold narrow throat. I stepped closer to the casket, my heart thudding like some awful battering ram trying to shatter the walls of my chest.

There was a metallic click when I forced the wire clamps apart; the silky rasp of glass on glass as I drew out the stopper. I held my breath and heard the blood singing in my ears.

"*I do not want the sorceress to profane my body. Give me peace. Be my son.*"

I looked on Joseph's face for the last time, while behind me Constantin's cries filled the night.

Time seemed to stop. I saw the acid pour from the spout, followed its sparkling trail down and down. When it struck the flesh with a crackling sound, I turned my face away. A thin steam rose up, and on its white smoke I smelled blood. The vitriol foamed and bubbled. I shut my eyes, but I knew that with each quick hiss, it ate inward more deeply. Under my upraised arm, I felt a dreadful heat being given off, a sickly warmth that penetrated the cloth of my jacket and made my skin clammy. My stomach churned, I couldn't bear the rank smells, the sound of that viscous gurgling any longer; and finally I twisted my wrist sharply and upended the bottle.

The last drops sputtered out, then I raised my arm and flung the bottle as hard as I could. It struck a tree, and I heard the glass shatter with a thick pop.

My mouth went dry. I broke out in a fit of shivering so hard the spasms wracked me. I sat heavily, my face turned up to the sky, my back slumping against the casket. The stars began to flicker, and I watched the dazzle of bluish light. In a little while I was aware the low seething sounds inside the coffin had stopped and I knew he was gone. It was over.

I did not look. I shut the lid softly, my fingernails clicking lightly on the wood, my mind conjuring his gaunt face, his dark penetrating eyes. Driven out, he'd left Hungary all those years before. Now his end was here in the woods above Sibiu, where Strauss had been feted and Liszt had played tunes stolen from gypsies. Everything, I ruminated sadly, is taken—bit by cruel bit—from each of us. We're all of us, always on the edge of bereavement. His life, his time had been measured by loss; and I'd lost him.

When the last person who remembers you dies, I thought, *you die again.* Bending low, I wet my lips and whispered. "Here there is a body, but in our memories, Joseph—in our hearts and memories lives the man."

I caressed the top of the coffin briefly, and my tears came suddenly and fell in a hot rain.

48

I woke to a brilliant yellow glare, and at first I thought it was the morning sun streaking through the glass. Torchlight. I was alone. Mimi was gone. I sat up in the dark, my heart suddenly pounding, listening to the sound of snapping twigs, voices shouting. There was a sharp crack, another. The sound of padding feet whispering on the grass. The lights receded in the distance.

Seconds later something first brushed, then caromed into the side of the caravan, and I felt us rocking lightly on the wheels. Through the thin walls came a husky, labored breathing.

I crept to the door, jerked it open. She lay on her back, sprawling on the tiny wooden stoop, one bare foot plunged into an icy puddle at the foot of the stairs. Mimi rolled her eyes up at me. "Help me, Imre," she breathed. "Don't let Lenore see me like this." Her dress was soaked in blood. There were dark shiny splashes on the steps and dripping off the short rail.

It was then I saw she was cradling her elbow, her face fierce with pain. She moved her hand aside, a small geyser of blood bubbled between her fingers, and I realized she'd been shot.

"What happened?" It was still too early to risk a light. I had summoned Constantin and together we bandaged the wounded arm as best we could. Lenore was sleeping in his caravan. Mimi sat propped on a mound of pillows sipping hot tea.

Closing her eyes, she leaned back against the headboard. "Anyeta came to the fore when I fell asleep," she said. "I couldn't help it. I saw her get out of bed, moving softly, careful not to wake you."

I grunted. "Then what?"

"She was angry. I don't know."

"Don't know—or won't say—" I said, pacing toward the window, then pointing out. "Those men shot you—they were chasing you."

"No, her," Mimi said in a tight voice. "Anyeta used her power and sent them away, confused them. Then she left me to deal with the pain."

"What put them on her trail, Mimi?" I fumed. Constantin made a coughing noise, and when I glanced at him he gave me a signal, saying, patience. "Can you heal the wound?" I asked more gently.

"No." Mimi whispered, her eyes dark with fear. "She'll come out."

I raked my hand through my hair, then moved alongside her. I took her good hand in mine. "Try and remember as much as you can," I said, and she nodded slowly.

"Anyeta—she was, she was in the woods."

"What do you see?"

"Nothing. I can't see anything, but I feel her." She shuddered. "She was boiling. Furious." Mimi's eyes opened wide in terror. "I hear the sound of hinges creaking. It's Joseph's casket." She cringed. "Oh my God, oh God, I hear her voice," Mimi said, suddenly fixing her gaze on Constantin.

I followed her eyes. He was sitting quietly on the chair, idly toying with the old man's ring as it swung on a ribbon against his dark shirtfront.

"No, no." She moaned, staring at the ring, winking and bobbing in the dim light.

"What is she saying, Mimi?"

Her voice, when it came, had a sickly sound. "She's saying over and over, '*I will wear your daughter like a bauble on a string around my neck.*'"

None of us said a word. In the dreadful silence that seemed to fill the room we felt the weight of the sorceress' revenge. Anyeta had been running with the wolves.

Constantin's face went white in the early morning light. He nudged me, pointing at the print of a bloody palm against the pale gray trunk of a thin sapling. Anyeta or Mimi had leaned against it, resting, I thought.

"Me-mee," he said, miming a pistol shot. "We-ak."

I nodded. It was the second or third smear we'd come on. "Christ, how much blood did she lose?" I said, lighting a cigarette to calm my nerves.

"Nuh," he said, lifting his eyes along the leaf-choked path ahead. He made a gobbling sound, hooked his hands into claws, and I found myself looking at the red spatters and droplets splashed along the trail. He was saying not all of the blood was my wife's—some of it had come from the kill. Joseph's words circled round and round my head. *First animals, then children.* Through the gray foggy shadows, I could make out the dark boxy shape of the old man's casket in the distance. My stomach cramped, and I ground out the cigarette, feeling a thick nausea.

We walked on, our boots slipping through the fallen rotting leaves. I saw a patch of hair stuck to a white stone. No, dear Christ, I begged, thinking of the men chasing Mimi through the woods, praying somehow it had been angry farmers who found the remains of sheep, cattle.

I stood beside the casket, my hand trembling. The lid was closed. Just behind my shoulder Constantin's warm breathing misted the air. I didn't want him to see the old man's remains, and I made him step aside.

Now I saw Joseph's coffin was covered with dark wet streaks I told myself might be night damp or beads of dew. No, it looks sticky, the wary part of my mind countered. But I shoved that notion aside, trying to convince myself it was new wood, the planks were bleeding sap, oozing . . . but in my heart I knew it wasn't so, I knew it was blood and with a moan I raised the lid.

"Oh JesusfuckingChrist!" I hissed.

A child's face stared up at me. The body was folded in on itself, like an overgrown fetus nested in the womb of the coffin. Skinny wrists crossed, small blue bumps of knees drawn high on the chest, it lay curled just above Joseph's shoulders—above the tattered shreds of burned cloth. It was there, the tiny back pressed against the acid scarred boards. Anyeta was vicious, this was a sickening grotesquerie, I thought, holding my breath: The child lay in that vast empty place—just where his head would have been.

I slammed the lid down.

"Oh Christ on the cross." This ravaged baby was little more than a year old. There was blood on its skin, but I wouldn't let myself think about the source of the wounds. No. Didn't want to envision the ragged marks inflicted by teeth—

The gorge rose in my throat, I leaned to vomit a thin sour stream that splatted weakly on the brown wind sucked leaves. I was on my hands and knees, unaware of the icy ground, my head rocked, my body swayed and I vomited over and over until there was nothing left in my belly.

"For I am the resurrection and the life," the blonde haired priest intoned.

Joseph's coffin rested alongside a shallow pit of a grave. My eye drifted over the wood that gleamed in the pale sunlight. We'd cleaned the blood up as best we could, I thought. My eye snagged at the large bleb of dark red wax I'd used to seal the lid. If you stared at it, you could make out his initial J where I pressed the signet in.

I wished the priest would hurry. I wondered if he knew he was reading the service over a child as well. Was it the housekeeper's grandson? We'd never

know, I guessed. The wind gusted up and I shivered. The baby curled above his .
. . above Joseph's—I closed my eyes, shut out the image.

My mind was hazy. It was the shock of these last days. I was tired, tired
unto death, I thought.

"He who believes in me lives forever," the priest said, his dark cassock
fanning out in the breeze. Constantin cried softly. I put my hand out and felt his
damp fingers twine through mine.

Both caravans—my bright green one and Joseph's canvas roofed wagon—
were parked too close to the rutted graveyard entry, looking gaudy, incongruous
I thought. Mimi was there, Lenore with her.

Mimi couldn't come to the service—not with a bandaged arm. The risk was
too great.

My gaze drifted to the far edge of the dismal field, past the rows of plain
wooden crosses, the patches of naked earth that were bare of any marker at all. I
saw three men walking slowly, eyes cast down; I wondered they could find the
graves of the friends they'd known.

"Grant him rest. We ask this in the name of the Christ Jesus, His Blessed
Mother, the apostles Peter and Paul, the holy martyrs, and all the company of
saints and angels who rest eternally in Your salvation." The priest's eyes were
closed, his chapped hands raised, palms out, to the level of his shoulders.

Constantin fingered the gold ring hanging on the cord, I saw a small ridge of
red wax clinging to the flat top. I glanced at the coffin, the mere scrape of a
grave. The ground was hard; the sextons had laid in a supply of stones and rocks
to cover up the casket and keep the scavengers away.

We were here, mourning Joseph again, I thought numbly. The priest droned
on. It didn't seem real. Lenore wanted to come. She cried when her mother and I
said no. We didn't speak of danger.

Behind me, I heard the two gravediggers shuffling their feet. One of them
absently scraped his shovel along the ground. The priest shook his head
frowning, and the man stopped.

After the funeral, this afternoon I was going to trade the horses—all of
them—for the swiftest team I could get. Then I'd hitch the wagons together and
we would leave right after—

I was suddenly aware of a soft spattering sound, like rain against glass. I
looked up to see the priest dipping a silver knobbed wand into a vessel of holy
water. He lifted it out, holding the slim tapered end, flicked it in time with his
voice, blessing the casket.

"In the name of the Father, the Son—"

He stopped. His eyes widened, and I saw his pink face turn a startling
deeper red. "What do you men want here?" he said.

I turned. Standing alongside the sextons were the three men I'd seen
walking through the field a few minutes ago.

"Why is the coffin sealed, Father?" A bearded man spoke up. His arms were crossed.

"How dare you profane this service? This is God's holy rite." The priest's blue eyes went hard.

He's the pastor. His word will carry weight. The old man's prophetic words roiled in me. The foggy dreaminess of the funeral scattered. I felt my pulse speed up. *Some things are better not known.*

"Gypsies always open the casket. Right by the grave." The bearded man gave me a sneering look, then he leaned over and spit on the ground. "They say good bye, they bury their dead with tools, clothes—all kinds of shit—"

"For the *journey*," a fat man with shaggy hair said. "In the *after-life.*"

It was true of course, and I'd sealed the casket in case the priest expected that gypsy ritual. I hadn't wanted him or one of the sextons to open it before I could—

"Christ, yes," one of the sextons murmured, tapping a rusted shovel. "Never seen one without they poured in wine and brandy. Even gold." His eye lit on the ring winking against Constantin's coat.

"But we're Catholics—not heathens," I said, turning away and motioning the priest to go on with the service.

The bearded man cut in. "There's a child gone," he said. "Know anything about it?" He stooped down, picked up a stone. He stood shifting it, almost casually, from hand to hand.

"We don't steal children," I said, deliberately twisting his meaning.

"Get out of here," the priest said. "There's an old man in the casket. A friend loved like a father. His name was Joseph, he was a Lovari, a horse dealer from Hungary." The priest put his hand on my shoulder. "And I tell you this man had tears in his eyes when he came to my church and spoke of his end."

The bearded man's eyes blazed. "That child was murdered. There was blood in its crib. Rudy here," he nodded toward the fat man, "shot at something in the woods last night. Where's the gyp woman? Huh? Why isn't she here?"

"My wife is ill—"

"Who sealed the casket? You?" He pointed at the priest, who shook his head. "I didn't think so."

"Give me your word," the priest said, "you had nothing to do with the child and I'll send these men away."

It was the barest of hesitations, I knew what they would find if they broke the seal and opened the lid. From the corner of my eye, I saw that now all three of them had sharp rocks.

"Give me your word, Imre," the priest said, stepping between us and the men. His fingers were very pale against the dark red of the seal.

"You stupid bastard! Get out of the way!" the bearded man screamed.

"Run," I shouted, yanking Constantin's arm, at the same time I saw a stone fly and strike the center of the priest's forehead. He swayed backwards, hands slipping over the smooth wooden coffin lid. There was a gout of blood, his blue eyes went glassy, his mouth dropped open. Then he toppled forward.

Panting, we ran for the caravan. I felt a rock sting the soft flesh of my ear. I got on the box, seized the whip and lashed the team, shouting. There was a hail of stones, the men gave chase screaming. One of the horses nickered in panic. We lurched forward, jolting over the curb and into the narrow street, then turned sharply heading toward the western road.

We were coming out of the turn when I heard the sound of gunfire. Behind me glass shattered in one of the windows, spraying onto the street. The horses pounded on. The men screamed obscenities, I saw their arms pumping furiously and I heard rocks pelting the wooden sides of the caravans.

It was then I turned to look at Constantin, white-faced, clinging to the box.

He looked at me, his lips moved slowly. His small hand came up, and he fumbled, grappling for Joseph's ring.

"Constantin," I said, seeing he was tugging at the folds of his coat.

"Im-re," he answered. The coat opened, and he tapped with one finger, pointing to the center of his muslin shirt.

A small star of blood bloomed there.

I felt a scream rise up out of my lungs. "NO! It can't be!"

The ring swayed against his chest; slowly he raised it toward his mouth. He pursed his lips to kiss it, and a bright red frothy bubble of blood burst between his parted teeth, then trickled down his chin.

His dark eyes sought mine. There was no fear, only a look behind the dulling light that said this was right, he would be with Joseph.

"No," I moaned. The caravans rolled past the cobbles and onto the dirt road. We were out of danger now; I thought sadly, we nearly made it, we were so close. The horses slackened their pace to a plodding walk.

In my mind's eye I saw Joseph the day we'd come to Romania, all those months before, his hooded eyes had been filled with a mystery I knew now was love. *I take care of him, Imre—as much as one man can care for another.*

"Oh, Christ, Constantin, don't—don't die now. You've got to stay with us." I swallowed, tasting salty tears. "Please," I said, groping for his small thick hand.

A faint smile touched his lips. His hand found mine.

He shook his head. "No leave Joseph," he whispered, and his eyes sank closed. "I stay. Jos—eph. No 'lone."

Under my fingers I felt the ebbing thread of his pulse, and I clutched him tighter. There was a huge erratic throb; and then, nothing more.

49

We drove west toward Gradistea, a remote place high above ancient pre-Roman ruins. Two days after we made camp, I began to dig the grave under an enormous beech tree on the edge of the woods. There was the smell of snow in the air, and the work was hard and heavy, my hands raw with the cold. There were no sounds except the grut of the metal shovel against the earth, the soft pattering spill of whatever soil I could dredge out. The sky grew darker and I hurried through the rest of the task; gathering stones to mound over the grave, carving their names, the date into the flesh of the tree. The epitaph was an afterthought, the words of a poem I recalled from childhood.

January 1864

Joseph of the Lovari and Constantin, a seer

Give us long rest or death, Dark death—or dreamful ease.

I thought it suited each of them well, knowing each of them had wanted the peace of the dark death—the dreamless sleep. And if there was awareness beyond death—then I wished for the other sort of peace: that they might lie in their easy dreams together.

At noon I'd set off to return to the potter's field, Lenore's and Mimi's voices rattling around in my head: You've got to go back for Joseph! None of us knew if Constantin had foreseen his own end, but his last thoughts had been with the old man. The huge sheltering tree was a place we would remember when we'd gone—something fixed to carry with us like a mental linchpin; but as the horse plodded on it began to snow, and I cast a wary eye toward the mountains. With each kilometer I began to feel more cut off, more isolated. I shivered under my cloak, the snow stung my skin, and as the heavy, muffled silence grew around me I knew we would never get through the icy steeps and snow-choked passes—not before spring.

By nightfall, the ground was covered, wrapping the potter's field in an undulating sweep of white that made the place seem emptier. I led the horse through the gate and saw at once that the townspeople had been at Joseph's coffin with hatchets. One joined corner stuck up out of the earth, like the ghostly hull of an old ship. In my lantern light I saw fragments of the red wax seal scattered over the snow, and I was half-afraid of finding his body hacked to pieces. But instead, they'd dumped him out. His body was a sprawled tangle of frozen limbs lying at the base of a low stone wall. Christ, they left him for carrion, I thought, wrapping him in a blanket I'd brought for the purpose. I had a mental picture of two greenish luminous eyes staring up at me over his body. A fox baring its teeth and slinking away. But there was nothing, and I hefted his body crosswise over the horse. We rode back carrying that uneasy weight, his loose-jointed limbs keeping time with the word carrion jouncing up and down in my brain. I recalled later that the word seemed to slice through me again and again with a peculiar intensity; of course, it's only later on that you can recognize a premonition for what it was.

We buried them together, their small grave marked with the heap of ancient gray stones rising out of the snow. I remembered the day, the anemic sun, Lenore's black hair fanning out in the breeze when she stooped down and wreathed the grave with a twig swollen with red winter berries. I traced the inscription carved into the old beech with my index finger, wished them well. I looked out over the bleak landscape above the ruined city with its silent monuments, toppled stones. There is always a deathly stillness in those places; it lies thick as a blanket, almost but not quite muting the awareness of once thriving life. As if only you turned quickly enough, you might catch sight of milkmaids laughing, men gathering in the squares, children roaming lanes and streets. It was both fitting and terrible that these two lay here, I thought. I remembered the day, the pale sun, the feel of those cold stones biting into my hands as I shaped the crude mound; but as the winter wore on cutting us off, and I had to shoot first one, then another of the horses for food, it was the huge tree that began to infiltrate my dreams. Mine and Mimi's—Anyeta was among us.

"Imre, Imre!"

I was startled out of a ragged sleep, could feel the sheets were damp and Mimi was huddled close by, trembling. The front door to the caravan was open; a chill March wind swirled across the threshold, the door swung on its hinges, and I heard the green curtain flapping. She's been out again I thought, at the same time her fingers closed on my wrist. They were cold and slick. I sucked in my breath, afraid it was blood and flinched away before I could stop myself.

"No, I was sweating," she said, leaving my fear unspoken between us. "It was a dream—a nightmare." Her voice trailed off, and I got up, closed the door, then lit a candle, and even in the soft light I could see her face was haggard. Her hair clung to her scalp in strings, her nightdress stuck to the damp skin. "I'm cold," she said, shivering, and the thought flashed through me that she was wet with being out of doors, that it wasn't perspiration.

"It's the same dream. Always the same, since the night you went back for Joseph. I'm afraid, but I can't stop it once it starts.

"There's a jagged flash of lightning, the sky and ground go silver bright and I see a towering tree, a heap of stones among the jumble of dark roots. And in the livid glare, I see a deep scar in the trunk where someone has carved their names and—"

"I have the same dream," I began, thinking their deaths last winter had left their mark on all of us.

"But Imre, how could I know . . ."

I stopped; my heartbeat seemed to fill the silence in the room.

"I wasn't there," she said.

"Lenore told you—"

She shook her head back and forth slowly. "Christ, I'm afraid." She bowed her head, her hair swung down covering her face. "The sounds," she whispered, "the sounds. The thick chunk of stone striking stone. White sheets fluttering in the wind. And then, then, the worst sound of all." She hugged herself. "I hear the wet snap of sinew and tendons, the soft purring sound of teeth ripping into decaying flesh." Her head came up, her mouth was drawn down in a rictus of fear and behind the begging look she gave me I saw the shadow of torment. "Oh Christ Jesus, help me."

Left him for *carrion*. "No," I said, feeling a sour nausea. "No, your hands, your legs, your nightdress—all clean!"

"Are they?"

I stared at her. None of us had been eating much, we'd all lost weight. And maybe it was a trick of the light, but it was then I saw that against her wasted thin body, her belly was blown out—hard and round and full—like the swollen gut of a man who eats meat once a year on a feast day, and cannot stop himself from gorging.

The rocks were scattered. One of the sheets I'd used as shrouds for their bodies was caught under a pile of the stony rubble; the other, a pale yellow in the early light, was a stiff, frozen wad; it lay partly revealed by the retreating snowcover.

I took a step nearer, and my stomach jolted. Their darkened skin had gone the color of bad wine. Constantin's face was glazed with an icy rime. His hair stuck out in white frosted clumps. His eyes were open as if he were terrified by his own destruction. The purplish cheek was gnawed through and I saw the whole length of the yellow teeth where the gums had receded. His throat was laid bare to the bone, the meat that was left looking clotted and torn. There were a few shredded bits of clothing here and there, but mostly their bodies were still clad. There was a long rent in Constantin's muddy shirt sleeve; it hung by threads where the tender flesh of the underarm was bitten through. Something had gone for the soft parts of both men. Joseph's innards were ripped wide, a forgotten hunk of intestine dangled near his hip. The white ends of the bones protruded through two of his fingers, gleaming against the sere black flesh.

Something picked them apart like carrion. My mind spun around Mimi's dream, the night in the potter's field and my knees buckled. I was hot and dizzy all at once. Not *something*, I groaned inwardly. I heard a harsh throaty caw, and a crow settled on the lowest limb of the tree, staring at me with bright black eyes, wishing me away. But it wasn't crows that had done this. They might peck at what had been exposed, but they hadn't moved those stones. No. Not crows or vixens or starving hunger-maddened dogs. Not something. It was Anyeta. And oh Christ, how was I going to tell Mimi?

Some part of her knew, I suppose; she'd climbed after me up the steep hillside. I'd stood over them a long while, twisting Joseph's ring against the flesh of my finger, my eye drawn again and again— unwillingly—to the carnage.

I wasn't listening for her. I didn't hear her at first, the snow muffled her slow steps. I heard her gasp and I turned, seeing her face go deadly white, taking all of it in at once. The huge beech tree she thought she'd seen in her nightmare, the fallen stones, the ruined bodies.

"Anyeta," I started to say, already regretting it...*when Anyeta comes out, where does your wife go? Does she watch, wait, sleep?* Thinking she can't live with this, not this guilt; she doesn't remember—not really. But she suddenly lunged forward and seized my shirtfront, clawing at me.

"Anyeta what! *What are you talking about?*" The spittle flew from her lips, her eyes blazed with a hellish light. The crow flapped off, its voice a rusty squeal.

"Anyeta—" I couldn't say the word, I flailed about uselessly, my voice sank, "took them—"

"She didn't! She couldn't have!" Mimi begged. There was a pause, and she turned her enormous violet eyes up to mine.

For her sake I wished it wasn't so. I nodded sadly.

Mimi's hands dropped away and she began to scream over and over.

She got through it, somehow she held on to herself and told me the story—the nightmare—that was her life all these long months since Anyeta had been running with the wolves. I like to think it was knowing I loved her that gave her the strength.

Because after that day, when we stood alone on the edge of the woods under a gunmetal gray sky near the ravaged grave she was often Mimi. But she never spoke again.

"I didn't know," she moaned, her face pressed down and against her palms. "I knew she was showing me the tree in my dreams for some reason, but I didn't know why." Mimi's thin hand snaked out and she clutched me. "Christ, you have to believe me, I swear it on Lenore's life, I didn't know!"

I swallowed uneasily, then nodded, and she went on.

"Anyeta—she let me see some of what happened when she killed—the animals—but never all of it. It was always distorted, like watching through bad glass. Things were wavy, sickening," she mewled, "but you never knew if you felt sick because of the glass or because of what you were seeing. I never tasted the blood—I think she was afraid I'd kill myself." Mimi licked her lips. "But I knew she loved it. She liked to feel the warmth, the wetness flowing over her—like a pampered woman naked in a spa. She liked to breathe the scent. Sometimes I woke up and found she'd cleaned herself off, and at first I would feel this chest-heaving relief. Then as I came more and more to myself, I would first become aware that my breath was foul, that my hands and arms were slightly sticky, and oh my Christ, I would realize she'd licked herself.

"I would hear a low evil snicker inside my head, and the fragmented image would come through. I'd see a blood covered hand, the pink tip of a tongue moving in the soft webbing between the fingers—lapping blood." Mimi looked up at me. "Do you know what she liked best—after killing— afterwards?" She faltered, I saw her mouth quiver, and felt an answering quiver inside.

"To take a man—to fuck him, Imre. She covered herself with perfume to hide the smell of the blood, and she rolled with a man; sometimes biting, always licking until all those smells mingled. Sex, dirt, blood. And then she slept.

"Each time I came up, I scrubbed myself. I ran to the river, not caring if the cold killed me. I plunged in, wearing clothes she'd stolen and bloodied. I stripped them off—watched them drift and snag on the downfalls and twigs, wash up against the rocks." She stopped, and I saw that her face looked blank, faraway, as if the image of the swift river water could blot out the terrible memories.

"But no matter how long I stayed in the icy water, no matter how much I rubbed myself raw, I couldn't undo her spells," she sighed.

"Pain helps. She's afraid of the hurt, and that holds her back— for a while." Mimi paused, slowly rubbing the gauze over the old wounds in her arm. "But it's a hard thing. It's hard to lose yourself,

your body—"

"I know."

"Do you?" Her voice was very mournful, and she shook her head. "I didn't think there was as much as that yet, I didn't think others saw it." Her hands flew up, pushing off a heavy fringed shawl, awkwardly tugging the neck of her dress. "Ah, God, where is it up to now?"

"Where is what?" I asked, but she was already going on, she couldn't hear me—

"To think she's turned me into an animal! To feel the stubborn creep of the beast flesh, to know I'm marked. Men will keep away," she nodded, biting her lip, "they will." She tore the dress apart, the buttons popping like fire crazed corn, and she looked down. "So much of me gone. Do you see it?"

My breath choked in my throat, my vision blurred and for a second, I did. Her chest was covered with a mat of thick black fur. Here and there, grayish patches of skin shone through. I saw the breasts had gone completely flat, shrunken to a row of small pips low on her belly. They can't be nipples, I thought wildly. She moved her finger through the mat of hair. "Six, now," she said. "Like a dog." Her voice was bitter.

Restlessly, she yanked at the hem of her skirt, and I saw the narrow feet of an animal drowning in a woman's leather slippers, the white stockings slipping down and the black satin ribbons tied and wound over a pair of hairy cocked ankles. The knees jutted like haunches. "Ah. I should've known you'd seen it over the last few weeks," she said, "by my walk."

My vision dimmed, and I tried to shake her. "There's nothing there!" I shouted. "It's an illusion! For Christ's sake, nothing's changed—"

"No?" she said, and I was aware of a peculiar glint in her eye. "Nothing," she began to laugh sharply. "But I've seen men draw back when I pass, cover their noses to avoid the rank odor of the animal hide—"

"You imagine it—"

She shook her head, whining deep in her throat. "Then the change is here," she said, touching her chest. I started to tell her that was so, but she cut me off. "I can only drink when I lower my head to the river. I snap up what food I find on all fours. My hands will not feed me," she said, turning them over to look at them.

And as she said the words I saw curved black nails, palms that were dark pads sprouting tufts of thick hair. Her tongue rolled out of her mouth, saliva glinting on the strong white teeth.

"No," I whispered, shaking my head clear, seeing the image waver. "No. It's an illusion. Don't let her infect us both."

"Keep Lenore away from me," she said, suddenly canting her head, then listening—as if she heard a low noise carried on the wind. Or, I thought, groaning inwardly, caught a sudden whiff of scent from the open grave.

"God has seen fit to punish me. How well it suits the crime! An animal shape for animal deeds." She nodded.

I stared, relieved to see Mimi, to see a woman's shape. But I couldn't put away the impression that her voice was a deep rumble in the well of her throat, or that her eyes had gone from their startling violet to a muddy brown that filled the sockets completely. I glanced up suddenly alarmed. Her eyes—the whites are gone—

"Like a dog," she muttered. "A carrion eater that feeds on anything it finds." Her face went blank and she lapsed into silence.

I saw her walking slowly back toward the caravan, her hips swaying crazily over ankles that looked unsteady. She took the mincing steps of some four legged creature trained to get up on its hind end, and my heart gave a lurch. I wanted to forget that pain. I made myself get busy, and I began piling the thick stones—one above the other—over Joseph and Constantin.

Anyeta had used the vision of that eternal unrest—of lying paralyzed with the cold weight of earth—to push Zahara aside. I thought at last she'd found the thing she needed to wreak her destruction on Mimi, to break her. A small rock rolled down the sloped side of the cairn, and I put it back.

With a pang I suddenly recalled the day Joseph had put Mimi into the trance. I saw Anyeta grinning, heard that evil snickering voice. *First animals. Bite deep. The blood fills your mouth. First animals. Then children.*

"And then! and then *what?*" the old man had cried out commandingly.

I saw her face go sly. *And then we will see what the other one turns into . . .* she chortled.

I remembered Joseph, his eyes hooded, his thin fingers tented as he sat considering. *Anyeta will use the secret byways of the mind to burrow deeply, to get at your wife's dreams, her fears.*

The memory faded. Joseph had been right, of course. Mimi was tormented, a broken thing. I recalled hearing as a child that Romanian gypsies turned their enemies into trained bears, and it always made me sad to see one performing its slow parade of tricks, the red leather collar around its neck, its huge paws shuffling. As a child, I always looked for— thought I could detect—a terrible grief behind a trained bear's eyes, the desperation of the human mind; dimmer perhaps but still aware. It was only a legend, I'd always thought, and yet here was Mimi locked inside an illusion that might as well be real.

For the first time, I understood the lure of the hand of the dead. Anyeta was sweeping over us all with the relentless savagery of a conquering horde. There was only me—and Lenore. If I owned that power I would make that she-bitch pay—for this, for everything! Angrily, I shoved the last few rocks back in place, finishing off the crude structure.

My gaze fell on the deep carving centered in the broad gray trunk of the copper beech. Through the bitter winter months the scar had gone dark and dulled. "Ah Christ—Joseph, Constantin, I need help, I need you to help me protect my little girl," I said aloud, but there was nothing. Nothing left but the mute jumble of timeworn stones and the bitter knowledge of how they had been desecrated.

There were gypsies—even *gaje*, I knew, who kept vigils over the graves of their loved ones for months on end to protect the remains from the resurrection men. If they could not keep watch, sometimes they filled the graves with chaff, because after body snatchers excavated, they used crowbars to pry open the coffin lids and pull out the corpses. But the chaff was soft: the grave walls collapsed, and there was no leverage for the resurrectionists to break through. It was a hideous fate; the remains were sometimes sold to unsavory medical men. In backwater countries the body parts were coveted, the eyes, fingers, even genitals hacked off for magic and charms. But what had happened to Constantin and Joseph was a thousand times worse. It was true that I had not been able to bury them properly in the frozen earth, that even if I'd guessed what would happen, I'd had no grain—but neither had I kept vigil—except perhaps in my heart.

And more than anything in the world, at that moment, I wished I'd never used the acid, that I might press the glittering ring on my finger and hear the old man's voice. And draw whatever small comfort might be there.

Part IV

Lenore

All men kill the thing they love.
                                        —Oscar Wilde

50

A month later the graves were still undisturbed. The light was graying toward dark when I started back to the caravan. Above the treetops I could see a milky film of smoke from the chimney. And as I approached, my feet getting wetter, sinking into the soft spring mud, I could see the yellowish glare of lamplight. I paused briefly, realizing there were none of the usual pleasant associations of going home, of going inside where it was warm, where dark and cold were kept at bay. Now moving closer, I saw how the green curtains had gone sun faded and pale. They had a ragged tattered look. The wagon itself slouched to one side. My eye fell on peeling paint, a cracked window I'd mended hastily one afternoon with cardboard that had turned mushy and swollen. Looking at it, it was hard to believe I had I preferred staying in the caravan; but I'd been reluctant to spend the winter the way some gypsies did, in a clay hut covered with branches, or in an earthen cave hollowed into a hillside. I stood in the shadows, breathing fast, my heart quickening—although at first I couldn't have said why.

The wind shifted and I heard the metallic pi—ping! of two rusty tin plates I'd wired up (thinking to myself when a poor man has too much time on his hands he gets to fooling with junk and castoffs) as a makeshift gong to call Lenore in for suppers—

—and then I had it. My mind drifted back to the first day we'd come to Romania, to Anyeta's dirty junk filled wagon, to the old fear I had of living in a wretched cave, to the first time Mimi and I had gone to Hungary all those years ago. The caravan wasn't our home any more. It was hers. And maybe, just maybe, I told myself, it was time to leave her country again and reclaim our own.

Two sets of eyes locked on mine when I opened the door. Mimi's violet eyes were cloudy with sorrow. Lenore flashed a look that said she was alarmed. She began talking in a high rapid voice.

"She won't eat," Lenore said, pointing first to Mimi's hand curled loosely around a blue-speckled enamel dish on the lap of her skirt, then to a short handled metal spoon lying on the floor a few feet away.

Lenore grabbed the full supper dish, grease congealing around the stew, and set it on the table with a bang. "I told her—her arm is all well! She can move it if she wants to, but she just sits there!" Lenore accused. "I put her fingers right around the spoon, she won't hold it. It falls off her lap and she just sits there! Staring! If I raise her elbow, she lets it hang in space. Why is she doing this, Papa? Why?"

I put my hand up for peace. Mimi turned those stricken eyes toward me and gave me a dreadful grin. A partly chewed chunk of what looked like meat fell out of the corner of her mouth and dropped onto the white bib Lenore had tied around her mother's neck and shoulders. A line of glistening brownish drool oozed down her chin.

"See!" Lenore said, lifting the edge of the stained bib and wiping Mimi's mouth. "See what she does!" She turned to me. "Even when I put it in her mouth, she won't eat it. Spits it out or keeps it under her tongue just moving and moving it around—like some kind of crazy cow—" Her voice hitched. Lenore's hand went flying up to her face and she began to cry.

Mimi's eyes met mine. You see how it is, the haunted look said. What can I do? I won't eat in front of her. *You know why, Imre.*

I smoothed Lenore's hair, her swollen blotchy cheeks, then cradled her against me. "She can't help it, sweetheart."

"Why not?" Lenore said into my chest. "Why can't she help it?" Lenore asked, smudging the back of her hand against her eyes. "She goes out at night—"

My heart missed a beat. Lenore hearing that low evil laugh, the sound of Anyeta creeping out the door. Feeding on God knew what. Had my daughter leaned to kiss her mother awake in the morning, then drawn back gagging on a cloud of blood and offal?

I put the thought aside, turned Lenore's face up to mine. "You've been a good nurse to your mother, honey, but now it's over."

"What do you mean?" Lenore's dark brows squinched down.

"I mean," I said, drawing them smooth with the tip of my index finger, "we're leaving. Going back to Hungary."

"Really?" Her face brightened, and I remembered a dead winter day when she'd cried to me she hated this country! Hated all of it! And the only good thing was the uncles, and they were—gone. And she'd prayed to God and the Virgin to make it spring so we could all leave, but God wouldn't do it. My little girl stood at the window, weeping—as if she were shocked to see the wet black tree limbs, the endless gray-white snow swirling, a row of icicles hanging from the roof like jagged silver teeth. "They won't let us leave," she'd cried hotly, pointing skyward. And I didn't know if she meant God and the Virgin, or the grinning row of frozen teeth that penned us in the mouth of the wagon.

"We're really leaving?" Lenore said again.

"Tomorrow," I said, putting my arm around her narrow shoulders and toying with a lock of stray hair. "I'll hitch the rest of the team, go south. Find a market town—it's coming on for spring. One of these godforsaken places will be having a fair. Trade these nags for good horses—"

"Can I come with you?"

"We'll all go," I said, catching Mimi's eye, sending her an imploring look that said, *Help me; if you can help at all, help us get out of here.* She shut her lids. I saw her nod a faint yes.

I walked Lenore to Constantin and Joseph's wagon where she slept. She pattered ahead, I heard the flap of the canvas, and she darted in. While she got ready for bed, I stayed outside, smoking, waiting for her to call me to tuck her in. I heard her pouring water into a basin, the drippy sound of the washcloth as she scrubbed her face.

She liked her privacy, she'd told me the day she settled in the small space for good, and I'd smiled at the time. Now I wondered if it had to do with the still childish part of her mind that said if I don't hear my mother stealing barefoot toward the door, the minute snap of the latch, the creak of hinges—if I don't hear it, if I can't hear it—it doesn't happen.

"Ready."

Lenore poked her face through the flaps, reminding me of a puppet at a fair, and I felt my face break out in a wide smile. We were going to find a fair, we were going to leave. Lenore would beg for coins, spend it on candy and useless truck, watch it all—the battling Punch and Judy puppets, the trained dogs and monkeys, the jugglers—with wide eager eyes.

The lamp on the night table was glowing. She sat crosslegged outside the covers. Her hands and teeth were busily working over the knots in the end of a soft cotton sock that jingled with money. Her face was fierce with determination, her hair a dark shimmering fall in the dim light, and it struck me all at once that she was caught in some shadowy space between childhood and womanhood.

The knots gave way, she thrust one hand deep into the worn sock and pulled out a fistful of coins. "Not bad," she said poking one finger through the money and making it chink.

"I'll give you more," I said, jingling some coins in my own pocket.

It was the child-Lenore that grinned up at me. "All of it." She put her hand out, and I filled it. We both laughed at the bright spill of gold.

"We're really, truly going?"

"Yes," I said, making her scoop up the money and get under the covers. She held the end of the droopy sock in one fist.

"Solemn promise, word of honor?" she said, beginning an old ritual she used when she wanted something very badly from me or her mother.

"Sacred promise, oath of honor," I said, rubbing my nose back and forth against hers to finish out the game. She heaved a little sigh of relief and let her lids fall closed. I smiled at the heavy fringe of sooty lashes against the round babyish cheek. Her fingers were still twined around the sock-bank. She opened one eye, checked its position, then lay back.

"Good night, honey," I said, blowing out the lamp. She gave the sock an idle flip, and I heard that pleasant tinkling shift of the coins.

"I love fairs," Lenore said sleepily.

"I know you do—"

"Going to dream about the colors, bright spangles on the ladies' dresses, and the booths and the food—" she broke off yawning, "and how much I love it all—"

"Yes," I whispered.

"—and know what, Poppie? I love you, too."

"I know," I breathed, feeling something inside my chest suddenly brimming with joy. I left quietly, not wanting to break the spell of her gentle sleep, not knowing the truth of our sad, human wishes. There's some of Lenore in all of us. We want small things, tiny joys. The feeling that tomorrow is going to bring us bright colors, shiny tinsel—the delicious smell of cooking, a moment's adventure in a sideshow. We want hope. We want love. And Christ, it shouldn't be too much to ask for in this cockeyed world—and yet it is. Somehow, it is.

I guess it was the lack of sex. For months Mimi slept in Lenore's berth. I slept alone in our sagging double. I'd blown out the candle, gotten into bed, and somewhere amid the happy run of my plans for tomorrow, I'd noticed a spark of excitement that quickly made itself known as a raging hard-on. Fantasies. The sheet, loosely draped along my naked inner thigh, was the soft down of Mimi's hair. The tip of one finger rubbing my flesh was the hardened red nipple of one heavy breast she nuzzled against me. I licked my palm, squeezing the whole wet length around my cock, and in my imagination, Mimi's mouth sucked and caressed—

—From beyond the kitchen came the sound of the wooden pocket doors sliding back. Mimi climbed down from the bunk bed, then ambled toward the kitchen.

In the dark, I stroked myself lightly now, keeping one ear out for footsteps coming closer. I slowed my hand and shifted the mental terrain a little.

Going to make you go wild and beg for it, baby, the fantasy Mimi crooned huskily. More saliva, and in my mind's eye she plucked a wet soppy washcloth from thin air and rubbed its warm soap-slick surface against my thighs and belly. Then I watched as the cloth moved in endless circles spiraling up her legs, her crotch, her chest. Teasingly, she slid against me. Delicious, and oh sweet saints, now I was aware of the feel of her lathered breasts—the hard buttons of her nipples poking through the foam. She was skimming over me, she was slipping downward, she—

A noise from the kitchen that sounded like the blue-specked metal plate being edged from the table, then falling and overturning with a wet clump onto the floorboards—

Oh for the love of Jesus, not now, I whined inwardly, I was nearly there, didn't want to stop, no, couldn't stop—

—Thump of knees, a small keening noise, the sound of the plate scraping—

I was aware of just how hot I was, my feet were tingling, the back of my throat was dry. On my tongue I tasted sexual excitement—as thick and hearty as wine. A musky smell rising from my flesh—

The enamelware plate was scraping against the floor, as if, I thought, she were nosing it this way and that. Trying to turn it back over, to get at the food underneath the rim. I had a brief mental flash of the stew meat lying in a puddle of cold grease.

My hand moved faster, and I felt myself on the verge. The fantasy Mimi pressed her wet lips tighter, drew me deeper into her mouth.

At the same moment, I heard the plate scoot tinnily across the kitchen floor.

I ground my teeth, shutting out reality. Focused on the imaginary feel of her tongue—like a soft damp pad cushioning me. The sound of it churning, lapping. I came in a long shuddering throb, my breath whistling through my lips.

A thick sound from the kitchen broke through. Jaws champing, a wet gobbling.

I shivered and went as cold as if I'd been suddenly doused with ice water.

I was in the bedroom pretending my wife was crouched between my legs licking my cock. She was in the kitchen, hunkered down on all fours, dog-like, eating her food off the floor.

"I heard you, you know."

I'd dozed off, and now I woke to dull candle gleam with a suffocating weight on my chest that held me fast.

"What?" I swam through layers of sleep.

Anyeta, naked, grinning, was astride me. "Lonely boy, wants to play, and has to play alone." She made a tsk-tsk sound, shaking her head back and forth.

I felt my face go bright red. "I don't know what you're talking about."

"No?" She giggled. "You can't fool an old hand like me," she said, then she tipped her head back, belly laughing at her own pun. "No siree," she lifted one thigh slowly, then slipped off me. She walked, flat hips swaying, a few short steps away from the bed. "Besides, I smell it on you," she said, letting one thin hand make a sensuous downward slide over the taut thigh muscle toward her crotch. "Just like," she said, rubbing herself lightly, "you smell it on me."

She was right, there was a ripeness coming off her in waves, a humid scent I'd thought was my own. I swallowed. My eyes flicked uneasily over her, and I saw how wet she was, the pearly flesh sheened over—

"I was playing with myself in that absurd little bed. Not bad of course, but why should either of us play alone? Hmm? Someone else's touch is always so much more exciting." Her voice dropped on the last word. "Isn't it?" she asked, nearing the bed.

I shut my eyes, half-enthralled, half-afraid. Her fingers made snail tracks against my lips and nose. I sat up and thrust her hands away. She chuckled again, eyes full of a wicked glee. She seemed to draw back, but now her hands found my crotch and she pressed her mouth against mine.

"You want it, you want her. I can give you that, you can see her—not the way she sees herself," Anyeta said, and for a second I saw the overlay of Mimi's features, her face half submerged beneath short bristling fur.

I groaned, but now I was staring at my wife, at her comely neat figure. The tiny waist, the dark thick nippled breasts, the flaring hips and shapely legs.

Anyeta spun around and now I felt her (Mimi's!) buttocks pressing against me, the soft flesh parting for me. She pushed backward.

"I like it this way," she said. "Go ahead," she urged.

My teeth and lips were buried against the nape of her neck. My hands floated up and lighted on the soft rounds of her breasts, my heart was hammering in my chest and God knows there was a part of me that wanted her. But the her—

"I'm not like her," Anyeta moaned, biting her lips and grinding against me. "I like it in the ass—"

—No, the her I wanted was Mimi, my wife. And my wife was not a foul talking whore, never had been. I thought of those times when Anyeta had tried to seduce me, when I'd asked for money, when Mimi had lost our first born, Elena. It was twenty years later and she was still playing games. "No!" I shouted. Roughly, I pushed Anyeta away.

She landed on the floor, then looked up at me with hate-filled eyes.

"If not me," she snapped, "then perhaps the gentleman would care to choose another." It was every whorehouse Madam's line. Though there wasn't a whore in the world who would say it in that venomous tone.

She began crawling away, and when she reached the stairs, she turned and looked over her shoulder at me, and I saw Mimi, her eyes a muddy daze. She began to slink off, bumping clumsily up the steps—and then it was Anyeta laughing, and I guessed she was imitating my wife to torment me.

"Any time you want it doggy style, daaarling," Anyeta smirked, getting to her feet.

Seconds later I heard the sound of the pocket doors slamming shut.

51

I t was the worst nightmare of my life. I was in a city whorehouse in Old Buda. The girls began to strut past me. I sat in the gaudy lounge, a black walking stick planted between my feet, a drink near my hand on a side table. A fat blonde with a baby face pouted her red lips, then turned to show off the plump contours of her white behind.

"Her?" The madam's black silk fan descended on my shoulder with a smart rap, and I shook my head. She made a shooing gesture with the fan, and the fat blonde sashayed off through a tatty velvet drape.

The madam leaned over, I saw the end of a long drooping silver curl and caught the smell of brandy when she whispered, "The next one is very special."

She clapped her hands, and the sliding door opened for the fourth or fifth time. A pretty Oriental girl minced through, her face done in white. She was wearing a heavy blue kimono. "Oriental," the Madam said, unnecessarily. "And quite clean. I found her myself."

I shook my head.

"If not her, perhaps the gentlemen would care to choose another," she said, and I heard the irritation in her voice.

She clapped her hands smartly, the fan swinging wildly from a black cord on her wrist. The door opened and now an entire line of women—all shapes, sizes and colors—began to parade before me, their high heels making lazy clacking sounds against the tiled floor.

"Perhaps—"

"There are no others. Choose," she said.

I looked up at the Madam, an old woman wearing a white wig, and for a second, I thought, *It's Anyeta, this is a trick.*

"Walk girls, walk quickly," she screeched.

They began to trot past.

I had the impression of jiggling flesh, lacy pastel undergarments, hurrying feet. They were moving out of reach, beyond recall. One by one the whores were disappearing through the red velvet drape.

"Her? Her?" The silk fan swatted my shoulder again and again.

I looked up at her, held my breath: If it was Anyeta, her piercing black eyes held me fast, and without even looking at the line, I raised my arm and shouted. "That one, I'll take that one in the pink chiffon. Her—third from the end! I want *her!*"

"Very good, sir. As you wish. A fine choice, the young lady is a virgin." The madam put her hands on her thick hips and smiled at me. Then she clapped her hands, and the scene shifted.

I was in the dark, pounding on top of the girl, my hands ripping at the flimsy pink chiffon, tearing at it. Oh my Christ, a virgin trained up into whoredom I thought, driving myself into a frenzy. I sucked her breast and she gave a groan.

"Please oh please," she whispered in a tiny helpless voice.

I was transported, wondering whether she was wanting it or asking me to go easy. I thrust deeper. The girl, a little chubby, bucked and squirmed beneath me, driving me madder still.

It went on and on. "Now like this," I'd shout, trying her this way and that, using her over and over. My mind was spinning. I pictured her short square body big with my child, her childish breasts milk-swollen, blue-veined.

It went on and on—'til a thin watery daylight came through the slats of the shutters, and I was still heaving on top of her.

"Please, oh please," she said again, and now I could see the tiny buds of her breasts beneath me, the heavy fringe of black eyelashes resting closed against the babyish cheeks, see the dark shimmering fall of her hair.

My heart jackknifed painfully in the cage of my chest.

"Please, Poppie. Please," Lenore begged.

And I sat bolt upright, a scream of terror locked in my throat. Never mind that it was a dream: guilt as noxious as the foulest cesspool lay in a black sludge in my brain. I heaved one quivering leg over the side of the bed, and snagged the chamberpot out. I leaned over it and squeezed my guts, gagging until my throat was a brutal rasp.

My heart slowed, I rocked, moaning softly to myself.

And oh Christ, I was sick at the thought I couldn't vomit it up.

52

"Sleep well, daaarling?"

I fumbled to cover myself with the bedclothes, then glanced up to see Anyeta leaning jauntily against the doorjamb, her obsidian eyes alight with malicious glee. Lenore stood at her side.

"Are you ill, Papa? Mother's ever so much better this morning," Lenore prattled, giving Anyeta a quick hug. "I think it's because we're going to the fair. I think she just needed something to look forward to—"

"We're not going to the fair. I'm going to trade what's left of the horses and come back for you."

Lenore uttered a little cry, but I wouldn't look at her. How long, I thought, as a sickly quiver rippled in my belly, before I found myself helplessly sleepwalking to her bed?

"Get dressed, Lenore," I said through gritted teeth, and she ran back toward the kitchen, Mimi's old white dressing gown flapping. When I heard the caravan door close I got out of bed, trailing the swirl of sheets and blankets, and moved toward Anyeta. She stood, unflinching, her face hard in the early morning light.

"You sent the dream," I said, feeling my anger rise.

"And wasn't it a dandy," she laughed, tipping her head back.

I seized her arm, tightening my fingers into the flesh. "I'd sooner cut my own throat than touch the child."

She never moved, but lifted her eyes and stared into mine. "I see. Is that why you were looking through the robe? Is that why you swallowed? Was it the shape of her thighs or the thought of her tits?" She lifted one hand slowly to the underswell of her breast.

"I'll kill you, you fucking whore."

"A virgin trained up into whoredom—wasn't that it?" she mocked, and I stepped away, suddenly drained. I couldn't leave Lenore—leave her with Anyeta. She was too young to cope with Mimi. A terrible weight squeezed my chest. My fingers knotted the sheets. Only a few weeks ago, at the breakfast table Lenore had told me she heard the Empress Elizabeth loved all the same things her father

Duke Maximillian had. Adored animals and traveling, learning languages and writing poetry. "I heard," Lenore said, "that her father liked to dress like a minstrel and visit fairs. When she was a little girl, he played the guitar and sang, while Sisi shook the tambourine, danced and caught the coins the crowds threw. Don't you think that's like the gypsies?" I was only half-awake, nodding over the steam in my coffee, answered uh-huh—more to keep her quiet than anything else. But charged with the early morning energy of a child, she prattled on. "Sisi is like her parents; and you've played the fiddle and mother has a tambourine."

She stopped, and at first I thought it was to get my attention, but then I realized there was something troubling her. "Sisi is afraid of madness; and I guess maybe someone in her family went crazy. So, what I want to know is," she said, picking at the tablecloth with her fingers, "since I like learning about herbs, and you always say I look like Mother. Well," Lenore hesitated. "Do you think when I grow up, I'll be like her?"

I heard the catch in her voice, and I saw she was frightened of Mimi, of the brooding mother with the haunted violet eyes who silently sat in the corner. I thought of the relief Lenore had shown just moments ago, because her mother finally seemed better. But if the mother Lenore feared was gone, the one I feared more was standing right in front of me. I looked up at her.

Anyeta chortled. "Play the odds, Imre," she said, ticking her fingers. "Leave her with me? Emm. Hard to say what she might see or learn." She grinned. "Take her with you? She wants to go to the fair, of course. But it's hard to know what might happen, isn't it? Hard to tell how much you can trust yourself. A man in your position gets to the bottom of his character quickly. Such a risk. But oh so interesting to find out how much character you have."

"Get out," I said, but she only crossed her arms and stood leaning against the wooden jamb.

"Are you afraid, Imre?" she taunted. "What's that old gypsy saying—*fear is the father to the wish.*"

"Get out of here you bitch, get out while I dress—"

The front door snicked open. "We're going, Lenore," she called out brightly. "I convinced your father." She gave me a wicked smile and swung away.

It had been on the tip of my tongue to say I was going to hitch the team, because we were leaving, but she'd stolen the words from me, said them aloud. I could hear her laughing to herself while I pulled my clothes on in a rush.

Daytimes were safe, I thought, standing under a large tree on the edge of the fairgrounds where I'd set up shop—so to speak—in order to conduct the horse trading. Around me was the noisy jangle of the carnival.

The nights though—I swallowed. I hadn't let myself sleep much. I was too afraid of the dreams. I was more frightened still I would fall under the sorceress' spell and act them out. *Please, Poppie, please.* That defenseless child-voice, and Lenore, I thought drawing a deep breath—she only called me that when she felt a sudden wellspring of love or when she was hurt.

A customer with a huge brush of a mustache idled toward me. This one was shabbily dressed; he had the look of a browser, not a buyer; and just as I expected, he shook his head that the price of the team I was offering was too high before he ambled off. I wasn't worried; I watched him disappear into the crowd.

"I've been looking just everywhere for you, Papa—" I turned to see Lenore beaming up at me, she put her face up for a kiss, and before I could stop myself, I flinched away. She popped the last bite of a *gogos*—a pastry like a doughnut—into her mouth, and went on. "How's the trading going?"

I felt easier. "All right." I'd been doing a steady business. I'd slicked up the nags we'd arrived with and sold them. I'd taken the money and bought a better team, then traded those horses for the ones—three roans and a bay stallion—now lazily cropping under the tree. I nodded toward them. "Can't really lose. It's the last afternoon of the fair. There'll be lots more stock coming in. If I get the price I want I'll pocket a profit—if I don't," I said shrugging, "these'll get us back to Hungary."

She nodded, and I noticed she was wearing a pair of oversized silver hoops in her ears.

"Where'd you get those?" I said.

"I bought them from a gypsy boy." One hand fluttered up and she set the earrings swaying.

"They're not real," I said. "They're *peche* and they'll turn your earlobes green before the week is out—"

An old man walked past, eyeing us, and Lenore whispered in my ear. "Well, Papa, it's like when you sell the nags. You mix ink and soot to hide the gray hairs in their muzzles or put coal tar into their molars so an old horse's teeth look like the black centers of a young one's. You always say 'I guess about a week from now the customer will be heaping curses on my gypsy head, but a trade is a trade.'"

She giggled, drawing back. "Anyway, I don't care, I love them." She twitched her head back and forth making them jingle, then took a small mirror out of her pocket and peered into it to see the hoops flash.

The thought flashed on me that it was something Anyeta would do. "Put that away," I said evenly, and she stashed the hand mirror. In the distance I heard the faint strains of the carousel tinkling like a music box. I looked up. I could see the tip of the gold-painted finial, part of the red striped pole.

Lenore turned too. "Oh," she said, "that's why I came. I wanted you to take me on the merry go round. A girl told me they're selling the tickets half-price because it's the last day—"

I felt my stomach knot. The carousel, I knew, was fitted out with animals from Noah's ark. They rode—camels and monkeys and horses and giraffes—two by two around the track of glittering mirrors and bright-painted murals that showed the whole motley crew getting into Noah's boat and fetching up in a landscape so green it looked like the jungle. I could imagine the animals mounted on their poles, moving up and down. "No. I can't—in case a customer comes."

"But you just said you couldn't lose—"

"You ride. I'll give you the money," I said thickly, putting my hand into my pocket for change.

"I want to go with you."

"No," I said, shaking my head. A sudden powerful image of her child's body seated before me on the whirling merry go round had risen in my mind. Her tiny back pressed against my heavy chest. My legs curved close around hers. "No," I swallowed.

"Go ahead, take your daughter on the carousel," Anyeta said, walking up, flat hips swaying like a cat's. A paper carnival fan dangled on a yellow cord from one wrist. She toyed with Lenore's curly hair briefly, then opened the fan.

"Oh, yes, please, Papa. Mother's ridden with me already. Please."

"No," I said huskily, but I didn't seem able to stop myself. Lenore laughed, tugging me by the hand and pulling me into the throng, while Anyeta watched us, her eyes glowing over the bright circle of the fan.

Daytime is safe, I told myself, looking at the crowd of children— their mouths smeared with jelly, their arms full of hideous stuffed prizes—as they clambered onto the merry go round, dragging mothers, fathers with them onto the giddy beasts.

"Help me up, Poppie!" a little girl chirped to her father, while one chubby hand patted the tall flank of a leopard.

Lenore settled onto the padded leather seat atop a white horse with a pink tongue and foam flecked teeth. She gave the gilded reins a flap. "Come on," she urged.

"I'll stand here," I said, curling my sweaty fingers around the striped pole the horse was mounted on. I got a sudden whiff of cooking and smelled hot sausage on the sun-warmed air as sharp as a premonition. *Don't. Don't get on behind her,* a sentient voice whispered in my mind. But I was only vaguely aware of trouble; I had no sense of the terrible sequence of events that led ultimately to my downfall, to contracting the foul disease that is wasting my strength and eating my flesh.

"Don't tell me you're afraid," she teased.

"No," I said, clinging to the pole, and shaking my head stubbornly. "I'll stand here," I said again.

"They won't let you," she laughed. "No standees, everyone has to ride." She pointed to an attendant, who was in the act of telling the very same thing to a big-bellied man with rolling eyes. I watched him huff, and the attendant gave him a leg up into the seat behind his grinning son.

"Hurry, Papa," Lenore said. "The music is starting."

Daytimes are safe. I felt the wide wooden boards spring lightly under my feet and I swung up in the saddle.

The carousel whirred up, spinning its dizzy circle. Lenore was laughing. There was the music, the twirling jungle landscape; the sounds of the crowd, their smiling faces reflected in the long glittering glass. I saw Anyeta's grin become a white blur and I seemed to fall into a spell, swaying lightly with the movement of the horse, jigging up and down, up and down, my hands riding the crest of Lenore's hips—and I was suddenly aware of her small face, looking puzzled, turning over her shoulder, peering up at me.

"Papa," she began, "there's something lumpy on the seat." She hitched her behind forward, trying to turn against the forward motion of the spinning carousel. She used one hand to feel beneath her—

My lap. Dear God her hands are in my lap because—I felt a thick horror as sudden and stinging as a slap. My cheeks burned hot, and I heard a low groan straining deep in my throat. She'd felt it: My prick, gone stiff, iron hard against her back. I saw the confusion on her face, she was (Oh dear Christ I prayed) convinced it was some oddment on the saddle, uncertain because the seat had seemed smooth before.

Oh God, God help me, I grieved, overcome with guilt and fear. I jerked away from her, leaping from the saddle. I ran forward in a stricken crouch. My steps were unsteady, the boards were spinning giddily under my feet, and I fled the carousel. I pushed my way through the crowd. Then I saw Anyeta's laughing onyx eyes peering over the edge of the yellow fan.

"You did it! For the love of Christ," I screamed, putting my face close to hers. "She's a twelve-year-old child!" There was a pause, the crowd stepping back from me, and I ran.

Behind me I heard the saccharine music grinding on and on, the sound of shouts: *What's the matter? Did you see that? That man suddenly jumped off the merry go round!* I glanced over my shoulder, seeing the kaleidoscopic blur of color and glass, the fantastic hazy shapes of the animals, and above it all, Lenore's tearful face beneath the cloud of her dark shining hair.

I got drunk and found a whore.

The drunker I got, the more it seemed to me that the only thing that could take the taste out of my mouth was to screw some low woman. There are always a few working the carnival crowds. Now, I stood lounging at a booth draped with bright yellow cheesecloth, drinking straight from the neck of a brandy bottle, waiting for someone likely to stroll by. I wanted someone blonde. I wanted her to be old. Above all, I thought, wiping mist from eyes, I wanted her not to fit against me—the top of her head close to the middle level of my chest—the way Lenore did. I watched the crowd, deliberately winking at a pair with raucous voices.

"Buy us a drink, lad?" the shorter one said. She was a skinny girl, no more than nineteen, wearing a huge bonnet with curling pink streamers.

"Sure." I nodded to the bartender and he set out two glass tumblers. They crowded close to me, lifting their glasses and nodding thanks. I kept my gaze fixed on the big one. Blonde and as wide and rolling as a box car. She was taller than me. Perfect. I spoke under my breath and transacted the business.

"Sure you wouldn't like us both?" said the shorter one. "I'm younger and spryer than Marta. It won't cost but a fraction more," she said, giving my thigh a surreptitious squeeze under the gauzy folds of the cheesecloth bunting. "Sure it has to be a blonde?"

"Shove off," Marta said. "He wants a ample girl with . . . experience."

"Says you." She sniffed, giving the pink ribbons a toss. "I call it lardy old pig-fat."

I bought another bottle, and we walked away, my arm circling her thick waist.

She brought me inside a kind of lean-to that was tacked onto the back of a wooden booth. On the other side of the canvas an old woman was selling a hodgepodge of pots and pans, herbs, jams, honey and teas. She did a brisk business, I guessed, by the sound of the jangling pots strung up on a rope around the booth. My whore did, too. The first thing she did was hike up her ruffled skirt, displaying a thick thigh, reach into the black roll of her stocking for money. She put it in a crock by the door. "I got an arrangement like," she said.

I sat down and started to undress.

"Uh-uh, can't use the bed," she said shaking her head at the dirty mattress where the old woman vendor slept nights. "She don't like me to use her bed."

So I did her standing against the wall. Three times, while she crooned in my ear, "Easy now, easy—the old lady don't like her customers on the other side to catch on, you know."

I kept my eyes open the whole time. Made myself concentrate on the heavy flesh, the coarse pores of her skin, the bright yellow hair. In between I swigged from the bottle, wiping the mouth with my hand before I passed it to her. She didn't drink much, only sipped when I pressed her.

"You ain't been gettin it regular, have you, pal? I can tell," she said, beginning to button up her dress. I made her stop. I wanted to keep Lenore safe, to force myself on her again, to drain myself until there was nothing left.

"Cost you extra," she said, and I nodded.

I battered away at her, but this time I felt myself shrinking in the wide used-up depths of her sex. I was drunker still and crying by the time she pushed me away. "Oh Christ, Mimi, forgive me," I wept. "I was afraid, so afraid, and there was nothing else I could do."

"All right, all right, that's enough now—you'll be pumping till Christmas before you're primed again." She pulled her dress closed. "Go on back to your wife now."

"I will," I said, sniffling tears, and wiping my nose.

"But if I was you, I'd take a piece of advice. Don't be singing out that there Lenore's name while you're doing *her*—"

"What—" I felt my face go white.

"Sure, the whole time you was slobbering on me, you was whispering your girlfriend's name. It don't sit with a *wife*." She sucked her belly in, and began fastening the buttons down her dress. It suddenly seemed very hot inside the small canvas tent. Outside the pots clanged and the old woman rang up a sale. My head rattled with a fierce pain, I felt queasy. "Men," she shook her head, looking up at me. "You're all the same."

Trembling, I took the bottle and left.

"Hey, I'm not in any rush," I said to a man wearing a brand-new black suit, a pair of shiny patent leather boots. There was a fancy pin in the white stock at his throat. I took a long swig from my bottle, then held it out to him. He shook his head, his eyes betraying a fleeting disgust.

"No?" he said. "I know every gypsy trick." He smoothed one gloved hand up along a brown mare's head; he glanced at the glove, then lightly pinched the flesh beneath its glassy eyes. "You use a straw to puff air under her eyes so they don't look sunken?"

"No," I said truthfully. The sun was hurting my eyes, making my head pound more fiercely. I didn't like this pompous man, I wanted to get a move on. I squeezed the bridge of my nose, grimaced. "Buy or don't. There'll be a hundred men who want these horshes come this afternoon," I slurred, wondering briefly if he'd caught it.

"Maybe. Maybe not." He tamped a cigarette against a flat silver case. "It's three o'clock now," he said, spreading his hands. "Where are they—"

I scoffed. "What do you take me for—some kind of rube? They hold this fair because of the annual drive for the livestock. The sheeps—sheep—going out to the spring pastures—"

He gave me a regretful smile. "Where'd you say you came from? Gradistea? Maybe you haven't heard. Lots won't be here—not this year—there's been glanders in the district."

"Glanders—"

"A disease found in horses, often passed to men who can infect others—"

"I know what it is," I said hotly, my head throbbing. The lesions and bloody crusts. Wet flesh gone runny with thick pus—I shoved the thought aside, took the last drink from the bottle and tossed it. It glittered in the grass.

He held up his gloved hands. "Your horses seem sound," he said at the same instant I heard a vague rustling behind me and turned my head, my eyes going a little blurry, to see Lenore and Anyeta moving slowly toward me.

The man talked in a low voice while he probed gently with one finger inside the mare's nostril, feeling for tiny nodules that would grow larger, thicker—

"Papa—"

"Not now, Lenore."

"Papa," she said again, "I only wanted to say I was sorry if I made you angry—"

And this time I turned all the way, hands on my hips, about to tell her I wasn't angry, but to let me conduct my business, but the words died on my lips.

Her eyes had a blank look. She arched up on tip-toe, and before I could shamble backwards, her lips brushed mine. I felt the point of her tongue, her small hands clasped tight to my waist.

My mouth fell open, I felt my face burning, I felt the curious eyes of the high class customer taking in the scene. Could hear him looking at our shabby clothes, thinking we were out of the backwoods where incest was so veddy, veddy common . . . . "Lenore," I croaked, smudging my sleeve across my damp lips.

Lenore giggled, then stepped back, and it was then I saw the blinding flash of the silver pendant draped around her throat. Oh dear Christ, she had that filthy crescent moon, the pendant Zahara had stolen and worn around her throat. Lenore was falling under Anyeta's spell. My child marked by the sorceress like a slave with a choker! Everything, all of it rose up in me in one furious mind shattering blast.

"Where did you get that, where?" I screamed, seizing her shoulders and shaking her. Her head bobbled like a rag doll's. Shamed, I let go. Oh Christ, why did I keep it?

Her hand clutched at the crescent moon. "Mother," she began, her eyes darting like flickering moths, then faltered. "She—"

"Take it off!" I shouted. Joseph's voice drilled in my brain. *Anything worn a long time becomes like the person, absorbing thoughts, feelings.*

"She said it would match the earrings—the hoops—"

I'd bought it for Mimi that day in Sighisoara, the first time we made love. Zahara had coveted it; and coveting me, had worn it for years maybe . . . Zahara possessed. *Anything worn over time.* The words swirled round and round. The same as if the she-demon had worn it, and hadn't Lenore kissed my lips, put her tongue and wet mouth on mine? Anyeta would take the child's body and I would be helpless, helpless and she would laugh when I cringed and whined and went mad with torment—and fucked her again, again.

"No," I moaned. In my head I was hearing Anyeta's threats and vicious taunts. *I will wear your daughter like a bauble on a string around my neck.*

"No." I seized the chain between my fingers and ripped it from Lenore's throat. Red marks like a line of tiny insect stings circled the tender flesh of her pale neck. I stood, stunned, the chain dangling loosely from my fingers, the silver crescent swinging to and fro.

"You're drunk, Imre!" Anyeta suddenly shrieked.

But it wasn't the drink, I knew—not really; it was her. "Not that drunk you goddamn bitch and you know it!"

Lenore's eyes went wide, her mouth dropped in a quavering O. Crying, she snatched the silver pendant from me, then she gathered up her skirts and ran.

"Lenore, Lenore," I screamed, tears flowing down my face. "Come back, don't you see, this is what she wants. She's trying to—Oh Jesus," I cried, sinking to my knees, then burying my spinning head in my hands. The sun burned and licked my scalp. I heard voices droning like the buzz of flies. I sank backward against the hot grass.

"He's drunk," I heard Anyeta say in the pathetic voice of a long abused housewife. "He fights with me or my daughter . . . drinks until he passes out."

"No," I tried to say, but my tongue was thick in my mouth.

"Please, sir," she said to my customer. "Won't you help us, take a little pity. He's been like this for days. I'm so afraid he hasn't chosen well—that these *grastende*—these horses are riddled with disease—"

"Sound," I murmured, trying to heave myself up. An invisible weight pinned me to the ground. The man—all patent leather and fancy jewels—I realized was a sham. He'd been looking for a drunk, a fool. Found me. And now Anyeta. No, by the bleeding, Christ, *no!*

"My team is here," the customer said. "Will you trade?"

"Yes, oh yes." I heard the eagerness in her voice.

And I knew what she was doing. I tried to protest, but I was powerless to stop it. Oh, God, it's not the drink, I thought, and a few minutes later I heard the man driving my sound, healthy horses off, their hooves churning up the turf.

Anyeta led four black stallions close by. I saw their varnished hooves—slicked up and glossy as the man had been himself. My eye traveled upward. Anyeta held the leather bridle snugly, one hand moving over the soft dark hide. The lead horse gave a sudden snort and a huge runner of snot dripped from its nose. I saw it shining dully against the grass. Oh Jesus! He's in the first stage of the sickness! I thought.

"What a shame," Anyeta said, shaking her head. "A *Lovari*. A horse dealer. Should've known better. But he was drunk, I'll say. So drunk he didn't know."

She flicked the hide lightly, and I saw its black flesh twitch as if it had been stung. The horse began to shiver. Its head drooped.

I watched in panic, my eyelids fluttering, my guts a nauseating spiral. Her glittering eyes met mine.

"No," I tried to say, and suddenly I felt as if my head was gripped in the claws of a vise. I thought of Joseph pinned, unmoving, against the wall. "Christ, Christ," I moaned.

Her face dissolved in a sly grin, her gaze never left mine, while her thin hand, with its long slim fingers disappeared up inside the black horse's streaming nose. She withdrew it and I saw the coat of viscous yellow slime.

"I won't get it," she whispered. "Glanders. But if I did I would use the power to bring myself a healing." She took two slow steps toward me.

And now my mouth was forcing itself open. As if inch by inch a stick pried my jaw wider, wider, wider. I could not move my lips. I heard a strange grunting noise—a terror stricken yarl—rising up and out of my paralyzed throat. No, I was shrieking, begging inwardly. Don't! For Christ's sake, don't! Please, Anyeta. *Don't!*

"Who owns the hand of the dead breeds destruction," she said softly.

I saw her pale cupped fingers held above my nose, my throat, my aching open lips. Saw glittering mucous; it hung suspended like a single strand of spider web—dripping with thick foul-smelling venom. My gaze—my whole being— was fixed on that wet running drool.

"A smear," she said. "A touch inside the nose, along the tongue— the same as eating death."

No! I screamed soundlessly, I felt my eyes bulging out.

"I can even cure the team," she said, "and drive us back to Hungary— daarling."

No-ooooooo!

Anyeta's eyes went as dull and black as the dead light in a cave. She raised her slip coated hand up. There was a stench from the yellowish clots, the ripe smell of bad cheese. I saw the evil rush of the glinting arc. Then her hand descended downward as quick and smooth as the executioner's axe.

I closed my eyes in dread.

And her dripping hand—a wet, suffocating cloud—closed in on me.

53
Nyiregyhaza, Northeastern Hungary: Late Spring, 1864

Three weeks after Anyeta infected me with glanders I found the first nodules inside my nose. I'd awakened early, pulled from a deep sleep with what felt like a bad cold: I was breathing heavily, I had chills and a fever, my eyes felt raw. I shuffled from the bed, and I was suddenly aware of a dry sensation inside my nostrils—as if tiny grains of hot sand had imbedded themselves under my skin. My steps quickened and I hurried to the mirror.

The light in the caravan was dim. I peered into the glass, craned my head up and down and side to side, trying to see inside my nostrils. I inserted a tentative finger and a sharp bolt of pain shot backward through my skull.

Shit, oh shit. I inched closer, leaning into the mirror and saw the nodules: hard, shiny, grayish. My heart sped up, my mouth dropped wide, and I saw thousands more coating my tongue, my lips, the inside of my cheeks.

I stared at the malignant rash of pinhead size bubbles; in the deepest recess of my brain, I knew they would grow and grow. Already the flesh they covered had a bloated look. I gasped, and my throat was stinging. I felt my heart double its pace. They were lining my throat, and with each breath I was drawing the disease deeper into my lungs. I wanted to vomit, suddenly caught on the memory of Anyeta's slippery hand smearing the foul clots over my lips, sliding up inside my nose, moving over my tongue. The taste and smell of mucous—like something low and rotting—drowning me. My stomach roiled.

Easy, easy now, I told myself, slowly hunkering down then lowering my head between my knees. Got to keep it down, acid in your stomach, it'll sting like fire, I thought drawing a light breath. A second pain roared inside and down my throat—as sharp and grating as if an invisible hand plied an emery board to the soft tissue. Dying, Christ you're going to die! Easy now, I thought just as a mindless fear gripped me and I threw up; choking on curds of vomit, the burning sensation, an agony.

"I'm afraid," I whispered.

Mimi turned my jaw delicately between her fingers and examined me. Her eyes were dark with sorrow.

That afternoon, the first of the nodules had swelled and burst with a tiny wet pop! that sounded like a miniature cork being slowly drawn from a glass bottle. My hand went to my upper lip and I felt a soft runny substance there.

"The horses," I said, as she pushed a stack of washcloths that lay on the night table closer to me. Without looking I wiped what I guessed was thin pus from my fingers and mouth, then dropped the cloth into a straw basket. At the end of the day, I thought sickly, when the basket was filled with those wet odorous cloths, she'd burn it.

"Shhh," she mimed, putting one finger to her lips. Her eyes said don't think about it, about what's going to happen. She held up a heavy white cup filled with soup but I shook my head, I didn't want it.

"I've seen the way it goes," I said, "with the horses—bodies shrunken to skeletons on their huge frames, the mass of lesions spreading, running one on the other. Until there's no more flesh, only scabs and dark maroon weeping sores—"

Mimi put her hand up but I went on. "Even their breathing's painful to watch. Their chests move in and out like slow leaking bellows. And the sound." I paused, hearing that high thin shriek of air wheezing through lungs that were breaking down.

"It eats through the flesh," I said. "We both know it." I felt my mouth twist in a lopsided sneer. "And when the skin is gone, it attacks the cartilage, finds its way to organs and bones." I shuddered, recalling a horse I'd seen in that final stage. "It didn't resemble an animal, a living thing," I rasped. "It was a heap of bleeding rags mounted on sticks."

Stop, her eyes begged. *Can't you stop?* But I couldn't.

"There was no tongue to hang from its mouth, only a dark lump of ulcerated flesh. Its eyes were fused shut with greenish pus. I remember I was amazed, because somehow it had gotten back up on its tottery feet and it was listing to and fro; rocking back and forth, too weak to nicker its pain. All the other horses in the barn around it were dying, bleating in agony, their voices echoing off the rafters. Then it collapsed all at once—as if its legs had been cut off underneath it. It crashed into the side of the narrow wooden stall, two of its legs a splintering mass of bone and ruined flesh. It was dead— and the others dying—when they burned the barn around it." I shut my eyes, beginning to cry.

"Shhh," she soothed, her hands cool against my brow.

I felt a sudden wetness ooze under my lids. And I found myself praying inwardly with all my might that the sticky damp gliding down my cheeks was only tears—and not the gluey track of pus.

I lost all sense of time. The fever was on me again. Waves of chills followed by a fierce heat that burned into me steadily, until it felt like my bones were iron rods laid in a forge and glowing orange-white.

From far off, I heard Mimi pour water into a basin. She bathed me when she could to keep me comfortable. I felt her hands moving over me. She pulled the coverlet down. Then she began undoing the row of buttons on my nightshirt, her fingers dibbling over them one by one. Down and down. Her hands stopped suddenly, and she gave a short gasp.

My eyes flew open, I raised my head.

My chest was a muddy sea of flesh, studded here and there with crusting scabs like dull rubies weeping blood and thin yellowish fluid.

"My face," I rasped. "What does my face look like?" I began to hack, my brain spinning. Was it this morning my wife showed me my face in the mirror? Yesterday? She broke it, I remember that. Smashed it right against the floor.

"My face? Is it worse?"

Mimi wouldn't answer. She only leaned over me and shook her head, putting her cool hands down over my both wrists, pinning them to my sweaty sides in a gesture that meant lie quiet. She narrowed her eyes, her mouth shaped, *Save your strength.*

"You're hurting me," I whispered, squirming. She stepped back, her face flushed red.

Me, she gestured. I did this to you—

"No," I had a vague memory of her trying to heal me, then crying because her powers had fled. "No," I coughed, and my hand went up automatically to cover my mouth and catch the sputum. I stopped. We saw it at the same time.

Joseph's gold ring was buried in a puffy swell of flesh. I turned my palm over, angry reddish knots rose up, giving it a misshapen look. It was spreading to my hands. I looked up, my pulse ticking with vague dread like a slow watch. "How long? how long do I have?"

Mimi's huge violet eyes said I had to hurry because there was something— something she wanted me to do.

My head was dull with fever, I couldn't remember. "What do you want?"

Lenore, she mouthed, her face taking on a kind of urgency. I saw the terror in her eyes. She's frightened for me, I thought, because there isn't much time—

Mimi uttered a low cry. Her eyelids fluttered, and I was suddenly looking into Anyeta's leering face.

She nodded toward the ulcers on my chest. "Coming along nicely now," she said, her voice purring with satisfaction. She said it loud enough for Lenore to overhear; then she laughed softly, because what she really meant was that I was dying.

I felt my mind burning with anger.

"I brought you home to die," she whispered, leaning over me. "Why don't you do it? Give in, let it take you. Do you know what you look like?" Her obsidian eyes gleamed.

I shook my head. "Lenore," I croaked, my tongue hot lead in my mouth.

"Mine for the taking. Didn't Joseph tell you?" she mocked. "You were the only one standing in my way. And now of course you cannot even stand."

Filthy bitch. I lunged toward her, then fell back, coughing, spraying droplets of blood over my chest, the quilts.

"It smells in here. It smells of your rotting flesh, Imre. Even outside, the breeze carries your stink to us in a gagging cloud. I don't think Lenore will ever forget this stench." She wrinkled her nose in disgust. "Not even when I *yag* the caravan."

"Why don't you kill me and be done with it."

"Soon. It will be soon," she said, and I had the sense she meant more than my death. She stared at me.

I stared back through rheumy eyes. Daytimes, Anyeta was letting Mimi nurse me, but as the long afternoons dragged on, the light dying toward evening, she came out.

"Yes, I think Lenore will see you once more—just once before you die. She knows her mother is not afraid of falling sick; and I don't think she will be either—"

"No—"

"If Lenore knew how sick her father was, I think she'd want to help," Anyeta said, rubbing the purple bracelet of scar tissue that wound over Mimi's wrist.

And then before I could answer, she was gone, and I lay there, knotting my lumpen hands uselessly. "The scar," I whispered, thinking of Anyeta caressing it so reverently. Terror seized me, I began to shake. I knew what Mimi wanted. She wanted me to claim the hand of the dead.

I craned my head and saw the copper box with the glass top lying on the low table where my wife left it for me. The dried wrinkled flesh of the hand was black with age, a vague shape against the maroon velvet. Anyeta missed it in the shadows, but now it seemed very bright to me. I sat up, staring. The copper took on a sharper gleam, beginning to be edged with a fantastic greenish light. It seeped up through the glass, and now the hand itself was luminescent. It flickered and danced like a firefly.

"Claim me," it whispered. It began to sing, a soft thrumming sound. I saw a moonlit garden where a golden fountain played in a yellow mist over the white, waxy blooms; where naked women strolled, their eyes filled with hunger for me—

I heard Anyeta calling Lenore for dinner. The two of them scampered up the stairs of Joseph's rickety caravan and went in. I heard Anyeta rolling up the canvas sidewalls.

The wind carried the sound of their voices, gossiping over a long supper.

I swallowed. Oh Christ, oh saints, I'm cold. I huddled under the blankets, drifting in and out of an uneasy sleep that was more delirium than easeful dreams, while Anyeta and my daughter talked and talked—of love and illness and healing—and the June wind brought me the low sound of their voices, late into the night.

"What did you do today, Lenore?" Anyeta asked, and I heard the soft chink of silverware.

"Went to the village—"

"Didn't I tell you not to go there? Your father is sick—if they find out we'll be hounded out of town, maybe put in a jail." A glass rattled and banged against a plate.

"It was only to see the priest—"

"Priests!" Anyeta snorted.

"I'm glad I went," Lenore said, "and look, Mother, look what he gave me." The light sound of her small feet hurrying. A dresser drawer banged open, slammed shut. "See, it's holy water. From Lourdes." Her voice took on a sweeter resonance. "There's a grotto there—with red roses that bloom in December and a blue lake with miraculous powers. This cave—it's filled with crutches, thousands and thousands of them. Men and women and little crippled children bathe in that blessed water and the Holy Virgin cures them—"

"Your father's dying, Lenore!"

"I know it." There was the sound of quiet weeping. "I've prayed to the Holy Spirit . . . and Saint Sarah—because she was a gypsy, I've prayed to her, too. And after supper I'm going to go inside the caravan and say the prayer to the Blessed Mother—and sprinkle all this clear healing water—"

"It won't work—"

"The priest said—"

"Priests. I never put much stock in the clergy, Lenore."

I'm delirious—or dreaming, I think, hearing the door swing open. I can see Lenore's silhouette; the moon glows white and round over her shoulder.

"Papa?" she whispers. Her feet make a soft scraping sound against the threshold. She takes two steps into the room, her heavy skirts are rustling. "Papa, are you asleep?"

"Ugh," she says suddenly and I hear her trying to stifle her gagging. She pounds her chest, her hands flail. I see them moving like pale silver fish in the murky light. She is breathing through her mouth.

"Are you awake? I came to help you." The moon picks out a glass vial in her hand. It glimmers when she holds it up. The cork disappears in her pocket.

She tips the bottle against the pads of her fingers, like a woman coaxing expensive perfume from a narrow-necked flask. Lenore flicks the droplets gently. I hear them pattering against the floor as she moves through the kitchen toward the top of the stairs. Her voice is low, barely above a whisper. "Holy Mother, I humbly beseech you from the bottom of my heart to hear my prayer."

She moves more quickly, leather heels tapping down the steps, across the darkened room. And now I hear the first droplets falling on the bed sheet.

The glass bottle tips downward, there is a minute gurgling, and I would smile if I could because my daughter, Lenore, has saved most of her precious holy water for my tortured body.

I see the shadowy cloud of her thick hair, her head bent at a slight angle, her hand held aloft as she walks up and down the length of the bed, christening me. I cannot really feel it, except as a vague dampness, but I know by the sound, she is drenching me in the cool liquid.

"Oh Most Blessed Mother, I place this cause in your hands. Let my father be healed."

Her voice is a soothing murmur as pretty as a lullaby, I think, easing me toward a tunnel that is dark and inviting. Dreamless, perhaps—

"Papa?"

Lenore is whispering, and I realize there haven't been any sounds for what seems like a long time, and I wonder if it's the same dream or another. I hear scratching noises like a match against the stove. The dream shifts in time, it's morning. I'm bathed in blinding sunlight—

—The light! Not sunlight! It's a candle!

I throw my arm across my burning eyes, the light is a wavy, sickening prism searing me with lancing pain.

Lenore screams. Through a blur, I see her hands turn into claws and in her terror she is shredding the soft white skin of her cheeks. Three red lines of blood well up, two on the right, one on the left. She is shrieking louder and louder, her fingers tearing at her lip.

"No! No! Poppie! No!"

Her terrified gaze lights on the bottle of holy water at the foot of the bed, and she seizes it. I see it hurling through the air. It smashes against the wall high over my head. Fragments of glass suddenly spray over me, and the noise makes me sit up in alarm. My feverish brain is turning round and round. It feels hot and stretched—as thin as copper wire. I'm so sick, I think. Delirious. I don't want visitors, not even Lenore.

"Please go," I say. I move one leg sluggishly. I will see her to the door, I think incoherently. Her dark eyes gleam with terror, she takes two nervous steps backward toward the stairs, hands hidden behind her.

I lurch out of the bed.

"Your mouth, oh dear God, your poor mouth," she breathes, backing up.

"Please go, now," I say, at the same instant I hear my voice for the bubbling clotty thing it is: An oaty rumbling, as if I were sucking wet porridge instead of speaking.

"Pleash . . . gaw," I mumble, the sound cutting deeper, slicing through layers of delirium. I suddenly catch sight of myself—like a fading ghost—in the window glass. A balding, scabrous head welded onto tottering sticks. The lids are half-eaten away and I stare into a pair of crusty burning eyes, glistening, luminous above the blackened pit that used to be my nose and mouth.

My tongue is a rotting stalk. My teeth are worn to rounded nubs. Through the crumbling flesh, I see part of my dirty jaw bone. The roof of my mouth has gone . . . mushy . . . the holes that were my nostrils are sinking down and caving in—like a grinning face carved on a burnt out Halloween pumpkin that crumples down and sags in on itself.

"Ahhh," I moan. "Pleash . . . gaww . . . " I beg again; the motion causes a flaring red pustule to burst and a noxious yellow fluid spills out of me because there are no lips to catch it. It drips onto the floor with a thick splat.

I open my mouth to scream and I feel it filling with blood. There is no sound beyond a rusty caw. Instead, Lenore screams for both of us, and then she runs.

I amble back to bed, to the dirty sheets. I shake them lightly, dimly watching dark red scabs bouncing off and scattering on the floor. But even that feeble movement is enough to bring on coughing. I try for the straw basket, miss, and now there's a puddle of blood on the floor.

I lay down. Lenore's screams subside. I stare at the moon through the open door. Even if it's June it's cold, I think, and I wish someone would shut it. The drafts make me shiver.

In Joseph's caravan, the rolled canvas flaps like a sail. I hear their voices on the wind that sweeps and sweeps across the vast distance of the plains. Lenore wants to know if her mother is sure, very sure—

"Yes," the she-demon Anyeta answers for my wife.

"And it—this charm—can heal him, truly?"

"Yes. You can save him, Lenore."

My eyes fly open. Something that feels like a steel pike rams my chest. Oh, Christ. In my mind's eye I see Mimi weeping fit to break her heart. Telling me— this morning or yesterday or a week ago— the time was short . . . Christ, Christ, I should have done it! The copper box with the hand is lying on the table.

"If I'm brave . . . "

"A cut, here, and you can claim its power."

"The scar . . ."

"A scar is only a scar. A moment's pain for your father's life."

"The *mulengi maulo*, the hand of the dead," Lenore agrees, getting to her feet.

"A miracle that's not a lie."

In my caravan the open door creaks, swaying lightly in the wind. Never, I'll never get it locked in time! I think wildly. My pulse is suddenly racing, and in my terror I'm able to wrench myself out of the bed.

I hear Lenore's feet whispering through the grass.

I crawl for the door, my hands and knees scuttling over the wooden boards. In my bleary-eyed state it seems farther than it is. I creep toward it, ignoring the pain that is rumbling up my arms and shooting from my raw kneecaps straight to my hips. The entry wavers, glowing with eerie moonlight like the throat into hell.

Sweet Bleeding Christ, let me get there, get the fucking thing locked!

Her hand slides onto the banister, her foot over the first step.

I scoot forward with a half-lunge, and I feel the cold round metal knob—in the cup of my blistered palm—like a blessing. I slide the bolt, hear it rattle through the iron ring, slurring over the wooden jamb.

I turn around, leaning clumsily against the wood like a falling drunk, panting heavily. Thank Christ, oh thank Christ.

In the dark, like a green ship's lantern on the foggy sea, the hand begins to glow.

54

Calling my name, Lenore shakes the knob on the other side. Once, twice. Then she is racing back past the low glare of the campfire to tell Anyeta the door is locked. The sorceress will open it with a flick of her mind.

I use my shoulders, pushing myself away, taking heavy faltering steps, grazing the walls. I leave smears and blood on the chairs, the kitchen table.

A knife winks green on the counter, its blade catching the weird glint of the pulsating light. My breath is coming hard, my fingers are clumsy and stubborn when I try to pick it up. It gets away from me and plummets from the counter. For Lenore, I think, and get it in my shaking hands.

Voices raised; Anyeta will be here soon. The knob will rattle once. There will be a sharp flash of electric blue light, the dizzy smell of ozone. In that one instant, the blasted door will slam wide open, the metal handle crashing backward into the scant lining of plaster. The door will rock madly, bouncing against the punctured wall of the caravan.

"Imre," the hand croons softly as I move toward the stairs. Mimi was naked when she claimed it, I suddenly remember. I rip at the nightshirt, tearing my flesh along with the cloth, then use the knife to cut the buttons and it flaps around the jutting bones of my hips.

Three steps down and I am in the bedroom, bending over the table, my hand going the fertile green of a jungle inside the spill of vibrant light.

"Imre! Imre!" Anyeta's voice is close. Footsteps running up the stairs.

I spring the catch. The glass top jitters up like a jack-in-the-box. The hand glows against the velvet. There is the smell of lilies, tuberoses, jasmine. Garden scents. Sweet *lulagis*, Imre my love.

I kneel on the floor, holding the knife over the rotting wrist I've exposed against the boards like a surgeon at his operating table. I raise my right arm, hoping to get all my weight and strength behind one heavy chopping blow. The knife comes whistling down like a meat cleaver.

"Open this goddamn door!" The knob rattles. "You stinking piece of shit, *I'll blast you blind!*"

Take me now, lovemylove. Oh Imre, the hand calls, *May kali i muri may gugli avela* . . . Ah, the darker the berry the sweeter its juice . . . Imre

"IMRE-E-E-E!" Anyeta screams.

"I claim it," I whisper at the same instant the metal bites through skin, bone, wood. There is blood, and it geysers up in a dark red fountain. But oh, I tell you, the sound of Anyeta's frustrated shrieks is a heavenly music, and I never felt the pain.

55

N ow there is all the time in the world. Now I can keep the door locked, keep her out. The jagged bracelet of scar tissue circling my wrist is thick, lumpy and purplish—but it is the only scar. The disease is gone. The rest of me is healed, whole, unspoiled.

I light all the lamps in the caravan, boil water in a kettle, bathe, then dress myself in clean clothes. The open box that holds the hand of the dead sends its heady aroma into the room, overpowering the stench from my sickness.

I rummage in the cupboards for cheese, bread, wine and make a light supper. Never has food or drink tasted this way—as if all the warm, good flavors in the world—grapes and salty rennet and delicate yeast are exploding on my tongue. It's because I was sick, I think; then I feel an inner twitch and wonder: Is it because I claimed the power of the hand?

All at once, the wood and plaster walls of my caravan are wavering, turning into a formless mist. I can see Anyeta brooding, pacing back and forth inside Joseph's caravan. I feel her mind seething. Lenore is asleep. The cunning old *choovahanee* hasn't given up on the prize; if she could find some other way to convince Lenore—to trick her—to claim the hand of the dead, she could possess my daughter. Mimi is barely a shell, she thinks; it will be easy.

A sudden fury seizes me. I have power, now I want revenge. For sending me those obscene dreams; for corrupting my daughter; for possessing my wife, for turning her into a ghoul feasting on Constantin and Joseph—on their rotting corpses; revenge for the foul plague—for all of it! I narrow my eyes into a squint and stare at her. My mind teems with bloody fantasies. I want to rip Anyeta to shreds, I want to hear her moan in a begging voice, to tear her apart with my bare hands—

I pause, catching sight of the old man's ring shining in the lamp-light. And it seems to me I hear his voice cutting through the bubbling rage inside me. *"Think of Mimi,"* the voice murmurs. *"Don't use it for that—not revenge! Use the power to send the sorceress to sleep, Imre. Use it just this once . . . Once and then perhaps once more; because it's an evil thing, corrupting its owner over time. An obsession that eats at the mind and heart—like the worm of disease."*

He's right about Mimi. I feel the blood draining from my face, my anger goes flat and stale. "All right," I whisper. My vision blurs, and I peer through the thin haze into his barrel-topped caravan, sending Anyeta into a dreamless sleep. She sits woozily on the bed, then crumples all at once, dark hair streaming over the quilt. Her breathing is slow and rhythmic. I see the soft rise and fall of her chest, her lips flutter very lightly. The demon is sleeping, and now I call forth my wife.

We sit, Mimi and I, holding hands across the table in our caravan. I'm reminded briefly of the night all of this began; the chill autumn night we learned Anyeta was dying in Romania and had sent for us. Mimi's shadow is dark and tall against the wall, her hands are pale in the lamplight. She smiles at me; it's a tired smile, I think.

"Anyeta will—" Mimi breaks off, clearing her throat. She's been mute so long she's not used to speaking. I realize her throat hurts, her voice sounds dry, dusty. She starts again, her hand pressing mine. "Anyeta will not rest."

"What of it? I'll batter that bitch into gravel, I'll grind her into dust." I smile, tip back in my chair. I'm very proud of myself. I've freed Mimi of that hideous spell, of the illusion she was a cringing beast.

"No," she says, nervously biting her lip. Mimi's eyes are very dark, the color shimmering between violet and a deep brown. She gets up; I think she's going to pace, but she comes and sits on my lap, placing her hands on my shoulders. I caress her waist. "Don't you see? Even now? She's in me, Imre," Mimi says, touching her heart lightly. "She's sleeping—but it's the sleep of some foul worm that grows fat even when it dreams. And I feel it, here." She touches her heart again. "She's stronger than you or me."

"Her power increased over time, mine will too—"

"Spells and counterspells and what then? You'll be just like her—"

Just like her. I feel my heart dropping in my chest. *The hand is an obsessive thing that corrupts . . .* Joseph's words toll dully in my brain like bells made of lead.

"No, you're wrong," I say. "I'm not like her—and neither are you! It's the goddamn guilt!" I shout. "Why can't you understand she did it! All of it—killed Joseph, fed on animals, on children—"

"She is me and I am her. More and more we merge. She is sucking me up. And there's so little of me left. I'm dying, Imre. The day is coming—soon—when I won't exist. Lenore isn't safe with me, either."

"I don't understand," I say, "I have you, all I want is to hold you, to kiss you, to make love to you—"

"Then make love to me, Imre. Make love and free me." She touches her lips softly to mine. "The power of the hand is a terrible thing. Joseph knew it, he never claimed it. I didn't want this for you, I didn't. Our fate is the same—lying in a stinking grave; seething, screaming . . . forever . . ."

The hand. I swallow, feeling cold earth pressing down on me, suffocating me; see red grave worms gnawing my flesh—

"Make love to me," Mimi says again. Her small hand knots into a fist and she strikes her chest in the center; in the place that lies just above her heart.

It is the last time. We are everything to one another. Man and woman, lover and beloved, husband and wife. The world is our universe, our playground, I think, looking up at her, at her small kitten-shaped face. Thin and haggard as she is, she's beautiful when passion takes her.

She rocks lightly on me, and never, never has her skin felt so soft. It glows under my fingertips, warm and delicate. There's a musky scent rising from her and I drink it in, kissing her breasts, her mouth. I taste her lush saltiness and she mine. We love and love.

Perhaps, I think, because I've claimed the power my strength flows into her, and together we're driving the she-demon deeper and deeper into some dark recess where she's no more than a speck, a mote . . . nothing. Our bodies cleave, rising and falling in the rhythms of love. It seems to me I'm on the verge of discovering some previously unsuspected and wondrous secret.

Then, something that feels like a door or window inside my mind suddenly slides open or up, letting in a kind of soft yellow light like summer moonglow. It's as if the moon was a globe or a round Chinese lantern you could hang in your bedroom, just above your head—

Above me Mimi sways, her eyes closed, her thick lashes fluttering against her cheek, her expression as mysterious and graceful as a Madonna's. I have a sense of an impending vision, a future free of the she-demon. And in our sweet union, in my mind's eye, there is only my wife, there is only Mimi:

It's five years from now and we're done with gypsy madness, gypsy ways, the endless roaming she hated. We have a house, a cottage really, and I see her sitting in the blue brocade wing chair near the window of the small cozy parlor. I see the sunlight gleaming on the polished floor, a wool rug twined with ivy leaves. A carved clock ticks on the mantelpiece. She's singing, her small mouth touched with the beginnings of a smile. And now I see her slippered foot tapping out the tune softly, and looking closer I see her arms are cradling an infant. Brown skinned, with the fat reddish cheeks of a peony. He squirms, I see his head cant back, the thick mat of black hair on the crown. He waves an arm, opens his mouth to bawl for his supper. Mimi laughs at him, gives him milk from a bottle with a rag wick in it. The sound of his fierce sucking is very loud, and she tells him that even if he is a very greedy noisy kind of boy, she loves him.

He's an angel. She leans over, crinkles her nose, gives him a smacking kiss at the top of his forehead. "Ion," she croons.

There are tiny lines around her eyes; I see them when she grins, see the wisps of gray in the once-glossy black hair. At night in bed we laugh about the gray streaks, and always I tell her it's about goddamn time she caught up. I was getting sick of being the only one making a count in the mirror every morning. She counted for a while too, then gave it up—until, she said, giggling, counting would be easy again. And I knew she meant when there was only a sprinkling of black left to stand out against the white.

Ion, I recall, was the name of the boy she gave her gold anklet to in memory of that other lost baby, Elena. Yes, I think, a child to erase the years of sorrow, to free us both from the spell of the past— the horrors and evils, both natural and unnatural. And if now there are lines in that face, the face of the woman that I love, I say let them wear deeper and deeper over time; because that other line— the scar around her wrist—has dwindled and faded into insignificance.

Now I see Lenore entering the room, bending to kiss her mother's cheek, to squeeze and pat her brother's toes. She's grown up, I think, really grown up, she's lost her girlish chubbiness, but not her fascination with the Empress—

"And do you know, Mother," Lenore says, taking an apple from the wooden bowl near the divan, "Elizabeth is insisting her lady-in-waiting has to be Hungarian—"

"Lady-in-waiting—what's that?" Mimi asks, deftly bringing the baby up to her shoulder for a burp, smoothing his back.

"A companion, mostly. Keeping track of social engagements— that kind of thing. Can I try for it?"

Mimi nods yes, and smiles. Lenore dashes across the room, puts her arms around her mother and the baby, trilling, "Thank you! Thank you!" Lenore takes up the baby, waltzes him gleefully around the room. "Ion, Ionny, your sister's going to see the Empress!"

I see a trace of sadness in Mimi's eyes. Lenore catches sight of it, too. "Oh, I'm going to miss you, miss all of you," she says, and a little of her sparkle dims. "Of course, I might not get it, the Empress might not want me as her companion—"

Then Mimi stands up swiftly, reaching upward because Lenore is taller than she is. She lays her finger gently against Lenore's lips. "Hush, don't say or think such things. She may or may not choose you, but you have to try." Lenore nods a little uncertainly. "Now, I wonder," Mimi says, "I wonder what you should wear—something like the pale green gown Elizabeth wore this spring?"

"Oh, Mother, I've outgrown copying her dresses—"

"So you have," Mimi sighs, "so you have."

And I see now that at last Lenore has the mother she was meant to have, the mother she deserves . . . .

—the mother, my mind echoes.

And even now, I think, perhaps this vision of the future is nearer than you dream. Perhaps even at this moment, the seed is becoming a life.

And I thrust harder and harder up inside her, praying inwardly that my strength be contaged into her, that life might flow into life, make her a mother—

Above me, Mimi moans softly, hips drumming faster and faster against mine. I hear her whispering, saying, "Yes, yes. Deeper now, stronger my love, for I must make you see . . . ."

I feel her letting go, feel myself letting go. And all at once in that swift blackout that is the beginning of the end, I see deep inside her—

Mimi cries out. The dream-like vision begins to scatter . . . bright colors fading, as insubstantial as last night's confetti swirling in a gutter. I open my eyes.

My wife's dear face crumbles like a plaster of Paris mask that is suddenly crushed underfoot, and behind it—

(the mother . . . the hideous face of the mother)

—Anyeta's ancient sly face looms.

Oh Christ, Christ! I mourn, shaking my head, feeling the giddy vision dissolve completely, leaving me sad, disoriented. And it's Mimi I want. Where is she? My grief gives way to anger, and I think, *Fucking whore! The sex brought her out!*

"Ah," she grunts, lurching upward, then back down again grinding me against her, and the movement reminds me of the jerky hop of some wizened toad.

Under the white lank hair, her onyx eyes are cold. Her hands on my chest feel leathery, and I glance down at her flesh sagging from the bones of the parted thighs, and I'm suddenly aware that her meager cunt is sharp, dry as stones in the desert.

The only moisture is a thin rill of blood leaking out of her hole. Something in me turns over; my blood or hers, I wonder. She churns and writhes against me. I cry out in pain, blood dribbles over my thighs, and I feel my cock shrinking.

"Shall I let you see her, let you see what's left?" Anyeta's wrinkled lips draw back grinning.

I turn away from the sight of her rotting brown teeth.

"You think she's pretty? A little tired looking? It's an illusion you fool! This! This is what you're *fucking!*" she screams, riding me like some foul hag rocking on a broomstick, her white hair foaming around her scrawny shoulders.

An icy dread clutches me, and suddenly I remember the night in the tomb when I saw Zahara's image melting, flickering around and through the withered face of the old sorceress-whore. There is no Zahara, she was sucked up over time, Mimi's voice, Joseph's voice cry out together, like dead echoes in a cold vault. *"No Zahara, no Za—"*

"No!" I shout in a paroxysm of terror.

"Yes!" Anyeta caws in triumph!

Now, in the blur of shifting shapes I see Mimi's face—pallid but beautiful. Anyeta rides her, bony arms locked in a death grip around my wife. Mimi screams, a long quavering wail rising higher and higher.

Anyeta's mouth opens wider and wider. I see the ring of fierce pointed teeth. Her huge red tongue rides out of the center of that cavernous black hole and she sucks at Mimi, consuming flesh, blood, licking the skin, layers of muscles from my wife's face, her breasts—

I moan, and I see Anyeta turn her face up to mine. She snickers. Her black eyes glow with sickly shine, her rotting teeth are lined with blood, her fat tongue dripping.

"No, no—"

She dips her head again. I shield my eyes for a time, but her pull is inexorable, and I feel its drag, feel myself forced to look at the terrible commingling—

There is no Anyeta, I think. The sorceress waxes younger, fatter. There is no Mimi; I see her aging, turning forty, fifty, eighty . . . .to bones. There's nothing left of Mimi but a hideous wraith, a skeleton with tortured eyes peering out from a white skull. Only her eyes still burn, and they will dim when her bones crumble into dust.

There can be no future, no cottage hearth. No child. My heart feels near to breaking; but her pain is unspeakable.

Lenore, I think, Oh sweet Christ, her childhood—her adolescent dreams, her life—will be stolen from her! Anyeta will suck up her youth until my daughter is no more than a pinch of gray ash swirling on a downdraft, scattered on the hot wind.

"No. *No!*" I suddenly scream, and my hands are around her throat, squeezing.

Anyeta's eyes bulge in their sockets. Her tongue lolls between her thin lips, and in a flash, I remember, I remember! The she-demon is afraid of pain, afraid of death, and in my mind's eye, I see Mimi slashing at her wrists to drive the sorceress deep inside, to keep the bitch at bay. My nails sink into the dirty wrinkled skin, drawing blood, and I push them deeper.

"Haaahhhhnnnn!" she croaks, seeing blood running down her sunken, bony chest, and dripping thickly over the deflated flaps of her shriveled breasts.

"Die, you bitch!" I say in a dark voice. "Mimi's as good as gone you say? Then *die!*"

She bucks and rocks, her hands scrabbling madly, beating and flailing around my forearms. She tries to jerk backward out of my grasp but the blue veins and corded tendons on my arms are standing up like thick ropes and my hands squeeze, squeeze—

I hear a choking sound, deep coughing, rapid breathing and wild gasps filled with terrible pain. Dark hair bobbing like a mop being shaken up and down.

Mimi twists and writhes above me. My hands, throbbing and twitching, drop away.

"You know," Mimi rasps, the mask—thin and fading, but there— is in place again. "Oh God, you do." She sinks feebly against my chest. I put my arms around her back and, mourning a vision that never was, can never be, we hold each other a long time.

"Free me," Mimi says, sitting up slowly, "what little is left. There isn't much time. Don't let her win, don't send me into that eternal torment. Christ. Please. You've got to end it. For my sake. For Lenore's. For your own."

I sit up, sighing. And at last, I know, I've come to it. My eyes brim with tears, my hands shuffle and skitter in my lap aimlessly, not wanting to get on with what she's asking of me.

"Mimi," I steal a glance at her. "Please . . ."

She doesn't answer, only gets up. She begins to get dressed.

I see Joseph's ring, the deep graven Germanic J is dark against the gold. Imre, my son, I imagine he says, his voice a well of sorrow that tells me he knows how hard this is. Gentling is the only way.

56

Up in the loft there are canvas summer tents, Lenore's outgrown toys. We don't let her go up there. It was the place Mimi hid the copper box that held the hand of the dead. My wife and I tell Lenore it's dirty, dangerous. And it is, I think, drawing a deep breath, my chest shuddering: There are scraps of lumber, leather bands, spikes that can be hammered thin—the raw materials that are the black heart of the gentling box.

There's enough, I think as I look around, my testicles constricting, to make a dozen of the damned devices.

A little while later I come down the stairs, my arms laden. My boots make a vacuous clatter on the steps. In the stove the embers shift, knocking down against the grate; and hearing the noise, I nearly pitch forward with sudden terror, then catch myself.

Mimi hums softly, braiding her hair. She paints her lips, and uses rouge to make a bloom on her cheeks. Her face, I think, has never looked so lovely.

I lay out the awl, the drill, the hammer alongside the rest. Then I sit down tailor fashion, and I begin my work.

In my mind's eye, I see the wild horses running swiftly over the honey colored open field. A skinny black-haired boy with a gold hoop in his ear runs at them, arms waving, white shirtsleeves billowing in the wind, wanting them to stampede, crying out I love you, I love you, I didn't know what it was!

Close by, a shackled horse nickers in pain, then lurches onto its feet. The blood drips in a runnel down its nose. Its eyes are dead and dumb.

I see hair and metal and leather and blood. I feel a wave of faintness, my head reels, and the black leather cap I'm sewing falls from my numb hands into my lap with a heavy fflump. I blink back my tears, pick it up again.

What's the matter with you? Old Joseph says, his voice merging with that of my father, *afterward they don't remember.* No more demons, the wildness blotted out forever. They're *bilovem.* Free. And they find peace, gentle dreamless sleep and it's endless, endless, endless . . . .

"Line them up," Mimi says, and I twist the outer wooden band clockwise so its holes match those I drilled on the inner circle.

"Put them in," Mimi says, her voice a little hard.

With a tremor, I pick up the spikes I hammered and insert them one at a time. They feel greasy in my damp fingers.

Mimi sits on the bed. Her hand is moist in mine. The ugly leather cap is tight against her skull, mashing down her hair so her head seems to have taken on an odd distorted shape. The wooden bands rise over her brow like an evil mockery of a saint's halo. I swallow. I cannot bring myself to look at the metal spikes denting her pale skin, at the honed glinting points I sharpened until they were needle thin. I stare at her lap, at the hem of her skirt, at the tips of her velvet slippers.

I'm not a child anymore, I think, and oh God oh fucking Christ, I know what this is. My tears are hot and thick, running down my cheeks. I can hardly see, my chest is heaving with my broken sobs.

"Imre," she says, "I believe I'll be with Joseph and with Constantin. They're very close now, and it is to them you send me."

"I can't, I can't!" My whole body begins to tremble. "It's death, it's your death. Don't make me," I whisper.

"Think of the torment; of confusion and pain that's worse than death—"

"It's not even death! It's unbeing!" I cry out. "Nothingness, nothing . . . !"

"No," she shakes her head. "There is heart, spirit—"

"Heart and spirit are nothing without the mind!"

She gives me a thin smile, as if she had some inner secret. "Then tell yourself it's freedom, Imre. An eternity of freedom." She tilts her head back, gazing at a horizon I cannot see. "*Bilovem*," she says.

The sound of an anticipation I cannot understand gives a lilt to her voice. I drop my head into my hands and moan.

"Look at me," she says, and my wet eyes lift sluggishly, meet hers. There's no fear in hers, only a hunger for peace. "Give me what I seek."

Her body is very straight. She holds her shoulders back, her chin high. Under her dark brows her eyes have gone huge and staring, as if she were seeing into another world beyond this one.

Her hand presses mine—just once—my fingers spasm and jerk, but her touch is as light and free as the wing of a moth.

I kiss her lips. Her mouth moves, saying, "I love you, Imre," against mine. Her small face is wet with my tears. I cannot look into her eyes—shining violet eyes I know will soon go dead, dumb—

"Gentling," she says. "It just needs to be done quick." She echoes my father's long ago words. "Then there's no pain."

And then, my hands come up shaking. The cold metal flanges— like the outstretched wings of dead moths—are between my fingers, my knees have gone weak and watery.

"Mimi—" I stop. There are no words in me to say all that my heart holds. My fingers ache and throb bitterly against the steel flanges.

"Close your eyes, my love," she whispers softly, "and free me now. Quick ..."

"Quick," I echo my beloved.

Then, God help me, with a single twist I turn the screws and sink the hellish bolts deep in her brain.

EPILOGUE

Gentling. It's near dawn now. I sit on the bed. I'm still holding her hand. I'm talking to her, telling her I love her, I want her. She doesn't answer. She is so still.

I took off the hideous cap, and it was as hard to remove those dangerous spikes from her brain as it was to force them in. I don't think I'll ever forget that sickening sound like a knife being pulled from the wet meat of a melon. I shiver. "Christ," I whisper.

I sponged the blood from Mimi's cheeks, and every now and then I carefully stroke her soft dark hair. I combed it down over those two deep holes so I don't have to see them again.

"Oh Jesus. Gentling," I say aloud. I glance at Joseph's ring on my finger. It's pale blonde in the gray light. She felt him and Constantin waiting for her—an arm's length away. I do not.

I sit with the bloodied cap on my head, the black leather pressing my scalp, the metal points digging into my skin. I'm trying to scan the future, see beyond the earth. Mimi did it; she saw the peace beyond this time. But there's nothing for me, no future of any kind without her, I think, dropping my chin toward my chest. On the outer edge of my vision I can see the wooden circles; a jolt of terror courses through me, my heart jerks in a painful throb.

I have a power I dare not use and do not want. My gaze flits across the room and I catch sight of the vile charm, the blackened hand lying on its bed of maroon velvet. The hand has a claim on me, I think, and unless I make certain there's no mind, nothing left to churn, I face eternal torment.

Don't think about the gentling, just do it! I tell myself. But I'll never have the strength to turn those screws I think, and in my mind's eye, I see Mimi, the light gone from her eyes, the blood that dripped and ran in ragged red lines down her face, trickled over her lips.

In my imagination I see myself, lowering my head like a bull about to charge, then running full tilt and slamming into the wall. The spikes are driven deep into my skull. The caravan rocks heavily on its springs.

And then?

Then my daughter will find my body and her mother's. And if she creeps in silent pensive mood to gaze on us, will she find a box? A box with a hand? She will. And it will sing its siren song, and if she touches it, she will feel that low sick power, the sensation of slamming your fingers. Hot and cold and dizzying. She will be repulsed. And attracted. Again and again. Poisonous knowledge will seep into her brain.

I look at the lumpy scar on my wrist, like a thick worm fastened to my skin, my heart goes cold and I think Oh good Christ, she'll claim it. If you're gone, Lenore will claim it! Anyeta will win.

I lurch to my feet and rip the device from my head. It goes skittering across the room, the cap spins. The spikes fall out of the oak circles and roll back and forth on the floorboards, chattering like bones against the wood.

Burn it, a voice says in my head. Burn all of it. Lenore doesn't have to know about any of this, doesn't have to see her mother's body, broken, bleeding on the bed.

My gaze lights on the copper box, and my heart quickens with savage delight when I think of the evil charm consumed by fire. The livid scar on my wrist throbs. I ignore the pain. Instead, I begin emptying the oil lamps one by one. The fumes rise around me. In a high glee I douse the floor, splash the liquid over curtains. I race up the stairs, duck under the low ceiling. I soak the loft, hearing the oil dripping through the interstices, splattering wetly on the floor below. From downstairs, the sound of moaning rises like a dirge from the box. A banshee wail drills louder and louder when I near the mummified hand. Imre, *oh Imre!* it weeps. I shut my ears, drenching the flesh with greasy kerosene. I move on through the kitchen and finally return to the bed.

I look at Mimi for the last time. I want to believe, I hope she's with Joseph and Constantin—

And then I see it. I utter a little cry, the oil lamp falls from my hand with a thump. From far off I hear it gurgling faintly.

There is a small light, a golden spark blooming in the center of my wife's chest. Her heart, I think, mesmerized. Her heart is surrounded by rays of dancing light. Then I see hands—pale as milk—reaching for her.

A hint of ghostly grin materializes in a round face. The short squat body of a tubby man spills like moonlight into the room. I see the glimmering opal of a gaunt face dominated by piercing eyes.

"Constantin! Joseph!" I cry out.

Constantin turns and smiles at me—for just a second, I think— but their pallid gleaming faces are fixed on Mimi. Joseph reaches down inside her. Suddenly the yellow spark is a beaming mote in his hand, and then it's as if I'm watching her climb up and out of herself. Her face is young, the face of a child, a limber elf.

I rub my eyes, look up. But there's nothing.

"You're a fool," I say to myself, sniffling back tears. "It was the mist in your eyes, a hallucination. You can make yourself see anything you want. There's nothing and she's gone."

I stoop for the heavy glass oil lamp and bring it up to finish what I started. I stand over her, about to pour the kerosene, and at that instant something clicks and registers in my head.

"Her face," I whisper, reaching out, then drawing back. For it is not my wife's face, not Mimi's body lying on the bed. Anyeta lies sprawling there, twisted with time and age. Through the straggly white hair, I see two brownish blood clotted holes where the spikes were driven deep into the sere wrinkled flesh. The old whore's obsidian eyes are dead, dark.

My wife, my beloved is with them.

I go to the doorway, and I light a match, half recall a snatch of the poem that was Joseph's, Constantin's epitaph. "All things have rest," I say, "and ripen toward the grave. In silence—ripen, fall, and cease. Rest," I tell Mimi, "we will not wander more."

I flick the wooden match from my fingers. It simmers briefly against the old wide boards; then flares into brilliance when it finds the lamp oil. There is a shifting tide of blue flame that suddenly boils like a storm-ridden sea, the suck-whump! of oxygen being ferociously consumed. The fire begins to rise high and hot and yellow along the walls, racing madly toward the ceiling, the loft.

I shut the door quickly; go down the stairs, moving into sunlight.

I step away. Soon, behind me the caravan is a burning pyre, the flames roaring toward the pale morning sky.

There is Lenore to live for and love, I think. In a little while, I'll go and wake her. A knowing voice—Joseph's perhaps—speaks up, telling me I might use the power—I do not want and will never use—one more time.

I close my eyes and concentrate: Who owns the hand of the dead can bring healing. Lenore will remember none of it. Only that my wife loved her, that her mother died when she was young.

I think of the charm. The box is turning heat black, the copper is melting and running. Ashes. Lenore will be safe. Forever. Her future, her childhood dreams, safe. And who's to say my girl won't grow up to be a lady waiting on an Empress?

I hold my hand up, gazing at the thick hump of scar snaking unevenly around my hairy wrist. I know in the end, of course, I will go down into that eternal unrest—unless . . . unless I . . . I push the thought aside. Anyway, Lenore will be an old woman then, settled. A day will come when Lenore doesn't need a father. It's hard to say when. I'll be old myself, I think—

Gentling.

Shielding my eyes from the hot glare, I turn and look at the burning caravan. When the flames die out, I'll go up the stairs into Joseph's rickety caravan and wake my sleeping daughter.

I recall Joseph's words. The dead have secrets, Imre, but the more you know of the future the harder your task will be. He was right, of course; but now I believe it's the hardest things that set you free.

Bilovem.

I watch the dark smoke funneling up in a thick black cloud, and think to myself, yes, yes in the end I'll know the freedom of the gentling box.

Author's Notes and Acknowledgements (Past, Present and Future Varieties)

About a month before Necon—Northeastern Writer's Conference—which is one of my favorite conventions (and not least because it's always held right around the time of Lizzie Borden's birthday) I received a charming note from a young man named Brent Chapman who told me he'd heard wonderful things about *The Gentling Box*, that'd he just ordered it, and was looking forward to reading it. Would I be willing to sign his copy when we all landed in Rhode Island this past July?

I don't remember what I replied, but I'm sure it was polite because one doesn't spend six or seven years under the tutelage of the Jesuits through undergraduate and graduate degrees and half of a Ph.D. without being inculcated (or inoculated—take your pick) with a sense of the *importance* of courtesy.

I do remember thinking, "Isn't that nice!"

Brent also signed on ahead of time for the Lizzie Borden excursion which I've been running since 2002. Nicer still. This year's foray into the axe murderess's old homestead which included the usual gang— good friends like Corrine De Winter and Dennis Cummins and Beth Blue—and new friends like Heather Graham, and her husband, Dennis Pozzossere and two of their kids; and was—we all agreed—the most fun we'd ever had hanging out with the Fall River ghosts and shadows at 92 Second Street. Except, because I had a long drive ahead of me, I went to sleep early (there have been years I never went to sleep at all) and I didn't have a chance to really speak with Brent. Mostly I remembered he was indeed, very young. Also very tall and possessed of a hugely contagious, booming laugh.

About a month after Necon, Brent wrote to me again.

This time he wanted to let me know he was starting a new publishing company.

He intended to treat the writers with the utmost professionalism and respect and he hoped I'd consider signing on with him because he dearly wanted to launch his new venture, Shadowfall, with *The Gentling Box*.

Since my contract with my former publisher had recently ended, deciding to work with Brent turned out to be one of the easier decisions in my life.

A much simpler decision than, say, when one of my professors at Fordham, James L. Tyne, asked me half way through that half-baked Ph.D. what I intended on for a career and I told him I wanted to write and to teach. He looked at me very seriously, then said I'd never write the kind of fiction I *should* be writing if I kept pacing down the halls of Academia.

Dr. Tyne was right. I did teach for a while on the college level and discovered I barely had time to jot down grocery lists, send Christmas cards or write out checks for the electric bill--much less the stories and novels I imagined were incubating inside me.

So....

I'm deeply grateful to Dr. Tyne because he set me on a path that ultimately changed my life. When *The Gentling Box* won the Bram Stoker Award it was—absolutely—the proudest and happiest moment of my life and it's impossible really, to convey what it meant, what it *still* means to me every single day.

I'm also deeply grateful to my family: my Dad, Armand; my mother, Anne; and my older brother, Peter; and a myriad of cousins--Karen Salerno, Diane Steverman, Maryann Kolb, Carmella and Faust Siconolfi--who have always believed in me even when I didn't quite believe in myself.

Friends—like Barbara McGill Grant, Frank and Gail Orfei, Corrine De Winter, Beth Blue, Judy Comeau, Robert Dunbar, Michael Hughes, Dennis Cummins, Di Barron, and Janice Morgan--have graciously read my writing in progress; shared dinners, drinks, coffee, and too many cigarettes; laughed and cried with me, delivered the appropriate, well-deserved kicks in the rear when needed and, in the aggregate, have functioned as the cornerstone of my writing life, *and* the mayhem and madness that passes as my daily existence.

I also want to thank good friends and mentors who lent their considerable expertise and enthusiasm both to this book *and* tales yet to be told: Monica O'Rourke, Elizabeth Crow, Emily Hanlon, Dr. Jim Garner, D.V. M. (who literally vetted the original manuscript and made sure I didn't' wander too far afield when describing both gentling and glanders); Dr. Eileen Reale; Tom Monteleone, F. Paul Wilson, Alexandra Sokoloff, and Deborah LeBlanc.

Thanks, too, beyond measure to both Heather Graham for the stunning afterward she served up along with a bright heaping cumulus of generosity, camaraderie and sisterhood; and, to Glenn Chadbourne—artist extraordinaire, trooper and true friend—who has joined in on every one of my hare-brained schemes and projects over the years, and who produced the magnificent cover of this edition of *The Gentling Box*.

Best for last: Thanks to Brent and Alisha Chapman of Shadowfall Publications—who, like Dr. Tyne at Fordham University all those years ago, have set me on a path that will ultimately change my life.

Grazie.

Mille grazie.

—*Lisa Mannetti*
October, 2015

ABOUT THE AUTHOR

Lisa Mannetti's debut novel, *The Gentling Box*, garnered a Bram Stoker Award and she has since been nominated three times for the prestigious award in both the short and long fiction categories: Her story, "Everybody Wins," was made into a short film and her novella, "Dissolution," will soon be a feature-length film directed by Paul Leyden. Recent and upcoming short stories include, "Resurgam" in Zombies: More Recent Dead and "Almost Everybody Wins," in Insidious Assassins. Her work, including *The Gentling Box*, and "1925: A Fall River Halloween" has been translated into Italian.

She has also authored *The New Adventures of Tom Sawyer and Huck Finn*, two companion novellas in *Deathwatch*, a macabre gag book, *51 Fiendish Ways to Leave your Lover*, as well as non-fiction books, and numerous articles and short stories in newspapers, magazines and anthologies. Forthcoming works include additional short stories and a novella about Houdini, *The Box Jumper*. She is currently working on two paranormal novels, tentatively titled *Spy Glass Hill* and *The Everest Hauntings*.

Lisa lives in New York in the 100 year old house she originally grew up in.

Visit her author website: www.lisamannetti.com
Visit her virtual haunted house: www.thechanceryhouse.com

Made in the USA
Middletown, DE
21 November 2016